222589279179

CHANGE AGENT

ALSO BY DANIEL SUAREZ

Daemon

Freedom™

Kill Decision

Influx

CHANGE AGENT

Daniel Suarez

DUTTON

DUTTON

An imprint of Penguin Random House LLC
375 Hudson Street
New York, New York 10014

Copyright © 2017 by Daniel Suarez
Penguin supports copyright. Copyright fuels creativity, encourages diverse voices, promotes free speech, and creates a vibrant culture. Thank you for buying an authorized edition of this book and for complying with copyright laws by not reproducing, scanning, or distributing any part of it in any form without permission. You are supporting writers and allowing Penguin to continue to publish books for every reader.

DUTTON is a registered trademark and the D colophon
is a trademark of Penguin Random House LLC.

LIBRARY OF CONGRESS CATALOGING-IN-PUBLICATION DATA
Names: Suarez, Daniel, 1964– author.
Title: Change agent : a novel / Daniel Suarez.
Description: First edition. | New York : Dutton, [2017]
Identifiers: LCCN 2016030244 | ISBN 9781101984666 (hardcover) |
ISBN 9781101984680 (ebook)
Subjects: LCSH: International Criminal Police Organization—Fiction. |
Genetic engineering—Fiction. | BISAC: FICTION / Technological. | FICTION
/ Science Fiction / Adventure. | GSAFD: Science fiction.
Classification: LLC PS3619.U327 C48 2017 | DDC 813/.6—dc23 LC record
available at https://lccn.loc.gov/2016030244

Printed in the United States of America
1   3   5   7   9   10   8   6   4   2

Book design by Amy Hill

This book is a work of fiction. Names, characters, places, and incidents either are the product of the author's imagination or are used fictitiously, and any resemblance to actual persons, living or dead, business establishments, events, or locales is entirely coincidental.

For my mother, Jane Haisser.
You will always be my hero.

Full fathom five thy father lies.
Of his bones are coral made.
Those are pearls that were his eyes.
Nothing of him that doth fade,
But doth suffer a sea-change
Into something rich and strange.

—*The Tempest*,
William Shakespeare

CHANGE AGENT

Chapter 1

Before we begin, have you any questions about genetic editing, Mr. and Mrs. Cherian?" The counselor took a whopping bite from a vada pav sandwich as he clicked through their file.

The young Mumbai couple exchanged uncertain looks. In their late twenties, well-groomed, and dressed in crisp business casual clothes, they appeared a step above the cramped, dingy, and windowless office around them. Nonetheless here they were. The wife appeared especially ill at ease.

The husband shook his head. "No questions at the moment, no." He looked to his wife reassuringly. Patted her on the knee.

She spoke up. "How does the procedure work?"

The counselor answered with his mouth full. "Ah, an inquiring mind."

She narrowed her eyes at him.

The husband cut in. "My wife and I are *both* attorneys. Given the legal status of this enterprise, we were understandably reluctant to research the topic on our own devices."

"Well then . . ." The counselor finished chewing and wiped his fingers on a crumpled napkin. "I have something that should address your questions." He noisily rooted around in his desk drawer and in a moment produced a device the size and shape of a paperback book, which he placed on the cluttered desktop between them. When he pressed down on the device it unfolded into a pylon shape—sporting several lenses facing forward and back. It booted up, white light glowing within.

The wife drew stylish mirror glasses from her purse and donned them to shield her eyes. "A *glim*? You think we'd allow you access to our retinas? This is out—"

"No retinal scanning, I assure you, Mrs. Cherian. Merely a brief in-eye presentation."

The husband looked to his wife. "They have our DNA, love. Retinas are the least of it."

"Neelo, I want our embryo transferred back to the clinic."

"My love, we—"

"This place is a rat hole. A defunct export office by the look of it."

"All part of the disguise, Mrs. Cherian. We must not attract undue attention from the authorities. But rest assured, our labs are well funded—run by the largest genediting syndicate in the world, Trefoil. None are more sophisticated."

"My love, remember: they came highly recommended."

She grabbed her bag as if to go. "Neelo, we are law-abiding people."

"We've discussed this, cherub. Principled positions are admirable, but other parents are doing this. We as well must do everything we can to prepare our son for the world in which he will live." He gestured to the glim on the table. "Why don't we watch the presentation and see how we feel afterward?"

She sighed—and reluctantly removed her mirror glasses.

The counselor beamed. "Very good. Please look forward. It will find your retinas in a jiffy."

In a moment, from their perspective, the air above the desk filled with a highly detailed 3D model of the double helix of DNA. It rotated there, an utterly convincing virtual object—seemingly as real as the desk. Yet the floating DNA existed only as a rich, plenoptic light field projected directly onto their retinas and unseen by anyone not targeted by the glim.

Light field projectors like these had largely replaced physical televisions, computer screens, and mobile OLED displays in the last decade or so. Beaming imagery directly onto a viewer's retinas instead of spraying photons all over the place had many advantages—authentic augmented reality being one. Environmental sustainability another. Privacy another still.

A female narrator's voice came to them via a focused acoustic beam. *"Initially developed in 2012, CRISPR technology is a search-and-replace tool for modifying DNA—the blueprint of all living things."*

The word "CRISPR" appeared with the letters expanding into full words in turn.

"Shorthand for 'clustered regularly interspaced short palindromic repeats,' CRISPR derives from a naturally occurring process in bacterial immune systems—and it has been adapted by modern science to permit targeted genetic edits of plant, animal, and human embryos."

The 3D animation showed a labeled RNA molecule enter the scene.

"The process begins by seeding a 'guide RNA' with both a target and a payload genetic sequence . . ."

Labels identified them in turn as they were inserted into the RNA molecule.

"This guide RNA is then injected into an embryonic cell's nucleus . . ."

The RNA clamped onto the double helix of DNA, unzipping it.

". . . where it reads the embryo's DNA. Wherever a match for the target sequence is found . . ."

The 3D image highlighted a match between the RNA target sequence and a segment of the cell's DNA.

". . . a natural cutting protein acts as a molecular scalpel, severing the DNA chain . . ."

The animation showed the double helix of DNA cut.

". . . removing the matching segment . . ."

The animation showed it being removed.

". . . and inserting a copy of the payload DNA in its place."

The RNA's payload sequence copied itself into the gap, and the DNA quickly rejoined.

"In this way human embryos may be safely and reliably 'edited' in vitro to correct deadly heritable genetic disorders."

Moving music swelled as the scene dissolved to a life-sized 3D projection of a beautiful but despondent little African girl with cloudy blind eyes. She looked as real as if she sat in the room with them.

"CRISPR-developed cures for cystic fibrosis, muscular dystrophy, sickle-cell anemia, Huntington's disease, hemophilia, and more have

already saved or improved the lives of hundreds of millions of people world-wide . . ."

The scene dissolved into a new image—one of the now smiling girl with clear brown eyes, reaching up to smudge flour onto her mother's nose. They both laughed and embraced as they made cookies together.

"Ending a legacy of suffering and for the first time putting humanity in control of its own genetics."

The image tilted skyward to show a brightly lit horizon. A new dawn.

"Theoretically there is no limit to the desirable edits CRISPR can perform."

Dark clouds moved in, obscuring this glowing horizon. Ominous music rumbled.

"However, international law currently prohibits edits beyond those designed to correct a short UN-approved list of genetic disorders. Despite this, our expert researchers have perfected hundreds of highly beneficial CRISPR edits. Edits that increase both the quality and the quantity of human life."

The music rose as the image ascended, finally bursting through the gray cloud layer into an endless expanse of sunlight beyond. No horizon in sight.

"And unlike other gene therapies, CRISPR edits are heritable—meaning they will be passed down to all future generations of your family line—what's known as 'germ line engineering.' This means your investment today will pay rich dividends for all your child's descendants."

The scene transitioned to a life-sized and utterly realistic projection of a healthy five-year-old South Asian boy, who rotated slowly before them.

"For example, a minor edit to a human embryo's DAF2 gene could add thirty healthy years to a child's life. A change to BCAT1 could add even more."

The image of the boy aged to an adult and then beyond until he had a full shock of gray hair—but an otherwise healthy frame. He lifted up a laughing grandchild with ease as they ran toward a zoo exhibit.

The imagery then dissolved to show a young man, studious and attentive in a classroom.

"*A change to gene DLG3 can improve memory, while a series of edits within the M1 and M3 gene clusters can substantially increase intelligence.*"

The image morphed to the teen wearing a valedictorian cap and gown. He smiled as he took the podium amid applause, ostensibly to address his graduating class.

The imagery shifted to an athletic young woman running on a track against several close competitors.

"*A tweak to the MEF2 gene can bestow type II 'fast-twitch' muscle fibers . . .*"

The young woman outpaced the other sprinters, raising her arms as she burst through the finish tape to cheers.

"*. . . increasing physical prowess.*"

The imagery resolved again to a double helix of DNA, with segments snipped and replaced here, there, and elsewhere.

"*Other even more exciting edits are being developed to meet the demands of our increasingly competitive world. Be sure to ask your genetic counselor for a full list of edits in your price range. No matter which you choose, you'll be giving your child a timeless gift, one that they will be able to pass down to their own children—the first truly priceless family heirloom.*"

The DNA looped as the image zoomed out to soft, inspiring music, transforming into a three-cornered continuous shape.

Text appeared above and below the logo as it pulsed with life:

TREFOIL LABS

Evolution by design.

Moments later the virtual logo blinked out of existence as the counselor pressed down on the glim to fold it. He scooped the glim back into his desk drawer. "I trust that answered your questions."

The husband and wife both looked somewhat dazed at the sudden disappearance of the alternate reality.

The wife was first to recover. "Could such edits be done on an adult person?"

The counselor laughed, putting his sandwich down and clasping his hands. "Now that would be valuable indeed! But alas, no, Mrs. Cherian. Editing the DNA of one cell out of thirty-five trillion would not accomplish much. That's why these changes need to be made while your child is but a zygote—a single fertilized cell."

She nodded to herself. "I see."

"You and I will remain as we are, but your child has no such limitation." He studied her expression, pausing with the experienced cadence of a true salesman. "Shall we discuss the desired edits for your future son?"

The husband took his wife's hand. "Are you ready to proceed, my love?"

She visibly struggled with powerful emotions.

The counselor had seen it before. "Mrs. Cherian, all creatures select genetic preferences when they choose a mate. But science now gives you and your husband the ability to adjust your child's genetics just a bit further—*together.*"

The husband again placed his hand on her knee.

She shook her head. "It seems against Nature."

The counselor spoke softly. "This is the very same process Nature follows to eliminate viral DNA in bacteria. The same process used under the UN's Treaty on Genetic Modification."

"Yes, but to cure deadly genetic defects, not to tailor-make a child."

The husband shook his head. "We are not tailoring our child. We are correcting genetic weaknesses. Is not a weak memory fatal to a future doctor or attorney?"

"Where does this sort of thinking lead us, Neelo—eugenics?"

The counselor shook his head slowly. "No, no, Mrs. Cherian. There are three billion letters in the human genome. Most people edit six to twelve—minor edits indeed."

"Remember, love, what did you say when you saw the Persauds' little boy? Is that not why we are here?"

She fell silent.

The husband turned to the counselor. "We don't want many edits, of course."

"Nor would you need them, Mr. Cherian." He started tapping at an unseen screen. "But even minor edits can go a long way to help your child in a rapidly evolving world. Some edits are more costly than others, of course, but who can put a price on parental love?"

The husband studied his wife, who was literally wringing her hands, but he spoke to the counselor. "Which edits would you recommend?"

"I always suggest the DAF2 edit. Why not start your child out with up to three decades more of healthy living? So they can be there in your twilight years." The counselor made some entries on the invisible screen. "How could such a thing be wrong?"

The Cherians exchanged appraising looks.

"Longer life, of course, suggests related edits—LRP5 for extra strong bones, PCSK9 for a greatly reduced risk of heart disease . . ." He clicked unseen UIs.

"The next question is whether you prize intellectual excellence over physical prowess. Heightened intellect requires more complex edits— and is, thus, more costly. You can choose both, of course, budget permitting." He looked up at the parents.

They stared, frozen by the magnitude of the decision.

"Well, let us see what the Greek ideal—body and mind—would require." The counselor displayed the price to them.

"That's more than a year of university, Neelo."

"But with these edits our boy could very well win a full scholarship."

"I am uncomfortable with this."

"Why? Because some government bureaucrat says it's not allowed? Do you really think the wealthiest families are not doing this, my love?"

She sighed and looked away.

He took her hand again. "We must do it. For our son's sake—no matter how uncomfortable it makes us."

Just then they heard a *BOOM* that caused them all to jump in their seats.

The wife turned. "What was that?"

The counselor was already clicking away at invisible screens. "Oh, my . . . Mr. and Mrs. Cherian, please . . . a moment."

The wife grabbed her husband's arm. "What was that, Neelo?"

The husband stood as the counselor did. The sound of running feet and muffled shouts came from the hall. "Speak up, man!"

The counselor motioned for calm. "It would appear that the Brihanmumbai are raiding this facility."

"The police?"

"Do not be alarmed. We have made contributions to the appropriate authorities. This is clearly a mix-up. In any event, we have numerous concealed exits for just such a contingency." He gestured to his office doorway. "If you would please follow me . . ."

The counselor moved quickly out his office door and into a narrow corridor, which was quickly crowding with other couples and their counselors. Some clients shielded their faces from one another with handbags and scarves.

The husband clasped his wife's hand and followed closely. "This is outrageous."

"What about our embryo, Neelo?"

The counselor glanced backward. "Not to worry, folks. As I said, we'll get this mix-up sorted."

Someone shouted in alarm behind them. The Cherians looked back to see the door at the far end of the hallway kicked in. Police in black body armor poured through, shouting, "*Zameen par sab log!*"

Someone screamed and the crowd of clients stampeded.

A lab security guard emerged from a side door—pistol in hand.

The police shouted it in unison, "*Bandook! Bandook!*"—red laser dots clustering on the guard's chest as he stood slack-jawed. Deafening POPS filled the corridor. Screaming as everyone scattered. The security guard dropped like a bag of cement.

The husband pulled his wife down to the floor alongside him. "Down, love! Get down!"

People ran past them in a panic toward an unseen rear exit—some trampling the husband and wife as he shielded her. "Watch it, damn you!"

The police shouted again, *"Zameen par sab log!"*

Their counselor was nowhere to be seen. The husband spoke into his wife's ear. "We must say nothing until we've seen counsel, love. I need to phone Anish."

His wife was silent.

The husband noticed blood on his hand. Panicked, he padded his sides down. "My love, I . . ." And then, finding nothing, he looked to his wife.

A small bullet hole pierced her temple.

"No . . ." He cupped her head. Blood pooled beneath them both, expanding quickly across the cheap, dirty carpet.

He tried to form words—then finally screamed in horror as police approached behind him, guns raised. "No! No!"

He hugged her body close, shrieking in anguish.

The helmeted and armored police tried to pull him from her, but he would not let go.

"My love. No, my love!"

Chapter 2

C **hange comes. Inexorable.** Most times it arrives gradually—but sometimes change is an earthquake. Cherished assumptions crack. Rocks of stability crumble. Chasms of experience open between adjacent generations.

Thinking back on his childhood, Kenneth Durand remembered his millennial parents enduring their own technological earthquake—the disruption of every industry. Their college degrees useless and their student debt insurmountable, they fell, like many others, out of the middle class. His father's ready smile was replaced by a mask of worry that remained until the day he died. Automation and disintermediation rocked their world.

And everyone thought that was big change.

It was nothing—just a tremor.

Two even larger shock waves came for Durand's generation.

The first was mass adoption of light fields. Suddenly what you saw with your own eyes wasn't necessarily reality. Most of the consumer electronics industry disappeared.

The second and *far* more disruptive shock wave was the fourth industrial revolution: synthetic biology. What was once manufactured was now increasingly grown by custom-designed organisms—algae, yeasts, bacteria. Automobile bodies grown from chitin. Biofuels from custom *E. coli* bacteria. Deathless meat and cultured dairy products from sustainable cellular agriculture. *Biofacturing* instead of manufacturing. Life itself harnessed to the human will.

Societies that incorporated these advances moved on. Those that could not did not. Instead, they languished in the debt, political paralysis, and recriminations of the previous age.

Durand had made his own choice, and the memory of those he'd left behind still ached. No doubt migrants of prior eras had always suffered the same anguish. They saw a brighter future somewhere and someway else and walked the difficult path that led them there. He'd disappointed so many people. Violated beloved traditions of service and loyalty. But life was all about difficult choices.

Durand contemplated headlights from eighty stories above as the first light of dawn crested the Johor Strait. Singapore's robot rush hour was already under way far below. Autonomous electric cars packed the expressways, their LED headlights coursing over the landscape like rivers of white-hot lava.

He barely paid attention to the voice of a female newscaster in his ear, *". . . Korea prepares to celebrate the anniversary of its reunification, Seoul officials are rolling out the red carpet for Chinese dignitaries— honoring Beijing's pivotal role in the nearly bloodless coup and invasion that deposed the Pyongyang regime . . ."*

From the traffic patterns below, it was clear humans were no longer behind the wheel. No stopping and starting, but traffic flowing smoothly, closely coordinated, optimized.

"Mathematics on parade," his father had called it. Each vehicle informed by its neighbors, and by the whole. These days you couldn't drive yourself to work even if you wanted to. Manual driving was prohibited on the expressways. Humans could not keep pace.

That was something his father well knew.

Mathematics on parade. An experienced and talented civil engineer, his father spent the last ten years of his life getting downsized from entry-level retail jobs. He died of a heart attack while Durand was still in high school—leaving them in poverty.

The anchorwoman's voice continued in his ear: *"The Australian Coast Guard rescued passengers of a so-called zombie ship adrift off the Port Arthur coastline on Tuesday. Packed with hundreds of desperate migrants, the vessel had been abandoned without food or water after traffickers reportedly received payment to ferry the refugees to Indonesia, where they were told jobs awaited."*

Durand turned away from the skyline and back to the high-rise jogging path. A glance at stats glowing in the corner of his vision showed he still had a chance to maintain a seven-minute mile.

He resumed jogging as the news continued.

"Fleeing climate-change-related crop failures, civil war, and rising ocean levels, tens of millions of desperate migrants are on the move in what has become the largest sustained migration in human history . . ."

Durand's LFP glasses tinted against the glare of dawn. The tropical humidity was already bearing down. He jogged through fogs of atomized water that cooled him at intervals. The track arced rightward on a five-kilometer loop traversing the top of the Hanging Gardens residential complex. Lush jungle plants lined the inner edge.

Durand pushed himself harder, curving along the path. Fashioned of spongy metamaterial, the surface reduced the impact on his joints. An infinity pool ran along the outer edge, and he jogged past a swimmer in goggles and a water cap. A lush garden path ran below and beyond that—near the outer railing. Everything in sight had been meticulously designed—what urban planners had taken to calling "the built environment."

"The International Olympic Committee gathers in Tokyo this week to debate the coming generation of genetically altered athletes. At issue is whether CRISPR edits should disqualify competitors for participation in Olympic and professional sport. At present, no reliable test exists to reveal embryonic genetic edits, potentially putting in peril long-standing records of human physical achievement."

As he ran, Durand focused on the ubiquitous construction cranes studding the Singapore skyline. Two-hundred-story buildings were going up all over the CBD. Mute testimony that the boom was on.

It was difficult to pinpoint the year Singapore became the technology capital of the world. Economists usually placed that somewhere between ratification of the UN Treaty on Genetic Modification and the second wave of moon landings. But certainly by the dawn of the Gene Revolution, the technological crown had shifted from America.

Silicon Valley did not go quietly.

Palo Alto, Mountain View, Cupertino, and San Francisco ran through all the Kübler-Ross stages of economic grief. Applied billions in defibrillating tax breaks to jump-start investment. Held embarrassing VR publicity stunts. In the end the US government was practically giving away H-1B visas.

But nothing could stop the exodus. The Valley was done. Synthetic biology finished it—though, to be fair, that wasn't the Valley's fault.

Synthetic biology was the transistor of the twenty-first century. Yet political realities in America made it increasingly unfeasible for entrepreneurs there to tinker with the building blocks of life. Every cluster of human cells was viewed as a baby in America. A quarter of the population wasn't vaccinated. A majority of Americans didn't believe in evolution. Social-media-powered opinions carried more influence than peer-reviewed scientific research. In this virulently anti-science atmosphere, synbio research was hounded offshore before it had really begun. Activists crowed over their victory.

The rest of the world did not let the opportunity pass it by.

By then, Silicon Valley's forte—circuitry and software—had become cheap global commodities, created everywhere. Network-centric economic disruption was largely complete. Every nook and cranny of modern life had already been disintermediated. The gig economy and time-share rentals had cannibalized the US consumer base, low-bidding the middle class out of existence. It was what had done Durand's parents in. He still remembered them huddled in one room of their home, while debt-collection software rented out the rest of their house over the Internet.

The world moved on, hungering for answers to the pressing problems of a rapidly heating world. Looking for ways to feed the hundreds of millions of people rendered jobless by automation, skyrocketing global debt, climate shifts, and war.

Synthetic biology delivered—engineering yeasts, algae, and bacteria as the machinery of sustainable production. Growing and evolving integrated biofactory systems. Serving as a foundry for new pharmaceuticals and CRISPR-edited climate-change-resistant crops—like C4 photosynthesis rice—to feed earth's ten billion people. Built environments where cyanobacteria converted light into sugar and custom *E. coli* converted sugar into biofuel—organisms altered to feed into each other's processing loops. Bespoke *E. coli* that scrubbed the oceans of pollutants or sequestered carbon.

Innovations in xenobiology allowed for the wholesale expansion of the biological alphabet itself: xenonucleic acids (XNA) such as HNA, TNA, GNA, LNA, and PNA—sugars not utilized in the natural world that could create entirely new cellular machinery and compounds that did not interact with natural biological systems—launched entire industries in biological computing and bio blockchain tech.

Life itself had become the next systems architecture. And it was hard to argue with its accumulated uptime.

And so the Valley moved overseas, as did many of the people and firms in it, reconvening in a locale more receptive to science—if not quite liberal democracy. By the mid-2030s most synbio start-ups were Changi-bound. Within a decade, new trillion-dollar companies called Singapore home, replacing oil and finance as the main industries in the tiny island republic. And it had yet again transformed the city-state's skyline.

Durand noticed a line of urban farming towers in the distance. A hundred stories each and draped in vines, the dozen towers resembled overgrown postapocalyptic ruins—except for their glittering organometallic lights. Acre for acre, the towers produced ten times the food of a traditional farm on just a fraction of the water. Zero pesticides. Almost entirely automated.

Nearby stood "pharm" towers, whose crops had been genetically modified to produce pharmaceutical compounds.

Beyond the towers clouds of commercial drone traffic surged past on the aerial logistics highway wrapping the northern and eastern shores—headed toward Changi and the aerial interchange that fed into the CBD. Silhouetted against the glowing eastern horizon, the delivery drones resembled flocks of birds.

Durand's newsfeed went to commercial—an American man talking fast: "... *the premier IGEA-certified provider for all custom cell-cloning services, gene synthesis, subcloning, mutagenesis, bespoke promutagens, variant libraries, and vector-shuttling services. cDNA clones available in your preferred vector . . ."*

No skipping or muting commercials; they'd be there waiting for you next time. Better to let them play. Besides, his lap was nearly finished.

Durand ran between rows of bioluminescent trees on the rooftop approach to Tower Six. The soft glow from the trees had begun to dim as the first rays of sunlight touched their broad leaves. Engineered like everything else around him, the plants were as beautiful as they were functional, illuminating roads and sidewalks throughout Singapore.

He sprinted the last twenty meters, pushing with everything he had. The building security system recognized him, and glass doors silently opened, as he knew they would. Durand slowed to a stop as he entered the blessed cool of the rooftop lobby.

The tower's synthetic female voice spoke in Asian-accented English: *"Good morning, Mr. Durand. I trust you had a pleasant exercise."*

Durand ignored the voice. He knew it was just a narrow AI. Any input he granted it would be stored for later use or misuse, nothing more. It did not "care" about him any more than his soap dish did. Instead he checked his running time while he caught his breath and stretched.

The newsfeed resumed in his ear: *"Attorney and internationally acclaimed human rights activist Kamala Cherian was slain Tuesday evening in a botched police raid on a black market CRISPR lab in the Kurla district of Mumbai . . ."*

Durand stopped cold.

"Indian authorities claim Ms. Cherian, a client of the facility, was caught in the cross fire between police and lab security. Cherian's death will likely only increase public opposition to armed raids on illicit genetic editing labs under a mandate by the UN Treaty on Genetic Modification. Ratified in 2038, the agreement was intended to halt the global spread of unregulated genetic editing of human embryos."

Durand spoke to the newscaster. "Britney. Pause news."

The synthetic anchorwoman answered. *"Pausing news."*

He pondered the information for several moments. "Britney, phone Michael Yi Ji-chang."

The synthetic anchorwoman, now his assistant, replied, *"I'm ringing Detective Sergeant Michael Yi Ji-chang. One moment . . ."* A pause. *"I have Sergeant Yi Ji-chang on an encrypted line."*

A man's voice answered. He had a slight Korean accent. *"A call this early can't be good."*

"Tell me about the Mumbai raid."

"What's to tell? Trigger-happy cop killed a VIP."

"Does Claire know yet?"

"Yes, and I'll tell you what I told her: we shouldn't overreact."

"The Brihanmumbai were supposed to raid the lab—not the clinic. There wouldn't be civilians in the lab. Now an innocent woman is dead."

"Not entirely innocent."

"Come on, Mike."

"If she had obeyed the law, Ms. Cherian would still be alive. Would you rather a cop died?"

"Of course not, but that's not the choice."

"Look, we just provide the intel. National police conduct the raids. It's not on us."

"Bullshit. We have leverage over the NCBs. We should only share lab locations with them."

"If we expect full reciprocity, Interpol needs to provide national police with the ability to follow the money into these syndicates—to get to the kingpins. That means your whole link analysis."

Durand felt a familiar fear. "Do you remember what we said after Djibouti?"

"This isn't misuse of intelligence, Ken."

"Do you remember?"

"This was a mistake—and not even our mistake."

"The media is making these raids out as murdering hopeful parents. You and I both know what happens if the public turns against the Genetic Crime Division."

"Twenty years from now, when kids have hands growing out of their foreheads, the public will want to know why the hell we didn't do something to shut these illegal labs down."

"Agreed, so let's defuse opposition by making sure human rights activists don't turn up dead in the morning news."

A weary sigh came over the line. *"Ken, I know you don't want to hear this, but innocent people are going to get caught in the cross fire. No black market on earth right now is more profitable than baby labs, and the syndicates that run them are ruthless. They've killed journalists, police, politicians, civilians. Their bad press will far exceed ours. Mark my words: the public will stay the course with us, even if, like this morning, we have some bad news days."*

Durand drummed his fingers on a nearby railing. "It's more than a bad news day to me."

"Ken. You didn't kill Ms. Cherian."

Durand stared at nothing. "I wrote the algorithms that found that lab. She is dead because—"

"A cop with bad aim killed Ms. Cherian. She was just at the wrong place at the wrong time."

Durand paced in silence.

"We save lives every day by shutting down these labs. You know it's true."

Durand remained silent.

"Hang in there, buddy. Listen, I'll see you at the eight o'clock. Okay?"

"Right."

"Haeng-syo."

Durand closed the line.

The building's AI asked, *"Shall I summon an elevator, Mr. Durand?"*

Durand nodded, mopping sweat from his face with his Annapolis T-shirt. He resisted the innate human urge to thank the digital assistant and walked toward the elevator bank.

Chapter 3

Durand padded down a corridor lined with culture-grown hardwoods and printed metals. The decor had an elegant, Scandinavian simplicity. The door to his flat recognized him and *clicked* unlocked as he reached it.

He pushed inside and gave a tight smile. "Morning."

His wife, Miyuki Uchida, sat at her desk with a cup of tea, engaged in an AR video conference with people invisible to Durand. Actual physical, framed photos of family, friends, and colleagues, along with mementos from years of development work in Africa, lined the shelves behind her. Her long black hair shimmered in the morning light as she turned a smile toward him, then blinded the line. "Hey, you."

He kissed her on the cheek. "You're up early."

"My Accra team ran into permit problems. Now they're talking in circles."

"Can I make you something?" Durand went into the kitchen.

"Thanks. I already ate. There's a mangosteen in there for you."

Durand filled a bottle of chilled water from the fridge door. In a few moments his wife followed him into the kitchen.

"Birthday girl up yet?" Durand grabbed a white tropical fruit from the fridge.

"Pretending to sleep—which reminds me: don't forget to come home with her gift tonight."

"Why wasn't it delivered here?"

"She's scanning deliveries."

"Ah."

"Something's bothering you. I can tell."

Durand took a bite of the mangosteen. After a moment he shrugged. "Just work stuff."

She regarded him.

He squirmed under her gaze.

"I haven't seen that look in two years."

Durand blinked. "My analysis got a civilian killed. Last night. A young woman. Human rights activist."

She put a hand on his shoulder. "Oh, Ken. I'm sorry." She hesitated. "Although I'm guessing it's not as simple as that."

"I can't get into the details."

"I understand." She hugged him. "I'm so sorry."

"This is why I got out, Mi."

"I know, but this isn't the same thing, Ken."

"It's happening all over again."

"It isn't the same." She let go and looked at him. "No one's launching air strikes based on your analysis."

He said nothing.

She took his hand. "You know how guilty living in the Bubble makes me feel. There's so much trouble in the world. We promised each other that we would only do this if what we're doing here makes the world a better place for her generation." She pointed at the refrigerator.

Durand turned to see a printed photo pinned to the fridge of their daughter's robotics team competing at a local maker fair. Smiling young hopeful faces.

"I know you well enough to know that's what you're trying to do."

He stared at the photo and nodded reluctantly. Then he noticed one of his daughter's plesiosaur polygon models pinned up nearby. He tapped the teacher's gold star affixed to it and nodded to his wife appreciatively. "She's getting good."

"Of course. She takes after me."

He laughed in spite of himself. "I'm gonna grab a shower."

• • •

While Durand ran an electric razor over his face, the family cat sat on the bathroom counter, watching him. Genetically modified, the breed was known as a "toyger" because it perfectly resembled a miniature tiger. The cat's gaze unnerved him—as though a full-grown tiger watched from the far bank of some watering hole instead of the far side of the bathroom sink.

"Nelson, do you mind?"

The toyger answered with a rumbling meow.

His daughter's pet. For some reason it focused most of its attention on Durand. He wasn't thrilled with the idea of bespoke animals. However, neotenic pets—the cuter and more juvenile, the better—were all the rage these days. And golden retrievers weren't an option in HDB flats.

After shaving, Durand got dressed, knotted his tie, pulled on his suit jacket, and gathered his devices before heading down the hall. He knocked before poking his head into his daughter's room, Nelson still close on his heels.

His daughter's room was decorated with solar system mobiles, deep field survey posters, and 3D-printed robot dinosaurs she'd created. He gazed down on her sleeping form.

She looked peaceful, a plush dinosaur toy pressed against her cheek.

He whispered, "You're such a faker."

Mia opened her eyes and giggled. "You woke me up."

"Really." He sat on the edge of her bed. "If you were asleep, then what's this . . . ?" He reached under her pillow and produced a glim. Already powered up, the small dome-shaped device instantly located his eyes and projected a video game screen onto his retinas. A virtual aquarium suddenly floated in midair before him—alive with alien swimming creatures and fictional plant life.

"Remember that talk we had about the importance of sleep?"

She whined, "I *did* sleep."

"So if I check the log on this device, I'm not going to see you were up all night?"

"It's *gamework*. And it's due today."

"Gamework."

"Yes. But I couldn't solve it."

Durand examined the screen and the completion percentage in the lower-right corner . . . slowly decrementing: 72 percent . . . then 71. "Well, if I can make some suggestions. Your ecosystem is out of balance—that's why it's decaying."

She propped herself up on her elbows.

He pointed. "You need more diversity to close your life cycle."

"How do I do that?"

"Well, see how energy is draining with each generation? Who's cleaning the ocean floor and recirculating nutrients up the food chain?"

She frowned at the image, which the glim was now projecting into both of their eyes.

"You created big creatures—which is fun. But notice how they're dying off? Instead make tiny, simple creatures, and they'll evolve from there. Balanced ecosystems grow from the bottom up over time, not from the top down all at once. We don't *design* complex systems; we evolve them. It's what Nature does. And Nature is the best teacher."

She reached out to the virtual aquarium and started creating tiny organisms from building blocks on the ocean floor with practiced flicks of her hand—quickly getting engrossed in the simulation.

The percentage jumped to 83. Then to 84. Then 85.

"There you go." He swept her hair aside and kissed her on the forehead. "You're welcome."

She spoke without looking up from the screen. "Adele was wrong. I told her she was wrong."

"It's not Adele's job to do *your* thinking." He got up.

Mia looked up at him. "Daddy?"

"Yes?"

"Is it wrong to edit babies?"

Durand paused for a moment but then sat back down on the edge of her bed. "What makes you ask *that*?"

"Because I was edited. Does that make me a bad person?" Mia kept working on the simulation.

Durand sat in shocked silence for several moments. "Who says you were edited?"

"You did." She turned to him. "I heard you talking to Jiichan when he and Obaasan came to visit."

Durand closed his eyes in frustration at his own stupidity. "Well, first: you weren't meant to hear that."

"So it *is* wrong?"

"No. Well, *babies* don't get edited; *embryos* get edited—when they're just a single fertilized cell. And it's rare."

She looked up at him. "Adele's mom says babies—I mean, embryos—should never be edited."

"Editing isn't necessarily wrong, and it's nothing to be ashamed of."

"But you and Sergeant Yi arrest people for editing embryos."

He leaned down to press his forehead against hers. "No, hon. Daddy doesn't *arrest* anyone. All I do is help the police find people who break the law."

"But editing is against the law."

"Not all edits—just those that aren't safe."

"Was mine safe?"

"Yes."

"What kind of edit was it?"

"It was to cure a disorder—one that's hard to pronounce, but it's called Leber congenital amaurosis. It would have caused your eyes not to develop, so you'd be blind. The doctors made a tiny edit to your SPATA7 gene and fixed it so you could grow up and see the world."

"So it cured me."

He nodded. "That's right. There's nothing wrong with curing an illness. I'm sure Adele's mom takes medicine when she's sick. People correct bad eyesight and cure diseases. Right?"

She nodded.

"Well, that's what your mom and I did because we love you very much."

"Then why are people on the feeds so upset?"

"They're not upset at you, honey."

"What are they mad at?"

He paused again. "Like I said: it's complicated. That's why we wanted to wait until you were older to talk about this." Realizing she wasn't satisfied with this, he added, "Some people want to edit embryos even when they're not sick."

"Why?"

"Because they want to make their kids taller or stronger or smarter than other kids."

"But some kids *are* stronger and taller and smarter."

"Yes, but Nature does that."

"But Nature also makes kids sick—like I was."

Durand paused. "That's true." He laughed and thought harder. "But we don't fully understand how all our genes work together. They took millions of years to evolve, and any changes we make are passed down to all future generations. So the results could change our whole species in ways we didn't intend . . ." A thought occurred to him. "Like in your gamework." He gestured to the glim-cast image. "Do you see how traits in your creatures are passed down to following generations?"

She nodded.

"Well, that's how genetics works in the real world. When you took a shortcut and designed your creatures the way you wanted, they didn't fit the environment, did they?"

She shook her head.

"And even though they looked cool, they soon got sick, and their offspring even sicker—and soon your whole ecosystem got sick. The same is true in the real world. If we make edits that don't fit the environment— even though we think they're cool—then bad things could happen to future generations that we didn't expect. And we don't want that. That's why we only let sick people correct genetic errors—changes that will make them the way humans evolved to be. Any other edits are against the law. And those are the edits your daddy, Sergeant Yi, and Inspector Belanger try to stop—because we want to keep everyone safe."

She looked up at him.

He brushed her hair away from her eyes. "Someday I'm sure you'll know a lot more than I do about all this."

She laughed. "I don't think so. You know a lot."

"You'd be surprised." He glanced up at the time. "Now, if I'm gonna get to work on time, I've got to go." He kissed her on the forehead and confiscated the glim. "Happy birthday, kiddo. And don't fall asleep at school."

He went to the door. "I'll see you tonight."

She waved. "Bye, Daddy."

"Bye-bye, sweetheart." Durand closed the door and turned to see his wife standing in the hall.

She smiled as she approached him. Then she put her arms around his neck. "The birds and the bees are so twentieth century."

"The birds and the bees I *can* explain. Or at least I think I can. What do the birds do again?"

She kissed him. "You did great. It almost makes me forget how badly you screwed up."

He winced. "I know. She must have been eavesdropping with one of her drones. You know how she gets when there's company."

"Thankfully, it worked out." Miyuki held out her hand.

Durand placed the glim into her outstretched palm.

"See you tonight." She kissed him. "Don't forget her gift."

"I won't. I won't."

Chapter 4

nterpol's Global Complex for Innovation, or GCI, resembled a fortified modern art museum. Originally built in the teens of the twenty-first century, it had been expanded and hardened against attack over the years. It now covered several acres of prime real estate in Singapore's diplomatic quarter across Napier Road from the US embassy.

As he approached the entrance, Kenneth Durand nodded to armed guards watching from beyond transparent aluminum blast shields marked with Interpol's sword-and-globe logo. The entrance split into a dozen sealed chutes, only one of which opened to admit Durand. The chute doors operated on a randomized algorithm—with each visitor following a separate, illuminated path. The entire entry system was designed to identify and categorize people into risk tranches—moving them through without stopping and quickly isolating suspected threats. This way no one queued up, which itself would have presented a target to terrorists.

And the GCI was definitely a target.

Organized into financial, cyber, genetic, and counterterrorism divisions, Interpol's GCI employed advanced technologies in the fight against transnational crime—though, contrary to popular perception, Interpol agents themselves had no police powers (at least outside their home countries). Likewise, Interpol itself had only two facilities worldwide—this GCI complex and a headquarters in Lyon, France.

Instead, 190 national police organizations around the world maintained their own Interpol National Central Bureaus, assigning officers to liaise with Interpol's network, receiving and issuing a kaleidoscope of colored Notices—Red, Orange, Yellow, Blue, Green, Purple, Black—advising other nations on the activities of global criminals and the increasingly borderless world of crime. Whether other nations followed up on those Notices depended on local politics and priorities. But if national police organizations wanted cooperation from other national police around the world, ignoring Interpol Notices wasn't the way to get it. This quid pro quo arrangement had worked with varying levels of success over the decades.

Member nations occasionally assigned—or *seconded*—investigators directly to Interpol headquarters, usually to learn or teach about new types of crime. And when it came to catching the next generation of high-tech criminals, Interpol was prepared to recruit from more than just the ranks of police.

Kenneth Durand was fortunate to be one of those recruits. And it couldn't have come at a more propitious time for him, personally.

He cleared two more security checkpoints before arriving on the third floor and passing through another transparent aluminum blast wall emblazoned with the seal of the Genetic Crime Division—Interpol's standard logo with the addition of a twining double helix of DNA around the sword, itself an alarming mutation to Asclepius's staff.

Durand entered the busy offices, nodding at a passing lab technician. The floor plan was sleek, modern—but crowded with makeshift workstations. Proprietary DNA theft, custom viruses, and baby labs were fast becoming the world's most profitable criminal enterprises. That meant the Genetic Crime Division was growing fast, too.

Durand entered the small, windowless office he shared with Detective Sergeant Michael Yi Ji-chang. "Morning, Mike."

"Hey." Yi stared at an AR screen (or screens) only he could see. Yi was an athletic, handsome man. He'd been seconded to Interpol from the Korean National Police Agency in Seoul, which had been in turmoil ever since the reunification. He was here to share his expertise in embryo clinic cartels—and it was Yi who'd referred Durand to Interpol.

"Something up?" Durand removed his suit jacket.

"Oh, sorry. No. Just reading a note from my new cousin."

"New? They found another one?"

"Yeah. Ministry of Health ran his DNA. Confirmed he's related."

"Congratulations. You're getting quite an extended family."

"Wants to come live with me."

"Shit."

"Blew through his reuni check. No marketable job skills. Fan-fucking-tastic." Yi dismissed the virtual screen that was distracting him. "You look better than you sounded on the phone."

Durand hung his suit jacket behind the door. "Haven't changed my mind, though."

"Let's schedule an argument. Right now we've got our eight o'clock." Yi got up and grabbed his own suit jacket from the back of his chair, then headed out through the cubicles.

"Oh, right." Durand grabbed his coat again and caught up. "The calendar just said 'external briefing.' What's this about—the Mumbai raid?"

Yi shook his head. "Two hundred and sixty-three embryo mills shut down on three continents last month, and you think top brass is upset about Mumbai?"

"I'm telling you, it matters."

Durand's division lead, Detective Inspector Claire Belanger, stood at the head of the briefing room. She was a slim, elegant woman in her early fifties, with a sweep of gray hair and piercing blue eyes. She wore a tailored pantsuit and no jewelry save for a platinum wedding band. Durand knew it had been placed there by her late husband—before the bioweapon attack in Paris, an attack that not only killed Belanger's husband but also sterilized thousands of Parisians, Belanger among them. Calm but intense, originally a biochemist, she had joined the Police Nationale in France and was later seconded to Interpol—where she now led the war against genetic crime. Life had delivered her here. Durand could think of no one more capable.

Belanger spoke English with a slight French accent. "Good morning. I realize this briefing was called with little notice, but it will cover new intelligence critical to our mission."

Belanger studied the faces of the two dozen members in her section. Satisfied she had their attention, Belanger continued. "We are joined today by Detective Inspector Aiyana Marcotte, head of Interpol's Human Trafficking Task Force. She will bring you up to speed. Inspector Marcotte comes to Interpol from the US Federal Bureau of Investigation. She is an experienced field agent who, as you'll soon learn, has unique expertise in global human trafficking networks. I expect your full attention to all she has to say—because it will change what we do." Belanger nodded to someone in the audience. "Inspector Marcotte."

"Thank you, Inspector Belanger." A statuesque African woman in her early thirties stood, her skin dark black, hair cropped short. She had a strong jawline and slender neck. Marcotte wore a dark blue business suit. Interpol identification hung around her neck on a lanyard, though Durand knew this was primarily for the convenience of staffers—the GCI's security systems recognized all people within its walls.

Belanger took a seat in the first row as Marcotte moved to the head of the room to stand before Interpol's official seal. Marcotte gazed out at the expert agents and analysts.

"In 2039, sixty million people attempted migrations northward and southward, away from regions stressed by drought, groundwater depletion, rising seas, corruption, war, or economic despair. By 2043, that number had swelled to seventy million. This year, the number is expected to increase yet again.

"Trafficking human beings involves more than just transporting migrants over borders. When people leave behind everything they own and everything they know—language, culture, family—they become vulnerable to exploitation. And exploitation is primarily what human trafficking gangs engage in."

Marcotte gestured and a virtual map of the world's continents appeared in midair. Opaque and vibrant, the image was beamed directly into the retinas of her audience by the room's LFP—or light field projection—system. It closely tracked the eye movement of every person in the room, and was capable of beaming to a full audience.

Marcotte gestured to the map of the world. Moving arrows illustrated paths of human migration away from equatorial climes.

"You may be familiar with these migration routes. Prostitution, manual labor—or worse—awaits the unlucky at the end of these journeys. Stripped of their few possessions, many will have accrued massive 'debts' to the traffickers who smuggle them—debts that must be repaid wherever they arrive."

Marcotte waved and the map was replaced by a gallery of life-sized and extraordinarily lifelike 3D scenes of refugees from all around the world—Caucasians, Africans, Latinos, Arabs, Central and Southeast Asians—men, women, children. These life-sized, realistic forms brought the full emotional impact of poverty to the audience in a way mere photos could not. The victims, frozen in time, had seemingly been brought into the room, new scenes fading in as old ones faded out. A never-ending procession of hardship.

Marcotte walked among the virtual migrants and stood. She gazed out at her audience.

"I, too, was trafficked as a child. In Sudan, my mother sold me into slavery at the age of six—so that my brothers could attend school. I was sold to a wealthy family, consular officials, who later brought me with them to the United States as a domestic. And it was in their home in a gated suburb of Los Angeles that I worked seven days a week and was chained to a bed each night. It was only when neighbors became suspicious that the police were called and I was freed. The arresting female officer later adopted me. Raised me as her own. And it is her name that I took."

She met the eyes of her audience. "Slavery is not an abstraction to me. I have experienced it. I have firsthand knowledge of the despair it brings, and that it is not in our past. In fact, there are more slaves in existence now than at any point in human history. The question is: What are we going to do about it?"

The entire room sat in stunned silence.

"I've come to seek the assistance of the Genetic Crime Division. Your group is one of the few success stories in the fight against high-tech transnational crime. All of Interpol has much to learn from you."

She studied the faces in the room. "And today I'm going to show you evidence that the worlds of human trafficking and genetic crime are converging."

A brief susurration spread through her audience.

She motioned and the images of refugees dissolved, soon replaced by a dozen full-body, hyperrealistic 3D booking scans of heavily tattooed criminals slowly rotating as if on a vertical rotisserie. Each virtual prisoner held a plaque displaying their name and booking number. The group was ethnically diverse—Caucasians, Africans, Asians, Latinos—hard-eyed men, plus a couple of women.

"These are captured leaders of human trafficking gangs that my task force disrupted in the past year." She pointed. "Asia; Africa; Russia; Europe; North, South, and Central America. These gangs all have one thing in common: they've been harvesting genetic material from the refugees they traffic—and selling that data to a single genediting cartel, a group known as the Huli jing. Does that name mean anything here in the GCD?"

Durand nodded with others around him. "We're familiar with the name, Inspector. They're a black market, on-demand cloud computing service. Used by embryo mills for genetic modeling."

Yi added, "Their ties to human trafficking is news to us. You say they pay for DNA samples?"

Marcotte nodded. "Digitized samples. The per-head bounty varies by country. We first learned of it from informants who were being required to extract DNA samples from refugees—saliva swabs mostly. Petabytes of genetic information were being sent from four continents to the Huli jing on a daily basis in exchange for cryptocurrency payments."

Durand took notes on a virtual surface. "It sounds like they're building a global genetic database."

Marcotte nodded. "That's precisely what the Huli jing is doing, Mr. Durand. In fact, we have evidence they were involved in the recent compromise of the Chinese National Genetic Registry—the largest digital storehouse of human genetic information in the world."

More murmurs spread through the audience.

Marcotte paced. "The Huli jing is well funded, disciplined, and extremely low-profile—with a data-gathering operation that gives them globe-spanning influence over both illicit editing labs and human trafficking rings. So far they've fallen between the cracks because they don't directly participate in either activity. But it's time we realized how pivotal they are to both and put our heads together to deal with them. So who are the Huli jing?"

Her entire audience was tapping notes into virtual devices now.

"The name *Huli jing* refers to a mythological nine-tailed fox spirit from Chinese lore, an entity able to assume any form—able to perpetrate mischief while remaining undetected." With a gesture, an inset image of a stylized fox appeared:

"The fox spirit has long been a popular tattoo throughout Asia and the West. But don't look for it among the Huli jing; unlike most gangs they themselves bear no distinguishing marks. No tattoos or brands. Like the mythological fox spirit, they prefer to remain hidden. How do we know?"

She waved her hand and the nine-tailed fox image faded away—replaced by 3D morgue scans of a dozen dead men of many different races—their faces in various stages of decomposition. Nude, the bodies had not one tattoo among them. "Because until recently these men were members of the Huli jing's inner circle—referred to as the Nine Tails—and they bore no gang symbols whatsoever."

Yi grunted. "They're dead."

"Good eye, Sergeant. Yes, they are dead."

And then another set of equally dead faces appeared. And then another.

"And so are these. And these. This last batch from just a month ago. None of the Nine Tails live long. Many were already dead before they'd been identified by our informants. We only discovered their identities later."

Durand frowned in confusion. "Murdered by rival gangs?"

"No. Poisoned by the leader of the Huli jing—Marcus Demang Wyckes. Our best guess is that he *murders* his inner circle on a regular basis."

Looks of confusion spread throughout the audience.

Yi frowned. "Then who on earth would want to become one of the Nine Tails?"

"An excellent question."

Marcotte pointed at the rogues gallery. "These men were all refugees. Perhaps they admired Wyckes—because, like them, Wyckes grew up in refugee camps. And yet he rose to become a major arms smuggler to a dozen insurgencies and terrorist groups. Wyckes gave these men a life of unimagined luxury and power for a brief time. Let them send significant sums of money to their extended families back home. And when they were no longer useful, he eliminated them. Apparently there is no shortage of desperate people willing to make that deal. Only one man always survives among the leadership of the Huli jing—and that's Marcus Wyckes."

Durand watched the procession of morgue scans continue. Each dead face both a victim and a willing participant. "I don't see how men with little education or training could manage—"

"Neither do we, Mr. Durand. That's what I'm hoping your group will help us explain. The Huli jing is a highly technical criminal organization with complex logistical needs, and yet somehow it continues to operate even though its leadership is constantly dying off. It's like no other cartel we've seen. There's no way to place high-level informants. Or to make arrests. Anyone who knows anything important soon dies. All except Wyckes."

Marcotte dismissed the dead men with a wave of her hand. "And as ruthless as Wyckes is with his own people—he is even more terrible to his enemies . . ."

She gestured, and several gruesome, hyperrealistic crime-scene scans appeared onstage—as real as if they were in the room. Each depicted victims dead of some hemorrhagic agent, blood streaming from eyes, nose, mouth. The victims clearly died screaming. "The preferred weapon of the Huli jing is poison—specifically custom-designed synbio-toxins that are difficult to detect and which maximize the victim's agony."

The audience reacted with muted disgust.

Molecular diagrams appeared alongside each image. "We suspect these biotoxins are developed in Huli jing labs—possibly customized to exploit genetic weaknesses of individual targets, meaning doses can be microscopic. Government officials, police, journalists are all fair game— anyone who tries to interfere with the Huli jing's business, which is developing and selling new genetic edits."

The entire room was furiously tapping notes.

"They have, in effect, created a franchise operation—one where they do not directly operate genetic labs, but provide the logistical, research, and even marketing support to gangs that do. Huli jing partner labs ben-efit from access to the most sophisticated technology. They've even branded their select franchisees with a premium label." Marcotte waved her hand and a three-sided knot replaced the crime-scene images:

It rotated, showing the depth of the knot in three-dimensional space. "Do any of you recognize this symbol?"

Durand, Yi, and most people in the division nodded. "Yes. That's the logo for Trefoil Labs."

Marcotte walked around the image. "Trefoil *is* the public face of the Huli jing."

Durand captured the logo and pasted it into his notes. "That's a very useful piece of intelligence, Inspector."

Marcotte nodded. "Their impressive edit library is expanding because they use massive photonic computing clusters to comb through oceans of global genetic data, discovering novel, commercially valuable mutations."

Durand: "They're expanding the edits available to parents."

"Correct—meaning your challenge here at the GCD is going to grow."

Another murmur swept through the crowd.

"More worrisome, the Huli jing is performing unethical research to confirm the viability of the edits their computer models predict . . ." With a wave of her hand, grainy two-dimensional photos appeared, depicting hideously deformed infants. Horrifying mutations.

The audience reacted with gasps.

"These images were taken by hidden camera. This is what Marcus Wyckes is capable of. The Huli jing is mapping not just the human genome, but epigenetics—gene expression—turning genes on and off. And they're doing it with no regard for human suffering. They've also been paying human traffickers to steal the eggs of young women unfortunate enough to fall under their control. To provide raw material for their research."

Durand noticed smoldering rage in Belanger's eyes as she looked up at the images.

"They're developing new edits and searching for commercially valuable mutations present in the population at large. And as you know, mutation laundering can revise the provenance of genetic IP—potentially turning single mutations into multibillion-dollar commercial products. Providing a strong economic incentive for governments to turn a blind eye to their activity."

Durand felt a burden lift from him as he exchanged looks with Yi. The sergeant had been right after all—their work was indeed critically important. More important than he'd ever guessed. He felt a renewed sense of purpose.

Marcotte swept the images all away. "One individual lies at the center of all of this: Marcus Demang Wyckes. He is the single unchanging fact of the Huli jing—its founder and its reclusive leader. If we can locate him, I think we can break their organization—and remove its support of both illicit baby labs and human trafficking cartels."

Marcotte studied the faces in the room. "Here is the last known photograph of Marcus Wyckes . . ." Marcotte waved her hand and a two-dimensional, old-time police booking photo appeared. It showed a dark-haired, burly Eurasian teenager with tan skin. Still young, Wyckes was nonetheless physically intimidating, with broad shoulders, a square jaw, and menacing eyes. "This is from a 2029 arrest in Vietnam on weapon smuggling charges."

Yi piped in, "That picture is fifteen years old."

"Which is why DNA samples taken from Vietnamese and Australian authorities were so useful. We were able to extract his complete genetic sequence and model his physical appearance at his current age of thirty-eight. We've predicted his height within five centimeters precision, his BMI within eight kilograms of precision, his eye color, skin color, and his facial structure." She looked out at her audience. "This is Marcus Wyckes now."

A virtual, photographically real computer model of Marcus Wyckes appeared bald-headed and nude, rotating before them, hands held at his side—a modesty filter blurring out his genitals. His facial expression neutral. One could clearly see the Malay-Australian ethnic mix with his tan skin. He looked physically powerful. Average height, but muscular, with a thick neck and slim waist even in his late thirties. Wyckes's physical stats appeared in text alongside—height, weight, age, eye color, and more.

"Yesterday my group issued a Red Notice for Wyckes's capture in every Interpol member country. I'm hoping I can count on your assistance in that effort."

A strong chorus of assent spread throughout the room.

Belanger stood. "Inspector, I speak for everyone here when I say we will do all within our power to assist you."

"Thank you, Inspector Belanger." She turned to the other agents and analysts. "I thank you for your time."

Belanger turned to her division staff. "You will find the dossier for Marcus Wyckes, the Huli jing, and all relevant intelligence relating to their activities on the GCD Commons. Within the next forty-eight hours I expect to see action plans from group leaders on how to pursue the Huli jing—with an eye in particular on locating Marcus Wyckes. That is all."

As the briefing broke up, Marcotte approached Durand and Yi, extending her hand to Durand. "Mr. Durand."

Surprised, Durand met her eyes and shook firmly. "Great detective work, Inspector Marcotte. I hope you know you can count on us."

Marcotte nodded. "I have it on good authority that your data mining is the root of the GCD's success against embryo labs."

Durand cast a glance at Belanger, who just now joined them.

Belanger nodded the okay to Durand.

He turned back to Marcotte. "I prefer the term *geospatial analysis*."

"Call it what you like, it means culling through oceans of data—not unlike the Huli jing."

"I think it's very different. My work doesn't involve genetic data at all. Just data on human activity."

"Where do you get it?"

"We purchase it just like any marketing company—but instead of targeting customers, we're looking for criminal enterprises."

Marcotte studied Durand for a moment. "I was told that early in your career you helped locate serial killers by modeling honey bees."

Durand was surprised she knew of his master's thesis. Apparently Marcotte had done her homework. "I just found a useful behavior pattern shared by both."

"And what behavior do honey bees and serial killers have in common?"

"Bee brains are fairly simple, so it's easier to model how bees are recruited to flowers than it is to understand how serial killers are drawn toward victims. However, both follow certain elemental behaviors. Bees, for example, maintain a buffer zone around their hive—a zone where they do not forage—in order to avoid bringing unwanted attention to the location of their home. Likewise, the data indicates most serial killers kill in the region of their home, but not in the immediate vicinity of it, where they're more likely to run into someone who recognizes them. Therefore, mapping the geographic spread of a killer's victims helps to further pinpoint the home base of a killer—narrowing the search area with every murder. The mathematical model closely correlates with bee-foraging algorithms."

"Interesting. Your CV says you spent eight years with US Naval Intelligence—hunting down gene-drive bioweapons. Why'd you leave?"

Durand felt an emotional scar itch somewhere deep. "I can't discuss that."

Yi interjected, "Ken did his share, Inspector."

Marcotte relented. "Of course. In any event, it's Interpol's gain. Mr. Durand, your group has achieved more against the Huli jing in the past six months than the rest of Interpol combined. You've seriously hampered their lab network."

Durand nodded. "Good."

"Your success is one reason I've come. I'd like you to focus your data-mining skills on the effort to locate Marcus Wyckes."

Durand exchanged looks with Yi, then Belanger. Then he looked back to Marcotte. "We find criminal activity, not individuals."

"My task force wants to stop human trafficking, and you want to stop genetic crime. The Huli jing are now at the center of both. And Marcus Wyckes is its driving force. Without him, we're confident his group will splinter."

There was silence for a few moments.

"Without question we'll assist you any way we can, Inspector. But regardless of what you've heard, geospatial analysis is not suited to locating specific individuals. I learned that the hard way. What it is useful for is identifying a pattern consistent with certain activities."

"Wyckes must have a pattern."

"Which we can't possibly know." Durand felt old fears awakening. "Individuals are far too variable. Too specific. You will get false positives. Innocent people will die."

Yi touched Durand's shoulder. "Ken."

Durand took a moment. "My algorithms have located hundreds of illegal CRISPR labs in dozens of countries—but we weren't looking for individuals. We were looking for a pattern of illicit commercial activity— a specific location that attracted would-be or existing parents who matched a consistent profile. Parents who had recently deviated from their established behavior patterns. Spent money on fertility treatments. Changed their usual travel and social patterns—especially after meeting with friends who'd recently done the same. We've issued Orange Notices to police agencies based on that analysis, but not Red Notices calling for individual arrests. That lies beyond the data."

"There must be some way to narrow down the search area for Wyckes or for his center of operations, like you did with your serial killer algo-rithms."

Durand was already shaking his head. "Again, organizations don't behave like individuals, and in any event, I doubt that Wyckes is taking part directly in crimes. Those would most likely be these Nine Tails you showed us."

"Then the activities of the Huli jing create a pattern."

"Yes, and if the Huli jing are selling new edits to illicit genetic edit-ing labs on several continents, then our efforts will impact their busi-ness. However, locating Marcus Wyckes *cannot* be part of our mission—not directly." Durand looked up to realize he was raising his voice. "I'm sorry, Inspector. Perhaps in one of these lab raids we'll get lucky, and intel on Wyckes's whereabouts will be found."

Yi added, "You must understand, Inspector, Ken's analysis has been forced to fit a pressing need before. Didn't turn out so well."

Marcotte relented. "I understand."

Belanger stepped in. "Inspector Marcotte, what you've shown us today makes the Huli jing our most pressing priority."

Marcotte nodded. "Sorry if I pressed you, Mr. Durand. I'd heard that you have a knack for locating things hiding in the data. But I also respect that you know the limits of your tools." She reached into her coat pocket. "If by chance anything does occur to you—a moment of inspira-tion perhaps—don't hesitate to contact me directly." She handed Durand an actual physical business card.

Puzzled, Durand took it and examined the inscrutable email address on it.

"I gather you don't get handed a lot of business cards."

He laughed. "No. It's kind of quaint. So you still use email?"

"It's helpful for informants. Some of the people who need to reach me are very poor and don't trust social media platforms."

Durand blinked at the card, and his LFP glasses scraped the data into his contacts.

Before she turned to go, Marcotte touched Durand's elbow. "If you don't mind my asking, how did a guy who can't locate individual crimi-nals wind up finding so many of them?"

Durand thought for a moment. "No offense, but I think the mistake of traditional law enforcement technique is its focus on individuals. Here, we try to limit the damage and spread of *criminal activity*—and that's what drives arrests at the local level. Individual criminals are in some ways beneath our notice here. What we defeat are rising trends. That's why guys like Wyckes never see us coming—because, in many ways, not even we realize we're looking for them."

Marcotte stared. "I see. Well, I look forward to working with you in the future, Mr. Durand."

"Likewise, Inspector."

Chapter 5

Early evening, and Durand sat in the conditioned air of a private, autonomous comcar as it merged into the close coordination of rush hour. His daughter's wrapped birthday gift sat on the seat beside him. He leaned back and felt the stress of the day leave him.

In the distance he could see the glowing logos of synbio firms on the Singapore skyline. Licensed AR video ads played across the surfaces of several skyscrapers—although they were really only being beamed into Durand's retinas by his own LFP glasses. The contract for his LFP glasses required exposure to specific layers of public advertising. At least he'd opted out of the low-end ads, but opting out of all AR advertising was prohibitively expensive.

Just the same, Durand frowned at the shoddy data management employed by advertisers. He was clearly not in the target demographic for an ad gliding across neighboring buildings, alive with images of Jedis, Starfleet officers, and steampunk characters: *"Singapore's premier Star Wars™, Star Trek™, and steampunk cosliving communities . . ."*

Cosseted young professionals at the big synbio firms were a more likely demo for their product—single people with a couple million to blow on living in a theme park.

But by then the ad had shifted to CRISPR Critters. Gigantic, adorable neotenic cats cavorted from building to building, pursuing a virtual ball of yarn.

Durand decided to close his eyes.

He knew it was extravagant to have his own private comcar, but it was one of the perks of the job. And in fact, he treasured this time each day. He had never really had time alone growing up. Not enough space for that. No privacy at the Naval Academy, either, and certainly not in the service.

Durand considered turning on some music when he heard the car's familiar voice.

"*Rerouting . . . Revised travel time one hour and six minutes.*"

Durand sat up. His commute had suddenly tripled in length. The comcar was stopped at a traffic light. Hundreds of people passed on the crosswalk in front of it. He turned around to look through the rear windshield at smaller, older building facades. The towering buildings of the Central Business District stood behind him—which meant he wasn't heading toward the BKE anymore. The car was taking a new route.

"Shit."

Traffic must be backed up somewhere. In his LFP glasses he brought up the car's virtual map and expanded it. The new route brought him around a line of red traffic warnings on the expressway.

"Damnit . . ." Durand tapped his LFP glasses to phone home.

In a moment Miyuki's voice came on the line. "*Hi, hon.*"

"Hi, Mi."

"*I'm scrambling to get ready. Please tell me you remembered the gift.*"

"Yes, got it right here." He put a hand on the package. "Just wanted to let you know the comcar is routing around traffic. If it keeps going this way I'm going to be late."

"*What's your ETA?*"

Durand winced. "Over an hour, but I'm working on it. Just wanted to give you a heads-up."

"*Okay. Do what you can. Love you.*"

"Love you, too."

He clicked off and watched in surprise as the comcar signaled and pulled slowly over to the left curb. The car's interior lights illuminated as if he'd opened the door.

The car's AI voice said, "*This vehicle is experiencing technical difficulties. Please exit.*"

He shouted at the ceiling liner. "Oh, come on!"

"Please exit the vehicle. This vehicle is now out of service."

"Goddamnit . . ." Durand grabbed Mia's gift and got out. He glanced around to get his bearings. He was clearly in an older part of the city. He instantiated the virtual map again with his LFP glasses and studied it as it floated before him.

He then launched his car-hailing app and noticed that it had terminated his ride due to an unspecified vehicle malfunction. Oddly, the app had not summoned a replacement car. He clicked through and was rewarded with an estimated pickup time of forty-five minutes from now.

"No, no, no." The car service had just dumped him here, far off the main expressways. In the middle of rush hour he knew damn well the algorithms were going to triage him as the odd man out. There was no efficient way to collect him where he was.

"Not today. Goddamnit." He checked the time. Guests were showing up in an hour and a half.

Commuters passed him on foot. They, too, were focused on or talking to their own devices.

Just then the supposedly out-of-service comcar he'd exited closed its doors and drove away—merging into the traffic.

"Are you shitting me?" Durand ran alongside the car on the sidewalk, pushing through the foot traffic. "Excuse me. Pardon me."

But the car didn't stop. He glanced at the ride-hailing app again, but no, he'd definitely lost his link to the vehicle. It drove off with an out-of-service AR sign rotating above it.

Durand sighed in frustration as other commuters continued to swarm past him. In a moment it occurred to him that they all seemed to be walking with purpose. He opened the map again and zoomed in to his current location. He was close to the new Tekka wet market—and an MRT station. If he couldn't get a car, he could take the MRT. He examined the street detail.

There. MRT station two blocks away. Durand oriented himself and now realized why the passersby were turning down a narrow pedestrian lane between historic brick buildings of the Little India district. It was the shortest path to the train station.

The north-south line stopped just a few blocks from his building. This was salvageable.

He tapped his LFP glasses to make a call as he fell in line with the rest of the foot traffic.

Miyuki answered. *"How's it looking?"*

He laughed. "You're not gonna believe this. My comcar crapped out."

"You're kidding."

"Stranded me in Little India before it shut down, and it'll take forty-five minutes for another car to pick me up."

"That's ridiculous."

"Don't worry. There's an MRT station nearby. I can hop a train. This might turn out better actually. I might not even be late."

"Well, make sure they give you a credit."

"I have to pay attention to where I'm going, though. So I'm going to hang up. See you soon, hon."

"Bye."

He clicked off and followed other commuters down a narrow lane between old brick buildings. This MRT crowd skewed young—twenties and early thirties. Lots of expats. Well dressed and all talking to people who weren't there. Snatches of conversation floated past him in Hokkien, Mandarin, Malay, Tamil, English, Russian, Swahili, German, Korean—and more he didn't recognize. They'd no doubt come to Singapore to make their killing. To work threads in a blockchain corporation or license their own cellular machinery. XNA programmers. Genetic engineers. Entrepreneurs. And they all had to have impressive CVs to get a work visa in the city.

Looking up, Durand noticed the old Indian and Hokkien storefronts around them. He wondered how these shops and tiny exporters were hanging on. Singapore was not a town paralyzed by nostalgia. Durand had never seen poorly designed public spaces in the city, and that's what this historic district was. He got jostled and held tightly on to Mia's gift as the crowd grew dense. It surged toward the MRT station entrance. Streams of commuters pushed and shoved.

Carried along with the crowd, Durand suddenly felt a sharp sting at the back of his right arm.

It took a second or two to pivot around in the crush of people, but all he saw behind him was a sea of diverse faces wearing LFP glasses, pushing relentlessly forward and past him, headed toward the station entrance. No one reacted to his stare.

Durand tugged at the back of his jacket sleeve but could see nothing. The pain was still there. In fact, it was getting worse.

Shit.

He recalled reading an Interpol report a few months back on jabstick attacks in dense crowds—that they could happen right in front of security cameras without revealing the perpetrator. Psychologists theorized it was a form of rebellion against ubiquitous surveillance. Durand didn't recall any of the incidents occurring in Singapore, though.

He started to doubt himself. But damn, his arm hurt.

Durand struggled across the river of commuters to get to the nearest wall. Just downstream of a support pillar, he took off his suit jacket and checked the back of his shirtsleeve.

A spot of blood soaked through the synthetic silk.

He felt adrenaline surge. *Shit . . .*

Someone in the crowd had stabbed him. An accident? A random psycho? But then Durand realized he could feel more than just adrenaline. He recalled the first time he'd experienced a mortar attack in a CLU at Camp Lemonnier. Alarms wailing as thumps rattled the walls. *That* was adrenaline.

This was something else.

The urge to vomit. Trembling hands, yes. But something else was coursing through him, too. A burning sensation. He could feel it spreading. Was it psychosomatic?

I haven't been stabbed—I've been injected.

An injection under high pressure.

The Huli jing use synbiotoxins.

That's what Marcotte had said. Wasn't that what she'd said? He needed to get help.

Durand tried to tap his LFP glasses to instantiate a phone—but his arm muscles had begun to spasm. The more he tried to move them, the more disconnected they seemed to become. And then he noticed his fingers were swelling.

He tried to speak to his virtual assistant, but his tongue didn't obey him, either—it was swelling fast. His throat constricted.

Durand staggered out into the flood of passing commuters. He stepped in front of them, pleading wordlessly. Workers pushed past him as he howled at them for help, raising a swelling hand. He began to drool uncontrollably, his face suddenly numb. His muscles began to clench in excruciating spasms, causing him to call out in pain.

The commuters looked away—intent on their own lives and virtual interactions. Not wanting to get involved in his reality.

Durand looked up at the ceiling and parapets around and above him—where he knew security cameras would be. But in this precise spot, he could see none.

That's not a coincidence.

Only then did he realize just how well planned this had been.

Durand pitched forward and collapsed onto the concrete floor. He rolled onto his back, staring upward at the graceful, arched ceiling of the wet market.

Passing commuters finally reacted, shouting in several languages, edging around him, some holding the crowd back so he didn't get trampled.

Durand's throat continued to constrict. He struggled for air. Looking up at the concerned faces all around him, he could tell by their expressions that he was in trouble. He could feel the skin of his face tightening.

Someone had intentionally injected him. *The Huli jing use synbio-toxins.* He recalled the gallery of dead.

Still clutching his daughter's gift with a paralyzed arm, he struggled to raise his free hand. His fingers were now so badly swollen that his wedding ring had become a tourniquet.

A group of commuters cleared space around Durand, shouting. Curious onlookers knotted around the scene.

"Call ambulance, lah!"

"Serangan jantung?"

"Mite, sugoku hareteiru!"

"Stay back! He looks contagious!"

Durand stared at people's feet. So many expensive shoes. Sneakers were not popular in Singapore. His breathing became more and more labored. Men knelt close to him, loosening his tie, unbuttoning his shirt.

"Usake paas se door hato!"

Durand soon became aware of uniformed paramedics arriving. They wore visored helmets. One of them leaned in close, checking Durand's vitals.

Durand tried to speak, but his swollen tongue and constricted throat rendered him mute.

Mia and Miyuki would be so disappointed. His mother, too. She'd never wanted him to travel here. Durand also realized how disappointed he was. He closed his eyes and concentrated.

Please, not this way. Not now.

Radio chatter in an unknown language. The whole world was looking and sounding strange now. Distorted. Leering faces of professional men and women.

He couldn't move. His entire body was swollen in a violent reaction to something. His shirtsleeves and shoes squeezed him mercilessly. Unbearable muscle spasms increased. He groaned.

One paramedic pried the birthday gift from Durand's frozen arm. Durand's eyes tried to follow it, only to see the other paramedic lift metal clippers to Durand's hand—and snip the wedding band off of Durand's swollen index finger, leaving a red indentation where it had been choking off blood flow.

A toy poodle in the arms of a nearby elderly Chinese man started barking madly—and then struggled to escape as if in terror. It hopped out of the man's hands and fled between the feet of onlookers. The man shouted after it.

Durand watched reality with increasing detachment, his eyes wandering across the faces in the crowd above him. Then his eyes focused on one face just now leaning in close to his own—a handsome young Eurasian man. He wore a fine suit and had midlength black hair. He knelt just two feet away, gazing down, with both hands leaning on the engraved ivory handle of a full-length black umbrella. The double-Windsor knot of the man's pale yellow silk tie was perfect.

Durand stared into the young man's gray eyes.

They stared back with unflinching intensity.

Even though Durand struggled for air, his entire focus held on the young man. Though every way normal in appearance—refined even—an uncanny-valley effect pervaded him. The young man did not seem real. Some instinct screamed to Durand that the eyes regarding him were empty.

He felt growing terror as the man leaned even closer now, reaching across Durand. Every cell in Durand's body recoiled.

The young man picked up Mia's gift and tucked it underneath his own arm. With that, he drew back again to stare once more into Durand's eyes.

Durand could not turn away. Those cold gray eyes held him. He couldn't recall *ever* having seen eyes like that before. Unliving eyes. They watched as Durand's vision faded into darkness as an internal fire consumed him.

He could not even gather the breath to scream.

Chapter 6

Kenneth Durand knows it is August 2035. That already happened, but that's okay because it's a beautiful day. He's younger—in his midtwenties. O-3, Lieutenant Durand, on ten days' leave, walking in civilian clothes through the newly expanded Greenfield Terminal of Nairobi's Jomo Kenyatta International Airport alongside a younger *Sowi* Michael Yi Ji-chang. Yi frowns as he pokes at an actual handheld smartphone. They move through the busy terminal, dodging between Chinese businessmen and tourists. Durand's stride is easy and relaxed—though he has no reason to be relaxed.

"Ken, this connection's going to be frickin' tight." Yi motions for them to step it up.

They're catching a Safarilink flight from Wilson Airport to Amboseli—half a dozen other squad mates will be trying to hold the plane for them. They have yet to collect their bags, deal with customs, taxi across town.

Durand just cannot work up anxiety over it. He's not sure if that's the way he felt at the time. He suspects not. This trip was important to him. He bought an actual camera for this trip. Kilimanjaro. The game preserve. It all seemed really special. And it was special.

But not today.

They're pushing through the crowd at baggage claim. Durand sees his bag before Yi spots his own. Durand reaches for the handle at the same time that a young Japanese woman does.

She looks up in surprise as they brush hands. "This one's mine."

"American." It is an odd thing for him to say.

"Yes. And this is my bag."

Durand lets go. He looks down and realizes she's right. There's a bright red, embossed metal tag on it, held fast by a beaded chain. It's otherwise identical to his own bag—a matte black carbon fiber shell with the closest thing to off-road wheels. You could probably row the damn thing down the Nile. Now he sees his own bag coming up not far behind on the carousel. He points. "You have good taste."

She laughs.

He collects his bag. It is a highly practical bag. Only attractive for what it can do. Both their bags are scuffed from rough handling.

She telescopes the handle on hers and rolls it away—but only far enough to get clear of the crowd. She takes out a tablet and starts reconnecting with her world.

A glance. Yi still anxiously awaits the appearance of his own bag on the carousel.

Durand turns back. He studies the young woman. She is dressed for travel. Sensible shoes. Lots of pockets. She is not a tourist. She has been here many times before. He rolls up to her. "I have to ask."

She looks up from her tablet, her expression guarded.

"That's a serious bag."

"That's not a question."

"You must have a serious job."

"I do." She nods toward his bag. "And you?"

"Too serious. I've been considering a change. But then I'd have to give up the bag."

She laughs again. Her eyes smile.

The connecting flight is suddenly not so important. "You're arriving from where?"

"Far away."

"I've been there."

She points at her tablet. "I've got to get my drilling robots clear of customs, and then I'm headed to Mombasa with my project team. So . . ."

"Right. I'm meeting friends, too." He moves away and then circles back after going just a few meters. "But here's the thing: I'll be on the coast at the end of this week, and there's this great place on Diani Beach."

"Ali Barbour's Cave."

He laughs. "Right."

"I love that place."

"There's lots of people there. Come join me."

"I'll still be with my project team."

"Bring them. I'll take your whole damn project team out to dinner if it means you'll say yes."

She laughs again. He could get lost in her eyes. "There's a fine line between persistence and harassment."

He nods, a slight smile on his face. "There is. But this is probably the only time our paths will ever cross. Unless I ask you." He searches her eyes. "So I'm asking you."

She eyes him back. "Do you have a name?"

"I do." He extends his hand. "Ken Durand."

She shakes his hand with a firm grip. She has calluses on her hands. "Okay, Ken Durand. I'm Miyuki Uchida."

"Miyuki. Good to meet you."

And it was true. He knew it the moment he first saw her.

Chapter 7

Kenneth Durand found himself staring at a soft white light. It took a long while to focus well enough to discern the frame around it.

A ceiling light fixture.

He then slowly resolved the ceiling tiles around that. Eventually he cast his gaze downward and saw that he was in a modern intensive care unit—medical machines beeping and pumps hissing.

What the hell?

His entire body was racked by dull pain, as though he'd pulled every muscle. He noticed that he was wearing a hospital gown. An IV ran into his arm and a catheter into his groin. No blanket covered him—so he could plainly see the skin of his arms and legs bruised black, blue, and yellow.

Confusion clouded his mind, and he looked up to see sensors and medical equipment looming around his bed. He felt something lodged in his throat and tried to swallow around it awkwardly. Panic rose as his gag reflex kicked in—until he saw the breathing tube leading from his mouth to a nearby ventilator. It hissed rhythmically, soothingly, and he felt air flow into his lungs. He could feel medical tape around his mouth securing it in place.

Durand closed his eyes again and tried to center himself. To remain calm. He had no idea how he'd gotten here.

He heard *beep-beep*ing as his heart rate settled once more. He opened his eyes and looked around the ICU. His bed was partitioned on the left and right by sliding curtains. He didn't hear any movement or talking beyond them, just the hisses of machines.

But then he discerned the whine of an approaching electric motor. A boxy wheeled robot soon came into view, emblazoned with a red cross. It rolled to a stop at the foot of his hospital bed, then turned to face him. A soft voice emanated from it as a soothing blue light pulsed: *"Please be calm. I have summoned assistance. Sila bertenang. Saya telah memanggil bantuan . . ."*

Durand focused on the pulsing pastel blue light and found it reassuring. He wondered what psychological research had led to its deployment. He decided the research was solid because he did feel soothed by its glowing, then fading—like waves lapping a beach. He had no idea what the hell was going on, but this machine apparently did, and that was some consolation.

Moments later an Indian woman doctor assisted by a Hoklo male nurse arrived to check Durand's vitals. The doctor tested Durand's pupils with a penlight. Satisfied, she looked closely at him and spoke in British-accented English. "Can you hear me?"

Durand nodded.

"I am Dr. Chaudhri." She placed a reassuring hand on Durand's shoulder. "You've been in a coma. Do you understand?"

The news hit Durand hard. After a moment or two of panic, he nodded slowly, despite the tubes leading from his throat.

The doctor squeezed Durand's shoulder again. "You've suffered a massive allergic reaction to something—we don't yet know what. However, we believe you're out of danger. Still, we're going to keep you in the ICU for a little while longer."

Durand studied his bruised and bandaged arms and hands. They looked almost alien.

The doctor followed his gaze. "The swelling receded only yesterday."

On Durand's effort to speak the doctor said, "I'm going to remove your breathing tube. Please just relax. This will not hurt, though it will be briefly uncomfortable."

The nurse moved in to assist, and after they removed the medical tape, Durand felt an alarmingly long tube snake out of his throat. He gagged a bit as the last of it came out, and felt again a dreadful soreness in his stomach muscles, ribs, and chest as he coughed. The agonizing coughing fit continued for several seconds.

The doctor's soothing hand was on his shoulder again. "You're safe now, but your heart stopped for a bit last week." She smiled. "You're quite the fighter."

With the tubes out Durand croaked, "How long have I been here?" His voice sounded as awful as his throat felt.

"Almost five weeks."

Five weeks? That was impossible. He'd just been talking with colleagues at the GCI. What happened? He looked back up at her. "What hospital?"

"Mount Elizabeth."

Durand stared blankly.

"Mount Elizabeth Hospital, Singapore. You were found without identification. Can you tell me your name?"

Durand struggled to process all this news. *Without identification?*

The doctor repeated, "You were found without identification. Do you remember your name?"

He took a deep breath. "I'm Kenneth Andrew Durand. Lead geospatial analyst with Interpol GCI. I'm a US citizen."

The doctor took notes on a totem device—an inert physical object commonly used as a handy surface on which to interact with virtual screens. "You're with Interpol?"

He nodded. "I don't know how I got here. Where are my wife and daughter? Are they okay?"

The doctor took additional notes. "You were found alone and unconscious in a stolen car parked in Boon Lay."

"Boon Lay?"

"Were you with your wife and daughter?"

Durand shook his head absently, recalling that he hadn't been. "No. No, they weren't with me." He wasn't quite sure how he knew that. But he did. He looked up. "I've been here five weeks?"

She nodded.

He struggled to understand. "No one came looking for me?"

"The police came."

"Police? Why didn't they contact my family? Or contact Interpol?"

"No one could ID you."

Durand looked up at her incredulously. "That makes no sense."

"You're not in our national DNA registry. Now we know why: you're American."

"The American embassy should have been searching for me. Interpol. My family."

The doctor leaned close and spoke slowly. "Understand, Mr. Durand, we were initially concerned you'd been infected by a contagious pathogen—a hemorrhagic fever or new synbio organism. You were black with bruising—your entire body and face badly swollen. Your skin scabrous. Not even your ethnicity was apparent. Even your hair fell out. Yours has been a curious case."

"But . . . fingerprints."

She lifted his left hand and opened the palm toward him. He could see bandages wrapping his fingertips.

"The swelling split your skin at the extremities. It's still healing. Some required stitches."

Durand studied his bandaged fingers and now discerned the soreness underneath. He looked up at her.

"Your eyes hemorrhaged as well—so we couldn't scan your retinas. They're still alarming to behold. We've ruled out contagious disease, but we don't yet know what caused your body's violent reaction."

He searched for words. "My name is Kenneth Andrew Durand. I live in Woodlands with my wife, Miyuki Uchida, and our daughter, Mia." Durand got emotional. "I need to see them. They must be frantic." He paused. "It was my daughter's birthday."

"A birthday is the least of your concerns at the moment." The doctor touched his shoulder again. "I'll contact your wife immediately, Mr. Durand. Do you have a number I can call?"

"You don't have my phone? I . . ." He realized this, of course, must be the case. "I had no identification on me? Nothing?"

Forgiving of his disorientation, she shook her head.

He saw that even his wedding band was missing. "They took my wedding ring."

"Someone robbed you?"

He clutched his bandaged hand, but could clearly see the ring was gone. "I remember a young man with an umbrella . . . He was terrifying. And paramedics. I remember paramedics."

She stared back.

"My wife's number is 9-3-9-3-9-4-7-8-7."

She jotted it down. "You're safe now, Mr. Durand. We think you'll make a full recovery. Though we'll want to continue tests to pinpoint the source of your allergic response."

As she turned to go, Durand clutched at the hem of her coat with his bandaged hand. "Interpol. Please contact Interpol here in Singapore. Ask for Detective Inspector Claire Belanger. They need to know where I am. It's critically important."

"The number?"

He paused. Security protocols started to come back to him. "Call the main Interpol line here in Singapore. Tell them who I am, and they'll direct you."

"Inspector Claire Belanger." The doctor wrote the name down.

Durand felt suddenly exhausted.

The doctor moved his arm back onto the bed. "Get some rest, Mr. Durand. We'll contact the authorities and your family. Your job now is simply to get well."

He nodded weakly. "Thank you, Doctor."

She and the nurse departed.

Exhausted, Durand dozed off.

Durand awoke to the sound of someone clearing their throat. He looked up to see Inspector Claire Belanger and Sergeant Michael Yi Ji-chang standing at the foot of his hospital bed. Neither of their expressions looked particularly friendly.

Durand straightened in the bed. "Claire. Mike. Thank god." His voice sounded gravelly and hoarse.

They exchanged concerned looks and resumed staring.

Durand then noticed that he was no longer in the intensive care unit but in a private room. It was evening outside. He wondered how and when they'd moved his hospital bed, but then decided it didn't matter.

"I was poisoned." Even his tongue felt odd, making it difficult to sound out words. "A jab-stick in the middle of a crowd near the Tekka wet market. I think the Huli jing did it."

They said nothing.

"My comcar malfunctioned and dumped me near downtown. Somebody must have been following me. Which means we've had a security breach."

They still did not react.

"We should get techs down here to pull a blood sample. There might still be traces of the biotoxin they used in my system." He winced as he sat up slightly. "Also, Anna and Gus should do a pattern analysis on all telephone calls radiating out from my location immediately following the assassination attempt. Geolocation data on all comm devices in the area, too—and communities of interest going out two generations at least, one minute before and after, looking for echoes."

Belanger and Yi continued staring at him.

Durand pressed on. "And a protective detail. They tried to kill me once, they'll try again. I think the only reason I'm alive is because I was brought in here as a John Doe. And for god's sake, put a protective detail on Miyuki and Mia. Better yet, put them on a plane to the States. Her parents will be glad to see them."

Durand regarded the unfriendly eyes of his colleagues. "This is typically where you guys say how *great* it is to see me alive."

Neither of them did.

As he tried to lift his arm, Durand's wrist tugged back to the rattling of metal. He looked down to see that he was handcuffed to the bed rail. "What the hell . . . ?"

Yi moved toward the bed, pulling a document out of his jacket pocket as he approached. He unfolded the paper and dropped it into Durand's lap.

It was a familiar Interpol Red Notice—with text and DNA profile information and also the photo of a familiar, thuggish Eurasian man—labeled with the name Marcus Demang Wyckes.

"We know who you are, Mr. Wyckes. Matched your DNA. And we'd like to have a word with you regarding the whereabouts of Kenneth Durand."

Chapter 8

nspector Belanger, Sergeant Yi, and Dr. Chaudhri stood in a radiology lab, examining a wall of virtual medical imagery on an AR layer shared through their LFP glasses. Floating before them were X-rays, 3D scans of bone structure, dental records, MRIs.

"Why didn't you confirm the patient's identity before contacting Durand's wife?"

Dr. Chaudhri cast an annoyed look Belanger's way. "I had no way of knowing who this man was. Not even the police could identify him."

Yi interceded. "She's right, Claire. The SPF must have gotten their samples mixed up. I came here last month hoping this guy was Ken— been to every hospital and morgue in Singapore and Johor a dozen times. City police gave me his DNA profile. I ran it through CODIS. No matches."

Belanger thought out loud. "And today—"

"I watched Dr. Chaudhri draw two different blood samples. Ran the GlobalFiler assay myself, and the DNA profiles were both perfect matches for Wyckes. I nearly fell over. The first test had to be a lab mix-up."

Belanger mused, "And the only reason we're here is because he claimed to be Ken. Wyckes called us here himself."

Yi shrugged. "Strange, isn't it? For Wyckes to do that."

"There must be some reason." Belanger held up her hands. "Apologies for my ill temper, Dr. Chaudhri. But our missing agent's wife and daughter are more traumatized than ever by your call. I'll need to go see them."

Yi turned to Belanger. "Claire, what was all that about in there? Why is Wyckes trying to convince us he's Ken?"

The doctor folded her arms. "Could be psychosis. The man did suffer swelling of his brain. Did he know your missing agent?"

Belanger said grimly, "He knew *of* him."

Yi studied the medical imagery. "But how does he know all that personal stuff about Ken? And about us?"

"The Huli jing were clearly planning their abduction of Ken for some time. We must assume they have the entire GCD team under close surveillance."

Yi frowned. "But even Ken's mannerisms, Claire. The *way* Wyckes talked. It's so much like Ken."

Belanger grabbed Yi by the shoulders. "Michael, I need you to function. I know you're hurting about Ken. So am I. But to think that the man in that hospital bed is Ken is not rational."

"It isn't . . ." Yi looked to both Chaudhri and Belanger. "Right? I mean, full-grown people can't be edited."

Belanger shook her head. "Modifying the genetic sequence of the thirty-five trillion cells that comprise a living, breathing human being— it isn't possible. You'd kill the person."

Dr. Chaudhri nodded. "Retroviruses modify the DNA of living cells, but only to replicate the virus. Even that small degree of editing can kill the host. The human immune response is—"

"This subject isn't worth discussing. What we need to figure out is why Marcus Wyckes is in that hospital bed. And how it relates to Ken's disappearance."

Yi nodded reluctantly. "Wyckes was puffed up like a dead whale when I came here last month—like his body was fighting off some type of poison."

"And poison is the preferred weapon of the Huli jing," Belanger mused.

"Maybe Wyckes got an accidental dose. This was around the same time Ken disappeared. Inspector Marcotte said even microscopic doses could be fatal. Maybe it damaged Wyckes's memory somehow."

Dr. Chaudhri instantiated a virtual lab report for their review. "We considered biotoxins. Didn't find any—although there were trace amounts of XNA in the initial toxicology report, which was strange. They didn't appear in subsequent tests."

"Synthetic DNA."

"Right. Since XNA doesn't interact with normal cells, it's sometimes used as a delivery mechanism for printed narcotics, date rape drugs, nanomachines—but it doesn't make much sense for a poison. If you're trying to kill someone, you're not worried about preventing an immune reaction."

Belanger pondered the situation. "There's something here we're not seeing."

Yi examined the lab report. "Is there anything else that might help us, Doctor? Anything you haven't already told us?"

Dr. Chaudhri thought for a moment, then looked up. "The patient's caloric needs while he was in his coma."

"What about them?"

"After a few weeks he was burning more calories than an Olympic athlete. At one point he was getting nine thousand calories a day in his drip. I've never seen anything like it. It was almost impossible to keep him hydrated, and his fever was close to fatal. His body was literally burning itself up."

Durand lay wide-awake in the private room, the door closed. Each time he moved, the handcuff chain rattled. This was a waking nightmare.

With his free hand he picked up the Interpol Red Notice still lying in his lap and studied it. DNA ladders, physical description, criminal history, extradition info—and a color computer model of a bald-headed, thick-necked Eurasian man.

An insane fear began to form in Durand's mind. The reaction of Yi and Belanger to him. Their insistence that he was Wyckes. Durand lay numbly for several moments, his heart beating faster.

Durand shouted at the top of his lungs: "Nurse!"

A nurse did not immediately appear, so he found the call button and pressed it with his bandaged fingers.

After a few moments an unfamiliar Caucasian male nurse opened the door and poked his head in.

Durand spoke, emotionless. "I need a mirror."

"I can't give you any hard objects."

"I want to see myself. I need to see my face."

"I can't give you—"

"Then *you* hold the mirror. Please. I need to see my face. I need to know I'm okay."

"It's just bruising, sir."

"I need to see my face. Please!"

Something about the desperation in Durand's voice caused the nurse to nod. He left and after a minute or two returned with a round, polished metal mirror with dull edges.

The nurse moved along the left edge of the bed, on the side opposite of where Durand's hand was cuffed to the rail. The nurse remained out of reach as he raised the mirror up to Durand at head level.

"See? It's just bruising. You'll look fine in a week or so."

Durand took a deep breath and looked up into the stainless-steel reflection of his face.

What he saw there drove him insane.

The face in the reflection was not his own. Not even close. His cheek-bones were different. His nose, his neck, and his jaw—all different. It was more than plastic surgery could ever change. Even his race was different—no longer Caucasian but Eurasian. The shape of his eyes and his eye color—though still bloodshot red—was different. Instead of blue, his eyes were now brown.

He was without doubt the Marcus Wyckes in the photo on the Red Notice.

Durand started hyperventilating, and then he shrieked in anguish.

"Sir! Sir!"

"What have you done to me!" Durand felt his adrenaline surging. He looked down at the catheter extending into his groin and took a deep breath.

He began to carefully pull it out, screaming against the pain. He got splashed briefly as the tube fell away from the bed.

"Sir! Stop!" The nurse smacked an alert button on the wall. "I need help in here!"

Durand was already clawing at the bandages holding his IV in place on the back of his hand. He screamed again in anguish as he pulled out the IV needle, toppling the IV stand.

"What have you done!"

Just then Durand noticed dark, curving lines had begun to appear on the surface of his bruised arms in several places, lengthening as though some mysterious force was writing on his skin with ink. He turned his arms over, staring at them in horror.

Elaborate tattoos began appearing up and down his arms. Chief among them was the nine-tailed fox of the Huli jing just now solidifying on his right forearm, with Asian script and a stylized trefoil knot on his left arm. It was as though they had floated to the surface from within him.

Several orderlies and a male doctor rushed in. They came to a full stop as they beheld him in shock.

Durand screamed, holding up his arms. "What have you done!"

The nurse pointed. "Those weren't there—"

Durand shouted, "What have you done to me!"

The doctor motioned to the orderlies. "Strap him down."

Durand screamed again and again. "What have you done to me? What have you done!"

The orderlies swarmed him.

Durand struggled as they grabbed his arms.

More orderlies arrived to help get Durand under control.

"What have you done!"

Back in the radiology lab, Dr. Chaudhri pointed. "What's going on there?"

Belanger and Yi followed the doctor's gaze toward a bank of virtual surveillance screens—one for each bed in the ward. Belanger expanded the screen where Wyckes wrestled silently with orderlies as they strapped him down. At the screen's edge a doctor prepared a sedative.

Belanger pointed to the elaborate, curving tattoo lines that now ran along Wyckes's neck, across his bald head and his arms. "Gang tattoos?"

Yi examined the surveillance image. "Where did they come from?"

"It appears Inspector Marcotte was wrong. The Huli jing are using some new type of tattoo to identify their members."

Yi nodded numbly.

Belanger turned to him. "Do you still doubt this is Marcus Wyckes?"

Yi gazed at the violent struggle on-screen. He hesitated—but then threw up his hands in frustration. "I still don't understand how Wyckes knew some of the private things he mentioned in there. He knew about a conversation Ken and I had before my *wedding*."

Belanger put a hand on Yi's shoulder. "Michael."

"You think they tortured Ken."

"I'm hopeful we can still find him. What I don't understand is why the leader of the Huli jing would come to Singapore in the first place. Wyckes is wanted in a hundred and ninety countries. Singapore has extradition, ubiquitous surveillance, a highly trained police force. There are a million safer places for Wyckes to be."

Yi tried to control his emotions—to concentrate on the case. "He doesn't seem so happy to be here now."

On the room monitor orderlies finished strapping Wyckes down. A doctor administered a sedative. Wyckes looked to be convulsed with sobs.

"Call in the Singapore police, Michael. Let's get this man into custody. And contact Inspector Marcotte. Tell her that Ken Durand found her man after all."

Yi pondered the surveillance image for several moments, then nodded to Belanger.

Chapter 9

The encrypted line rang several times before it picked up without a word.

The caller spoke into the silence. "The transformation ran its course, but hospital staff revived him at the end."

A digitally altered voice replied, *"Then he's still alive?"*

"Yes. He's been positively identified as you. They're transferring him into police custody to face charges."

After several moments, *"The change agent was supposed to kill him after it completed."*

"It stopped his heart, but apparently the doctors at Mount Elizabeth have talent."

Several more moments of silence, filled with encryption static.

"Finish it. Make it look like an escape attempt."

"I'll take care of it personally."

"No. I don't want you under scrutiny. Let other police do our work for us—preferably in public."

"I understand."

"And, Detective . . ."

"Yes?"

"Make his escape violent. There must not be a shred of doubt who this man is."

The line held for a moment in silence.

"Consider it done."

The line disconnected.

Chapter 10

Durand lay disconsolate, strapped to his hospital bed. It occurred to him he might have suffered neurological damage from the biotoxin—that he might not be perceiving reality.

He looked at his arms, strapped down at the wrists. No tattoos in sight on his bruised forearms.

Hallucinations. If he was honest with himself, brain damage seemed increasingly likely. He knew it could manifest strange symptoms. Men and women who were convinced their spouse was an imposter—identical but not genuine. Or people who could no longer recognize facial features for even the most significant people in their lives—fathers, sons, wives. What if he was unable to recognize *himself*?

But that didn't explain his colleagues. Why didn't his colleagues recognize him? Was he misperceiving that, too?

And would it be any better to be insane? After a moment's thought, he decided insanity would be preferable to what he'd seen in that mirror. What *had* he seen in that mirror?

Heavy footsteps approached in the corridor outside. The hospital room door opened. Half a dozen uniformed Singapore police officers entered, hands resting on the butts of their holstered pistols as they checked out the room.

Strapped down and helpless, Durand looked up at them.

The officers acted as though he wasn't there. Instead, one of the policemen called out in Malay, *"Memberselikhan!"*

A pair of uniformed constables wheeled a gurney into the room and alongside Durand's bed. More officers and a dour-looking detective with facial moles and designer LFP glasses crowded around the doorway. Durand could hear police radios squawk in the corridor beyond as well.

The detective spoke in British-accented English. "Marcus Demang Wyckes, you are under arrest on multiple counts of murder, racketeering, extortion, human trafficking, tax evasion, unlawful genetic editing, and kidnapping. You are to be remanded to a prison infirmary to await arraignment."

Durand closed his eyes and shouted, "I'm not Marcus Wyckes! I'm Kenneth Durand!"

"Do not test me, Mr. Wyckes."

"I'm Kenneth Durand! There must be a way to—"

"You will be silent or you will be silenced."

Four officers grabbed Durand's arms and legs, while another two officers unfastened the bed's restraining straps.

Durand did not struggle, but he looked up at the detective again. "Please. I'm not who you think I am. I'm—"

"Silence this man."

"Wait! Please—"

An officer fitted a seizure muzzle over Durand's lower face. It had a plastic mouthpiece apparently designed to prevent a patient from swallowing or biting his tongue—which effectively made it impossible to speak as well. The officer tightened the Velcro straps. Moments later Durand could only emit muffled noise.

The police lifted him from the bed, transferring him to the waiting gurney, where they cuffed both hands and both feet to the railings. They then wheeled Durand out the door and down the corridor—past lines of uniformed police amid the crackling of radios.

Durand saw Michael Yi and Claire Belanger standing among them, looking down at him as he rolled past. Durand struggled to speak through the muzzle. Yi watched Durand go with what looked to be an odd mixture of animosity and concern. Belanger was stone-faced.

The gurney rolled noisily into a hospital elevator, attended by two uniformed officers. Durand's prolonged stare at Sergeant Yi ended only when the elevator doors closed. He then slumped back onto the gurney, without hope.

One of the officers turned a key in the panel and the elevator descended. The radio on one officer's belt squawked, "*Transport five ready in loading dock. Area secure for transfer.*"

The officer responded in English. "Descending elevator four. Prisoner secured."

Durand lay staring up at the harsh ceiling lights. *Secured.* Yes, he was definitely secured—hand and foot. Gagged. Trapped in an alien body. Clearly this was not happening—some fever dream. It had all the surreality of a dream.

They traveled for perhaps thirty seconds in silence until one of the officers muttered as he worked the elevator key.

The other snorted. "You missed."

"Fuck off."

The elevator doors opened to reveal a subbasement corridor. A tactical police officer in body armor, helmet, and balaclava looked up at them. He approached, submachine slung across his chest. The word "Police" was printed in bold white letters on his black vest. He pointed upward. "You're supposed to be on one, lah."

The officer sighed and looked closer at the markings on the elevator panel. "This damned thing . . ."

The tactical officer chuckled and leaned in. "If it's in fire mode, it'll go to the basement. Here . . ."

His gloved hand moved forward, but instead of operating the panel, it held a disposable polymer revolver—which he fired from the waist upward into the throat of the nearest officer. The shot hammered Durand's eardrums in the closed space.

The other officer scrambled for his holster, but two more deafening shots caught the man in the eye and the jaw—splattering blood over the back wall and onto Durand's feet. The officer's hat fell off as his body collapsed onto Durand.

Durand struggled, screaming into his muzzle.

The tactical officer placed the printed gun alongside Durand's bandaged hand—and fired one more shot into the second officer's scalp.

Durand let out another muffled shout as blood streamed onto him from the bullet hole.

The tactical officer then pivoted the gun and fired two more shots into the first officer on the floor nearby. After which he stowed the revolver in his weapon harness.

Durand's ears rang.

He felt the gurney pulled out of the elevator and into the corridor. The tactical cop aimed his MP6 from its strap and stared menacingly at Durand as he worked a key to unlock all four handcuffs.

Durand's eyes darted in confusion. Finished, the cop tossed the key into the elevator, then put his booted foot to the gurney and kicked it over—rolling Durand onto the concrete floor. Every bruise and ache flared up anew as he tried to raise himself up.

The tactical officer grabbed him by the hospital gown, dragging him forward. Durand felt a gun barrel shoved into his ribs. "On your feet!"

Durand stumbled, at first barely able to walk after weeks on his back. But adrenaline flowed through his system. He found reserves of strength he didn't think he had as he glanced back to see blood spreading across the floor of the open elevator. He limped forward.

"Move!" The tactical officer practically dragged him up a short flight of concrete steps. At the top, he kicked open a fire door.

Fire alarms immediately squealed. Strobe lights flashed.

The tactical officer shoved Durand out into the darkness beyond. Durand tumbled onto pavement, pain blinding him for several moments.

But then Durand rolled over to see the metal fire door swing slowly closed as the tactical officer spoke into his shoulder radio. "Officers down! Officers down! The prisoner escaped—he has a weapon!"

The steel door slammed shut, muffling the fire alarm and leaving Durand on a concrete sidewalk behind the hospital amid the humidity of a tropical night. There was no door handle on this side.

Durand got shakily to his bare feet and tore at the Velcro fasteners of the muzzle—finally pulling it off.

"Fuck!"

What the hell is happening?

This nightmare refused to end. His mind raced as he tried to understand. But then he heard police sirens over the muted fire alarm. Lots of sirens.

If this was real, then two police officers had just been murdered. In a city that often went *years* without a single officer fatality, that was going to result in a massive manhunt. And he was clearly supposed to take the blame.

But why? Wasn't he already headed to prison as Wyckes? It dawned on Durand that now he wasn't likely to survive long enough to reach prison.

Durand gazed out at the skyline of downtown Singapore towering around him, at autonomous vehicle traffic, bright street lights. The navigation strobes of drones flitting about on delivery runs. He tried to get his bearings, but without LFP glasses, he realized, he wasn't as familiar with the Central Business District as he had believed. Hell, he didn't even have shoes. All he was wearing was a blood-spattered hospital gown with his ass hanging out—blood spattered his bare arms and legs, too.

The sirens drew closer.

Durand chose a random direction and fled into the evening streets. It hardly mattered which way he went since there were cameras everywhere.

Chapter 11

Durand clambered through a hedge line and crossed onto a three-lane road busy with autonomous cars and buses. He waved his arms and the autonomous vehicles lurched to a stop—as he knew their algorithms required. Comcar passengers shouted at him to get out of the road.

"What, you crazy?"

Durand could see nightsun searchlights already stabbing down from approaching aircraft in the distance. Strobing police lights passed on nearby blocks. Sirens grew louder.

Durand's bare feet slapped across the pavement, moving toward crowds of people—toward restaurants and cafés on the next block—and deeper into the Central Business District. He loped along, wind kicking up his hospital gown—his near nudity making him feel even more vulnerable.

Hallucinations be damned; he was propelled by instinct now. How all this had happened wasn't clear, but if he wasn't brain damaged and imagining all this, a police officer had just set him up. Set him up and reported him as an armed escapee who had already killed two cops. With that added to the other heinous crimes committed by Wyckes, he had no doubt the Singapore police would shoot on sight. They'd have to assume he was a clear and present danger to the public.

As futile as it felt, Durand ran. He needed time. Time to figure out who to talk to. There had to be a way to straighten this out. But he had to reach friends to do that.

Durand glanced up at Ping-Pong-ball-sized surveillance cameras on every light pole. Facial detection would make short work of finding him. How long would it take to load his likeness into the SPF surveillance system? Minutes?

Pedestrians stared at his bloody hospital gown as he passed by.

Durand wiped blood off his face and arms. More passersby gazed after him and shouted in alarm as he fast-walked past. He hoped that he looked like a runaway surgical patient.

As he rounded a corner, Durand noticed autonomous vehicles up the block turning away en masse—avoiding the area. A synthetic voice spoke from a passing car as its windows automatically rolled up, "*Rerouting vehicle. Police activity, this area . . .*"

"Shit . . ." He was beginning to realize the foolishness of all this. Running would not help him escape. At most it could buy a few minutes. Yet a few minutes might help him find an answer.

The roadways rapidly emptied of autonomous cars as sirens surrounded the area. Durand moved more calmly now as he tried to slow his breathing. He passed cafés and bistros lively with a dinner crowd. A discordant alarm tone sounded on every device in his vicinity. A synthesized voice announced, "*Alert: police activity in your immediate area. Be on the lookout for this suspect . . .*"

Durand noticed people glancing up at virtual screens he could not see. Others were gazing up at the sides of buildings, where he suspected the normal AR ad rotation had been replaced by his likeness displayed forty stories high.

The same voice echoed on dozens of devices as he walked. "*. . . do not approach. Suspect is armed and extremely dangerous.*"

Durand noticed his new strange face filling a lone physical screen still active over a nearby bar. His image was bordered in red and marked "Extremely Dangerous."

While looking through the glass, Durand suddenly focused on a stranger's reflection staring back at him—a brooding scowl. An intimidating visage.

He raised powerful hands to the window—the reflection moving to meet him. It was him. He could feel horror gripping him again, his heart pounding. This was him. It really was him.

And even as he watched, on his forearms the lines began again to draw themselves across his bruised skin—like something floating up from the deep. Within seconds he had a full complement of black, red, and green Thai or Malay letters, Chinese characters, as well as images of a nine-tailed fox on his left biceps, a trefoil knot on his right. Another tattoo of Asian script on the left side of his neck, and more running across his scalp. He was as menacing a character as he'd ever seen on an international arrest warrant.

It had to be an LFP projection—a virtual trick. He shielded his eyes with his hand—protecting against an unseen LFP projector, but the tattoos did not disappear.

Someone shouted, and Durand turned back to the street to see someone pointing at him from a café.

The synthetic voice could be heard all around him: "... *if you see this suspect, alert police immediately. Use the hashtag ME9_PURSUIT. Repeat: hashtag ME9_PURSUIT.*"

Others pointed at him. There were shouts of fear as the patrons of cafés and restaurants moved away from him, even as they turned their LFP glasses and thumbcams onto Durand. Pedestrians ahead on the sidewalk dodged out of Durand's way and collectively started filming him as they crossed the now empty roadway.

Durand turned and walked briskly in the opposite direction—only to be met with more pointing people and more thumbcams. He glanced up to see searchlights of approaching police drones weaving between two-hundred-story skyscrapers—en route to his location. The roar of racing police cars and sirens converging.

Dozens of people filmed him from all angles. He knew what was about to happen; crowd-sourced policing was kicking into action.

"Great. The system works . . ."

In the Singapore Police Force Operations Control Center on Ketam Island, technical officers tracked dozens of virtual objects in their light field projection glasses—manipulating their perspective with gloved hands.

Already the ME9_PURSUIT hashtag was trending in local social media, and video streams were pouring in—pinpointing the suspect's location with a hundred different feeds.

Police software immediately identified the hashtagged video, pulled it from public streams, and stitched it together into a live 3D video feed of Durand's chase from constantly shifting civilian perspectives.

The officers gazed down on the live 3D projection and highlighted Durand in the shot. The system tracked his movements from there on. The police had him zeroed in.

"All units, positive identification on Marcus Wyckes moving eastbound on foot along Orchard Road."

Durand noticed more people holding up thumbcams on the sidewalks ahead—the entire city bearing witness, triangulating him. This was about to go very badly.

He fled the sidewalk, clambering over a wooden construction-site security wall painted with utopian visions of the multihundred-story office tower to come. At present beyond the fence was a fifty-story maze of exposed girders and decking, lit up at intervals by laser sintering robots that were printing the carbon lattice girders as they went. Work carried on around the clock.

Durand hit the ground on the other side, skinning his knees. He carefully navigated in bare feet across rock-strewn soil and onto the concrete foundation. Sintering flashes stabbed at Durand's eyes, and sparks sprayed downward on him from above.

Directed by civilian camera streams, truck-sized police quadcopter drones roared overhead, converging on the construction site—blinding nightsun lights stabbed down, bathing him in white light. A thunderous voice shouted from loudspeakers, *"Marcus Wyckes, stop where you are and place your hands over your head immediately!"*

Durand fled between robotic construction machinery as a dozen police cars arrived beyond the perimeter fence on all sides of the construction site. He jumped onto another inner security fence, climbing up and over it with surprising ease. He was amazed at what the human body was capable of under circumstances of life and death. He couldn't believe he was standing upright, much less fleeing.

Fleeing to where? was the question.

Durand could see body-armor-clad tactical police units streaming out of a truck as it pulled up. They looked ready to deal with a terrorist attack.

Durand fled beneath the decking of the unfinished office tower, moving up an open stairwell. He triggered several alarms on the way. Warning sirens whooped. Robotic machinery in his vicinity shut down for safety, allowing him to pass.

As he glanced down at the streets from the fourth floor, Durand could now see dozens and dozens of heavily armed Singapore police surrounding the site, with more vehicles on the way. In the air, large police drones descended from between neighboring office towers, moving into support positions.

"Goddamnit . . ." Looking out, Durand realized there was nowhere to run, no escape. And for what reason?

He caught his breath and pondered the situation. He needed to talk rationally—to get authorities to understand who he was and what had happened. Lie detector tests or some other method. There had to be a way to prove his identity. There had to be. Because he really was Kenneth Durand.

Durand heard boots clattering on the decking just a couple floors below—could see the darting beams and shadows from tactical lights. He raised his hands and began walking down the stairwell.

"I'm here! I surrender! Don't shoot!"

Almost immediately a tactical squad in black body armor rounded the stairwell. Startled, the point man raised his MP6. "There!"

Durand instinctively jumped aside as bullets sparked off the metal deck and girders, the shots thundering in the partially enclosed stairwell.

Shouting of police. "Shots fired! Shots fired!"

More deafening gunfire.

Durand crawled up the stairwell and then broke into a run. "Stop!"

His voice was drowned out by more gunfire. Bullets whined past him as he kept rounding the corners on his way up the stairwell.

In the lulls between, he could hear echoing radio chatter on his heels.

"Suspect in south stairwell."

Durand ducked down as several shots came up from street level. One snapped close by, and the others disintegrated in sparks against a girder.

"Hold your fire on the ground! We've got people up here!"

Exhausted as he reached floor fifteen, Durand moved at a crouch out of the stairwell and across the metal decking. He ducked behind a pallet of construction filament and tried to stifle his panting as he heard boots not far behind him.

The lead tactical team moved past in the stairwell, headed upward, gasping for breath. He could hear a couple of them linger in the doorway—tactical lights scanning the deserted floor. But in a moment, they, too, passed, clanging farther up the stairwell.

Durand sucked for air. He glanced around the pallet toward the far stairwell to see tactical lights approaching on that side as well. He took the moment to move at a crouch between pallets—heading toward a third stairwell on the east side of the building.

Behind him, tactical lights shined across the floor. Durand ducked into the east stairwell as police spread out and more lights approached from below.

He broke into a run, panting almost immediately as he kept climbing.

Powered by adrenaline, Durand managed to get to the thirtieth floor before he collapsed onto the decking, gasping for air. Covered in sweat, he could hear the turbofans of the police drones thundering below. Flashing lights reflected from the mirrored glass on neighboring office towers. Scanning searchlights cast stark shadows everywhere.

Durand had no idea what to do. The extra minutes had clarified nothing. Solved nothing. Surrender clearly wasn't an option.

He dragged himself to the far edge of the thirty-first floor and hid behind a refrigerator-sized sintering robot covered by a tarp. Durand caught his breath as the noise and blinding lights of his pursuers closed in all around him.

He could see in the reflection of nearby towers that the police drones were circling the building several floors below—their nightsun search-lights stabbing out, clearing each floor. He knew they were scanning in infrared as well. Their lidar memorizing the geometry and zeroing in on the movement of human-shaped objects. The drones were large—bigger than comcars, with powerful turbofans in cowls on each corner. Bundles of antenna masts on top, and arrays of searchlights, cameras—and a pod containing both nonlethal and lethal weapons—on the bottom.

Durand felt what little hope he had vanish. Wyckes was a cop killer. A slaver. They would not take him alive. And as far as the SPF was concerned, he *was* Wyckes.

Drone turbofan engines drowned out the radio chatter and shouts of approaching police teams.

It wouldn't be long now. He closed his eyes for a moment. How had this insanity happened?

He thought about his mother back in Colorado. His brother and sister. He should have stayed in the States. But then he wouldn't have met Miyuki or been blessed with Mia.

Then again, he wasn't going to have them, was he? He was going to die here. Tonight. As someone else. A villain.

Could he really just give up? He thought about his wife—and about his daughter growing up without him.

He looked around. He was not going to simply let this happen. He had to do something. Durand's eye fell upon the tarpaulin thrown over the inactive sintering robot. He ran his hand across the tarp. A thought occurred to him.

He crawled toward the edge of the building and, from behind a girder, looked down at the drones rising as they scanned each floor with their blinding nightsun lights. They were only two floors below—the closest one marked with a bioluminescent number 16, its engines unbelievably loud. The air around it rippling with heat distortion. Durand studied the half dozen antenna masts clustered at the center of its upper surface, in the flat portion between the four turbofan engines.

Durand looked lower on the mirrored face of the building opposite to see reflections of tactical teams moving upward from the floors, close behind and below the drone scans. He rolled back into darkness and grabbed the plastic tarp. He started rolling it and wrapping both ends of it around his bandaged, thick-fingered alien hands many times—linking his arms together. Muscular arms that were now covered with a profusion of gang tattoos.

The turbofans of the drones grew louder as they ascended—scanning the floor just below Durand.

He moved into a crouch near the edge of the decking and could see drone 16 edging in from the left—still fifty meters away, its searchlights and sensors scanning for him below. He leaned out, while gripping a girder, and saw that the police drone flew perhaps fifteen feet from the building.

Fifteen feet.

Durand looked below, at a thirty-one-story drop. A sea of flashing police lights ringed the building.

He could hear the drone roaring in from the left.

Durand looked up at the nighttime skyline of mid-twenty-first-century Singapore glittering around him. He soaked in the beauty of the scene, taking one last deep breath of this life.

Durand stepped back ten feet or so, feeling more than hearing the howling wind of the drone's turbofans.

I love you, Miyuki. I love you, Mia.

With that, Durand ran and launched himself off the decking, across the fifteen-foot gap. As he fell, he stretched out his bound arms toward the drone's antenna masts. His vision narrowed and the noise—previously so deafening—suddenly dimmed.

His focus was total. Sounds muted.

Durand landed hard on the quadcopter's broad back, between all four rotors—knocking the wind out of him. He couldn't immediately tell if he'd succeeded in wrapping his bound arms around the central antenna cluster. But almost immediately he felt the drone yaw aside, losing flight trim. The world around him started to spin.

Durand slid toward one of the four large rotor wells, but he was suddenly jerked back by his wrists. He felt as though his arms were going to come out of their sockets as he spun faster, veering this way and then that.

He gripped the plastic wound around his hands as hard as he could.

Suddenly Durand's forearm pressed against a burning hot motor cowling. He screamed in pain and pulled away from it as the drone's spin reduced—though it was still yawing from side to side. Durand heaved himself up and away from the deafening rotors and toward the center of the drone. The machine veered a bit more, trying to stabilize itself as Durand looked up and out at the world.

They had already gained altitude and cleared the top of the unfinished tower. It looked like the pilot was edging away from all the surrounding buildings.

In the Singapore Police Operations Control Center, Technical Sergeant Zhang put down his tea and tapped at alert messages on a virtual screen. His LFP glasses gave him a full virtual reality view of the Central Business District—as though he was inside the cockpit of the vehicle. Normally it was a view he relished, but right now he was struggling to keep on a projected flight path as Tail 16 yawed from side to side.

The software would normally find an optimal, safe route, but his bird was suddenly behaving unpredictably. A series of anomalies had turned his virtual board red.

"Lieutenant! I seem to have an undefined technical failure on Tail 16."

He could hear his commanding officer take a seat and mimic Zhang's POV with headgear of her own. "Ground fire?"

"Negative. Engines and avionics are good. Uplink good, but trim is all over the place."

Error alerts warbled.

"I'm having difficulty keeping Tail 16 on the glide path."

"Can you land safely?"

He considered the risks. "Negative. Not in the tight quarters of the CBD."

She nodded and spoke into her radio. "AOC, Tail 16 returning to base on a code 3-3-7. Repeat: Tail 16 returning to base on a code 3-3-7."

Zhang heard her voice focused back on to him. "Bring 16 back to base via the logistics airway. If you need to ditch, do so over water. Understood?"

He nodded. "Understood, Lieutenant."

• • •

Durand clung to the deafening police drone. As he felt his adrenaline receding, the true magnitude of noise and vibration on this machine was becoming unbearable. Suddenly the engines increased in tempo, and he looked up to see the two-hundred-story towers around him pulling away.

Durand lifted his head long enough to see that they were ascending and departing the area. Looking behind and below, Durand could see several other police drones and hundreds of police converging on the half-constructed building.

He struggled to hold on as his own drone wobbled, then pitched forward, heading across town and toward the north coast.

The entire city shimmered below and around him. After several minutes of rushing wind, Durand realized the drone pilot was bringing them toward the drone logistics highway that ringed the northern and eastern coasts of the island. They'd dropped considerably in altitude as they turned to merge into it.

The logistics highway covered a fifty-meter virtual tunnel at roughly 150 meters altitude.

Durand's heart leapt into his throat as the drone tilted forward during its descent, causing him to swing around the antenna mast and hang from his hands on the far side. This only accelerated the drone's downward glide—which the software immediately overcorrected for. Durand got swung around several sides of the aircraft as it yawed this way and that.

By the time the police drone leveled out, he could see he was surrounded by dozens of commercial drones of all shapes and sizes, soaring over the water just off the coast. The idea was that if any of these machines fell from the sky, they'd be falling on water, not taxpayers' heads—at least for most of their journey. Plus it was much safer than risking midair collisions over populated city blocks.

Looking to his right, Durand could see a Domino's Pizza drone, an Amazon drone, and several FedEx ones as well.

Gazing back at the coastline, Durand could see Woodlands—the neighborhood he called home. He soon spotted the Hanging Gardens complex, but it receded behind him in the night.

Rounding south toward Changi Airport, the police drone veered shakily left, away from the logistics highway, descending on a glide path toward a well-lit police aviation islet that Durand knew of. It was roughly a quarter mile off the coast, near the Tekong military island.

Gazing down now, Durand could see he was about twenty meters off the water and cruising along Singapore's industrial coastline at seventy, maybe eighty knots. There might not be a better opportunity to jump ship. He could hardly cling to the craft as it landed in the middle of a police base (if it landed without crashing, that is).

Studying the dark water racing past below, Durand unlooped one hand from the rolled-up tarp, and then—before he could even prepare himself—suddenly slipped off the edge of the drone and into free fall.

He heard the deafening engines recede—then it felt like somebody hit his entire body with a two-by-four. After several moments insensible, he started clawing instinctively for the surface and burst forth gasping for air and thrashing.

Back in the Police Operations Control Center, Sergeant Zhang reacted in surprise. His entire control board suddenly cleared of anomalies. Normal flight characteristics had resumed.

He frowned in confusion. "Lieutenant, the malfunction to Tail 16 seems to have cleared. I'm fully operational again."

"Return to base just the same. Let's have the techs check it out just to be on the safe side. Let me know when you're landed, and we'll review the black box."

"Will do."

In the water Durand oriented himself and started swimming back toward Singapore. It was only a couple hundred meters away. Exhausted as he was, he was thankful not to be fully dressed. The extra weight of wet clothing might have pulled him under. He glanced back at the police drone. It was landing at the distant base. He couldn't stay in the open water long. Other drones might spot him.

The short swim to shore nearly killed him. Several times Durand almost slipped beneath the surface of the water, spitting out salt water. He wondered if his wounds would attract sharks, but then remembered that there were hardly any sharks left. He struggled, alternately kicking with his feet and pulling with one hand against the water.

By the time the moon had crested the horizon, he tumbled through a mild surf and eventually stumbled out of the water onto a trash- and seaweed-strewn beach dotted with boulders. He crawled on all fours over debris in the darkness, finally reaching a cement seawall that ringed the north coast. He collapsed against it. He was shivering—not something he often did in Singapore. But then the water no doubt was cold— a fact he hadn't concretely noticed at any point. Durand lay facedown on rotting seaweed and tried to gather the energy to move.

Parasympathetic backlash was hitting him hard now. He'd been running on adrenaline for the past hour or more. He'd never felt such exhaustion. Durand couldn't even turn himself over. Instead, his consciousness drifted away.

Chapter 12

Durand's mind snapped back into focus as he felt hands rummaging over him. Then somebody turned him over.

"Hey!" Durand shouted, as he got to his feet and grabbed at a thin, old Chinese man. "What the hell are you doing?" His voice sounded less hoarse now. Deeper.

The elderly man backed away. Durand saw the man clearly in the moonlight.

Not an old man—just an emaciated guy in his thirties in a threadbare sleeveless vest and shorts. Tattoos of molecular diagrams covered his sinewy arms.

A synth addict.

Durand, wide-awake now, watched the man back away in fear, and in that moment it all came back to him. He examined his own thick-fingered hands and beefy forearms.

He was another person. Still.

He glanced up at the thin sliver of moon—a dozen degrees higher into the sky than when he'd come ashore. He'd been out cold for at least an hour.

Looking past the retreating junkie in the semidarkness, Durand could see more figures moving along the base of a seawall, along the coastline.

He turned around and realized he was near an industrial road traversed by autonomous semitrucks leaving automated container yards. Facing back toward the junkies again, he could see in the moonlight where the beach ended a few hundred meters beyond. It wasn't apparent where the junkies were heading, except maybe to drown themselves in the Johor Strait.

Durand ducked down as a police drone roared past not far away. He saw that it was heading toward the police aviation facility just off the coast. Gazing back at the skyscrapers of Singapore, he could see more police drones in the sky—their searchlights stabbing down. The search for him wasn't over yet.

He started carefully stepping across the rocky, trash-strewn beach in his bare feet, following the junkies. As he proceeded, Durand saw a circular opening in the seawall ahead. He noticed the Chinese junkie glance back at him with concern before disappearing into the opening.

Durand continued toward what soon resolved to a drainage tunnel—capped at its end by a series of galvanized steel bars, bent to permit people to squeeze through.

Around the edge of the opening, Durand could see broken motion sensors and proximity lights. The entire area had been wired for security at some point, but apparently that was just on paper now. He made a mental note to pass this intel along to the Singapore Police Force.

As he peered into the darkness, Durand could see soft light in the tunnel ahead. He could also hear music thumping.

Music?

He moved cautiously forward and felt plastic crunching underfoot. Kneeling down, Durand could see bubble paks strewn across the sand in the moonlight.

Drug printing.

It made sense. He'd always wondered where in the hell on the island this happened. Drug smuggling was a thing of the past in most countries now—not because of any great advances in drug treatment or human nature but because of synthetic biology. Just as algae, yeast, and bacteria were being custom designed to grow food, chemicals, and products—so, too, were they being harnessed to synthesize narcotics.

No need to store or ship large quantities of drugs. No need to smuggle. Synthetic opioids a hundred times more powerful and pure than organic heroin could be synthesized from a surprising list of mundane, common-use ingredients. All you needed was the right genetically designed organism—one that consumed sugar or iodine or any number of substances to produce a pure molecular narcotic. Nearly impossible to stop. Nearly impossible to police. Also far more deadly.

And that's where the drug printers came in.

Durand entered the tunnel and began moving toward a distant light. He stepped carefully to avoid cutting his feet on glass or rocks, crunching across trash. He passed alcoves where rail-thin shadows of people hovered, their crazed eyes catching a glint of reflected moonlight as they watched Durand pass.

For a place to hide from the police, he could do worse than here. Invisible from the air, it already existed in defiance of the law—and in Singapore that was no mean feat. Durand was surprised he'd never heard a whisper about this place's existence. But then again, he wasn't really a cop. Not like Michael was.

It did seem odd that authorities would let a coastal industrial drainage tunnel go open and unmonitored. Wasn't there a risk of bioterrorists using this tunnel? As a data scientist, he was always shocked at how little of reality seemed to be modeled in the data—Internet of Things be damned. This place shouldn't exist. And yet here it was.

After traveling a hundred meters in darkness, Durand came to an intersection of three tunnels marked by bioluminescent light sticks. Green and blue and yellow light sticks formed an arrow leading down the center tunnel. The festive lights illuminated people rolling on the edge of darkness in the side passages. Shadows moaning. A grinning man with a bald head with wires inserted into drill holes at his temples leaned into the light, watching Durand pass. He laughed maniacally as he reached out to touch Durand.

Durand batted the man's hands away. "Off!" Durand had heard of biohackers who electrically stimulated the pleasure center of their brain. Stim addicts. Wireheads. They usually starved if the surgery was successful. For every one of them who'd suffered an unendurable loss that made them pursue the wire, there were others who were just pleasure addicts. Once the wire was in place, the motive made little difference.

Durand moved deeper into the tunnel. The music grew louder—

cacophonous, disjointed, and thudding. Laser lights flashed ahead. He soon entered a chamber thirty meters or so in diameter and five meters high, all smooth concrete. It was a junction for several tunnels radiating outward. Dozens of people languished in the preternatural twilight of light sticks, some trance-dancing alone in their own worlds, others staring into space at the margins. No one seemed to be talking.

A thin man wearing glowing lipstick approached Durand. "Blow job, baby?"

Durand shook his head, moving past into the crowd. He could see the dealers wearing LFP glasses, while the junkies carried cheap flexible phablets. Gazing around in the semidarkness, Durand saw glowing screens—actual physical screens. But it figured. After all, any junkie who'd had an expensive light field device had probably already sold it for drug money.

Instead all around him were cheap-shit, thin film screens. Addicts laughing as they watched movies and TV shows. Porn. Played games. No photonics in here, he guessed. Just old-school silicon.

Durand passed along a line of dealers. As he watched, an emaciated junkie pointed out a tattoo of a molecular model on his left arm to a drug printer. The dealer scanned it under the bioluminescent light, and a moment later the molecule appeared on a disposable phablet screen— ready for synthesis somewhere nearby.

He'd never actually seen this in person—only read about it. Custom highs were the drug business now. Your drug was synthesized as you ordered it—specialized just for your DNA, to create the perfect high. To gauge the precise dose, to avoid death. At maximum purity.

Buyers had to have their genome analyzed only once—a free service from dealers, of course. Genomic analysis software could compute the perfect drug structures for that person. A tiny change to a molecule here or there went a long way, kicking the high up to the next level. And what better way for dealers to write down your preferences than on your own skin? Something that wasn't going to get pawned off or stolen when you were stoned out of your mind. Tattoos were forever. Another free service of the printers.

Light flashed and another drug printer scanned another tattoo.

Within ten or fifteen minutes, the junkie could have a small hit of his choice drug produced somewhere in these tunnels and transported straight here by drone.

It didn't take much to get high these days. Just a few milligrams would knock you on your ass for hours. Any more could kill you. But then, drug printers knew the precise dose their customers could handle. Big data had entered the black market, and the drug printers knew more about their customers than social media companies knew about theirs. The printers also knew dead customers weren't repeat customers.

By now some of the synth addicts had taken notice of Durand, backing away warily as Durand passed through. He still had bloodstains on his wet hospital gown and looked like an escaped lunatic even among the clientele here.

Sofyan Taniwan monitored his synth dealers with one eye and the Gujarat Lions cricket match with the other. He had serious money riding on both. The virtual screen created by his LFP glasses could have filled his vision, but as a pudgy, diminutive man he needed to keep at least one wary eye out while inside the Drain—the slang term for Singapore's underground drug printing market. The place certainly drained the detritus out of Singapore, human and otherwise.

Taniwan raised his fist and stifled a shout as the inimitable McAllister shipped in with his fifty-third run on the video inset, making the spread. Taniwan smiled briefly before erasing his emotion. It never paid to express emotion among the losers spiraling through the Drain. Emotion was a tell, and tells could be exploited. But he had just won a substantial wager.

Just then Taniwan focused his left eye beyond his dealers, onto a thuggish, thick-necked Eurasian man wearing—of all things—a hospital gown. He'd seen all types in the Drain. People escaped from rehab clinics. The rich. The poor. But they had a gaunt, zombified look about them. You could see the hunger in their eyes. This man, though, looked like the opposite of a synth addict. In fact, he looked like trouble, and if anything had earned Taniwan the trust of his bosses, it was his nose for trouble.

Taniwan reluctantly dismissed the virtual cricket screen with a gesture and focused both eyes on the man, who was now passing by his dealers with the gawping air of a tourist in the bad part of town. And yet somehow this man looked like he brought the bad part of town with him wherever he went. Something was amiss here. What resembled bloodstains spattered the man's hospital smock. Taniwan was willing to bet it wasn't this man's blood, either.

Taniwan moved his hands with subtlety, so as not to attract undue attention, bringing up his gang's facial recognition app (like any business, they kept track of their customers—especially the troublemakers). This sort of thing could readily be misunderstood here in the Drain. It was a poorly kept secret that the drug printing labs were tolerated by the SPF; they kept the synth addict problem out of the public eye, and no doubt greased a few palms as well. However, being a police informant was part of the deal.

The positive match was almost immediate, and the man's virtual, closed-eye 3D headscan and name soon rotated before Taniwan. Taniwan did not like what he saw—not one bit . . .

Marcus Demang Wyckes, leader of the Huli jing.

Implicated in hundreds of murders, kidnappings, human trafficking—and just two hours ago personally murdering two Singapore police officers. Every damn cop in the city-state was searching for this man. Taniwan wiped away the virtual bust of Wyckes as though it was a letter from his ex-wife's attorney. True fear gripped him for the first time since he'd left the slums of Johor. Why hadn't he just minded his own damn business? Why did he have to spot this man? *Now he knew.*

Normally Taniwan would order his men to grab felons the police really wanted and, depending on the situation, dump the perp behind a police station, beaten to a pulp—or dead. But that's what you did with unconnected nobodies. This was a different kettle of fish altogether. The leader of the Huli jing had no doubt put out a call for his people, and they would be here soon enough.

And so would the police. Some junkie was going to spot Wyckes sooner or later, and a whole goddamned anti-terror squad would storm in here—the very last thing Taniwan wanted in the Drain. It was bad for business. Getting into the feeds. Increasing taxpayer awareness. No, no, no. This would not do.

But worse still would be the Huli jing finding out that Taniwan had ordered his men to turn Wyckes over to the police. This was a quandary. If he pretended he'd never seen Wyckes, then the police could come storming into the Drain any minute. If he turned Wyckes in, then the Huli jing would track Taniwan down and torture him to death on camera as a warning to others.

But this was why Taniwan was in charge here—to make the tough calls. After a few moments' consideration, he decided to split the difference; he'd take action—but make sure no one knew the real reason. Plausible deniability.

Taniwan glanced toward his dealers, where one of the Indo-Australian enforcers shoved away a dancing synth addict. Taniwan spoke to the man over a radio link. "Tok. See that mental case in the hospital gown?" Taniwan watched Tok scan the crowd of addicts. "No, to your right. By the vuck pit."

Tok zeroed in on Wyckes near the VR sex machines. "*Got him. Watchu want?*"

"Take your mate and find out what hospital he escaped from and dump his ass back there."

"*You havin' a piss?*"

"Just do it."

"*Can we keep whatever we find on 'im?*"

"Sure. Just get him the hell out of here. Crazy people are bad for business."

Durand moved past the printers, following light sticks into the tunnels beyond and away from the crowd. There, he found more junkies and homeless. Durand stepped over legs and around makeshift cardboard shelters. As he walked, his shadow cast along the tunnel walls—but then he noticed other shadows behind his. Turning around Durand could see two wiry-looking Southeast Asian men. They didn't look like addicts and wore faded digital camouflage military jackets in the cool air of the tunnels. No one else seemed to have jackets.

Durand saw the glint of a knife catch the light as the men kept on his tail. Other addicts retreated into the shadows.

"Oi! Mate!" The lead one had an Australian accent.

Durand turned to face them.

"You a mental case?"

The man's companion clattered across trash as he moved to flank Durand. A metal pipe slipped down into his hand from within his coat sleeve.

Durand eyed them both warily. "I don't have anything. I just want to be left alone." Durand turned in place, arms extended, most likely revealing the crack of his ass at the back of the hospital gown.

"Yeah? Let's have a look at that wrist bracelet."

Durand noticed the hospital patient bracelet on his right wrist for the first time. "It's a printed bracelet."

"Could still work to get meds."

"Meds?" Durand looked at it and saw the name Marcus Wyckes printed on it along with computer codes. He had literally been wearing a name tag this entire time. He tried to pull it off, but the material was tough.

"I'll cut it off ya."

Durand felt anger rising in him—as if he hadn't had a bad enough day, now he was dealing with these two scavengers. They appeared well used to preying on loners.

"Don't seem interested in the printers, do ya?"

The other one snorted. "Doesn't look like an addict."

The first nodded. "Right. So watcha doin' down here, mate?"

Durand studied both men. He was half a head taller than both.

"Looks like you got in one hell of a fight."

The other laughed. "And lost."

"Right?" The first chuckled as he rolled a curving, clawlike knife in his hand.

Durand felt an unfamiliar calm again as adrenaline flowed. He felt focused. Clear-headed. This was not how he usually felt in life-threatening situations. "I just want to be left alone. I don't have anything."

"Let's see the bracelet, sweetheart." He motioned with the knife. "You turn around. Hands on your head, yeah?"

Durand shook his head slowly.

"We're not askin', mate."

They rushed Durand, the second man raising his foot-long pipe as he came in.

Durand felt oddly detached from fear as he rushed toward the second man fast enough to get inside the arc of his swing. He grabbed the man's wrist and kneed him in the groin—then pulled him in front of the oncoming man with the knife.

Durand twisted the pipe out of the second man's grip and pushed him toward his knife-wielding partner—who pulled back out of range as his friend collapsed, groaning in pain.

"You're proper fucked now, mate!" The first man lunged forward with the knife, slashing.

Durand ducked back, raised the steel pipe—then hurled it at the man's face, connecting with a resounding CRACK. He followed it in.

Durand rained haymakers to the man's head, stomach, and ribs. The knife fell to the ground as the guy collapsed. Durand grabbed the pipe from the floor of the tunnel and continued beating the man with it—a soggy ringing sound echoing in the tunnel.

"Happy now?" Durand panted heavily as he turned the man over, raising the pipe again.

The sound of gasping and shoes sliding on concrete behind him. Durand turned to see the second scavenger trying to get to his feet.

"Aaaahhh!" Durand raced after the man before he could even fully stand.

"No! Wait!"

Durand struck him in the stomach, and then continued beating him until he collapsed—then still continued beating him.

"I just wanted to be left alone!"

After a few more blows, Durand tossed the pipe to the ground, where it clattered and rolled across the tunnel floor. He stood panting, and then turned around to see the eyes of gaunt addicts in the semidarkness.

He pointed at them. "If any of you fucking get near me, I won't be as kind."

The reflected light on those eyes disappeared, and he heard people pull farther into side tunnels.

Durand caught his breath and looked down at the motionless bodies in the glow of light sticks. The men were crumpled and bloodied but breathing. As his own pulse slowed, Durand could barely believe what he'd done. He'd just badly injured two men, beating them into unconsciousness.

He'd been schooled in hand-to-hand combat at the Naval Academy. And he'd taken the odd karate and jujitsu course. But it had always been theoretical up until now. He hadn't had a real hand-to-hand fight since high school. And never with an actual enemy.

He examined his thick, bloodied hands. The tattoos had reappeared along his forearms.

Then it occurred to him that there must be police informants all over the drug printing markets. How could he have been so stupid? Junkies were among the most pliant of informants. Soon this place might be crawling with police.

He had to keep moving. He didn't have the luxury to dwell on this. He started rifling through the first man's overlarge camouflage jacket. He found a vape pen case and several blister paks with custom drug process codes on it. These he tossed aside.

He heard the man groan.

Durand pulled a cheap phablet from the guy's inside pocket. A thin film device. Common with drug users and low-level criminals. Prepaid. Solar-charged batteries. A couple millimeters thick at least.

In other words: obsolete crap. It would still be useful, but if either of these men spoke to police, they'd be able to track this device. Durand tossed it into the nearby puddle of water.

What Durand needed most was clothes. He pulled the hospital gown off and dropped it at his feet. Feeling vulnerable in his nudity,

Durand stripped the shapeless sweatpants and gray hoodie from the larger of the two men and put them on. He also slipped on the man's overlarge camouflage jacket. It was tight in the shoulders, but it would work.

He then grabbed the second man's well-worn military boots. These were uncomfortably small, but they were infinitely better than bare feet.

Now clothed, Durand searched amid the trash for the fallen knife. He saw it lying in a puddle of brackish water.

Picking it up, he could see it was a *grown* knife—probably a keratin-silica hybrid from some vat in Thailand or Vietnam. Highly illegal in Singapore. Nonmetallic and thus difficult to detect on scanners. He squeezed the handle where it felt soft, and the blade retracted like a cat's claw into the handle. He squeezed it again, and the blade reappeared. It felt organic, like some hunter's souvenir from a big game hunt. He retracted the blade again and stored the knife in his jacket.

It was a felony to carry a concealed weapon in Singapore, but that was the least of his supposed crimes. And he guessed these men would have friends.

Durand then rifled through the second man's pockets. He found another thin-film phablet device, but also a dozen or more bitrings in a plastic pouch—probably stolen. These were disposable cryptocurrency devices popular with undocumented migrants, itinerants, and synth addicts. They served as wireless wallets for small amounts of digital money. They typically required physical contact between a terminal or another bitring to transfer funds—and were usually tethered to a parent device for loading money or setting up transactions. Bitrings were no safer than carrying cash really but were never loaded with much. It certainly beat connecting your main device to a potentially malware-infested point-of-sale terminal. And they were easily concealed by junkies.

The only question was what type of currency was on them. There were a dozen popular blockchain cryptocurrencies now—ChiCoin, ThaiCoin, Biocoin, SinCoin—most linked to a central banking authority. Cryptocurrency providers had concluded in the early 2020s that it was better to sell blockchain software solutions to central banks than to enter the heavily regulated banking industry on their own. More libertarian-minded flavors, like Biocoin, still existed (named because it used cell division and mutation inside a bioreactor as a calculation engine to unlock coins, while simultaneously generating intrinsically valuable biomass). But whatever money was on them should work.

One of the men groaned again.

Durand decided he'd figure the rings out later. Right now Durand had to be anywhere but here. He headed off down the tunnels, moving past more homeless camps and dozing addicts clustered in twos and threes. Those awake watched him warily, but avoided his menacing stare.

Durand collected several light sticks from the tunnel floor as he walked and held them up as a torch. Looking down a darkened side tunnel, he decided to follow it, going deeper into the maze beneath the city. He wondered how far the tunnels stretched.

After walking several minutes, turning down occasional side tunnels, Durand spotted the glow of two phablet screens in the shadows ahead. He continued warily and the glow suddenly disappeared.

Durand put his hand on the knife in his pocket and held up the light sticks. "I know you're there. I don't want trouble. I'm just passing through."

He proceeded and soon he could see two outlines in the semidarkness. Passing by them in the tunnel, he could see they were young Burmese or Thai men clad in cheap printed clothes—both of them thin and clearly nervous. One of them held a piece of steel rebar.

Durand studied them. "Either of you speak English? *Nǐ huì shuō pǔtōnghuà ma?*"

The men turned to each other uncertainly.

Durand raised the bag containing the bitrings. "I want to buy one of those phablets." He pointed at the phablet still in one man's hand. "I'll pay. *Wǒ huì fù.*"

The man on the left said simply, "How much?"

Durand reached into the bag and fished out a bitring at random. He tossed it over.

The man caught the bitring warily, and then touched it to one he wore—he then consulted his phablet screen. He shook his head. "No good. Much more."

Durand tossed another one. "That's what I've got." It wasn't, but he hoped it was enough.

The man checked this ring like the first, then looked at his companion. They both seemed either pleased or offended. It was hard to tell which.

The second man nodded. He tossed the cheap phablet over to Durand, who caught it without dropping the light sticks.

"You go now!" The man raised the rebar menacingly.

Durand nodded and continued down the tunnel, glancing behind him to see that the glow of their remaining phablet had returned. He also thought he could hear gleeful laughter.

Okay, maybe they got a deal. But he got what he needed, too: access to the Net.

After twenty minutes of walking, and taking several more turns, Durand entered a small chamber that bore evidence of past human habitation—plastic tarps, spent light sticks, excrement, and trash. But nothing recent from the look of it. A small pool of brackish water occupied the center of the chamber. Small drainage pipes fed into the room from two walls, but the tunnel continued through the far wall. He had a means of escape if someone came from either direction.

Durand tossed the light sticks onto the floor and then dropped onto a fiber pallet next to the pool of dirty water. He felt his exhaustion coming on him in waves.

He caught sight of a stranger's face reflected in the puddle's surface next to him. He gasped and reached for the knife—but then stopped.

It was his own reflection again.

The surreal nature of his situation hit home.

The Eurasian face staring back at him was bruised. Square-jawed and thick-necked. His bald head scratched and cut. His dark brown eyes intense.

Who was this? Was it really Wyckes?

Durand felt more bereft than he had ever felt. Even worse than the night his father died, back when he was in high school—and he had to grow up so suddenly. No, this . . . He didn't even know what this sensation was. Utter loss. The death of *himself.*

How was this possible? It seemed like just last night that he'd been reading to Mia. But that was weeks ago now.

The magnitude of all he'd lost became clear. Mourning gripped Durand. Examining his own thick-fingered hands again, he began to weep. Everywhere he turned made him feel more lost. Could he even convince his wife and child who he was? How could he ever get back?

Durand wept for an unknown time, teetering on the edge of insanity as he gazed at the bruised and beaten stranger in the water's surface.

There was no getting back.

Images of his wife and daughter came to his mind. But they now soothed him. They would know him. He was sure of it. He could convince them.

And then something occurred to Durand: he was still himself.

His mind was unchanged. His body and face might have changed, but he was still himself inside. So his brain hadn't been altered. Was it the blood-brain barrier?

This comforted him. There was a limit to the transformation.

Durand took a deep, calming breath, then looked down into the pool of water at the stranger's reflection. The analyst inside him wondered.

How was it done?

And more importantly:

Why was it done?

Someone had somehow edited his genomic sequence—trillions of living cells, each edited in hundreds of ways. CRISPR edits on an unimaginable scale. Edits on an embryo were one thing, but edits to a living, complex organism? This was light-years different. The human body had evolved over millions of years to resist invaders. Attempts to change DNA—say, by a viral infection—were quickly detected by RNA within the body, the invaders destroyed. If a virus somehow managed to make edits, these wouldn't match the DNA template in the cell's nucleus—and if enough changes occurred, the cell would effectively commit suicide in a last-ditch effort to protect the rest of the organism.

No, humans—and life in general—had evolved serious genetic security. That's what made biology so robust as a manufacturing platform. If you tried to break it, it resisted.

So how had they done it?

Durand examined his bruised arms and neck. He recalled that when he awoke the doctor said the swelling had only just receded—that he had *whole-body* swelling and bruising while he was in the coma.

His body trying to fight something off.

Edits.

His body must have been trying to resist massive, contemporaneous edits.

Dear god.

Someone had really figured it out. They'd figured out how to edit the living.

Durand sat back and contemplated this. If that was true—and he had firsthand evidence that it was—then it had major implications, not just for Durand but for all of humanity. For the future of life on earth.

Anything could be changed now. By comparison, embryo edits were child's play.

Durand looked closer at his reflection in the water. Even the bones of his face and jaw had changed. He opened his mouth. His teeth had been slightly altered as well. DNA was the cornerstone of criminal forensics. Of legal identity itself. If you couldn't rely on DNA staying the same, how could you hold anyone responsible for anything?

It suddenly dawned on Durand: *That's why Wyckes did this.*

Durand pulled the cheap phablet from his coat pocket and searched public newsfeeds. Durand saw his new face all over the headlines. The top item on the *Straits Times* described the Singapore Police Force's massive manhunt aimed toward preventing Marcus Wyckes from escaping Singapore.

Durand quickly found the Interpol Red Notice, too.

There he was—the man reflected in the water's surface.

The Huli jing had literally *made* Durand into the criminal he was hunting. Durand recalled Marcotte's briefing. How arrests and turnover of Huli jing ringleaders had no effect on the cartel's rapid expansion.

He lowered the phablet in sudden realization.

The Nine Tails of the Huli jing weren't dying—they were changing their DNA. Perhaps killing someone else in their place.

Then a startling idea occurred to Durand: if the Huli jing could edit him once—*they could do it again.*

Couldn't they? If they changed his DNA, then they could probably *change him back.*

Durand caught his breath.

There still might be a way to get back to his family. Back to his life. Durand's mind raced, despite his exhaustion. He looked at the stranger's reflection in the water.

He nodded, and the stranger nodded back. "The Huli jing could change me back."

However, it would require one critical component he was currently missing. Some of his original DNA . . .

A slight grin creased the stranger's mouth. He knew just where he could get that.

Chapter 13

Detective Inspector Aiyana Marcotte approached heavily armed Singapore police tactical units guarding a subbasement corridor. The masked sentry there noted her Interpol ID with suspicion but nodded her through.

She walked toward bright lights and evidence technicians 3D-scanning the scene of two dead policemen in a blood-spattered elevator car. Several Singapore police detectives conferred nearby. Hospital attendants waited with gurneys since the scene was just down the hall from the hospital morgue.

Detective Sergeant Michael Yi Ji-chang stood beyond the yellow police tape and saw her approach. "Evening, Inspector."

Marcotte stopped alongside. "I had planned on congratulating you for locating Marcus Wyckes."

"You still can." He grimaced. "Though he got away again."

She nodded toward the scene. "I'm told the Singapore police had two dozen men managing the transfer."

"I personally watched them chain Wyckes hand and foot." He pointed at the unlocked cuffs still wrapped around the rails of a toppled gurney.

"Have they found the gun?"

"No. No idea how he got one, either. Probably a polymer piece— maybe printed here in the hospital. They're checking printer logs." Yi shook his head. "I *had* Wyckes. I should have just stayed with him."

"Then you'd be dead, too. If I'm not mistaken, you have no gun."

Yi said nothing.

"Too bad we don't have police powers here." Marcotte studied the scene. "It's pretty clear Wyckes had inside help."

"I'd agree with you except there's street camera imagery of Wyckes fleeing alone, barefoot and bare-assed—looking confused and afraid."

Marcotte pointed. "Elevator security camera cut out during the escape."

Yi considered this news. "I hadn't heard that."

"And one of the police drones was taken off station at a crucial moment due to some 'mysterious' malfunction—giving Wyckes a blind spot to escape into."

Yi looked around and spoke softly. "You really think Wyckes had inside help?"

"I think the Huli jing is a multibillion-dollar transnational criminal organization with eyes and people all over."

"But you think people inside the SPF helped?"

"I don't know. But I do know the Huli jing crossed a line on this one. The rest of the SPF is on the warpath—as we speak, they're raiding every Huli jing safe house, bordello, and lab on the island looking for Wyckes."

Yi grunted. "Suddenly the SPF has actionable information."

"I think even the crooked cops are with us on this one. Wyckes can't murder SPF without consequences—they'll tear apart Huli jing operations until the gang coughs him up."

"Nice to have their full cooperation."

They stood for a moment in silence.

"I read Inspector Belanger's report on your initial interview with Wyckes."

Yi just stared.

"That Wyckes claimed he was really Kenneth Durand."

Yi remained stone-face. "None of it made sense."

"That Wyckes knew personal information about you, her. That he knew classified information about the GCD."

Yi hesitated before responding. "It was uncanny. That's the only word for it. He knew things. He knew . . ." Yi paused. "It wasn't just that, Inspector. He had Ken's mannerisms—you know what I mean? I used to do a wicked impression of Ken—to make fun, like you do. But this guy . . . he had Ken down cold."

Marcotte studied Yi's expression. "And then he killed two cops and fled on foot."

Yi deflated. "Okay, maybe part of me *wanted* to believe him. Like I said, none of it makes sense."

"For the record, Sergeant, what he claimed isn't possible with any known technology."

Yi looked at her sideways. "So you checked into it?"

"Didn't have to look far."

Yi hissed, "When I saw that DNA match for Wyckes, I thought: *Dae bak*. This is my chance to find Ken."

"Inspector Belanger says you haven't given up the search for Agent Durand."

"I'm not an idiot. I know Ken's dead. I know. But I still need to find him. I owe him that." He searched for words. "Have you ever heard of the concept of *Han*, Inspector?"

She shook her head.

"We Koreans have been invaded and tossed around by forces beyond our control for centuries. It's built in us a feeling of resentment about our helplessness—a desire to strike back against any injustice, no matter how futile it might seem."

"That's Han?"

He nodded. "And we Koreans all have it. I will find Ken. I won't rest until I do."

She studied him for several moments. "You knew him how long?"

"Since before Interpol. Coalition forces, Africa. We were bug hunters together."

"Biological weapons—like the one released in Paris."

Yi nodded. "Clearly there were failures. Ken usually blamed himself."

"Is that why he left the service?"

"He met Miyuki. Saw a future worth living. Miyuki and Mia were *everything* to Ken." Yi's expression clouded.

"Sergeant, I've asked Inspector Belanger to loan you to me."

Yi looked up.

"I know you want to locate your partner, and I respect that. But frankly, you're no use to the Genetic Crime Division in your current state. However, you did locate Marcus Wyckes once. I'd like you to help me find him again."

The determination on Yi's face was obvious. "That's convenient—because I was planning on doing that anyway."

"Where do you suggest we begin?"

"By trying to find out what Wyckes was doing here in Singapore . . ."

Chapter 14

What Otto liked most about the capital was its lack of humanity. Its buildings were empty monuments. More akin to a mausoleum than a city.

From inside the autonomous Tesla Model-L limousine, he watched through blacked-out, bulletproof windows as the sanitized streets passed by. The sprawling, ultramodern metropolis glittered in the sunlight, boasting sixteen-lane boulevards and gargantuan, outlandish architecture—each building separated by wide, ornamental parks. All of the pathways and park benches devoid of people. Robotic landscaping machinery roamed here and there, trimming hedges and lawns. Cleaning windows. Sweeping streets. Tending flower beds.

No cafés or bodegas. No shops. No billboards or logos. No pedestrians. A planned cityscape utterly bereft of human beings.

It was a marvelous achievement.

Otto noticed his own reflection in the window glass. Somewhat Slavic this month—perhaps Russian-Mongolian extraction. Last month he had appeared more Southeast Asian than Mongolian. The genetic engineers could tell him his current genetic mix, but in truth, it didn't interest him. He smiled an alien smile. Whoever this face belonged to did not matter. Change itself defined Otto now. His only immutable feature, gray eyes, anchored him. Helped him know his own reflection. Eyes, after all, were the windows to the soul.

The Tesla rolled to a stop beneath the marble portico of a fifty-story building hundreds of meters from its nearest neighbor. The tower had organometallic lights bright enough to trace its outline even in daytime.

The gull-wing limo door rose automatically. Otto emerged into the sunlight. He wore a well-tailored gray suit. His pastel pink double-Windsor knot, as always, perfect. He might not choose his face, but he carefully chose his wardrobe.

Otto mounted wide marble steps, atop which stood uniformed, heavily armed soldiers of indeterminate Central Asian nationality and ethnicity. They bore no insignias or unit patches on their randomized, digitally printed urban camouflage uniforms. Were they Kazakh? Turkmen? Mongolian? It was difficult to know.

As he reached the top of the steps, a K-9 patrol passed on its circuit of the building. Two vicious mastiffs snarled and strained against their masters' leashes.

But as they drew near Otto, the dogs raised their ears, drew back, and then whimpered before straining with all their might to flee. Soon the soldiers were shouting commands as the dogs pulled free and fled in terror into the wide, empty street, yelping like puppies.

The feeling was mutual, as far as Otto was concerned. Animals were simply more honest than humans.

The entire line of soldiers avoided Otto's gaze, and glass doors hissed open to admit him into a high-ceilinged lobby hung with ornate crystal chandeliers. The world's gaudiest gold-and-mirrored service robot vacuumed rich red carpets that were trimmed in gold tassels.

Otto trailed his hand affectionately over the robot's polished surface as he passed by. He had a soft spot for robots. They weren't as off-putting as humans.

He entered an elevator car paneled in mahogany, crystal, and brass. Without his selecting a floor, its doors closed and whisked him to the penthouse. There, Otto exited, walking between grim security men in blue suits bulging from gel body armor. The final two guards stood before closed oak doors richly carved with Asian dragon motifs.

The guard on the left, a six-foot-eight, bearded mountain of a man, held his hand up to stop Otto. "He's in a private meeting, Mr. Otto. He asked not to be disturbed."

Otto let a crooked smile crease his face. He then walked right up to the guard while the man's colleague gazed nervously elsewhere. Otto held out his hand as if to shake. "And who are you?"

Uncertain, the first guard extended his own massive hand. "I'm—"

Otto swiftly clasped the guard's hand, watching closely as a sheen of sweat appeared almost immediately on the guard's face. Seconds later a dark wet stain spread from the guard's crotch, urine dripping onto his dress shoes.

The man pulled free from Otto's grip and backed away from the door—and then away from Otto entirely. Existential dread was written on his face. He gasped for air. "I'm sorry. I'm sorry! Please . . ."

The other guard swung the doors open without a word, still avoiding Otto's gaze.

Otto calmly entered the penthouse office. It had a sweeping view of the unpopulated city below. The double doors closed behind him.

He heard voices to his right and turned to see an Indian bioengineer in a white lab coat speaking to the owner of the office—who stood with his back turned inside a large, ornately fashioned conservatory. The enclosure was alive with fluttering silver, black, white, and orange butterflies and was easily twenty feet wide. It contained potted trees, a fountain, and flowers.

Otto would recognize Marcus Wyckes anywhere by his commanding presence. He didn't need to see the man's face. In fact, Wyckes's face, like Otto's, was forever changing. But Wyckes's presence never changed. And it was why this human was the closest thing to a father that Otto would ever have.

Otto approached silently.

The researcher spoke haltingly to Wyckes. "We did as instructed . . . prepared a . . . a lethal change agent . . . a revision to your birth DNA."

Wyckes observed a silver-gold-and-black butterfly crawl across the back of his hand as he replied with an Australian accent, "I didn't instruct you to include my chromatophores. Now this man apparently has my unique mark of rank. He's already displayed it in public."

The bioengineer stammered. "We . . . we have never performed a lethal transformation outside this facility, Master Wyckes. And it has never been raised as an issue before."

Wyckes's voice remained calm. "Was I born with chromatophores?"

"No. Of course, you were not, Master Wyckes. But I assumed you wanted him to be mistaken for you."

"*After* he was dead—not *before* he was dead."

"But, Master Wyckes, the added processing to remove chromatophores would have been—"

As Otto quietly came alongside the researcher, the man drew back as if he sensed something *wrong* nearby.

The butterflies within the conservatory suddenly took flight en masse, fluttering from the back of Wyckes's hand. Every one of them clustered at the farthest point from Otto that they could manage.

Wyckes spoke without turning. "Otto." He turned and smiled, revealing a mix of Slavic and Chinese features—ruddy-faced with short black hair. He wore a cashmere sweater and tailored slacks. "Humanity's last hope has returned."

Otto smiled slightly.

Wyckes nodded to the researcher. "Leave us."

The man happily complied, clearly eager to get away from Otto.

Otto opened the conservatory door for Wyckes. They did not touch as Wyckes exited, but Wyckes smiled warmly before moving toward a massive mahogany desk a dozen meters away, near the tall bank of windows. The desk was carved with Chinese dragon motifs and entirely out of keeping with the modern architecture of the office.

"I'm glad you're back so soon."

Otto's voice was measured. Calm. "Our new partners were very cooperative."

"Well, that's fortunate, because a problem has come up that requires your unique talents." Wyckes sat in an ancient-looking leather wing chair.

Otto sat in one of the two modern guest chairs in front of the desk, unbuttoning his suit jacket.

"Do you recall administering a very important injection for me in

Singapore last month? Into the Interpol agent responsible for locating so many of our partner labs?"

Otto considered the question for a moment, then nodded. "Yes. In a crowded train station, I recall."

Wyckes nodded. "Yes. The dose was meant to be a lethal change agent to transform the man into someone very special: me."

Otto contemplated the event. "That was uncomfortable—being among so many humans."

Wyckes's expression softened. "You know how much I appreciate your sacrifices, Otto. Our research would not be possible without you."

"Has there been a complication?"

"Yes. Unfortunately, the target did not perish after the transformation completed. He survived. And what's worse, he's now running around loose."

Otto pondered this news. "As you?"

Wyckes shrugged. "As what I once was. At least partially so. And worse still, he's got this . . ."

With that, a full complement of green, blue, black, and orange tattoos faded into existence on Wyckes's neck, forearms, and knuckles. Within seconds they stood out in vibrant color. From a mild-seeming businessman, he now had the appearance of an arch Yakuza or Triad warlord.

As if by reflex, Otto's chromatophores responded in kind. He saw his own Huli jing tattoos surface on his hands, but knew they were activated across his chest, back, arms, neck, and legs, too.

They both had unique patterns. Their own signature.

Otto nodded. "Your marks of rank. That is a problem."

Wyckes nodded back. "Yes. It's a problem. One I need you to resolve." He made several hand gestures and a desk-mounted LFP beamed virtual images into Otto's retinas.

Internet newsfeeds floated before Otto. One headline read, "Cartel Kingpin Kills Officers in Dramatic Escape," with a scan of police boots sticking out of an elevator door. The other article showed an Interpol Red Notice and photo of a bald, fierce-looking man that in no way resembled the Marcus Wyckes sitting in front of him. That headline read: "Infamous Gangster Loose in Singapore."

Wyckes nodded toward the images. "I'm not sure how he did it, but this Interpol agent is now on the run. Our friends in the police failed to do their job."

"Will they find him?"

"We can no longer rely on the police. But the media should make it easier to locate this person. His face—that is, my old face—is all over the news. I'm now wanted in nearly two hundred countries. It'll be difficult for him to hide." Wyckes passed the virtual Interpol Red Notice to Otto—who examined the image carefully.

"I want you to do what the police could not: find this imposter, kill him, and leave his body where it'll be quickly found by the authorities. It's high time for Marcus Demang Wyckes to finally die—and his lengthy criminal record along with him."

Otto nodded. "It also eliminates our most troublesome enemy. There is a beautiful symmetry to your plan. I will see it done."

"Good." Wyckes smiled, closing his eyes in relief. "I knew I could count on you, Otto. You know there is no one I trust more in this entire doomed world than you."

Otto stood, and with a nod, he headed for the elevator.

Chapter 15

The junkie's phablet was cheap, Tanzanian-made shit. And Kenneth Durand wasn't used to tapping at a physical screen as he walked. AR light field displays were a much more natural way to interact with information. But then nonretinal displays had huge advantages to criminals (which Durand now technically was); they couldn't easily rat you out.

Durand had been walking for several kilometers down a long drainage channel, headed northward. Holding up the phablet screen and comparing his location to a city map, he turned down the next side tunnel and edged around motion sensors, lowering his head as he passed a camera.

These, too, appeared to be out of commission. It was obvious that the criminal element moving about the tunnel system beneath the city regularly broke the devices and sabotaged locked entry gates—although the locks were disguised to appear intact. Durand was surprised the SPF tolerated this. He remembered all the security data being fed into his systems from Singapore officials, and he wondered to what degree any of it was true. He found it hard to believe that Singapore would tolerate malfunctioning motion sensors and bent gates in a drainage channel going out to the Strait—allowing passage by random people unchecked. How could they permit junkies and transients to wander across the city unobserved via the drainage channels?

He wondered if this was a state of affairs Michael Yi would recognize. Had the SPF relegated security to informers among the junkie population? Had they come to terms with criminal gangs to keep an eye out for terrorists moving through? Human intelligence was something streets cops infinitely preferred to IoT data.

Durand was starting to realize they might have a point.

He passed by a couple of Filipino teens strutting to Thai retro-funk. The music echoed confidently in the tunnel, but the young men turned their music down and moved warily around Durand on the far side of the tunnel as he glared at them. They looked petrified. Urban explorers? Future synth addicts? Difficult to say.

Durand made sure the teens didn't double-back on him, and then, referencing the phablet map again, he turned down a side passage that ended in a steel gate with a thick lock built into it and menacing-looking alarms. Beyond it, he could see MRT rails and diamond-plate stairs. He pushed against the locked gate, and it came open, as the previous ones had—maximum-security appearance notwithstanding.

In a moment, Durand moved up the maintenance stairs and found himself walking on a catwalk alongside an MRT subway track. Up ahead there was another gate, and he could see bright lighting with commuters and transit police moving on a station platform.

There would be working cameras here, so he inserted phablet-linked earphones, tossed the camouflage jacket, and pulled up the hoodie on his sweatshirt. He then flipped his phablet screen to anime he'd found in its library—no doubt torrented. He turned the volume to zero, then pushed through the maintenance gate and let it close behind him with a bang—as if he didn't give a damn who saw him.

He moved out onto the subway platform with other commuters, head bobbing to imaginary music as the cartoon titles played.

Woodlands station—his MRT stop. He wasn't far from home now.

He kept his head down, ostensibly engrossed in the animation as he passed what he knew were numerous surveillance cameras—running real-time facial recognition in a photonic cloud.

But Durand knew more than most people about these systems—knew what they were and were not capable of. He also knew what the algorithms were searching for. Loitering, rapid movements, recognizable weapons—all of these set off alarm bells. So did positive matches for wanted felons— particularly those who'd been headscanned, like he'd been. However, an overreliance on automated systems meant that second-order anomalies weren't caught; whereas a human might think it odd that someone was wearing a sweatshirt with the hood up on a warm day, algorithms weren't yet sharp enough to connect those dots—at least not the systems used by MRT security.

Durand also knew it was common for commuters to read and keep to themselves, avoiding eye contact with others as they pushed through the crowd. He tried to recall security conferences where vendors described what type of "suspicious behavior" their algorithms looked for.

Durand headed up the stairs to street level. Two transit police passed by him, and he laughed to an imaginary phone companion, turning away. He was relieved when they paid no attention to him.

Durand reached daylight. It was wonderful to be in fresh air again, partly sunny and in the midseventies. To smell familiar smells. He kept his head down, but activated the phablet's front-facing camera as a form of periscope—allowing him to look ahead without lifting his face to street-level surveillance cameras. He knew there were camera pods on every sign pole and streetlight in this neighborhood. It had been a selling point actually.

He angled the phablet across Woodlands Terrace road, revealing the six eighty-story towers of the Hanging Gardens complex where he lived, linked at their summit by a ring of greenery. The Woodlands district was popular with expats and biotech folk. The neighborhood was a showroom for the built environment. And its security infrastructure was also constantly searching for trouble.

As he crossed the street, it only just now occurred to Durand that the prior owner of the phablet might have problems that would flag him as trouble to local police. Had the man ever been arrested? Was he a known synth addict?

The analyst in him tried to derive what Singapore's algorithms might be watching for in his neighborhood. Durand hoped that walking head-down, gazing at a *physical* device, wasn't going to make algorithms suspicious of him as a low-rent invader. And yet someone walking facedown could be looking at a map or having a conversation with a child or eating. There would be just too many errors on a typical crowded street to react to them all. It was one of the reasons why automated facial recognition systems were imperfect at best—why so many other data points needed to be cross-referenced to identify people: their phone IDs, the NFC chips in their credit fobs, Bluetooth IDs, and a dozen other technological tracers. IoT data frequently overwhelmed authorities.

None of these currently connected this device to Wyckes—and Wyckes was the one everyone was looking for, hopefully elsewhere (like at the border).

Durand passed by his own building and surreptitiously viewed the lobby through his phablet camera. He could see no additional police presence in front of the building or inside.

This actually made him angry. There should have been a security detail guarding his family.

Though, of course, Interpol had no police powers to provide one. And he'd been missing over a month.

Maybe Miyuki had taken Mia back to her parents' home in Chicago. He felt a pang of homesickness but also relief at the thought of their being out of harm's way.

Durand, on the other hand, needed to get into his flat, and precisely how he was going to do it without getting arrested (or, more likely, killed) was an open question.

There was a rear service entrance to his building. He'd cleared the delivery of their new refrigerator through there a year ago. Durand walked purposefully around the block and turned down the side street, passing the building's service alley. An elevator company service truck was parked some ways down the alley, as were a couple dozen electric scooters—probably from domestic workers. Nannies. Maids. Tradesmen and domestic help went in and out of his building all the time. As he glanced at the service entrance, a young Filipina maid walked out, obviously poking at a virtual screen to catch up on messages.

It occurred to Durand that although his building used biometrics—analyses of face, walk, voice, and a dozen other traits—to recognize flat owners, biometric recognition didn't actually grant access; it just made the building polite, allowing it to greet tenants by name and make them feel cared for. It was actually a chip in a key fob that granted access to the building. If someone the building did not recognize tried to gain access with a key fob, it would alert human security, but could also still grant access. People had guests all the time, and operationally it was just too difficult to manage all the exceptions.

Plus, biometrics had fallen into disfavor back in the 2020s. Once spoofed by a hacker, they were burned, and an individual couldn't very well invalidate their own retinas and get new ones (with the sole exception of Durand perhaps). So instead, biometrics were used in combination with revocable credentials—fobs, chips, passcodes, and one-time codes. A whole mix.

Which meant he actually had a way of granting himself access to his building: he could schedule a service call through the concierge console. All residents had an account.

It took him a while to search out the landing page with the phablet— particularly since he wasn't familiar with older, two-dimensional browsers. His first login attempt failed, but he guessed right on the second try (and confirmed why passwords were so awful from a security point of view). The scheduling screen came up, and he navigated to a grid showing the maid's schedule. He noticed there was a cat nanny listed as well, arriving daily in the midafternoon. A cat nanny—had Miyuki and Mia indeed headed for the States? Quarantine would have prevented them from taking Nelson, so it made sense.

Durand felt horrible for his daughter. First losing her father, and then parting with her toyger. But then he realized the more time he stood here, the more likely he was to appear suspicious.

Checking the time, Durand noticed the cat nanny's visit was only a couple of hours from now. He tapped at the physical screen awkwardly but managed to create an appointment for an electrician just a few minutes after the nanny. He typed in a fictitious name.

Roderick Feines.

Good enough. Durand walked a few blocks away on side streets, occasionally stepping aside to use the phablet to search online for uniforms, tools—everything he needed. Singapore was the global capital of same-day drone delivery, and "current location" was always a delivery option. Lots of expats worked out of coffeehouses and cocktail bars these days. Tradesmen on job sites. It shouldn't raise any red flags, and Durand still had quite a few bitrings on him for payment.

Food!

Durand suddenly realized just how hungry he was. He hadn't had solid food in over a month. Best to start with liquid nourishment since his digestive system would need time to restart. He checked the time again and then searched for a local juicing kiosk that offered drone delivery.

A couple hours later, Durand entered through the service entrance at the back of his home building wearing a new work shirt, boots, and work pants and holding an electrician's toolbox. A brand-new olive drab cap shielded his face from most of the cameras as he looked for his business card.

He nodded to the security guard and signed in. The guard checked to confirm Durand was expected and provided a visitor's fob that granted access to the floor that had requested him—and only for the scheduled time. The guard absently told Durand to use the service elevator.

In a few moments, Durand was at the fifty-sixth floor. He exited into familiar environs from an unfamiliar direction. The building didn't bid him good afternoon—and neither did one of his passing neighbors, Raz, an Indian geneticist in his thirties who worked from home. There wasn't a hint of recognition in the man's face.

Good.

Durand walked past the door to his own flat without seeing any additional police presence. He then pulled out and studied his phablet diligently—appearing busy.

In a couple of minutes he heard his flat door open behind him. But what he heard next set his heart racing . . .

Miyuki's voice.

She sounded tired and stressed as she told someone, "The vet information is on the cupboard door. With the food."

A young woman with a Malay accent answered, "But I need feeding information—"

"I . . . I'm sorry. I can send it to you. I'm not normally this disorganized. I'm sorry."

Durand turned toward them, still holding the phablet in his hand. He froze as he caught sight of his wife just meters away. Her eyes looked puffy, and he instantly knew she'd been crying. She'd received false hope about her husband just yesterday.

"What do you do?" A little girl's voice—one Durand would recognize in utter darkness.

Durand looked down at his six-year-old daughter, Mia, staring at him from near her mother. They both pulled rolling luggage behind them.

They were leaving.

Seeing the complete lack of recognition in his own daughter's eyes, Durand felt further away from them than ever before—even though they were right here in front of him. This was everything he'd been hoping for, but now that he was here—he could not come back to them like this. Not this way.

His daughter gave him a quizzical look.

Durand cleared his throat. "I'm the electrician."

Mia pointed at him and looked at her mother as she smiled. "Cooool."

Miyuki looked to the nanny. "We have to go. I will send you a message with all the information." She glanced down. "Mia, please stop bothering that man. Inspector Belanger is waiting for us." Miyuki placed a hand on her daughter's head, and they both moved toward the elevators.

Durand watched them go, on the verge of chasing after them. But to what point? To terrify them? He noticed the hand holding the phablet now bore his tattoo-like markings again. He tugged up his sleeve and saw that they continued up his arm. The deep emotion he felt at this moment had caused them to reappear. This much he now knew. There was a logic to them, then.

He looked up to see his wife and daughter enter the elevator. His daughter stared back. She waved, nearly crushing him.

And then the doors closed.

Durand stood in the corridor alone, only then noticing that the cat nanny had reentered the apartment. Gathering his resolve, he approached his flat door to knock, but just then it reopened. He ducked to the side as the young woman exited. He could hear her music playing in headphones, and she was already engrossed in her LFP glasses as she walked down the corridor, also headed to the elevators.

Durand lunged toward the door, managing to catch the lever handle just before it shut. He then slipped inside.

The alarm was *BEEP-BEEPING*, but he tapped the disarm code into the keypad—glad that he hadn't had the old physical interface removed. Durand felt tremendous relief when his own front door latched closed behind him.

He looked around his living room, and then over to his wife's office, with its glass wall. Her desk was cleared off. The photos on her back wall gone.

The place felt emotionally empty. Glancing into the kitchen, he could see that the photos and 3D-printed models were gone from the refrigerator door as well. There was fresh food and water for the cat, but no other sign of recent habitation.

Miyuki had taken Mia and gone somewhere with Inspector Belanger. Durand was relieved. They hadn't moved, but clearly they weren't staying here anymore.

He was glad they were somewhere safe—with someone who loved Mia almost as much as he did. He had to take care of this impossible situation.

He moved through the dining room and past the laundry room. Durand passed by his daughter's bedroom and nudged the door open.

Her solar system mobile and horse-themed comforter were still in place. But the room was much neater than it normally was. Her desk, too, was immaculate—something that had never happened before.

Durand restored the door to its previous, half-opened position, and then entered his own bedroom. He closed his eyes and inhaled deeply. The familiar scents brought powerful memories of who he was—of Miyuki lying next to him in the darkness.

He turned to see a framed photograph on their bureau dresser—of his real self smiling with his wife and daughter at Hong Kong Disneyland. Durand picked up the photo frame and touched it with alien fingers. He looked up at the strange reflection in his own bedroom mirror. Perhaps the face of the man who had done this to him.

Desperation began to resurface. Was there any hope of getting back? Was he just kidding himself? Kenneth Durand was gone.

He was startled by his daughter's toyger, Lord Nelson, leaping up onto the bureau dresser. "Nelson . . . you scared the shit out of me."

Durand slumped in relief as the cat rubbed against his hand, purring loudly. Durand put the photo frame down and picked Nelson up, lifting him to his face while holding him under his forelegs. The toyger bumped his head affectionately against Durand's nose.

Durand sat down on the edge of the bed, nestling his daughter's cat close. "Nelson, Nelson."

There was still some of his original self left to detect apparently. There was still hope. He hugged the cat for the first time and then held him up to look him in the eyes. "Thanks, buddy. I really needed that."

He gently placed Nelson on the bed.

He had urgent business to attend to here. Durand went to the kitchen and retrieved small, resealable plastic baggies. He then entered the master bathroom and carefully retrieved strands of his own hair from his hairbrush and electric razor—looking especially for strands with the root. He sealed all the individual bags into a larger one.

Lord Nelson sat on the bathroom counter, observing impassively. Durand had never been happier to have the cat's company. "If I ever complain about you again, go ahead and scratch me."

Finally leveling a gaze at himself in his large bathroom mirror, Durand sighed deeply. He looked like hell. Aside from being a thuggish stranger, his face was bruised, and taking off his uniform, he could see the second-degree burn on his forearm from the hot cowling of the police drone.

Glancing at the shower, Durand decided there was no time like the present.

He took a long, hot soak, and felt relief cascade over him. He hurt all over, and the burn in particular was giving him trouble, but there was nothing like being home.

Once out of the shower, he glanced in the mirror at this new body. He'd never been physically intimidating—Durand had more of a runner's physique—but he now had a substantial chest, brawny arms, and a thick neck. He looked like some Eurasian middleweight wrestler. Looking more closely at his face, he was still amazed that his ethnicity had been changed. He was part Asian now.

He turned forward and back and could find no trace of the massive array of tattoos that had reappeared on him just minutes before. Strange. But then, that was the least strange thing that had happened to him lately.

He took out a first aid kit. The Naval Academy had drilled organization into him until it was habit. Durand knew where everything was in his flat, and it was well organized. He treated his burn with a synbio skin spray, then dressed his other wounds as best he could.

Looking back into the mirror, he was glad he was bald. He didn't want to see what Wyckes's hair would look like. From the shadow of growth forming, it was probably going to be black. His own hair was a dusty brown.

Durand entered the walk-in closet and could see that a portion of his wife's wardrobe was gone, along with her luggage. Durand couldn't help but wonder what her plan was. To get out of here for now, certainly, but what then?

He contemplated what he would have done if the reverse had happened—if one day his wife suddenly went missing. He realized it would consume him—even as he would have to care for Mia's well-being, too. He decided his wife had it tougher than he did right now.

Durand moved aside some of his suits. He felt closer to his real identity again, touching the synthetic gabardine, but felt a pang of melancholy when he discovered his dress shirts no longer fit—too narrow in the neck and shoulders.

Durand glanced at Nelson, who was shadowing him. He rubbed the cat under the chin. "Looks like we're going casual."

He put on one of his looser-fitting tracksuits and a pristine Colorado Rockies baseball hat.

Lastly, Durand went to the bureau dresser, where he took the family photo out of its frame. He examined the precious image of his wife, daughter, and finally his real self.

He *would* get back to his family—and to himself. He folded the photo and slipped it into his pocket. Durand then went into his wife's office and took one of her old-timey ink pens and quality vellum from a drawer where he knew she kept them. He glanced admiringly at her handwriting on a note there. It was something she did that he had always adored. Her writing was feminine and yet so confident—bold, graceful strokes.

His own handwriting was childish and crude—but then, he was a technology guy. As Durand lifted the pen, he wondered if his wife (or anyone) actually had a sample of his handwriting with which to confirm the authenticity of this note.

Durand placed the tip of the pen on paper, took a breath, and then wrote the following:

> *Dearest Miyuki and Mia,*
>
> *I am alive and safe for now—but as you probably guessed, I'm on the run from very bad people. You must stay away from home and in protective custody—preferably back in the United States. Ask Claire and Michael for help if you need it. Please tell my mother, brother, and sister that I love them. Do not try to look for me. I promise you, I will come back to you both. You are all that I live for.*
>
> *Your loving husband and father,*
> *Kenneth Durand*

Durand left the note against the empty photo frame in the bedroom. With one last look at the stranger in his own bedroom mirror, he pointed at his reflection.

"I'm coming for you, asshole."

With that, he exited his flat, and hoped it wasn't for the last time.

Chapter 16

Now equipped with proper exercise clothes, Kenneth Durand flipped up his hoodie and jogged as though he intended to work up a sweat in the humid heat.

The Singapore police were still looking for him, of course, but he knew where he needed to go. It was only a kilometer away. Durand aimed for the north waterfront and the line of farming towers covered in greenery. As he drew closer to the massive structures, he noticed aggie drones flitting around them like bees pollinating flowers.

The exterior of the towers was mostly public relations—displaying walls of flowering plants and supporting bee populations. But the real business was inside—highly productive, automated, aquaponic urban agriculture. Plants not visible from out here.

Soaked with sweat from his jog, Durand walked with an easy confidence toward the loading dock at the back of Farm Tower Four. It was owned by a company named Agriville—its logo a stylized flowering tree. Durand passed autonomous trucks and vans carrying racks of produce to local markets.

He nodded to a security guard in a shack near the rear gate. "Headed in to see Mr. Desai."

"Very well, please sign in, sir." He presented a ruggedized thirty-year-old tablet for Durand to sign.

Durand tapped in a random name on the visitor form and handed the device back. "I know where it is." He pushed through, and the bored security guard didn't object. Instead the man went back to watching something on a light field device.

Durand knew the route inside well enough, and he knew how to act among the very few human workers on the ground floor. He moved immediately toward a shipping clerk's office and reached inside the open doorway. Without looking, he pulled a yellow composite hard hat from a rack next to the door. He also grabbed an ID badge on a lanyard from an unlocked locker and looped it around his neck. The photo on it distracted him momentarily—it showed his old self above the name Martin Peele.

Durand then grabbed a work tablet and headed toward the large freight elevators. Autonomous forklifts moved pallets of produce to and fro, their warning lights flashing. He entered the elevator and watched as the button panel turned green to show he had access. Durand tapped the button for the seventy-fifth floor.

As the open elevator car rose, he saw floor after floor of purplish light illuminating endless racks of lush, highly diverse plants. Purple was a frequency of artificial sunlight alien to human eyes, but divine to plants. Here, Agriville grew produce to order for restaurants and markets all over the city, with the entire operation managed by a data-driven logistics system. Each row and each shelf might grow a hundred different plants for a dozen different clients. Or a single client. Specialized, track-mounted robots managed seed retrieval, planting, germination, and plant care.

As the floors zoomed past, Durand saw only one or two human beings moving about—monitoring autonomous operations mostly. On the whole, the entire facility and the surrounding towers just like it were almost completely automated. Not many people necessary, really. That created opportunities for the more enterprising.

Durand glanced back at the impressive skyline behind him—Johor Bahru across the Strait. Autonomous ships plied the water. Security drones patrolled the coast. He had no doubt the search for Wyckes was still in full swing—that they were expecting Wyckes to flee the country. To get back to his people.

The elevator came to a stop with a loud musical tone that could be heard halfway across the rack-filled floor. Durand exited and moved with purpose along the wide aisle at the head of the racks, glancing at the numbers.

At aisle forty-two, he turned in, squeezing past several robots that rolled past on rails built into the shelving. They sprayed water, pruned leaves, and searched for blights and parasites with microscopic care.

Durand walked a hundred meters to the end of the aisle, where he saw a cage door with no markings. He approached with his head down, eyes on the ruggedized tablet, knowing full well there was a camera watching the doorway. As he reached the gate, he raised his ID badge up to the lens.

The gate clicked open and Durand pushed through. The metal cage slammed behind him as he slipped next through a fire-rated security door marked with a biohazard symbol and the text "Danger" in multiple languages.

Durand entered a space where classical music played on hidden speakers. As the door eased shut behind him, he surveyed a sprawling laboratory where white lab robots holding racks of microtubes rolled past on rubber wheels. Centrifuges whirred, their payloads a blur. Cooling fans of DNA-sequencing machines hummed. This place was noticeably cleaner and more technical than elsewhere in the building.

Durand walked past flowering plants growing in the shape of company logos or broad tropical leaves bearing advertising slogans. He nudged past another potted plant bearing juice boxes as fruit, replete with branded packaging, scan codes, and ingredients listed on their biodegradable skin.

This was, in fact, an illegal embryo-editing lab—albeit one for making illegal edits to plants.

Staring via LFP glasses into the virtual screen of an advanced-looking microscope, Malaysian geneticist Radheya Desai sat on a lab stool, his back to Durand. The man was slightly overweight, balding, and wore a white lab coat. Without turning, Desai held up a rubber-gloved hand. "Marty. I'll be with you in a moment."

The classical music continued to play.

Durand cleared his throat and tossed his hard hat onto a nearby counter. "Rad, I need your help."

Desai turned in alarm, his face registering fear at the sight of this burly stranger in his lab. "Shit." He killed the music with a wave of his hand. In the silence he glanced over at a wall-mounted alarm button several meters away.

Durand moved to interpose himself between Desai and the alarm.

The geneticist held up his hands. "You do know whose lab this is, right?"

"Just listen." Durand approached Desai and pulled the LFP glasses off his face. "No phone calls, either."

Desai held up his hands. "Okay. Okay." He pointed to Durand's ID badge. "What happened to Marty?"

Durand pointed to a lab stool. "Sit down, and I'll go over it."

Desai looked around for some way to call help. "Look, I can pay. Whatever gang you're with, agreements can be struck. We're businessmen, here."

"I'm not here to shake you down."

"How did you even know this lab was here and what to—"

"Just calm down."

Desai was starting to hyperventilate. "I support my entire extended family. Okay? I've got kids. Nephews, nieces. Aunts, uncles. Grandparents. I—"

Desai swept a metal tray off the counter toward Durand—and then made a run for the opposite end of the lab.

Durand deflected the tray with his arm. Angry at the pain, he sprinted after Desai, his baseball cap flying off as he caught up to the fifty-year-old scientist with ease. Durand grabbed Desai by the collar and pulled him up sharply—shoving him back against the long lab counter and cabinets, rattling glass vials and beakers. "Would you calm down, goddamnit? I'm not here to hurt you. I'm here to ask for your help."

Desai's eyes went wide, and he suddenly looked more amazed than afraid. "Oh my god."

Durand looked up at his own reflection in the glass cabinet just behind Desai. His complement of tattoos was reappearing, arching across his scalp, neck, and hands. Apparently the sudden pain of getting

hit with the metal tray had set it off. He looked menacing as hell—
scowling with a bruised face and bloodshot eyes. He tried to soften his
expression, but it was difficult.

Desai stared closely. "What is that?" He straightened and held up his
hands in a gesture of reconciliation. "My apologies. Apologies. My god—
they're getting darker." Desai laughed in spite of himself. "Those are
amazing."

Durand released Desai, who immediately tried to touch Durand's
face. Durand swatted his plump hands away. "Never mind the tattoos.
I'm here for a different reason."

"But those are incredible. That synbio IP is worth more than this
entire lab."

"I came here because you're an informant for Interpol."

Desai suddenly went back into panic mode again. "Whoa! I don't
have any contact with Interpol, my friend. I swear to you. I am
completely—"

Durand grabbed Desai by his lab coat lapels once more. "Would you
shut up? I'm trying to tell you something."

Desai fell silent, but Durand could feel the man shaking.

"I'm not asking you whether you're an informant. I know you are."

"No, I promise."

Durand pounded the counter. "Shut up!"

Desai fell silent again.

He jabbed a thick finger into the man's face. "You are Radheya
Desai, black market geneticist. You work for Pinjab, but you are a police
informant."

Desai shook his head.

"Your handlers are Ling Ho and Martin Peele—aliases for agents
with Interpol's Genetic Crime Division."

"No, no—"

"I know this because I'm the man you know as Martin Peele."
Durand held up his ID badge, with the photo of Kenneth Durand on it,
along with his alias name.

Desai glanced at the two different faces. "I don't understand."

Durand released his grip on the man's coat. "Neither do I. That's why I need your help."

"You look nothing like Martin Peele—if I even *knew* a Martin Peele. Which I do not."

"Rad, I instructed the Singapore police to raid this facility in March of last year. Since then, you've been passing me intelligence on chemical compounds, holding companies, and shipping addresses for embryo clinic suppliers."

Desai shook his head vigorously. "We don't edit human embryos here."

"I know you don't. But DNA is the same across all species. You use a lot of the same precursor materials as human embryo mills. Your usefulness to me is the only reason the SPF tolerates your existence."

Desai now looked grim-faced. "Okay, for the sake of argument, let's pretend that was true. What do you want from me . . . 'Mr. Peele'?"

Durand got right into Desai's face. "Someone edited my DNA. I think that someone was Marcus Wyckes—the leader of the Huli jing. You've heard of the Huli jing, right?"

Desai nodded.

"I need your help."

Durand was expecting more resistance, but instead Desai simply put a rubber-gloved hand to his mouth. "Wow . . ."

Durand observed Desai warily.

"The Huli jing edited your DNA."

Durand nodded.

"You do realize that's impossible—to edit a living, breathing organism. The changes would—"

"Yes. I know. The template wouldn't match. The organism would die before— I know all that. And yet apparently the Huli jing's bioengineers figured out a way."

Desai just stood shaking his head slowly. "I still—"

"Five weeks ago they injected me in the middle of a crowd of commuters. I woke up yesterday as a John Doe in an intensive care unit. Apparently the transformation happened while I was in a coma. They said I was all swelled up."

Desai considered this. He gestured toward Durand's tattoos. "And those?"

Durand examined his arm. "Whatever these are appeared at the same time. I don't even know why they come and go. They seem to be linked to my emotional state."

Desai motioned tentatively. "May I see your arm?"

"Sure." Durand warily extended his arm onto the counter as Desai grabbed a head-mounted magnifying glass from a nearby shelf.

"We'll go old-school since you've taken my LFPs . . ."

Desai peered closely at Durand's skin. The tattoos were beginning to fade right before their eyes. "Remarkable. This is remarkable work." He looked up. "May I put your arm under my microscope, Mr. Peele?"

Durand nodded.

"I will need my LFP glasses. They're linked to the device—but I assure you"—he held up his hand—"I will not misuse its connection. I simply want to confirm what I'm seeing."

Durand glowered but then passed the LFP glasses lying on the counter over to Desai. "I'm not in the mood for any tricks."

Desai put them on, and they both moved over to the sophisticated microscope.

Looking gleeful, Desai removed samples he already had in place and expanded the viewing area. He motioned, and Durand eased his hand into place beneath its lens. "Palm down on the counter, please. There. Be still." He examined the virtual imagery in his glasses. "What have we here . . . ?" He gasped. "My, my, my . . ." He looked up and smiled in genuine amazement.

"What do you see?"

"I did not think it possible. What year were you born?"

"Two thousand ten."

He waved it away. "Of course, of course, way too old to have received these edits in vitro. CRISPR didn't even exist then. Somehow you have specialized cells known as chromatophores seamlessly woven into your skin. My microscope just confirmed their structure."

"What are they?"

"You could think of them as *genetic tattoos*. They appear identical in structure to that of a chameleon—the topmost layer transparent with subsequent layers containing various pigments; xanthophores for yellow, erythrophores for red, cyanophores for blue, melanophores for brown— you get the idea. In a chameleon the colors are locked away in tiny vesicles so they don't normally appear. But they react to the central nervous system and are sensitive to chemicals in the bloodstream, making their colors visible when under duress or—"

"Excitement. Emotion."

"Precisely. Mood. Most people think the color changes of a chameleon are for camouflage, but they're actually to convey information to enemies and potential mates. Fascinating creatures, really."

Durand pulled his now normal-looking arm clear. "And you've seen this type of thing before?"

Desai lifted up his LFP glasses and rubbed his eyes. He shook his head. "No. And up until this moment, I didn't think such a thing was technologically possible." He turned to regard Durand. "You say that someone genetically edited you?"

"These tattoos are the least of it. They changed my ethnicity. My body. My face."

Desai examined Durand closely. "You mentioned your body swelled up—after receiving an injection?"

"I could barely breathe. Then I blacked out. The doctor said my skin got scabrous while I was in the coma."

Desai pondered this. "Like a chrysalis."

"I don't know. The hospital staff couldn't ID me. It's like my DNA got scrambled. I woke up to this . . ." Durand gestured at his reflection in a nearby glass cabinet.

Desai picked up the ID on Durand's lanyard and held the photo up alongside Durand's new face. "No obvious likeness. At all."

"My vocal cords. My hands. My body. Look, I know this sounds insane, but somehow the Huli jing figured out how to edit the living. Do you realize what this means for humanity?"

Desai seemed focused on his own thoughts. "I'd heard whispers in certain circles."

"What kind of whispers?"

"About in vivo edits."

"Hold it—you've *heard* of this?"

Desai nodded. "They say the increased processing power of photonic computing provided a window into epigenetics."

Durand didn't know whether to hug the man or punch him in the face. "Why the hell didn't you tell Interpol?"

Desai shrugged. "Because it was ridiculous. The type of thing one hears from synth addicts. From wishful-thinking trustafarian transhumanists."

"Back up. What did you hear, when, and from whom?"

"Whispered rumors of an elite black market where they edit the living."

"Who's 'they'?"

He nodded sheepishly. "The Huli jing . . . I'll grant you the rumor was about the Huli jing."

Durand pulled his phablet out and displayed the Interpol Red Notice on its screen. It displayed Durand's new DNA, photo, and listed his name as Marcus Wyckes.

"Apparently the Huli jing edited me to match the DNA profile of their leader, Marcus Wyckes. So now I'm wanted for all his crimes in one hundred and ninety countries. They turned me into the criminal I was hunting for."

Desai picked up the phablet, studying the Red Notice. "I saw the news. And here you are."

"I'm not this man, Rad. You have to believe me."

"Something tells me that if you were this man, I would already be dead. And the real Marcus Wyckes wouldn't need my help, in any case."

Durand looked at his reflection again in the cabinet glass. "I need to get back to who I was. Is that possible?"

Desai studied the photo on the front page of the Red Notice. Then he looked up. "Wait a minute. I think I know your real name. You're that Interpol agent who disappeared a month or so ago." He started searching the news. "It starts with a 'D.'"

Durand grabbed the phablet.

Desai held up his hands in peace. "You must forgive me, but your cover is, as they say in America, 'blown.' It is just a search away."

Durand sighed. "Durand. Kenneth Durand."

"Ah, Mr. Durand. Pleasure to finally meet you. And I might have good news for you."

"Let's hear it."

"The good news is that a GlobalFiler DNA profile consists of a minuscule percentage of a person's entire genomic sequence—just forty-six letters out of three billion. And that's all *noncoding* DNA—meaning it doesn't have any effect on physical appearance."

"Okay. So . . ."

"To make your DNA profile a preliminary match for Marcus Wyckes's, the Huli jing wouldn't need to change your physical appearance at all. They'd just have to change forty-six noncoding letters in all of your thirty-five trillion cells—a tall order, of course, but it's all relative."

"But they *did* change my appearance, and it's obvious why: to rob me of my identity and to make me a wanted man."

"Because?"

"Because I was a threat to them. I've been shutting down their labs."

Desai nodded. "And yet a complete transformation to this Wyckes fellow would not be necessary to frame you. They would likely restrict their edits to purely phenotypical traits—skin color, facial features, eye color, musculature—because changes to your organs would probably start to kill you."

"Meaning you don't think I'm *completely* changed."

"Right." He raised the Red Notice and pointed at the DNA ladders. "This minuscule GlobalFiler DNA profile would usually be sufficient to convict you. But I think a more complete sequencing would reveal that much of your original internals remain."

"How much of my DNA do you think the Huli jing edited?"

Desai studied Durand closely. "If I had access to some of your original DNA, I could tell for certain. But you must realize that all of humanity is 99.8 percent genetically identical. Just one-fifth of a percentage point is all that comprises our individual genetic identity."

"That little?"

Desai shrugged. "But we could compare your current genomic sequence to that of the real Marcus Wyckes—assuming the authorities have his original DNA."

"They do."

"I'm guessing there'll be a difference. That should prove to the authorities that you aren't Wyckes. But to prove your identity as Kenneth Durand we'd need a sample of your original DNA."

Durand produced the plastic bag containing his original hair. "I lifted it from my flat just before I came here."

"Marvelous." Desai held the bag up to the light. "It'll take a few hours to sequence. I'll need to draw blood from you as you are now—we can run the sequencing in parallel. Afterward, assuming I'm correct, I could approach the authorities with the evidence—perhaps your partner, Mr. Ling?"

Durand took a moment to consider his options. After several seconds he shook his head. "No."

Desai looked surprised. "No?"

"We're not doing that."

"I thought you wanted to get your identity back."

"It's not just my identity I want back. I want my physical form back. My own DNA."

Desai put a hand to his chin. "Well, if this sort of change is occurring somewhere in the world, then the technology will eventually—"

"You don't seem to understand the full implications of live editing."

Desai laughed ruefully. "Oh, I do. I realize how much this innovation is worth, certainly."

"Think beyond that. The ability to edit living people undermines the very foundation of authority—namely the ability to *uniquely* identify human beings. If DNA can be edited in living people, there's no way to hold anyone accountable anymore. For *anything*. This procedure will be *far* more illegal than embryo edits ever were—by a long shot."

Desai contemplated this.

"I know the law. They won't make an exception for me, Rad. They might promise to help me, but they'll never do it. I'll be a casualty in the war on genetic edits. They'll tell me to just accept it."

Desai said nothing.

"How can I make love to my wife as Marcus Wyckes? Or have my six-year-old daughter accept me? I *must* get back to the way I was. I need to get this man's DNA out of me. Do you understand?"

Desai proceeded cautiously. "Is it the Asian aspect that—?"

He pounded the counter again. "My wife and child are Asian, you idiot. I'm not a racist—I just want my self back."

"I see." Desai spread his hands. "I'm sorry, but I don't see how that's possible, Mr. Durand."

"The Huli jing already showed it's possible. They edited me once. It must be possible to be edited again."

Desai paced his lab. "Look. To be entirely honest, I'm not an actual geneticist. Not really."

Durand narrowed his eyes at the man.

"I'm more of a glorified technician. I tell people I'm a geneticist because—"

Durand felt himself getting mad. His tattoos began to reappear.

Desai held up his hands. "What you need to do is talk to a full-fledged *genetic engineer*. Fortunately, I know an excellent one. He could tell you whether it's possible to get changed back."

"Who is he?"

"A man who can be trusted."

"How do you know he won't turn me in?"

"Because, like you, he's a wanted man. One problem, though: he's not in Singapore."

"Can we get him on an AR conference line?"

Desai winced. "He avoids phones."

"Can you get him to come here?"

"Mmm . . . that's the thing. Singapore is one of the countries where he's wanted." Desai clapped. "Fortunately, though, he's just across the Strait in Johor Bahru."

"You expect me to cross the border into Malaysia? How the hell can I get across the Strait? Every cop in Singapore is expecting me to cross the border."

Desai patted Durand's shoulder. "Not to worry. We cross the border all the time."

Chapter 17

R adheya Desai and Kenneth Durand arrived via a freight elevator at a subbasement of the Agriville farm tower. They then moved through several locked doors, and finally through a hidden panel disguised as a plain cement wall.

They entered a large concrete chamber with an open pool of water in the center. The space was lined with metal shelving packed to overflowing with fiber-optic and electroactive polymer extruders, photonics boards, and rebreather gear. Likewise, an entire aquarium of lifelike robotic fish hung on racks or splayed across shelves. It was like a robotic theme park storage room.

"What's all this?" Durand sifted through the shelves as two Hoklo workers entered from a doorway on the far side of the room.

Desai barked at the men in Hokkien. Then he turned to Durand. "Underwater air lock. Leads right into the Strait of Johor. We use this to smuggle biotech wares out of Singapore via autonomous subs."

Durand felt the rubbery fin of an artificial marlin. "Robotic fish?"

"Electroactive polymers. Soft robotics." Desai shrugged. "The SPF and Malaysian officials have lots of drones searching for other drones. But *fish*—especially endangered species—get a free pass. Except with poachers, of course, but our fish are not likely to wander into purse seine nets because they monitor fishing trawler radar signals—and avoid them. Something real fish do not do."

Durand studied the shelves and wall pegs overflowing with robotic fish. "How does this get me to Johor?"

"Ah . . ."

Durand turned to see that the two Chinese workers had left, and now he heard the scraping rattle of metal as they pushed open twin rusting metal doors to a neighboring room—revealing a life-sized replica of a great white shark. It was at least twenty feet long and suspended in a harness, secured by chains to a rusting overhead rail system that squealed as the men pushed the artificial shark along the track.

"You have got to be shitting me."

"No! We've only rarely used it. Most of our shipments are deliberately small. However, 'Bruce' here sometimes comes in handy." Desai motioned for the men to bring the soft robotic shark all the way into the room and alongside the opening to the pool of water.

"You're yanking my chain."

"No, indeed."

"You've sent a human being in that thing across the Strait of Johor?"

Desai hesitated. "Not a *living* person, no. But at least we know you'll fit." He clapped Durand on the back. "We'll set Bruce to a neutral buoyancy for your weight." He escorted Durand onto a scale.

Durand was fifteen kilos heavier than he'd ever been. Given his build, it certainly wasn't fat.

"You're a bit heavier than our last passenger, and neither did he need breathing apparatus. But I'm sure we can get it to work."

One of the Chinese workers opened a locker and pulled out rebreather equipment.

"You know how to use a rebreather?"

"Yes. I learned in the navy." Durand eyed the robotic shark skeptically. "How do I know you're not just trying to kill me?"

"There are cheaper ways to kill you. But you must also realize that I have more than a passing interest in whether this in vivo editing of yours is real. I'm every bit as eager as you are to learn more. And my friend will be able to tell us both a great deal."

Durand felt irritation at Desai's implication, but he decided not to say anything. Instead, he stared at the robotic shark as one of the workers tapped at an old, ruggedized computer tablet—causing the shark's mouth to open wide.

Durand could see all the way down its gullet.

Desai turned to him with a smile. "It can accept a payload of a hundred and fifty kilos. And we haven't lost it yet."

Durand looked into the creature's mouth and tested its rows of teeth with his finger. They flexed. *Rubber.*

Desai leaned in next to him and winced at the odor coming out of the depths. "Wang, you should have kept it stored with its mouth open, lah. It never dried out from last time. There are puddles inside."

They began to argue in Hokkien.

Durand studied the interior. "You disposed of a body with this. Who and why?"

"A Yakuza—mortally wounded in a gun battle with Singapore police. His family wanted him back in Japan for burial. We helped spirit his remains out of the country, so to speak."

"All the way to *Japan?*"

Desai laughed. "Of course not. Just across the Strait. It's just a few kilometers. Liquid metal batteries give this a range of approximately sixteen kilometers, so you'll have plenty of power. We have a matching underwater airlock in Johor. You'll be able to get past all the underwater scanners, border control drones. You name it."

Durand again leaned into the shark's mouth. The reek was revolting— a mix of rotten fish, dirty socks, and ozone. He could see a pallet-like platform six feet long and two feet wide, with straps for securing a load. It was perhaps a foot high. It was going to be tight indeed—especially with his new body. "I lie down on that?"

Desai nodded. "Have any fear of closed spaces?"

"No."

"You will." He then reached in and pulled out the platform like a drawer—although it more accurately resembled a shark's tongue depressor.

One of the workers behind him held up the rebreather gear and spoke with a thick Hokkien accent. "Ready, lah?"

It took about fifteen minutes for Durand to get suited up. He then lay on his stomach on the pallet platform as Desai went back over the procedure yet again. Durand was filled with anxiety; lying in the mouth of a great white shark brought to mind the end of some classic movie.

Desai patted Durand's shoulder. "Don't worry. The shark will take care of everything. It will evade boats and drones on its own. It's programmed to know where to go. We think we've got the buoyancy calculations right, so you shouldn't sink to the ocean floor."

"You *think* you've got them right?"

"It's math. You trust math, right?"

"It's not math I'm worried about."

"You'll travel at a depth of ten meters—roughly two atmospheres of pressure. So decompression won't be a problem. That is, unless some major evasive action is necessary—in which case you might need some decompression time. But not to worry! We'll sort all that out if necessary. There's a VR display in your face mask that's hooked into cameras in the front and sides of the machine—so you can get a solid visual of the swim."

"How long?"

"Twenty minutes—give or take depending on tides, currents, and evasion of authorities, smugglers, poachers, and fishing nets."

"The little details."

"I'll be honest with you: this will not be pleasant. I want to be clear on that. But given how wanted you are by the police, it's the only way to smuggle you across the border."

Durand reluctantly nodded.

"I'll meet you on the other side."

With that, Desai slapped Durand on the shoulder one more time and put his full-face rebreather mask on, which Durand began to adjust. Desai made a circular motion with his hand to the Chinese workers.

Durand felt the pallet platform move slowly into the gullet of the shark—and the rubbery electroactive polymer material suddenly squeezed in on him from all sides. He felt a growing panic of confinement. It was like climbing into a rubber coffin. Massive electroactive polymer muscles constricted on him as the machine went through its diagnostics.

And then the mouth of the shark closed. Complete blackness.

Durand heard whirring winch motors and felt the shark swaying back and forth. A moment later a video image projected into his retinas—and light streamed in. He could see a wide-angle view forward and to the sides of the shark's head.

Desai stood near the air lock, next to a worker holding the winch controls. He smiled and gave a thumbs-up sign.

Durand could hear only his heart pounding in his ears. Air had started flowing from the rebreather, but he still felt like he was suffocating.

And then the bottom dropped out.

From the video he could tell that someone had detached the harness and let the synthetic shark drop into the pool of water. Durand nearly panicked as the artificial musculature of the robotic fish launched into action, noiselessly squeezing him like a vise as it twisted right, then left.

And then cold water poured in all around him.

He tried to disregard the feeling of drowning, but being unable to draw breath every time the shark's muscles clenched didn't help.

But he was locked in place. He couldn't move.

He opened his eyes to see in the video feed that his artificial shark was sweeping forward through a tubelike concrete tunnel. Up ahead, he could see a steel gate opening slowly with a grinding sound. There were barnacles and smaller fish all around—some of which fled at the looming terror of this six-meter fish.

With each sweep of its tail, the artificial muscles squeezed the air out of Durand, causing him to cough as he sucked for oxygen—and then get a mouthful of salt water through the distorted rubber seals. Then the shark's musculature would relax, and Durand would gulp air before the cycle began again.

The shark plunged downward now. Durand tried to take in the underwater scene, but constriction crushed him.

It was an advanced design, he did not doubt—no moving parts, just electroactive polymers contracting like muscle tissue under the guidance of a computer brain—but it was clear this machine wasn't designed for a living passenger.

The shark leveled out and began swimming across the murky, sandy seabed. The depth gauge in the corner of his video feed indicated that he was at ten meters depth almost exactly. But the seabed was dropping out beneath him.

And yet everything seemed under control. Durand tried to calm his rising sense of claustrophobia. He looked down and could see the trash-strewn seabed of the Strait of Johor. There was the rusted shell of a car. A sunken fishing boat. Various steel barrels and barnacle-encrusted bill-boards.

Not as many fish as he'd expected, though. Lots of jellyfish—some of them huge. The artificial shark didn't seem to notice any but the larg-est of these. They were vast translucent organisms, some of them tens of meters long. They caught the sunlight from above as they floated, their gossamer-like stingers trailing. Durand had to admit they were beautiful, but he knew why they were proliferating. He'd read about acidification of the oceans—how the rising acidity harmed fish and the formation of shells, fostering what was called "jellification" of the seas; jellyfish thrived in the new environment, whereas more advanced life-forms—like fish—did not.

Ahead he could see an endless field of jellyfish, dotting the depths like eerie spaceships.

And then Durand saw something else—a torpedo-like craft surging along in front of a whirring screw. Even deep within the belly of the arti-ficial shark, he could hear the shrill piercing of its sensors scanning as it passed below them, from left to right, heading along the coast. A black torpedo with the logo of the Singapore Customs department on its flank.

The shark leaned to the left, and then dove down in a move that put Durand's stomach in his throat. He resisted the urge to vomit—which he knew would probably cause him to suffocate. He couldn't even raise his hand to his face. His robotic monster swam deeper and Durand could feel the pressure in his ears. But they moved clear of the customs drone.

As he looked downward now, Durand saw they were much closer to the seabed, moving between piles of garbage and rocks. Here, too, he could see lidar, radar, and heat sensors of all types—hear their ear-drilling sonar beeps and frequency scanning. The place was a solid wall of under-water sensors.

The anti-terror security measures were for good reason. Not everyone in the world was pleased about Singapore's success, and not everyone wished it well.

The shark undulated forward, sweeping its tail tirelessly as it headed off a cliff and out across the much deeper channel. A murky abyss yawed below—not more than sixty meters deep, he knew, but due to the low visibility it might as well have been a thousand.

Then the hiss of a ship's propeller and the drone of a big engine rose above all the other sounds. Durand turned right and left to see where it was coming from. It seemed almost upon them, but then it kept getting louder. Something truly huge was headed his way.

When it had become almost deafening, he finally saw ahead a black wall moving into his view from the left—with a range of numbers printed on it that, having been in the navy, he knew well. They were depth measurements, in meters. The numbers went to fifteen—and that's when he realized it was a monstrous container ship, with a draft in excess of forty-five feet.

It was sliding in front of them at a distance of a hundred meters, a rolling wall of steel—followed, he well knew, by three or more propellers five meters in diameter, moving fast enough to kill with cavitations alone anything that came close to them.

Durand turned his eyes as far left as they could go to see the approaching propellers—horrified that the shark wasn't yet diving deep. It needed to dive! He struggled with rising panic, but could still not move. The damn shark was heading right toward the wall of the ship, and if it only dove just beneath it, the propellers might roll in right on top of them—cutting them to ribbons.

Durand felt panic and started hyperventilating—but then the shark dove, and he mentally urged it to continue diving as the water pressure closed in on him, making it still harder to catch his breath between vise-like constrictions of the shark's musculature.

And then Durand saw the whirling cavitation patterns of the quad screws rolling in above them—and not nearly far enough away.

The impact of their pressure wave crushed the top of the shark down into him, squeezing every ounce of breath from Durand's body as the shark was swept aside like a bathtub toy. He heard straining metamaterials creaking all around him as the shark continued to struggle, and finally rolled over.

The video feed went black.

The entire machine simply stopped functioning. Limp, it began to sink, still buffeted by the deafening roar of the propeller wash above.

No!

Durand strained against the impenetrable skin of the robotic monster and cursed himself for not asking for a diving knife. He might have been able to cut himself free. Instead, he watched in horror as the video feed stayed black. The shark kept rolling, rolling. The water pressure increased. Then the shark thumped onto the seabed.

His ears felt the crushing depth, and he knew he was finished. It was all quiet now, with the ship's roar receding fast, but the shark was still in utter darkness.

And then he heard beeping and felt constrictions in several of the shark's muscle groups. It was a pattern that a computerphile instinctively knew.

A reboot.

A terminal cursor appeared in his vision, and then computer scripts rushed past.

The shark had crashed. That must have been it. Maybe it didn't like the readings it was getting. Maybe something got a voltage spike. Whatever it was, the great artificial shark started to come back to life, and with relief Durand felt its crushing wave of muscle contractions come over him again. Squeezing the air out of him once more.

He was never so happy to feel partially suffocated.

Nearly an hour later—about three times longer than he'd expected—the synthetic shark ceased its slow, upward decompression spirals and finally entered the mouth of the Sungai Kim inlet across the border in Malaysia. He could see a couple of customs sensors on the ocean floor, but nothing compared with the great array monitoring Singapore.

Before long the false shark was swinging its tail against a current and into a smuggler's cove. Durand heard the whining screws of smaller boats, but after his experience with the monstrous container ship, he wasn't nearly as concerned. Instead, he was struggling with real suffocation. His rebreather mouthpiece had become partly dislodged from the air hose during one of the shark's muscle contractions—and now every time he had to draw air, he barely got enough. He felt himself near to hypoxia and knew that if he passed out he'd die—since he wouldn't be able to time or maximize his breaths to the shark's movements.

Durand closely watched his progress into the cove on the video monitor as the shark moved into shallower and shallower water—finally reaching a depth of barely ten meters. He could see pier piles ahead, and the shark moved directly into their barnacle-encrusted forest-like depths.

And then suddenly the shark surged upward, finally relaxing its muscles as Durand heard a hissing sound—actuators releasing compressed air.

In a few moments, the video feed revealed that he'd surfaced in another air lock, one not dissimilar to the air lock he'd left in Singapore. He realized that identical portals would suit a robotic shark. Robots liked predictable apertures. The shark bobbed in the sloshing waves of the small opening.

Durand felt the shark get winched out of the water, and finally watched as workers with hard hats motioned for others to lower the shark onto a concrete floor.

Only then did the shark's mouth open, and Durand immediately used the freedom of movement to pull the rebreather mask off his face. He sucked for air as fast as he could, coughing out seawater.

After his breathing calmed, he looked up to see Desai, now wearing a fedora, suit, and tie, and clutching a gold-handled cane.

Desai smiled. "Your tattoos communicate that you are upset with me. But in my defense, if I had been honest about how unpleasant that journey would be, you might not have done it. And now look: you are in Johor Bahru, my friend."

Durand resisted the urge to punch Desai's smiling face.

Malaysian workers activated the platform inside the shark, causing

Durand to emerge from the shark's mouth as though it were regurgitating a surfboard.

As soon as he was free, Durand shakily got to his feet. Desai helped hold him upright. Durand took a deep breath as he looked around. No police or armed men about. Desai had apparently not betrayed him.

Durand finally nodded. "You're right. I wouldn't have gotten in there if I knew what was coming."

Desai slapped him on the back. "That's the spirit! Now come on. Let's get you out of those wet clothes. We have someone to see."

An hour later Durand and Desai exited an electric van driven by one of Desai's confederates. Durand wore a wide-brimmed bush hat, baggy cargo shorts, a plain button-down shirt, and sandals. He gazed at the cityscape around him.

Durand had been to Johor Bahru several times. As far as he was concerned, it was a cheap shopping destination for Singaporeans—ringed with shopping malls, restaurants, low-cost entertainments. The last time he'd been here was to buy furniture for Mia's bedroom.

But he'd never wandered into the industrial backstreets—which was where they were now. He could see the additive printing houses, bio-manufacturing plants, and photonic part suppliers that no one had ever heard of. Hundreds of migrant workers moved around him interacting with invisible AR objects and speaking to invisible people back home. He heard a smattering of Bengali, Indonesian, Vietnamese, and Burmese. It was a pale imitation of Singapore's synbio industry—but the spillover was still substantial.

Desai led him down a narrow lane of smaller shops and teeming apartment blocks. They passed a row of laser vision-correction vending machines. Real-world signage was on display all around him, but also rogue light field projectors, creating ghostly "adparitions" of Asian models hawking beer and energy drinks, with captions in various languages scrolling in midair.

Desai pushed a pair of mirror glasses into Durand's hand. "The ad mix gets aggressive here in Johor."

Durand slipped on the mirror glasses and half the advertising disappeared. But one sign close at hand did not. It cast a glow over them both in the fading light of the humid evening. It was an old-fashioned, real-life neon sign buzzing the word "Twisted" into life letter by letter, with a double helix of DNA serving as a swizzle stick in a martini glass.

Durand cast a doubtful look at Desai.

"Never heard of it?"

"No. And if it mattered, I would have."

Desai laughed. "Embryo labs aren't the only things of interest in this world, Mr. Durand."

Durand followed Desai down a dark flight of stone steps.

They entered through an ancient wooden door into a dimly lit vestibule—and were immediately deafened by cacophonous guitar and synthesis sounds. Durand winced at the random musical gibberish.

Desai motioned and pulled Durand farther inside. After a few moments they passed through a sonic wall and immediately found themselves in comparative silence. They moved through a velvet curtain into a darkened, ornate bar buzzing with conversation and soft ambient music.

"Apologies for the sonic assault at the entrance. Protein music discourages casual tourists. That sounded like tomato DNA actually . . ."

Durand removed his mirror glasses and surveyed the place—an eighteenth-century Asian watering hole, with curtained booths and a crowded British-colonial-period bar, beveled mirrors and carved teak wood. In an earlier century it might have been an opium den. Original gas lamps barely illuminated the room—and its unusual clientele. Strangely attired patrons with anti-facial-recognition paint in stylish Día de los Muertos patterns, electronic tattoos of Chinese characters or animated cartoon characters glittering across bald scalps, motorized piercings (earlobe-mounted gear mechanisms seemed popular), ornate cosmetic surgical stitches, and other enhancements from devil horns to fangs filled the room.

"And they said bio-punk was dead."

"Don't mock what you don't understand."

Durand's gaze moved from person to person. They spanned all ages and races; male, female, and transgender. "Biohackers."

"I'm told they prefer the term *extra-humanists*."

"These aren't geneditors, Rad. They're tweakers. Surgical and chemical modification isn't going to help me. What are we doing here?"

"Patience." Desai led him farther into the establishment, squeezing past the crowd at the bar. Durand edged past a buxom Caucasian woman in a corset and a Victorian hat—her skin glowed softly in the semidarkness as if she were a ghost. Durand shielded his eyes to see if she was an AR projection, but she remained.

Desai whispered, "Bioluminescent elixirs—popular with party people. Wears off after a few hours. Many's the office worker whose midnight proclivities are revealed when they arrive, still glowing, to the office the next morning."

The woman's gaze followed Durand with obvious interest. It shocked him how unabashed she was, and what was stranger was how magnetic he felt. Confident as he strode through the crowd, which was something he'd never felt in crowds before.

They moved through another sonic compartment of the open room, where the ambient music was replaced by thumping dance music and lights.

Desai leaned back to speak as he continued to move through the dancers. "They augment themselves, you see. Imbibe chemicals, endure radical surgeries. All to extend their natural senses, abilities, and appearance—some of it only temporary. But all in an effort to make their physical form match the person they see in their mind's eye."

Durand watched as he passed a booth where black-eyed young men speaking in Russian watched one of their number inject a companion in the eyeball. The liquid turned the man's eye completely black in seconds.

"Ocular reagent—gives a limited ability to see invisible spectrums of light. Ultraviolet. Temporary, of course. The body metabolizes it."

"And just think, all you have to do is inject yourself in the eye."

"The world has all types. I think it's marvelous." Desai brought them onward.

"How's this place stay open? I thought Malaysia was a conservative country."

"Malaysia has its own method of dealing with human nature. Almost nothing is allowed. But that's what fines are for. None of this would be tolerated in Singapore, of course, but many of these people work for the biggest synbio firms in Singapore. 'Straities,' they're called. There is money in this room, my friend."

Durand pushed past a young man with artificial horns protruding from his skull. Durand nodded to him as he edged by.

Another man sitting in a booth wore a thin film display on his chest, revealing an ultrasound image of his heart beating and trachea swallowing as he downed his drink.

Desai pointed. "Chip implanters, body modders, quantified-self addicts. You'll find all types here. Perhaps some of them have edited somatic cells—blood, sperm, and so on. But nothing as ambitious as what you've experienced."

The vibe was clearly more relaxed than in Singapore. Durand had been aware of this at some level but had never seen it firsthand—and he found it fascinating. More than a few women—and also a few men—cast looks his way. He strode through and others made way for him. He was intimidating, and with shame he felt elated by it.

Desai led Durand toward a roped entrance to a back room, guarded by a burly Chinese bouncer in a pin-striped suit and black derby that Durand guessed was loaded with sensor gear. Maybe even nonlethal weaponry. The huge man stared at Desai for a moment—getting a face-rec match apparently. His expression suddenly softened, no doubt after the CRM system told him to smile courteously and unhinge a velvet rope. "Mr. Desai. Good evening, sir."

Desai motioned. "This young man is with me, Ferar."

"Very good, sir. Will you be—"

"No, we'll be joining Dr. Frey this evening."

"Very good, sir."

Durand squeezed past the bouncer, avoiding the man's stare lest management get a face-rec match on him as well.

Desai led the way down an aisle of Persian carpet, bordered by closed velvet curtains and richly carved mahogany dragons. They caught glimpses of smiling faces, the sharp scent of atomized narcotics, and laughter through narrow openings. Then Desai stopped and knocked with his cane on a wooden dragon head—the number "13" clutched in its fanged mouth.

A man's voice called from within. "What sort of idiot knocks on a curtain?"

Desai nodded to Durand and pushed through.

Durand followed.

Inside, instead of the private booth he had expected, there was a small sitting room, with normal-sized chairs arrayed around a shorter-than-usual table, at which sat a dwarf with a brooding, handsome face and tousled brown hair. He wore a collared silk shirt and LFP glasses adapted to fit antique frames. The room was otherwise covered in Persian carpets, velvet throw pillows with tassels, and oil paintings of twentieth-century Asian businessmen in suits and ties. It was as though someone had furnished the place entirely from the bankruptcy auctions of pre–fourth industrial revolution companies and raided bordellos.

Durand guessed the dwarf was under a meter and a half tall. Except for his diminutive arms and legs, he was normally proportioned and clattered away on a totem keyboard. Several other inscrutable totem devices stood on the table beside him. Durand knew those inert pieces of plastic would look quite different through LFP glasses.

A piece of crystal stemware also stood on the table, its mouth bridged by an ornate silver spoon holding a sugar cube. An open bottle of absinthe stood close by along with a pitcher of water. Vapor wafted upward from the man's 1930s-style vape pen. A blister pak of printed pharmaceuticals also sat open on the table, with two tabs out of four empty.

Desai and Durand eased into rattan chairs on the far side of the table. The dwarf's unwelcoming stare followed them both.

He took a pull from his vape pen and spoke with a mid-Atlantic American accent as vapor curled around him. "Radheya Desai. Not a face I've seen in a while. I heard you were farming juice boxes back in the Bubble."

"We all have bills to pay."

"I see you brought a menacing stranger along." He resumed tapping at his totem keyboard. "Unannounced."

Desai smiled. "A business opportunity, Bryan."

Durand cast a wary look Desai's way.

"Dr. Bryan Frey, please meet . . ." Desai gestured to Durand. "Let's just say a most fascinating friend."

Frey continued typing. "I have yet to meet any friend of yours I'd call fascinating."

"Then this will be the exception." Desai turned to Durand. "Dr. Frey holds a degree in genetic engineering from the University of Bonn. His specialty is bioinformatics—computer modeling to develop new CRISPR edits for numerous species."

Durand watched Frey still tapping away. "Human edits?"

Frey spoke without looking up. "No, those would be *very* illegal. What I do is considerably less so."

Desai gestured. "He is an editor for hire—jail-breaking closed-loop proprietary agricultural sequences. He also creates edits for house pets and the occasional chemical biohack for humans—synthesized supplements, things of that sort."

"Anything that hardens dicks is a big seller." Frey glanced up. "In the humans, not the pets."

Durand eyed Frey dubiously.

"Look at it this way: I'm saving the rhinos."

Durand spoke to Desai. "You brought me to a back-alley gene hacker?"

Frey pointed to the door. "Piss off, 'most fascinating friend.'"

Desai motioned for calm. "Dr. Frey has an open mind, and he is an engineer of considerable talent."

Durand nodded to the printed pharmaceutical blister pak. "Yeah, he looks real solid. I crossed the Johor Strait to meet this guy?"

"I can think of no one better suited to answer your question."

Frey studied Durand. "Crossed over from Singapore, eh? The Orange County of Asia. Personally, I prefer my corruption a shade less self-righteous."

Desai turned to Frey. "A sonic curtain, if you please, Bryan."

Frey sighed. "Your mistake, Rad, is that you think anyone gives a shit about what you have to say." He fished in a nearby leather satchel and produced a metallic wand. With a click, three legs extended from it, and he placed it on the table. "This is a two-person unit, so we'll have to get chummy." He pressed a button. A high-pitched noise raced past them.

Durand was familiar with the devices—white noise projector. They generated a wall of scrambled audio—canceling vibrations within a sphere and generating random noise in its place. They'd be able to speak freely without being overheard by nearby microphones or eavesdroppers. Interpol's GCI was surrounded by them. The sonic walls near the bar doorway and the dance floor were based on similar principles.

As Durand pulled his chair close to the table, he and Desai passed through a field of noise that buzzed in their ears. Then the sound of the bar beyond vanished. The echoes now made it sound like they were conversing in a closet.

Desai leveled a stare at Frey. "Bryan, my friend here is wanted by the authorities."

Frey glowered. "You'd better mean *Singapore* authorities."

"Yes . . . among many others. And yet he is, himself, an Interpol agent."

Frey's face turned decidedly grim.

Desai continued. "He is, in fact, the lead analyst for Interpol's Genetic Crime Division. Possibly the man most responsible for the raids shutting down illicit embryo clinics worldwide." Desai gestured. "Dr. Bryan Frey, meet Agent Kenneth Durand."

Frey turned from one to the other man several times. "You brought an Interpol agent *here*—to my office? Are you insane?"

Desai motioned for calm. "There are reasons, Bryan."

"Reasons. I can't imagine any reason why you would bring a *world policeman* to see *me*—much less into this establishment." He gestured to the curtains. "Please leave, gentlemen. It is my sincere hope you do not get murdered on the way out. Although I wouldn't count on it."

Desai persisted. "This is a special case, Bryan. Look . . ." And with that Desai hauled off and slapped Durand across the face—the hit echoing in the closed acoustic environment.

The surprise of the slap was worse than its sting. Durand leaped up, grabbing Desai's wrist in a crushing hold. The table shook, toppling the bottle and pitcher.

Frey stood. "Careful, goddamnit!" He grabbed for the water pitcher.

Durand used Desai's tie to pull him close. "What the hell, Rad?"

Desai winced as Durand's powerful fist held him. "Look, Bryan! Look." Desai pointed to Durand's face and neck.

Sure enough, Durand could see the tattoos fading into place on his forearms and the back of his hand as he held Desai in a crushing grip. No doubt they were doing the same on his neck and elsewhere.

Frey righted the spilled bottle, and looking up, his face went slack. He focused with new interest on Durand.

Durand released Desai. "You goddamned idiot."

Desai straightened his tie. "My apologies, Mr. Durand. But a picture is worth a thousand words, as they say."

Frey stared closely at Durand's arms as he wiped liquid off his inert keyboard. "I must confess I'm curious. What am I looking at ?"

"Chromatophores, Bryan. Genetic tattoos. Integrated into his skin."

Frey gave an incredulous look. "No . . ."

"I have microscope slides. It's seamlessly integrated into his nervous system."

"How in the hell . . . ?"

Desai looked giddy. "Isn't it incredible?"

"Well, it might be incredible, but I'm curious why a 'wanted' Interpol agent is fronting exotic synbio. Are you offering the IP for sale, Mr. Durand?"

"The tattoos aren't why I'm here."

"Undercover—is that it? Thus the whole 'wanted man' nonsense?" Frey dropped the keyboard onto the table. "If you came here to recruit me as an informer—"

"Bryan, listen: these tattoos are nothing. *Nothing.* Mr. Durand is here to request your help on something much bigger."

Frey laughed ruefully. "Well, you can go screw yourself, Agent Durand—or whoever you are. You may have some impressive Straitie toys, but I don't talk to cops and no doubt the gentleman out front has already pegged you for a cop."

"I'm not here for Interpol. I came to ask for your help."

"Well, I don't want to help you." Frey jabbed his vape pen at Durand.

"World-government types like you are the reason I wasn't born both handsome *and* tall. My achondroplasia could have been corrected in vitro by my mother. A fairly straightforward mutation in the fibroblast growth factor receptor three gene that could have easily been modified. But no, because it wasn't on the 'UN-approved' list of genetic edits, I get to stare at people's crotches my whole life. Asshole."

Durand felt his temper flaring.

"The tattoos are intensifying, Bryan. See how they're linked to his central nervous system?"

"That is pretty impressive—"

Durand leaned across the table—almost up to Frey's face. "Listen, you shit. You have no idea what I went through to get here—"

"I pay rent here. If you so much as touch me, they'll find your body in the—"

Desai tugged at both the men's sleeves. "Please! Please. Gentlemen. Sit, Mr. Durand." Desai turned to Frey. "None of this matters. Bryan. Look at Mr. Durand—whom does he resemble?"

Frey glowered. "*Homo neanderthalensis?*"

"No! If you check the news, you will see that an Interpol agent named Kenneth Durand went missing over a month ago—presumably kidnapped by the Huli jing. Today Mr. Durand sits before you, physically transformed."

Frey glared. "I'm not in the mood for cryptic games, Rad. I'm busy. Now leave, both of you, before I have management throw you out."

"Mr. Durand was genetically edited, Bryan. The Huli jing edited him in vivo. *In vivo.* A mass genedit to a living organism. To a *living* adult human being."

Frey stopped cold. He looked intensely at Durand—then back at Desai. "Get the hell out of here."

"You've heard the rumors, same as me."

"People say lots of crazy shit, Rad. It's just talk."

"Is it?" Desai put his hand on Durand's muscular shoulder. "The Huli jing modified Mr. Durand's DNA, making him both a forensic profile match and phenotypical match for Marcus Wyckes. Look . . ."

Durand removed the phablet from his cargo pocket. The Interpol

Red Notice was still displayed on its screen as he slid it across the table to Frey.

"But I don't think it was a complete transformation—I think his vital organs remain unchanged. If we run a genetic sequence on this man and compare it to his original DNA, there will be massive overlap. You don't have to believe me; run bioinformatic models on both samples and the similarities should be obvious."

Frey watched Durand closely, and then snatched up the phablet, his eyes scanning the printed DNA ladders and the mug shot photo.

Desai pressed. "Search the newsfeeds. You will see photographs confirming that the man sitting before you is the infamous Marcus Wyckes—and yet he is not. Ask yourself: Why would Marcus Wyckes come to you for help? Marcus Wyckes has an army of bioengineers."

Frey scrolled down, quickly reading through. He finally looked up again. "Yes. I've heard rumors about living edits, but around here everyone wants to be something or someone else. Desperation makes them willing to believe any rumor." He slid the phablet back to Durand, eyeing his guest closely.

Durand stared back.

Frey then picked up his phone totem.

Durand's hand shot out to grab Frey's wrist. "You're not calling anyone."

Frey looked with impatience at the massive hand clutching his wrist. "I'm checking newsfeeds to confirm a few things. I'm sure a world policeman like yourself can appreciate the need to gather evidence."

Durand released Frey's arm.

"Keep your sausage fingers off me." Frey became engrossed in his virtual screens. He looked into space with the dreamlike trance of someone engaging with a private light field projection. He slid something unseen in line with Durand, apparently comparing reality to the virtual. "Well. There you are. Marcus Demang Wyckes. A twenty-first-century Pablo Escobar. Mass murderer. Slaver."

Frey lowered his arms, clearly engaging with the reality in front of him now. "I'd like to apologize if I have in any way—"

"Bryan! He's not Marcus Wyckes. I'm telling you."

Frey pondered the situation. "Well . . . there seems to be a reward of ten million yuan for his capture, dead or alive—though I don't imagine there will be many takers."

"The reward is nothing—*nothing*—compared to this technology, Bryan!"

Durand leaned forward. "I'm not Marcus Wyckes. I'm Kenneth Durand. The Huli jing hit me with some sort of injection that put me into a coma. I woke up like this, and I need to get changed back to my original DNA. What I need to know is whether that's possible. You're a genetic engineer. I need some answers."

Frey let out an exasperated laugh. "I'd be guessing."

"The Huli jing edited me once. Could they use my original DNA to change me back?"

Frey pondered the question. "You claim that you—an adult human—have been genetically edited, even though it's never been proven possible. My immediate reaction is that you're a raving lunatic."

Desai interjected, "You can sequence his DNA—"

Frey held up a silencing hand. "*Except.* Except your face is also undeniably all over the feeds as Marcus Wyckes and you've got some incredible synbio tech woven into your skin. Which means you're no run-of-the-mill lunatic." He sighed. "If you're really this Kenneth Durand—I would give anything to know what biotech was in that injection. It would have to be virally based—possibly XNA machinery—to get around the immune response."

Desai interjected. "He was swollen up like a balloon, Bryan."

"Like a chrysalis . . ."

"Yes, I thought the same thing!"

"Interesting . . ."

Durand ignored their apparent excitement. "Just answer my question. Could the Huli jing change me back to myself?"

Frey took a big pull on his vape pen. "If—and this is a big if—if Huli jing genetic engineers have developed the ability to edit *living organisms*. If they have somehow decoded gene expression, figured out how to evade all the body's natural defenses and rewrite genetic code even as you lived and all without instigating a necrotic cascade. If they can do that . . ."

Durand hung on Frey's words.

"I see no scientific reason why they couldn't reverse it."

Durand slumped in relief.

Desai leaned in. "Think about it, Bryan: editing the DNA template is the Holy Grail. If we could reverse engineer their change agent—"

Frey interjected, "We're not about to go into competition against the Huli jing, Rad. I rather like being alive."

"No, of course not. But what about selling the tech? Anonymously. In the blockchain markets. It would be worth a bloody fortune."

Durand cast a dark look Desai's way. "What the hell are you talking about—selling *it*? Selling what?"

"The technique only, Mr. Durand. Just the technique. A blood sample is all we need."

Frey was nodding to himself. "I will say it makes sense that the Huli jing would be the first to have this. They have more unwilling human test subjects for genetic experimentation than I care to contemplate. They've got hundreds of billions of yuan."

"It is unethical, without question, but think if they accomplished it, Bryan. Think what it would mean."

"I wonder what they're doing with it."

Durand looked closely at Frey. "Will you help me?"

Frey sighed. "I'll need to confirm it first. I'll want to do as Rad suggests and compare your current DNA with the original Durand DNA." He looked to Desai. "You say you have it?"

"Yes. Mr. Durand has some hairs with the root attached."

Frey searched in his bag and came up with a sterile test kit, which he ripped open. "A saliva sample, if you will, Mr. Durand."

"How do I know you'll even help me after you get this sample?"

"Because if I can confirm what Desai says, I'll want to take you to meet some people."

"What people?"

"People with the resources to actually do something about this."

Durand thought for a moment. "A baby lab. You mean a baby lab."

Frey held up his hands for patience. "A few years back I worked with an embryo-editing ring in Thailand—a gang called the Luk Krung.

These days they handle some pretty radical edits. There could still be some trace of this change agent in your cells. Some viral machinery. Something that would clue us in to how the Huli jing did it. Modeling even simple genetic edits for an embryo is computationally intensive. But for an adult living organism? I can't even imagine. Thousands of edits in a complex sequence to thirty-five trillion living cells? We must be talking exascale computing for a significant period of time. The Luk Krung would have the financial resources to access photonic supercomputing clusters for the modeling load—which will be huge."

"And then they'd have it. I'd be spreading this madness even further."

"Don't think for a moment that the Huli jing aren't using it already. Do you want to get back to yourself or not?"

Durand sat for several moments. How could he even contemplate giving this technology to yet another genediting gang? But then he thought about his wife and daughter. Of becoming the man he was once more. What he was about to agree to was outrageous. He closed his eyes and nodded.

"Good. If it makes you feel any better, Mr. Durand, I don't approve much of the Luk Krung, either. But I don't see any other choice—unless you want to go ask the Huli jing."

Durand said nothing.

Frey handed the swab to Durand. "A sample of your saliva, please."

Durand opened his mouth and swiped the swab along the inside of his cheek. He then inserted it into a handheld device Frey held toward him.

"Very good. A full sequence will be finished in four hours or so, and we'll know how much of you is Durand and how much Wyckes."

Durand brooded. "You do realize that this change agent will eventually make it impossible to hold anyone responsible for anything? It will render identity meaningless."

"I know that commanding the tides to cease does not work. That's what I know."

Durand felt ashamed that he had so readily crossed this line. It was something he'd thought he'd never do. But then something else occurred to Durand. He focused his gaze on Frey. "Why are you going with me?"

Desai laughed. "I should think that's obvious, Mr. Durand."

"I thought you were nervous about going into competition with the Huli jing?"

"I'm not competing against the Huli jing—I'm bringing it to the Luk Krung."

"And you really think this Luk Krung is going to cut you in after you hand it over?"

Frey tapped the table impatiently. "I'll negotiate a sizable finder's fee."

"Which you could do without going with me." Durand stared at Frey. "Why are you so intent on coming along?"

Desai frowned after a moment's thought and turned to Frey.

Frey still tapped the table with his fingers. Then he stopped. "Look around you, Mr. Durand. You're not the only person who would like to make some changes. This supposed 'change agent' would finally allow me to address my own condition. I could finally have my achondroplasia corrected—even as an adult. I could become morphologically normative. What I want in exchange for making this introduction to the Luk Krung is to cure my condition. Which is why my presence at any meeting is mandatory. And that's nonnegotiable."

Durand realized that perhaps his and Frey's interests were aligned, after all—regardless of whether the man could be trusted. He again nodded in agreement.

Desai leaned forward. "You'll still request a finder's fee, Bryan, yes? I did bring Mr. Durand to you, after all, at some considerable risk to myself."

Frey cast a look at Desai. "Yes—especially since your risk is not yet over."

"What do you mean?"

"You'll need to figure out how to get Mr. Durand across the Thai border."

Durand shook his head. "I'm not climbing into that goddamn fish again."

Frey laughed. "I won't even ask."

"Mr. Durand, Bruce has very limited range. It wouldn't help."

They both looked to Frey.

Frey shrugged. "Don't look at me. All I send across borders is encrypted data."

Durand gestured. "How are *you* getting to Thailand?"

"Qantas business class. I'm not a wanted man in Thailand. Meet me in Pattaya City, on the Thai coast."

"Pattaya City."

"That's right." Frey jotted something down on a piece of paper. "When you get there, message me at this number—no names. Do not use it more than once. Memorize the number, then destroy it. Hell, recycle it—love Mother Earth. But definitely *do not* keep it on your person. I don't want any connection between you and me until you're safely over the border."

"All right." Durand examined the number. "You write like a doctor."

"I *am* a doctor."

Desai looked concerned. "Smuggling people isn't what I do, Bryan. It took everything I could think of to get Mr. Durand across the Strait."

"Well, if you watch the news, there seem to be tens of millions of undocumented migrants on the move. Spend some money with the right people, and you should be able to get Mr. Durand to Pattaya City. That's like smuggling someone to Las Vegas—they rather *want* you to be there."

"What right people? I don't know *human* traffickers."

"You could get him a fake passport with sufficient investment."

"A false passport is not going to help Mr. Durand. He's all over the news, and they've got three-dimensional scans of his head, face, everything. He can't go through airports or border crossings."

Frey shrugged. "Traffickers it is, then. Ask your smuggler friends. They must know *somebody*. Offer a 100 percent bonus once our friend reaches Thailand safely. That will incentivize whoever takes him to make sure he arrives safely."

"And who will pay for that?"

"Consider it an investment, Rad. After all, I'm the one putting my neck on the line to meet with a criminal element in Thailand."

Desai leaned in. "Perhaps I should go with you as well?"

Frey shook his head. "My contacts are *my* contacts, Rad. Certainly you don't anticipate that I'd cheat you?"

Desai said nothing in reply.

Frey scowled. "What do you know about me?"

Desai considered the question. "That you are a highly talented, undisciplined genetic engineer who consistently overpromises and underdelivers. That you eventually wear out your welcome in whatever country you find yourself, and must eventually flee upset clients."

"But I *do* deliver. Maybe not precisely what the client wanted or when . . . but I deliver."

Desai nodded reluctantly. "Yes. Yes, you do."

"Good. Then you and I will be equal partners in whatever results. Are we agreed?"

With some hesitation Desai finally extended his hand.

They shook on it.

Durand sighed in irritation. "Already dividing the spoils, I see."

"Yes, and after you take advantage of this technology for your personal gain, I'm sure you'll see it declared illegal." Frey leaned back in his chair. "Now for god's sake, get Mr. Durand out of here—and use the rear exit. I've no doubt that the management of this establishment—and possibly others—recognized Mr. Durand on the way in."

Desai shook his head. "I don't think any of them would be foolish enough to betray the Huli jing, Bryan."

"Regardless. Keep him out of sight and get him to Thailand."

Desai grimaced. "I'll figure it out."

Frey raised his absinthe glass. "I will next see you in Pattaya City, Mr. Durand. Safe travels."

Chapter 18

A **pounding noise roused** Durand. He rolled onto his side. He lay on a sofa in a living room that seemed familiar—though it was new to him.

The sound came again. *Boom. Boom-boom.*

Durand looked up to see Mia. She was just a toddler in a purple jumper embroidered with dinosaurs. She stood on a stuffed chair on the far side of the room, pounding a wooden spoon on an African djembe drum that stood as decoration in the corner.

Boom-boom-boom.

Durand rubbed his face, awaking from a nap. "Mia. Honey."

Boom. Boom-boom-boom.

He couldn't help but laugh. "Mia, sweetie. Please stop."

Boom-boom-boom.

Durand's head cleared, and suddenly he realized he wasn't in a living room at all.

Mia was nowhere to be seen. A spartan microtel room surrounded him. He leaned up to see an intimidating stranger's reflection in the mirror on the far wall—just a meter from the foot of his bed.

Reality came rushing back to him. But the pounding sound remained.

Boom-boom-boom.

Durand looked to the microtel room door. Someone was beating on it.

Durand sat up. The dream had left him with devastating homesickness.

He thought about Miyuki and Mia. About his mother. His brother and sister back in Colorado, too. About his friends. His colleagues. What were they doing about his disappearance? He knew the authorities were searching for him, but did they already believe he was dead? He couldn't imagine what that would do to his little girl. Or to his wife.

And how long would it take for someone to find the note he'd left in his flat?

The pounding on the door came again. *Boom-boom-boom.*

Durand glanced up at blackout curtains. He had no idea what time it was—or even what day it was. A glowing red clock face in the darkness told him it was 7:22 something. Morning? Night?

Boom-boom-boom.

Durand took a deep breath. He felt more rested than he had since this had all begun. He noticed daylight under the door and could see the shadow of two feet shifting impatiently. It was morning, then. He must have slept about twelve hours. He wasn't even undressed.

Durand went to the curtain and peered through. Desai was out front preparing to pound on the door again. The man held a plastic bag and a cardboard tray of takeout coffee. Durand opened the door and stepped aside.

Desai entered quickly, locking the door behind him. "*Ko ni lubang pantat betul, lah.* I've been hammering on the door for five minutes."

"I was asleep."

"More like a second coma."

Durand stretched and looked in the mirror. He noticed that the majority of his bruises seemed to have faded in the night.

"Well, you look better, at any rate." Desai peered through the door's peephole warily. Satisfied, he turned and offered a coffee cup and a plastic bag sealed with a strip of raffia. "I bring refreshment."

Durand grabbed the bag, tearing it open. "Excellent. Roti canai. Thank you." He dipped the grilled flaky flatbread into a container of lamb curry that came with it—then paused. "Is this deathless?"

Desai raised an eyebrow. "You're a *degan*? You surprise me, Mr. Durand. But yes, it is cultured lamb."

Durand tucked in and spoke with an overstuffed mouth. "Thank you." He chewed noisily.

"Go slow. Your system might still be in distress."

Durand suddenly realized that the food tasted odd to him. He slowed his chewing.

"What?"

"This doesn't taste right."

"It's from the best mamak stall in Johor, man."

Durand smelled the curry again. "Oh god . . ."

Desai snapped his fingers. "I'll bet your taste buds have changed, too. That must be it."

Durand closed his eyes. "When will this end?"

"Fascinating. You must have the taste buds of this Wyckes fellow. Things you once enjoyed may no longer be palatable to you—or at least they may taste differently."

"Yeah. Fascinating." Durand resumed eating. He was just too hungry. Roti canai was among his favorites, but this simply tasted okay. Even that small pleasure had been robbed from him.

"Arrangements have been made."

"How and where?" Durand opened the coffee lid and scowled at the contents. "This isn't coffee."

"Soya cincau—you Americans call it a 'Michael Jackson,' soy milk with little strands of grass jelly."

"Whatever. Maybe Wyckes will like it . . ." Durand took a sip. To his consternation, he did like it.

"There's an autonomous hire car waiting in the alley out back, to take you north."

"A car? *To Thailand?* That's at least a thousand kilometers."

"It's two thousand to Pattaya City, but the car is just to the state of Kelantan here in Malaysia. There you'll be hidden in a truck by smuggler friends of mine and smuggled over the border."

"I won't get that far. Hire cars have interior cameras. Facial recognition. I won't get out of Johor."

Desai patted him on the back. "This isn't Singapore, Mr. Durand.

The car service is owned by smugglers. This car makes a trip up the coast a couple times a week. There'll be some contraband in the panels, but that's the price of pseudonymous travel."

Still eating, he cast an annoyed look at Desai. "Don't even start with me, Rad."

"Custom plant embryos in cryo. Nothing to be overly concerned about."

"I'm trying to avoid the police, not attract them."

"Smugglers make their living with the *cooperation* of the police. This way you're just another mule among many. Your journey will arouse no suspicion."

Durand considered this. "What did you tell your smuggler friends about me?"

"Only that I've a shipment and an associate willing to go along with it. It saves them the trouble of finding a mule. Empty hire cars on long-distance runs are routinely stolen."

Durand tossed the bag in the trash as he finished the roti canai. "Why not a boat across the Gulf of Thailand like all these refugees? A straight shot."

"The Gulf is risky. And I have no contacts with human traffickers."

"Still, the Malaysian peninsula is crawling with climate refugees. The southern provinces of Thailand are under martial law. Muslim separatists. Bombings. There are military checkpoints. It's not exactly a Sunday drive."

"It's not a *war*. It's just a 'zone of heightened security,' is all. Thai soldiers are looking for terrorists, not smugglers. Which is why they accept bribes. You'll be on the back of a military truck all through Southern Thailand."

Durand contemplated this. "How many days?"

"Two. Three at most."

Durand had to admit that it sounded like a reasonable plan. He stood. "What's in the other bag?"

"Oh . . ." Desai opened the bag he held in his hand and produced a theatrical-quality hairpiece with dramatic sideburns. "I thought it best to alter your appearance. I've a friend who works for a low-budget film studio near here."

Durand went to the mirror and tried on the hairpiece. He turned this way and that. He resembled a Eurasian Clint Eastwood. Desai passed him a false mustache and a container of spirit gum.

"Really? A mustache."

"You want to look as different as possible to casual inspection."

Durand used the spirit gum to affix the mustache and then slipped on the mirror glasses Desai had given him the day before. Looking at his reflection, he now resembled a Bollywood action hero. "Won't fool near-infrared facial recognition systems."

"Of which there are few to zero in rural Malaysia."

"Nor is it likely to fool the police."

"Then don't talk to any."

Stepping out into the morning heat, Desai led Durand around the side of the prefab microtel to an alley where a budget autonomous car was parked. The humidity—even this early—was stifling. A fetid stew of odors emanated from nearby overflowing dumpsters. It was gag-inducing. Crowds of Bangladeshi and Burmese immigrants lucky enough to have found illegal employment walked through the alley on their way to work.

Desai extended his hand to bump bitrings with a preteen kid who was sitting on the car—apparently watching it. With that the kid scurried off. "Here we are."

Durand examined a blue grown-shell chitin car wedged in with a row of other poorly parked vehicles—part of the haphazard pattern of life in Johor. The car was a two-seater—a popular low-budget model called a Shrimp (because the body was grown from the same chitinous material as shrimp shells). Painting them wasn't necessary since they were grown with their shells in many colors. Lightweight. Strong. Eventually biodegradable. This one was blue with a mother-of-pearl iridescence and OLED headlamps.

Desai waved a prepaid credit fob to unlock it, and then handed the fob to Durand, who climbed inside. Glancing around, he saw no one taking any notice of them. But then, almost everyone in the city seemed to be from somewhere else.

Desai handed Durand a new phablet device. "Take this—and give me that old one."

Durand hesitated. "Why?"

"Because I've loaded a substantial amount into a digital wallet on this one. You can access the funds here." He pointed. "For god's sake, secure it with a passkey. I've given you far more money than you'll need just in case anything goes wrong. But I expect to be paid back."

Durand handed over the junkie's phablet and took the new one.

"I can also track that device in a pinch if I need to—although I'm going to avoid that if at all possible. I'm not keen on being linked to you."

Durand nodded.

Desai offered his hand. "I wish you luck in returning to your former self, Mr. Durand."

Durand took Desai's hand and shook it. "I appreciate your help, Rad. I really do."

"If you succeed, remember: we could convert this live editing technology into billions of American dollars. The three of us. Literally *billions*, Mr. Durand. Imagine retiring young to your own compound."

Durand stared coldly for a moment—then smiled tightly. "I'll bear that in mind."

Desai shut the door. He saluted, then merged into the foot traffic passing around the Shrimp.

Durand looked at the vehicle number on the front visor and spoke to the car without taking his eyes off Desai. "Comcar 6362, start current journey."

A synthetic voice with a male Indian accent said in English, "*Commencing journey from . . . Johor Bahru to . . . Endau. Estimated travel time, two hours and nineteen minutes, charged to your Sinco card. Please relax and enjoy your journey. You can request to pull over at any time by announcing 'Unscheduled Stop.' Stops will incur extra charges.*"

A digital map appeared on a cheap video sticker screen adhered (slightly crooked) to the car's dashboard. No light field projectors here. The interior was as low-budget as they came.

The car began to roll forward, lightly honking its horn to alert the undocumented workers to make way.

Advertisements started playing on the map screen almost immediately. There was no mute button.

The tiny, bulbous Shrimp car cruised among other autonomous and manually driven cars and trucks on the AH18, headed north and out of the dense urban sprawl of Johor. Morning rush hour was a mix of crowded autonomous buses, a few Shrimp cars like his own, and colorful dump trucks and freight haulers—most still diesel.

The curving windows of the Shrimp didn't give Durand much privacy. He suspected this was by design. Malaysian society was fairly conservative, and providing roving rental rooms for sexual trysts wasn't going to happen. Thus, the budget comcars were wide open to public view. Durand lowered the bush hat over his face as if nodding off, though he couldn't help gazing through his fingers at the world passing by.

A huge building boom in Johor had been sparked by the rocketing fortunes of Singapore across the Strait—doubling Johor's population in the past two decades. What the real estate agents called "Singapore-adjacent."

As Durand gazed through the windshield, the malls, condos, and chain restaurants went on for kilometers—many of them named in English. Though he recognized few of the brands, the signage looked similar to almost everywhere, as did the sleek retail fronts. It occurred to Durand that perhaps this sort of consumer culture was just a natural consequence of modernity—that perhaps it had nothing to do with American culture. Modern civilization created convenience and comfort, and this is what that looked like.

What was once dense, malarial jungle was now condos, malls, office towers, and golf courses. The burgeoning cities of Africa were much the same.

The inevitable poor walked past robotic construction equipment, selling fruit or begging for alms. The modern world no longer needed manual labor—at least not labor anyone was willing to pay for.

Durand wondered where it would all lead. It was the main reason he and Miyuki had striven to get Mia into the best schools. Specialized knowledge, after all, was what had saved him from his fate as the North American middle class shriveled away. Specialized knowledge was the way you became an expat instead of a refugee.

After thirty minutes or so, the Shrimp cleared the outskirts of Johor Bahru. Here, the road narrowed to just two lanes and traffic thinned out considerably. The landscape was relatively flat. Telecommunication towers, the occasional jungle-choked hill, and broad mud-brown rivers separated defunct palm oil plantations with fading signage and tattered fence lines.

The sound of the Adhan—the Muslim call to prayer—could be heard over loudspeakers in the distance. The tiny car rolled through small towns of mildewed buildings with peeling paint. It looked as though there were hard economic times hereabouts.

Rain clouds loomed ahead. Monsoons were unreliable lately, but when they came, they came with a vengeance. Judging by the blackness of the clouds and occasional flashes of lightning ahead, they were going to be torrential today.

The first fat raindrops began to pound down on the bulbous windshield. Disquietingly, the comcar did not have windshield wipers. That would have required another maintenance item—wiper blades—and economy cars didn't bother with such niceties. He was quickly blind to the road ahead.

With one last glance at the blurry, expressionistic view of cascading water, Durand tried to doze off despite an annoying parade of ads on the dashboard screen. He concentrated on the sound of heavy rain—amazed at how exhausted his body still was even after twelve hours' sleep. His traumatic physical transformation had no doubt taken its toll. Perhaps he had not yet fully healed.

Durand awoke some time later to the sound of clicking on his side window. He jerked up to see a mix of Burmese and Bangladeshi men—with their hands cupped, faces pressed against the window glass. They each wore a colorful lungi—a simple kilt-like cloth tied at the waist by a twist knot—and clicked bitrings against the windshield for his attention. Some were shirtless, but others wore T-shirts bearing the logos of sport brands or cartoon characters with Chinese text. The moment they noticed Durand was awake, they started calling out in beseeching voices.

"Forty ringgit, sir!"

"Ringgit to travel, sir!"

Why the car wasn't moving was a mystery. The rain had stopped. It was partly sunny out. He glanced at the clock on the dashboard screen. He was two hours out of Johor, apparently in the countryside on a rural stretch of the AH18 lined with palm oil plantations.

In the middle of the roadway in front of the Shrimp stood half a dozen young men with bare feet and cheap phablets; a couple even had low-end LFP glasses. They blocked the way. The comcar's horn beeped lightly several times but was ignored.

A truck horn howled from behind as it crossed the middle line and passed by Durand's stopped vehicle—causing it to shudder. The refugees ignored the truck—apparently knowing full well that trying to stop a human-driven truck would get them killed.

But they knew algorithms. Algorithms could be counted upon to stop if human beings stood in the middle of the roadway.

"Forty ringgit, sir!" A Bangladeshi man in his early forties sporting a graying beard clicked his bitring against the window.

Durand realized to his dismay that this group wasn't going to move unless he paid them. And looking up ahead at the empty road, he could see dozens more refugee groups moving in the tree line. The smoke of cook fires was visible in the distance as well.

This was going to be a long damn ride.

The refugees clicked their bitrings again on the window.

"Sir. Fifty ringgit, sir! Please, fifty ringgit to travel!"

The price was rising the more he waited. They knew their business.

Durand nodded and held up one hand. He pulled out the phablet Desai had given him and accessed his digital wallet. He wished he had a set of LFP glasses so he could do this in AR, but after clicking clumsily around, he transferred several fifty-ringgit-sized chunks of ChiCoin to one of his bitrings. Each bump should transfer fifty ringgit—with a delay between for safety.

He found a window slot and pulled its handle back to create a small opening—apparently panhandling had been anticipated. Either that or it was meant to pass ID to police.

The fortyish bearded man was the first in line. He was sinewy, with chocolate-brown skin—and what looked to be a nasty machete scar on his forearm. His jet-black hair was streaked with gray. He bumped bitrings with Durand, then checked his phablet device. He nodded and caused the phablet to speak for him in a synthetic English translation: *"Bless you, sir. Long life to you."*

Several more young men pushed in to bump rings with Durand, but after a certain point, the fortyish man pushed them away, shouting. He then motioned with his hand, whistling. He was clearly their leader.

Looking ahead, Durand could see the men on the road had not moved aside.

"Hey! I paid you."

The group leader spoke quickly as young men around him rushed to a ditch by the side of the road.

Durand waved his arms. "Get out of the way. I paid you!" He picked up the phablet and repeated the command, translating it into Bengali. And then into Burmese.

Three or four young men ran up to the Shrimp on all sides.

Suddenly a loud *BANG* startled Durand. It was followed by squeaking. The car rocked, and Durand looked up at the glass ceiling to see two makeshift benches linked with cord straps had been tossed like a saddle over the bulbous car's body.

"You have got to be kidding me . . ." Durand pounded on the side window himself. "Get that off my car!" He was about to unbuckle and go out to muscle them off when he heard a shout.

The sinewy older man leaned up to the window and spoke into his own device. It repeated in English, *"If not us, there will be others."* He gestured down the road.

Durand's gaze followed, and he realized the man was right. Hundreds of migrants lined the road ahead.

Young men started piling onto the bench ledges, clambering onto Durand's car, rocking it severely. One boy wearing a tattered e-sports

T-shirt still stood in front of the comcar to keep it from driving on while the others piled on top.

Durand stared at the kid, who couldn't have been more than twelve. The kid stared back, then smiled. Finally, a shout went up, and the kid moved aside. The comcar began to move, and the boy ran for the outstretched hands of his comrades as they pulled him up and onto the top of the little car.

An alarm went off on the Shrimp, and a synthetic voice warned, *"Car overloaded. Car overloaded."* A pause. *"At the current payload, energy surcharges will apply. Recharge stops being recalculated . . ."*

"Of course . . ." Durand leaned back in his seat as the comcar slowly—and laboriously—accelerated with its new passengers. He had to hand it to the refugees; they were resourceful. Preying on autonomous vehicles like ticks would never have been tolerated in Singapore, but Malaysia had a long coastline, and millions of people were on the move. The law was stretched thin here.

Dirt-covered bare feet now dangled over the windshield. The men and boys outside the car were involved in a raucous discussion in several languages, pointing at distant objects, sharing food. Poring over their phablet devices. They were a networked tribe, and now that they'd scored a ride, they all but ignored Durand.

Well. It was good cover, wasn't it? Durand realized he now looked more like a harried tourist than a wanted cartel leader.

More refugees loomed out of the bush on the road ahead, but as they tried to step into the roadway and cause the car to stop to beg for money, Durand's passengers shouted at them, and the newcomers beat a retreat back into the tree line. The car continued down the highway, still gaining speed.

So his ticks were useful at least. A symbiotic relationship, then. Durand settled in for a long journey.

Chapter 19

After traveling for another half hour, Durand grew concerned about his vehicle. The Shrimp was driving slower and slower with its extra passengers—apparently to conserve charge. They hadn't passed any liquid metal battery stations in a while.

The Shrimp's video screen didn't give him access to a charge indicator, either. The roads in Singapore had chargers built into the surface and the distances were short. But this budget comcar company apparently considered passengers freight, and freight had no need to know the status of its vehicle.

Suddenly two young men on the roof hung down from the benches, waving their feet before the car's bumper.

The lidar sensors triggered, bringing the car to a sudden, lurching halt. The two men leaped off and stood in front of the car as others hurled bundles and packs down to them. The rest of the men jumped down, and they began unharnessing their makeshift benches.

Durand was apparently losing his ticks. He watched with curiosity as they disembarked. Beyond them was actual jungle—not palm oil plantations but wild trees and undergrowth. A glance at the map indicated they had just entered the Gunung Arong national coastal forest. He could see many more cooking fires in the distance.

The forty-something leader of the ticks approached the side window, leaning down. He tapped his fingers to his forehead and bowed greeting—then held up his phablet device. As he spoke, the device translated his words: *"It may not matter to you, but there is a police checkpoint ahead. Not immigration. Serious national police."*

Durand sat up straight and looked ahead. There was a curve in the road not far on. He could see only trees.

The man pointed. *"Three kilometers north. Our people have eyes on the coastal highway."*

This explained why his ticks were bailing on him. Durand decided to pay more attention to the behavior of these refugees. They seemed to have a solid information network. A digital diaspora of mobile intelligence.

The man slapped the side of the Shrimp affectionately, nodded again to Durand. Then he and his people crossed a drainage ditch, heading into the jungle.

As the last refugee moved aside, Durand's car began to move once more.

He spoke immediately: "Unscheduled stop."

The car replied, *"Unscheduled stop requested. Pulling over at the next safe location . . ."*

But the car did not stop—instead it kept moving forward slowly, its lidar scanning the narrow shoulder for someplace to get clear of the traffic lane, its hazard lights blinking.

"Screw it . . ." Durand opened the Shrimp's door. Alarms went off. Durand jumped clear, running to a stop. He then looked back at the group of refugees heading into the jungle.

The forty-something leader of the Bangladeshis noticed Durand and motioned for him to follow.

Durand gazed back at the autonomous Shrimp, which was locked in some sort of ethical dilemma—it had lost its passenger, but without an obstruction in front, its algorithms were escalating the priority to pull clear of traffic lanes . . . which wasn't possible on the narrow road. He left the AI to its shuddering confusion and instead leaped over the dry drainage ditch.

He approached the jungle edge, and the older refugee placed a hand on his chest and spoke into his device. The phablet's dry artificial voice said, "*My name is Mahfuz.*" He gestured to two younger Bangladeshi men in their early twenties standing next to him—one was wiry and in good health, the other smaller with facial scars. "*My nephews, Abul and Azam.*"

Durand nodded to them. He produced his own phablet and fumbled for the translation app. It was already open. He spoke into it: "Call me"—he hesitated—"Jim."

Mahfuz nodded to him, repeating, "Mr. Jim."

"Thank you for the warning. I don't have papers." The computer voice translated. He gazed down the path. "Where does this lead?"

Mahfuz motioned for Durand to follow, and they all moved under the cover of the jungle, following a path worn by many others.

Mahfuz spoke into his device. "*There is a migrant camp. Eight kilometers away. You can obtain food. Medical care. Lots of people from many places there.*"

Durand fell in behind the men.

They walked in stifling heat and humidity. Mahfuz and his nephews insisted on sharing their water bottles with Durand. He became increasingly grateful, especially as the path began to climb a steep jungle hillside—the only hill he'd seen in a while.

Sometime near sunset they reached the crest of a ridge, and there was a break between young dipterocarp trees. Mahfuz waited on the trail for Durand, and then pointed down on the lowland plain and the highway. He offered a Ping-Pong-ball-sized thumbcam to Durand. Durand lifted its viewfinder level with his eye and scrolled the zoom wheel. Molecular lenses with no moving parts were dirt cheap now, available all over. It still amazed him how broadly technology had diffused.

He zoomed in on a police checkpoint several kilometers below. Dozens of vehicles blocked the highway. Military tents stood nearby. Satellite dishes. Generators. The vehicles bore the insignia of the Royal Malaysian Police. Anti-terror units stood by out of sight from the road. It was a major op.

Durand removed his eye from the lens.

Mahfuz studied him closely.

The man knew more about what was really going on in this region than either Durand or Radheya Desai—that much was clear. Durand held up his hands, as if clueless.

Mahfuz collected his thumbcam, and they walked on.

They hiked down into a shallow jungle valley, and Durand saw the dark shadow of the South China Sea over the next rise. Lights of resort islands off the Malaysian coast twinkled as the sun set at their backs. Closer at hand, in the jungle below them, white LED lights glowed beneath the tree canopy.

The voice of a muezzin announced the Maghrib, the evening call to prayer, on a loudspeaker somewhere. Abul and Azam glanced to their uncle. He spoke softly to them, and they continued down the path.

It wasn't until darkness fell that they reached the edge of a large migrant camp. Here, hundreds of refugees were bedding down beneath plastic tarps. As Durand passed through, he saw faces and heard languages from all over the world: Yemenis, Syrians, Afghans, Iraqis, Cambodians, Laotians, Vietnamese, Filipinos, New Guineans. It was an incredibly diverse group. Here was Inspector Marcotte's briefing come to life.

Observing the weary, dejected faces, Durand knew these people had no choice but to take their chances and hope that something broke their way. Perhaps they had family beyond a border somewhere. Someone who could sponsor them. But he suspected that too often even the cousin or uncle in Africa or China couldn't help. There were fewer jobs all over these days, and refugee camps grew on the borders of everywhere.

And yet nearly all of the refugees huddled with their devices in the darkness. Their sole link to scattered families, scouting the world for a place to call home.

As Durand, Mahfuz, and his nephews neared the center of the camp, they saw a Red Crescent flag on the side of a large white kitchen tent. People there queued up for food. A medical clinic stood nearby in a separate tent. Work lights starkly illuminated the area, with swarms of bugs circling beneath.

A multiethnic crowd of migrants stood near the tents debating something—each of them holding up devices to translate a dozen languages as they shouted simultaneously. Pointing and gesturing passionately, while dispassionate robot voices on their handhelds tried to make sense of this modern Tower of Babel.

Mahfuz gestured to the group and spoke to Durand through his own phablet. The device repeated in English, *"There is no path to Johor or Kuala Lumpur. Immigration police. Some will try for Jakarta. But without money, they will not get far."*

Durand spoke into his device. "Where are you and your nephews headed?" A delay as the device translated.

"That is a question we are asking ourselves."

Durand studied the grim, mostly male faces of the migrants. The journey was no doubt unsafe. Robberies and extortion common. He guessed they would send for their families only when they'd secured a place somewhere—anywhere—and set aside enough money to bring family by safer means.

He realized his own personal crisis was just another in an ocean of calamities. Every person here faced a seemingly insurmountable obstacle. And this was just one camp.

The only difference was that he had money. Desai said he'd loaded a ChiCoin account for emergency use. Its transactions were tracked by the People's Bank of China, but that was hardly a problem short-term, and the account holder was presumably fictitious.

Azam motioned for his uncle, brother, and Durand to follow. They joined the chow line. Clearly nothing else was available out here. After a considerable wait, they emerged with cultured plastic bowls of steamed rice, tofu, greens, and bottled water, passed to them by aid workers. The same volunteers were also handing out pocket chemical stoves, rations wrapped in biodegradable plastic—apparently an effort by Malaysian authorities to stave off waves of immigrants burning wood and hunting in the national forest.

After they had eaten, Mahfuz chatted softly with his nephews in Bengali. Durand kept his translator app turned off to allow them privacy. It was clear they were working through some difficulties. The young men sounded despondent. But they were also tired, and soon they rolled on their sides to sleep on the still-moist ground.

Lots of refugees around them were doing the same, whole constellations of device screens winking off. Durand slapped mosquitoes off his neck.

Then he heard Mahfuz speak softly in his direction. The man's device translated into English: *"What are you, Mr. Jim—a smuggler?"*

Durand looked up to see reflected screen light illuminating Mahfuz's eyes in the darkness. Durand spoke into his own device. "Same as you: I need to get somewhere. And I don't have documents."

A murmuring of Bengali followed by, *"You had a private car."*

"It was owned by smugglers. I was just a mule."

"They will be angry with you."

"I don't care. I need to get to Thailand."

"Borders mean little to gangs. And they do not forgive debts."

Durand almost laughed. If the man only knew. He looked more intently at Mahfuz. "Do you have family back home?"

There was a moment of silence.

Then, *"My entire remaining family is there."* Mahfuz looked down at the young men. *"We spent all we had to reach Penang, but I did not want my nephews to get indebted. So we remain."*

"Indebted—to traffickers?"

Mahfuz nodded grimly. *"Abul has an architecture degree. Azam was pursuing a degree in engineering. What does it matter? There is no work outside the cities."*

They sat in silence for a time.

A commotion began in the center of camp. It looked like a convoy of electric all-terrain cycles was moving through. A whining nafiri combined with thumping techno music synchronized to laser lights awoke the camp. Lights flashed through the trees. There was shouting in many languages.

Mahfuz gestured and spoke into his device. *"Traffickers. They come at night—when their boats leave. They will promise work, but only the foolish get in their debt."*

Durand watched the commotion. The laser lights whirled. It certainly drew attention. "I have no intention of getting in their debt." He stood. "Because I have money." Durand opened up his phablet. "Mahfuz, what's a reasonable sum for me to pay traffickers to reach Northern Thailand?"

Mahfuz was taken aback. *"From here?"* He thought for a moment. *"They will probably want at least twenty thousand ringgit, half up front, half on arrival. But you must give them the transfer code for the second half on arrival, or you will never escape. They may cheat you still. And admit to no family—say you are alone in the world—or they may kidnap you for ransom. Keep your bank codes memorized. Write nothing down."*

Durand checked his ChiCoin account. "They bring people by boat?"

"They will bring you out to one of the trawlers supplying the fishing fleets. But do not board a fishing boat—no matter what you do. And do not ever board a container ship—especially those at anchor in international waters. These they call Hulks because they never move."

Durand tapped at his device. "What's on the Hulks?"

"Factories. They seal slaves into the shipping containers. Make them assemble devices like the one in your hand. I'm told it's even cheaper than factory robots. Because they do not feed anyone. No one leaves alive."

Durand stared at Mahfuz in shock. "How could that be happening? What about the coast guard or—"

"In international waters, the disposable are disposed of. No one wishes to know."

Durand shook his head. His own problems seemed so insignificant amid all this. He then looked back down at his phablet. Desai had made a substantial sum available for emergencies. It was time to put it to good use. Durand transferred about ten thousand US dollars' worth onto one of his several bitrings. After receiving a confirmation code, he handed the bitring to Mahfuz.

Mahfuz looked warily at Durand.

"There should be enough on here to get you and your nephews into either Johor or Kuala Lumpur. To buy documentation."

"You would have us be in your debt?"

Durand had forgotten how menacing he could appear. He shook his head. "I am in your debt, Mahfuz. Consider this repayment."

Still wary, Mahfuz took the ring and touched it to his own. He then checked his phablet to confirm the amount it held. After a moment he looked up. He placed his hand to his heart and lowered his device—speaking man-to-man. *"Bhalo thakben,* Mr. Jim. *Jani dekha hobe."*

Deriving the sentiment from the tone and solemnity, Durand nodded. He then turned and walked toward the music and whirling laser lights of the traffickers.

Chapter 20

Durand stood on a stone pier in darkness on the shore of the South China Sea. The coast curled away in both directions to form a sizable cove hemmed in by steep jungle hills, devoid of lights. Wispy casuarina trees sighed from an onshore breeze, their trunks extending into the gentle waves. Semisubmerged huts and abandoned resort cabins stood in the water as well. Parking lot signs stood half submerged.

The water had indeed risen over the decades. Malaysia was relatively lucky. Low-lying, heavily populated countries like Bangladesh were in a much deeper crisis.

The night was moonless, but Durand gazed up at the brilliant field of stars above—the Milky Way at the edge of his vision. Around him the jungle thrummed with insects and whooping night birds. He felt eager to reach his destination. To see this deed done.

Close by, an Indian teenager in stylish clothes sat on an electric all-terrain cycle. He'd used it to bring Durand through jungle trails to this location. But right now, the kid was playing an invisible AR game through his designer LFP glasses—ignoring the breathtakingly beautiful night around them.

Durand heard the crunching of tires over gravel, and soon an electric SUV rolled into view through the trees. It moved like a shadow through a half-submerged parking lot and came to a halt at the end of the stone pier.

Several people got out. They removed luggage from the cargo area.

Before long they approached, and Durand's companion turned off his LFP game, sitting up straight.

The kid's boss had evidently arrived.

Four men joined them. Two dour-looking Malays in wide-collared shirts, shorts, and sandals. The other two, clearly paying passengers—like Durand.

The first was a portly Hoklo man in his sixties wearing a white suit that almost phosphoresced in the starlight. He clutched a Panama hat to his head while his tie flopped around in the breeze. A businessman jumping bail? A dirty politician on the lam? Anybody's guess.

The second passenger was a twenty-something Thai man with spiked hair, wireless piercings, designer LFPs, and trendy clothing. A long-tailed macaque crawled around his shoulders, chattering. The man clutched a refrigerated metal case in one hand.

Durand knew a case like that could hold a thousand microscopic samples of proprietary synbio lifted from firms in Singapore, Johor, or Kuala Lumpur.

And this one probably did.

Lights flashed in the forest. And soon the low silhouette of an electric cigarette boat glided silently across the cove like an eel. A crew of two stood in the black boat, and they brought the vessel alongside the pier with practiced ease—not even bothering to tie it off.

The traffickers on the pier slid a small ramp out onto it. They then motioned for Durand and the others to board.

As he descended, Durand felt something sharp scratch across his forearm. He looked down and could see a shallow scratch on his skin, visible even by starlight.

"What the hell was that?"

One of the Malays was busy inserting something into a small device. "DNA sample. Get ass on board."

The other trafficker scraped a skin sample from the next passenger.

Durand looked back down at his arm.

"Hey! Shit for brains . . ." It was an Australian accent. The pilot of the boat was a young Aussie in cargo shorts and LFPs sporting a night-vision nodule.

Standing next to him was a wiry Filipino man—an old Skorpion machine pistol hung on a strap at his chest and a metal-detecting wand in his hand. He spoke Aussie lingo with a Filipino accent: "Oi! Hold out your arms for scan."

With no room to argue, Durand stepped aboard. He held out his arms as the metal detection wand was waved over him.

"He's clean." The Filipino pushed him toward an open seat. "Sit down."

Durand sat. His grown knife had indeed passed through. No wonder they were illegal. He sat pondering the significance of the DNA sample that had just been taken from him.

The seats were surprisingly comfortable—plush white faux-leather upholstery. He guessed the boat was a stolen pleasure yacht. Perfect for smugglers. Low radar signature. Quiet. No doubt fast.

The second mate scanned the other two passengers with the detection wand as well, while the traffickers stowed the businessman's luggage on deck. The Thai man held his metal case close. The monkey crawled over him, though now it was clear it was on a leash.

"If that monkey bites me, mate, I'm going to serve you monkey tartare on a fucking cracka. You hear me?"

The Thai man spoke in heavily accented English. "Monkey does not bite."

The detector wand warbled on the businessman's coat, and the second mate pulled a .357 snub-nosed revolver from the man's belt. "Fuck's this?"

"Protection."

He shouted in the man's face: "You don't need potection. We yo potection." He shoved the man forward, passing the revolver to the Aussie pilot, who placed it on the dash.

The men on the pier pulled the ramp up. Without a word, the pilot brought the boat about. A whoosh of water jets, and the boat accelerated. An ocean breeze rolled over them, and they headed out into the South China Sea.

Looking back, Durand watched the dark line of jungle recede. The smell of rotting vegetation faded with it.

The wind picked up. Soon they were doing at least thirty-five knots. The pilot fastened a safety harness as the boat continued to pick up speed. Durand searched for his own seat belt and fastened himself in. No one else appeared concerned.

The silhouettes of mountainous islands rose a few kilometers ahead. The biggest of these, Durand knew from examining his phablet map, was Tioman—with a pair of rocky peaks, about fifty kilometers out. It was visible only as a dark smudge on the horizon against a field of stars.

Once they were clear of the cove and in open water, the powerful cigarette boat picked up even more speed—its electric water jets moving them at sixty knots or more. The boat had no dashboard lights or gauges. Durand guessed those were all beamed into the pilot's LFP glasses as virtual displays—though the boat did have a physical throttle and wheel. It skimmed across the surface of a calm sea, the wind whipping over them.

The businessman's hat finally broke free of his grip and disappeared over the stern into darkness. The Filipino second mate laughed as the elderly man cursed under his breath.

Durand leaned down to activate his phablet map. At their current heading, they appeared to be aiming for Tioman. And at this speed they'd reach it in just a half hour or so—and then it was out into the open sea, and the supply trawler already moving north, toward Thailand.

Durand's mind wandered as the whine of the electric motors sent up a geyser behind them. He fixated on the phosphorescing water. Before he knew it, the rocky peaks of Tioman loomed in front of him, black silhouettes. The earthy scent of jungle reached them. He could see the lights of resorts stretching along its coastline. No doubt refugees were quickly whisked away from here.

In ten minutes Tioman fell behind, and they headed out into the open water of the South China Sea.

Durand started from a light snooze as the young Thai smuggler shouted against the wind. "There! Hulks!"

Durand sat up and saw what appeared to be a glittering city ahead. There were hundreds of bright lights reflected on the water. After a few moments he realized it was a flotilla of huge container ships, moored in place. Smaller boats moved about between them. They were probably a kilometer or more away.

The Thai man's monkey hunkered down at his feet, sheltering from the howling wind. But the young man pointed again and shouted to Durand. "Slave city!"

Durand watched with disbelieving eyes as they passed the collection of rusting retired vessels. The ships were massive. And there must have been forty or fifty of them, each a thousand feet or more long, stretching to the horizon. The most distant ones were illuminated by flashes of far-off lightning. These also revealed dark, towering clouds.

But the looming weather could wait. Durand instead focused on the Hulks. Decommissioned after the collapse of global shipping, no doubt. When he was a child, they'd transported the products of distant factories. Now they *were* the factories.

Even over the roar of the speedboat, he could hear voices on loud-speakers from the Hulks. Talking in a foreign language. Heavy machinery pounded rhythmically. Human forms moved along the railings. Men with guns. Cranes lowered containers onto ships, while others lifted containers from ships.

How many flotillas like this were in the oceans? How many refugees were disappearing in transit, never to be heard from again? Durand checked his device and noticed there was no signal. Or perhaps they had jammers? This place was beyond calls for help.

His own boat powered on, heading farther out to sea.

After five minutes or so, Durand heard the water jets rev down, and the cigarette boat's speed reduced by half. And then half again.

Durand turned to see the pilot studying something unseen in his own LFP glasses. Apparently the man had a satellite uplink. He had that blank virtual-presence stare. A moment later he looked up and focused on Durand.

The pilot reduced the boat's speed again and motioned for the second mate to come close.

Durand felt a surge of adrenaline.

The two men conferred, and at one point the Filipino glanced furtively over at Durand, too.

The Hoklo businessman shouted from a forward seat, "Why we stop? Let's get moving!"

The pilot was reading something in his LFP glasses again. "You're confused, mate. I'm in charge here . . ."

The boat began to turn, looping around to head back toward the Hulks, still glowing a couple kilometers behind them. Durand spotted lights moving out from the Hulks to meet them.

Boats.

The Hoklo man shouted again, "Why are we turning around? The trawler is north! My associate is on board."

The second mate now brandished the Skorpion, aiming it. "Shut up!"

The man blanched.

The young Thai pulled his macaque up onto his shoulder. "You know who I'm with?"

"I said shut up, asshole!"

Durand felt a renewed rush of adrenaline. He unclipped his seat belt and stood, gazing out toward the lights of distant boats coming to meet them. They were still at least a klick away.

The Filipino unsteadily aimed the Skorpion at him as the boat rolled through the waves.

"Big fish, eh? They want for you. They pay big."

Durand felt an eerie calm as the adrenaline bathed him with clarity. He knew without having to see. He could feel them on his skin. His marks revealing themselves.

The second mate lowered the gun slightly as a look of shock came across his face. "Holy shit. You seeing this, Mackie?"

The pilot stared in shock at Durand.

The boat pitched sideways as it hit another wave, and in that moment Durand launched himself at the pilot. He brought his hand up with the grown knife already in his grip. The pilot, still strapped into his seat, came up with the businessman's .357 revolver. Durand caught the man's wrist and buried the knife under his armpit.

There was a loud CRACK from the pistol. Durand glanced back to see the Hoklo businessman roll sideways on a seat, choking as blood spread on his shirtfront.

The macaque screeched, and the Thai man dove for the deck, covering his head.

Durand turned toward the second mate—who struggled to maintain his footing as he brought the Skorpion to bear. The boat rolled through another wave.

Durand grabbed a metal rail and jammed the throttle forward.

Everyone else slid sternward; the businessman's choking body slid across the desk and slammed into the second mate, followed by the Thai smuggler. Only the monkey held on, climbing into a storage cabinet.

Durand rolled the wheel, turning the cigarette boat in an arc away from the approaching searchlights and the Hulks in the distance—on a heading back north.

The boat now roared ruthlessly over waves, thumping over the ridge of each and making it difficult to stand.

Durand saw his own reflection in the windshield as a searchlight passed over the boat. Tattoos covered Durand's neck and chest now. They were as dark as he'd ever seen them. He felt as fierce as he looked. The dead Aussie pilot was still strapped into his harness, and Durand drew the grown knife from the sucking wound in the man's chest. Durand then moved sternward using handholds, toward the pile of men struggling to their feet.

The Thai kid clambered away from the Filipino second mate—who himself was trying to get out from under the portly businessman. Blood stained the white upholstery and decking.

The second mate crawled free of the dead businessman just as Durand reached him—and they all lost contact with the deck as the boat impacted another wave.

They landed on the deck hard, and both Durand's knife and the

Skorpion fell away. The macaque screeched somewhere. Durand grabbed the second mate's arm.

But the Filipino drew a knife from his own belt and tried to stab Durand in the chest. Durand's new reflexes surprised him—his hand shot out and twisted the mate's wrist. The knife clattered to the deck. Durand head-butted him. They both rolled kicking and punching each other, tumbling over the businessman's body.

Multiple searchlights were on them now. Loudspeaker voices shouted angrily in a foreign language.

Durand screamed as he pulled the second mate's head back from behind. He spotted the grown knife rolling past on the deck. He grabbed it—plunging the razor-sharp claw into the second mate's shoulder blade.

The second mate screamed, "I fucking kill you! I kill you!"

Durand repeatedly plunged the knife into the man's back, feeling the air leaving his punctured lungs. But he kept stabbing. He lost track of how many times.

Durand felt the strength in this new body. Blood ran down his own nose, and he shoved the body of the second mate onto the deck—then buried the knife in the back of the man's skull.

Durand stared at the dead eyes of the Hoklo businessman, who lay unblinking on the carbyne decking, blood washing from side to side over him as the waves rocked the boat.

The Thai smuggler screamed from somewhere as an ungodly bright searchlight played over the boat from one of the huge container ships. The air was white glare all around them.

The cigarette boat roared onward, thundering through waves. A dead man at the helm.

Tracer rounds snapped past.

Durand pulled the grown knife out of the Filipino's skull and retracted its keratin blade, stowing it as he grabbed a handrail. He pulled himself toward the pilot seat, holding on as the deck leaped and rolled. The dead pilot's body shuddered with the impact of each wave, the man's arms and head flopping forward. Durand reached up and unclipped the pilot's harness. He shoved the pilot's body onto the deck, climbing up in his place.

The blinding light did not waver. Tracers whined over the top of the windshield.

Without turret-mounted stabilizers, though, the men firing weapons aboard the boats pursuing him were bound to be wildly inaccurate. Still, if they fired enough bullets, they might get a hit.

Durand strapped himself into the seat, cinching the harness tight. He then turned the wheel slightly one way, and then the other.

They were almost instantly out of the monster spotlight.

He had no gauges, maps, or sensors to work with, but the lights of the Hulks behind him were to the south. That meant he knew the direction north. He adjusted his heading.

Durand screamed in defiance as the searchlights illuminated a series of larger waves looming ahead. The boat caught air and pounded into the water with punishing intensity. He glanced back over his shoulder to see that the boats giving pursuit were not gaining on him. In fact, they were already falling behind.

The troughs of the waves were getting deeper, and being low-slung, the cigarette boat occasionally dipped below visibility—the searchlights passing over him. No doubt he had a tricky radar signature, too.

But Durand didn't let up. He kept the throttle maxed out. He had no idea how much battery power he had left, but he wasn't going to fail by not pushing with all this machine could do. He needed to get over the horizon before dawn.

To the east lightning flashed, revealing towering thunderheads again. The wind had been coming from the east, and Durand knew if he could just keep heading north, his pursuers would have to factor in oncoming weather. The typhoons and storms of the South China Sea were getting more powerful every year. Right now that might benefit him.

Durand looked forward again just in time to see the boat launch off a wave and over a deep trough.

The sharp carbyne prow of the cigarette boat pierced the next wave at fifty or sixty knots—submerging the boat completely for a moment before it burst out the far side of the wave. A scouring deluge swept through the passenger compartment and nearly sucked Durand out of his harness. Only the transparent aluminum windshield and carbyne hull kept the boat intact. And though he'd momentarily lost half his speed, the motors jetted him forward again, causing the hundreds of gallons of water in the passenger compartment to pour over the stern in a sucking tide.

Looking back behind him, Durand could see that the bodies and blood were all gone. The luggage was gone, too. Glancing all around the boat, he didn't see the Thai smuggler or his monkey, either. Everyone was *gone*.

The pursuing boats seemed to have disappeared as well.

Durand reduced throttle by 15 percent, and then tried to get his adrenaline under control. With the reduced speed he would be able to go farther.

Good.

Durand focused on the waves ahead, illuminated by occasional flashes of lightning from the east. He tried to forget the young smuggler he'd just swept into the sea. Or the men he'd just killed.

As he gripped the wheel, he noticed the tattoos on his wet arms fading.

Chapter 21

Radheya Desai hummed along to the soaring chorus of Johann Sebastian Bach's Cantata BWV 19. The music resounded through the racks of healthy plants stretching away in both directions. Of course, Desai could have listened on headphones, but then the plants wouldn't have been able to enjoy it with him. He was convinced that beauty nourished them just as it nourished him.

While it was true that the cantata was a choral presentation of strife from the Christian Book of Revelation—"*And war was begun in heaven, with Michael and his angels fighting the dragon, casting out the old serpent, the Devil*"—none of that came across in the joyous music, whose vibrations he believed to be highly beneficial.

Besides, plants didn't understand German, and fortunately neither did his Muslim relatives.

Desai moved slowly along an aisle of aquaponic greenery bathed in indigo light, studying magnified leaves and stalks through his LFP glasses. Each aisle stood twenty racks high on either side. There were a hundred aisles like this on every floor, each a hundred meters long, and eighty floors in total. And that was just one tower. There were five others just like this one.

But this floor was his to manage as he pleased. His research racks.

Desai raised his arms, conducting an imaginary chorus as the voices rose in crescendo. This music was such an inspiration to him.

And as long as Desai delivered for his employers, he was free to make his own hours and his own work. Solitude—something that wasn't cheap in Singapore.

Of course, this entire place glowed with purple light. Love of natural sunlight was, he knew, an evolved trait of humanity. But he'd grown to love this perpetual, otherworldly twilight as well. Plants flourished in it.

Desai read augmented-reality labels that floated in an invisible, private layer in his LFP glasses. The labels identified the plants in front of him: "gRIA396," "Pu19L," "R193m"—a nomenclature denoting traits he was modifying. It was his own private language. No one but he needed to understand it. This was his job security.

Job security.

He chuckled to himself. That was something he might not need for much longer. He might soon be able to build his own farming towers.

This in vivo editing technology could revolutionize everything. And he would be among the first to have it—if Frey came through. Durand might even get back to himself. In which case, Desai would have done a good deed. Doing well while doing good. What was wrong with that?

And Frey was reasonably trustworthy. Reasonably.

A nagging doubt clouded Desai's sunny dream. Frey had *better* be trustworthy . . .

Desai paused. No. This was a joyous night. He had a lot to be hopeful for these days.

Moving down the row, he was suddenly surprised to see—of all things—a gorgeous flowering plant in the aquaponic rack. It stood out like an angel against the greens and browns of his other agricultural varieties.

"Hello, my lovely . . ."

He moved down to it. It was exceptional—morphologically a cross between a rose and a white lily. But more intricate. Its petals were iridescent.

It was breathtakingly gorgeous. What on earth was it doing in his research racks? Desai read the AR label floating over it, but frowned as he saw "Ub082A"—Araucarian, which this clearly was not. Clerical error? Did he accidentally cross the genomic sequence of a coniferous tree with something in the *Lilium* genus? If so, the result was a happy accident.

Perhaps this was his year after all. First encountering in vivo genetic editing, and now stumbling into one of the most beautiful flower designs he'd ever seen.

He reached out to touch its fragrant petals—and felt a sting in the tip of his finger.

"Ah!" He drew his finger back and saw blood oozing. He laughed and sucked it for a moment, and then more carefully examined the flower's stem to see unusually vicious-looking black thorns concealed beneath the petals.

Okay, that's a trait that can be removed.

A sudden feeling of dread stole over Desai—as though he could sense a dark presence.

A man's voice behind him said, "Beautiful."

Desai spun around to see a man standing a couple meters behind him—blocking the aisle and the way back to the lab.

The man wore a tailored black pin-striped suit and a blue pastel tie with a precise double-Windsor knot. The stranger looked to be ethnically Slavic-Mongolian or perhaps Inuit, with a broad face yet fair skin. His black hair was slicked back. He stared at Desai with the unliving eyes of a doll.

The chorus of the cantata swelled again.

Then the man's hands rolled in time with the music, and he closed his dead eyes in contentment. "What is this called?"

Fear radiated through Desai. He made a single hand gesture that ended the beautiful music. In the sudden silence Desai's heart pounded in his chest.

The man's doll's eyes opened again—his contented expression gone.

Desai struggled to speak. "Who are you?"

The man reached toward him.

Desai sucked in a breath.

But instead of touching Desai, the man reached for the beautiful flower, brushing its petals. "The thorns are deadly." He spoke English with an undefined accent.

The man then plucked the flower and brought it to his nose. "But the pollen is far worse. The merest touch brings death."

Desai gasped.

The man held the flower against the light. "Designed specifically to appeal to the visual cortex of the human brain. Leveraging highly evolved traits of *Homo sapiens* to make it irresistible."

Desai tried to speak but could not. Something about the man before him was *wrong*. An affront to Nature.

The man reached into his jacket to produce a book-sized device. He placed it on the nearest shelf, pressed down, and it unfolded into a pylon shape. White light glowed from within as it booted up.

Desai managed to croak out, "What do you want?"

"You may find this interesting . . ."

Suddenly, a kneeling, pleading Spanish man materialized at Desai's feet—as lifelike and real as if the man were actually present. But Desai knew it was only a light field beamed into his retinas.

The apparition pleaded silently to someone offscreen. There was no sound. Only real-as-life imagery. Blood dripped down the man's forehead in rivulets. From his teeth and nose. From his eyes. He wept and screamed as blisters formed on his skin.

"The apaxi synbiotoxin breaks down cell walls. Attacks capillaries. And—most important of all—it binds to nerve endings, dissolving them like acid."

The virtual kneeling man began to shriek in silence—going insane with agony. He thrashed around uncontrollably. Pulling clumps of hair from his scalp. Pleading for mercy as he sweated blood.

Desai felt sweat dripping down his own face. He touched his cheek—and his fingertips came back stained red.

Fear enveloped him. He looked into the dissolving eyes of the silent, shrieking man. He, too, understood.

"Please . . ."

"There is an antidote."

Desai looked up, clasping his hands—and, yes, fell to his knees. "Please! Please! I beg you!"

The man folded up the glim, and the dying Spaniard winked out of existence. The man slipped the glim calmly back into his jacket pocket.

"The antidote, please!" Desai felt blood begin to run from his nose. A burning sensation began in his right arm. He looked up into the stranger's dead eyes. He was looking at the face of death. He realized that now.

"You brought him to Johor."

"Please, the antidote! I will tell you everything, but please . . ." Burning tingled in his fingertips. "Please!"

"I have video of you together there."

"Please!"

"Where is he?" The man studied Desai's increasing terror. "Where is Durand?"

It felt as though Desai's fingertips were starting to go through a meat grinder. He shrieked. Blood oozed from under his fingernails.

The man placed the flower under Desai's nose—somehow unaffected by it himself.

Desai wept in terror and pain. "Please! I beg you!"

"Where is Durand?"

"Malaysia! Federal Route Three! Headed to Thailand!"

"Where in Thailand?"

"Please!" Desai's sinuses began to burn. "It's spreading! Help me, please!"

The man tossed the flower aside and grabbed Desai's jaw. "Focus! Where is Durand? Details."

Desai tried to ignore the expanding agony. Tried to unsee the crimson color spreading beneath his skin. "Over the border. From Kelantan all the way to Pattaya City by truck."

"Pattaya City."

"Thailand!"

"What's in Pattaya City?"

Desai wept. And then he realized his tears were blood. His terror increased by an order of magnitude.

"What's in Pattaya City?"

"Dr. Bryan Frey! The man we met in Johor!"

"What about him?"

"He's going to bring Durand to meet the Luk Krung—a genediting ring." His eyes clouded with blood. "Please! The antidote! I will help you find them!"

"What does Durand want from the Luk Krung?"

"He wants them to change him back! To change him back into himself!" Desai's spine began to burn like a tree in a wildfire. "Please! OH GOD! PLEASE! The antidote!"

The man seemed unmoved. "Is that all you can tell me?"

"That's all I know! PLEASE!"

The man gazed at the racks of plants all around them. "What an abomination life is to me."

"PLEASE!"

He looked down on Desai. "I cannot wait until you are all extinct. You've poisoned this world. But your poisons mean nothing to me."

The man turned to leave, headed toward the freight elevators.

"WAIT!" Desai tried to crawl after him, blubbering. He pulled himself along by the plant racks, knocking plants onto the floor and breaking fragile aquaponic lines. As the fire spread within him, he lost control of his muscles. Blood now oozed out from between his pores—every drop of it feeling like acid.

"PLEASE! PLEASE KILL ME! MERCY!"

It felt as though fire ants were trying to eat their way out of him now. He began to shriek.

"KILL ME! PLEASE!"

The shrieks followed Otto toward the elevator bank. Singapore was normally a difficult place for him to conduct interrogations—too many witnesses. But this place had the virtue of solitude. And yet it was also infested with old life. He was eager to be clear of it.

Otto summoned the elevator.

An incoming encrypted call popped up on his display. As he stepped into the elevator, Otto tapped his LFP glasses to answer. The shrieks receded as the elevator descended. He turned to face a comforting view of the city—the built environment.

He spoke into the hiss of encryption. "Yes?"

Wyckes's voice came to him. *"Durand's DNA just appeared in the trafficking network. I need you to head to the eastern Malaysian coast."*

Otto remained silent.

"They tried to bring him to a factory ship, but he escaped. He seems to have killed some traffickers and stolen their boat."

Otto stared out at the city lights. "As you, he's full of surprises."

"I'm creating another twin, but it will be weeks. This fool has put my name all over the news. The police pressure is increasing on us everywhere. We need to put an end to this manhunt for Wyckes. I need his body."

"I understand."

"Bad weather is moving into the southern Gulf—the gangs there can't send up drone flights. But we must find him."

"We don't have to find him if we know exactly where he's headed."

There was a brief pause. *"Where?"*

"To the Luk Krung."

Only static came over the line. Followed by a rasping laugh. *"What would I do without you, Otto?"*

Chapter 22

Inspector **Aiyana Marcotte** had always been curious about the interior of these urban farming towers. They were appearing in more cities around the world, and had an appealing, earthy look.

However, it turned out they had no earthy aroma because they didn't use soil. Her corporate minder told her that the plants here were nourished by a special aquaponic solution that conveyed food directly to the plant roots in the most efficient way possible. Soil was unnecessary.

The result looked like a cross between a designer LFP store and a plant nursery.

As she emerged from the freight elevator, Marcotte saw Singapore police everywhere. Sergeant Michael Yi Ji-chang stood waiting for her in the bare concrete elevator lobby. Brilliant light flared as 3D scans were being taken of the murder scene behind him.

Yi nodded to her. "Synbiotoxin. Nasty one. Probably an apaxi derivative. Definitely Huli jing."

Marcotte nodded to an SPF detective she knew. The man didn't immediately move to throw her and Yi out, so she proceeded as if he'd given her the okay to stay.

Marcotte stopped at the end of aisle number seventy-four and looked down its length to see a body midway. Bloody handprints smeared the racks—with indigo backlighting making it all the more macabre. Around the body, the blood had channeled into drains in the floor.

The victim had clearly struggled for quite some time. He was surrounded by broken glass and torn irrigation lines.

Yi spoke. "Radheya Desai. Black market geneticist." He peered over her shoulder. "Security video's been erased. Two technicians and a security guard dead as well—though with fast-acting nerve toxin."

"Why are we here, Sergeant?"

"Desai was my informant. Mine and Ken's. SPF called me as soon as they found him."

"How long were you running him?"

"Couple of years. Not exactly a gangster. A low-level plant editor for Pinjab."

"So what is it you wanted to show me?"

Yi proceeded to move his hands around—clearly manipulating virtual objects in his LFP glasses. "Look at this layer . . ."

Marcotte received the layer invite, and she accepted. Suddenly a virtual 2D surveillance image appeared in front of her. It showed a narrow, cluttered city street bustling with scooters and pedestrians. A glowing neon sign for a bar named Twisted flickered.

"When I found out Desai was dead, I decided to go back and take a look at where he'd been the last few days."

"What did you find?"

"Turns out Desai took a trip across the border to Johor Bahru just yesterday. Not completely out of the ordinary, but take a look at this street camera video I got from the RMP . . ."

Marcotte watched the virtual image as a utility van pulled up to the mouth of an alley. In a moment the sliding door opened and Desai exited, wearing a fedora and carrying a cane.

A man in a bush hat and shorts followed, and as he looked up, Yi froze the image.

Marcus Wyckes.

"*Dae bak.*"

"*Dae bak*, indeed."

"They don't use much facial recognition over in Johor, so I ran the imagery . . ." The image showed facial pattern recognition markers highlighting the eyes and cheekbones, then a positive identification on Marcus Wyckes.

"So Wyckes leaned on Desai to get him across the border. Any idea how?"

"Not yet. But there's more." He pointed at the bar's neon sign in the image. "This place. I talked to friends in the RMP. It's a biohacker bar. No interior video available, and I've been told not to go there asking for it, either."

"Gang-owned."

Yi nodded. "But from the time code and location on this street video, I was able to have the RMP pull the International Mobile Equipment Identity of Desai's and Wyckes's devices. With that I was able to geolocate their movements from this point."

Yi brought up a 2D map of the building roof as seen from the air. Two highlighted dots moved into the building through a sea of other dots—all unique IMEI numbers. But then the highlighted dots moved toward the back of the building. Here Desai and Wyckes apparently met with a lone third IMEI number.

"Who's that belong to?"

Yi made several gestures and a 3D booking scan of Bryan Frey appeared, rotating in space before them. "Dr. Bryan Frey—unlicensed genetic engineer and minor lowlife. Designs plants, vanity pets, shit like that. Seems to be a talented fuckup. Lost his license. Wanted on low-level warrants here in Singapore, Vietnam, Laos, Indonesia, Australia, the US, and Germany."

"He gets around."

"He needs to. He's got angry clients all over."

"So why was Wyckes meeting with him?"

"I don't know." Yi pointed as the dots separated again. "But the meeting lasted about a half hour, and immediately afterward Frey booked a flight to Pattaya City, Thailand."

"How often does he travel there?"

"Hasn't been there since 2038."

Marcotte turned back to reality and Desai's dead body halfway down the aisle. "So why'd the Huli jing clip Desai?"

"Tying up loose ends, I expect. They'll probably do the same to Frey sooner or later."

Marcotte was unconvinced. "They were doing more than getting rid of a witness here. Apaxi variants are interrogation poisons. The technicians and security guard downstairs were killed quickly—but Desai slowly."

Yi pondered this. "Punishment?"

"For what? It looks like Desai helped Wyckes get across the border. You'd think that would earn him a painless death at worst. No, I think they were questioning him."

Yi frowned harder the more he thought about it. "What would Desai know that the Huli jing didn't? I mean, Desai is a minor leaguer at best."

She turned back to Yi and his dot map, which had frozen. "Where'd Wyckes go after the meeting?"

"Holed up in a microtel." He shifted the map across town. "His device goes dark there the next morning." He raised a finger. "But wait. A hire comcar departs from there at around the same time, carrying a device with this new IMEI. See?"

She followed it as it moved north, away from Johor Bahru and up the Malaysian eastern coast.

Marcotte paced as she pondered this. "So Wyckes was headed north, too."

"Yeah. Except Frey went business class. Wyckes's new device seems to have hopped a trafficker's boat across the Gulf. His device last pinged a tower on Tioman. Then disappeared for good."

She gazed at the map. "They're *both* heading to Thailand."

"That would be my guess."

Marcotte turned to Yi. "Excellent work, Sergeant. Reach out to the NCB in Bangkok. Tell them we need Frey followed. I want to know where he goes and who he meets with. You and I need to hop a plane there tonight. I have a feeling Frey's arranging something for Wyckes."

"You think Wyckes is going to meet Frey there?"

"Yes, I do. And if Wyckes shows his face, we need to convince the Thais to grab him."

Chapter 23

The sun was brutally hot, and the humidity made it worse. The cigarette boat drifted somewhere in the South China Sea, its liquid metal batteries exhausted. Kenneth Durand's best guess was that the Hulks were eighty kilometers to the south. A line of rumbling thunderstorms glowered on the horizon there. Hopefully that would hinder launching drone flights. Searching for him by boat would be much harder.

To the north Durand saw sun and clearer skies. No land in sight—though he had a rough idea where he was: still six or seven hundred kilometers south of Thailand. He didn't have a data link to the boat, and so couldn't access its mapping systems or its no doubt elaborate virtual console. The vessel was devoid of physical screens and gauges. But he had found a thirty-year-old GPS unit that morning in the boat's cabin along with a reverse osmosis water maker, and canned food, liquor, beer, and bags of chips.

He starting charging the GPS on the cabin battery, and though the internal battery didn't charge, the GPS still worked. Better yet, it was so old he suspected it wasn't going to be trackable, unlike the GPS in his phablet (which had gone overboard the night before along with his hairpiece, mustache, bush hat, and a lot else).

The GPS showed that Durand had dead reckoned his position fairly well. He was about a hundred and fifty kilometers off the coast of Kuantan, Malaysia. Well out to sea.

He felt a pang of guilt about the Thai smuggler who'd been washed overboard. And about the dead businessman. To his surprise, the long-tailed macaque had emerged at dawn from an open storage locker, chattering and poking around for food. How the animal had held on during the boat's scouring submersion was beyond him.

He fed it canned pineapple chunks, and it followed him around just out of arm's reach the entire morning, watching his every move.

"Sorry about your friend, monkey. Maybe he got picked up."

The macaque chattered in response.

Durand wasn't sure getting rescued by the slavers was a better fate. Still, he was glad the dead bodies and the blood had all been washed away. It made last night's events seem like only a nightmare, and he preferred to pretend it had been just that. Only the monkey remained as evidence that anyone else had been here.

But then he stumbled over the Skorpion machine pistol lying on the deck against the stern gunwale. That hadn't gotten washed overboard.

He decided he didn't have the luxury of sitting around. He searched every locker, cabinet, and storage well in the boat, including down in the small, unkempt cabin. He came up with blankets, a flare gun, a blister pak of military-grade amphetamines, clothing, water skis and ropes, and a high-end nitrox rebreather pack along with wet suit, fins, and a Hawaiian sling for spear fishing. He checked the rebreather tanks and saw they were half charged.

Why did the traffickers have diving gear? Did they cache supplies or bitrings on shallow coastlines? It occurred to Durand that it might be useful, and he decided to take time cleaning it up and making certain the rebreather functioned. In any event, it would give him something to do while the boat's batteries recharged.

Like any electric car, the boat could be quickly recharged by exchanging spent battery liquid at a service station. But if time wasn't a factor or there weren't battery stations available (or cost was an issue), the boat came with floating, inflatable solar cells for recharging the batteries at sea. Durand had set the solar array out and watched it automatically inflate. He should have a full charge by late afternoon.

That is, if slavers or pirates didn't find him first.

Throughout the day he spotted distant trawlers heading out to sea. None got within a few kilometers of him. Neither did he see any drones or other aircraft.

Exhausted but thinking sleep inadvisable, Durand took one of the amphetamines. He'd used them before on critical navy ops, where sleep also wasn't an option. He resolved to toss the drugs overboard at the first opportunity, but he might need to run for the next couple days without rest before then.

With new energy, Durand sat on one of the upholstered seats and started cleaning the rebreather equipment while the monkey watched his every move.

"Do me a favor and screech if someone gets near. Okay?"

The macaque chattered back as always.

Durand suddenly noticed dried blood under his fingernails.

He remembered all over again that he had killed people the night before. He'd actually *killed* people. The surreality of his situation made him momentarily unsteady.

They were cruel men, yes. But he'd murdered them violently. He wondered if he'd ever be able to lay his head down at night without thinking of this.

The monkey chattered at him again, bringing him back to the present.

Thunder rumbled in the south. Flashes of lightning. More thunder.

A quick check on the angle of the sun. It was nearing 1600 hours. Durand moved to check the LED meter in the battery well and saw he was at 87 percent charge.

Better to get farther away sooner than wait for a full charge.

Durand deflated the solar array and laboriously refolded it into the battery well. He could probably run a couple hundred kilometers in the night. But that still left seven or eight hundred kilometers to go—a few days' travel at least.

And that was if he didn't encounter anyone.

Durand traveled through the gloaming. A brilliant red sunset with towering clouds rose on his left. The monkey joined him on the dashboard just ahead of the wheel. They cruised on into the night at roughly thirty knots. He avoided the lights of distant ships and smaller boats and ran with no lights himself.

By dawn the GPS showed that Durand had reached the mouth of the Gulf of Thailand, where it narrowed to four hundred kilometers.

No doubt there was coastal radar and military drones patrolling here, but he had to hope this tiny boat wasn't worth investigating. That there were bigger fish in this sea.

Certainly there were other refugee boats motoring past in the distance, packed with people. He could hear their older diesel engines from a kilometer away. When one wooden-hull fishing boat moved closer, Durand stood with the Skorpion across his chest, and they veered away—heading off to the south. His own sleek boat certainly gave the appearance of a cartel smuggler.

The map showed the water was less than sixty meters deep, so after the batteries died in the predawn, Durand dropped anchor. He unfurled the solar array and kept an eye on the horizon and the sky.

By late afternoon he was off again, the macaque assuming a place near the helm. Before sunset, Durand smelled a rancid stench that he hoped was a floating whale carcass. But soon enough he saw bloated human bodies in the water. The macaque fled down into the cabin at the scent.

Durand slowed and used the fading sunlight to navigate around the corpses—several dozen of which floated on the current, clothed in bright colors. Scattered over hundreds of meters.

Men, women, and children. Impossible to tell their nationality.

People fleeing despair in an unseaworthy ship, no doubt. Had it sunk beneath them—or been sunk by someone else? Perhaps no one would ever know. Debris floated among them, but there were no survivors clinging to barrels or life jackets.

Durand wondered why none of them had been devoured by sharks or other fish. But then he recalled that fish populations here had crashed—predators more than all others. Sharks were almost unseen now. Instead, these bodies rotted in the empty water amid glittering flecks of plastic and constellations of small jellyfish.

He motored on.

• • •

By the time the rain came, Durand had been up for three days straight. He felt as if he was losing his mind. Hallucinating. Seeing faces in the darkness. But that was normal on so little sleep. He kept telling himself not to take seriously anything he saw that didn't make sense. But very little did make sense—even in reality.

The chattering macaque didn't help, either. Was it really here? Was he misremembering that the smuggler had a monkey, or did he retroactively add an imaginary monkey to his recollections?

Swallowing another pill, Durand motored onward—down through the center of the Gulf of Thailand in the night. Occasionally driving rains came across the water like a falling curtain, but he welcomed the rain. The rain refreshed him—brought him back to life.

He saw things in the darkness, though. Ships. Lights. He had no idea what was real and what was not. Reality felt stretched thin. Was he even really here? Perhaps he had died somewhere back there on the South China Sea.

The tiny GPS map glowed in the darkness as he neared the first land he'd seen in days. Two islands, Ko Phai and Ko Lan—the latter just a couple kilometers off the coast of Pattaya City, Thailand. His destination.

Durand kept an eye out for Thai Coast Guard patrols, but happily there were excursion boats moving all over here. So many, in fact, that he had to actively avoid their reckless antics. He flicked on his navigation lights just to fit in. Floating restaurants swept past, packed with tourists taking in the harbor sights. Pop music came to him over the water. He could see people dancing through the windows.

Had he actually made it?

The monkey chattered excitedly. Unless the monkey was a figment of his imagination.

Durand motored around the flank of Ko Lan in the dark, and the lights of Pattaya City spread out before him. Hundreds of high-rise condominiums lined its miles-long crescent of beach. Bright laser light played across the sky above it, and a Hollywood-esque sign erected in the jungle hills above the city proclaimed in large, illuminated English letters "Pattaya City."

Durand couldn't think of a stranger place for Bryan Frey to want to meet. It did look like Las Vegas of the Far East.

Pleasure craft and jet skis passed by him now. People waving beer bottles and screaming in celebration.

Durand had prepared the rebreather gear in case a police boat attempted to stop him—he'd jump overboard and swim for the beach.

But the cigarette boat fit right in with the party atmosphere. To all appearances, Durand was a rich expat living it up in vacationland. Replete with a pet monkey.

Durand decided to toss the Skorpion machine gun and the remaining amphetamines overboard. They would only bring trouble now. He wanted to get through this next part as cleanly as possible. Get a new phone. Message Frey and arrange a place to meet. Simple. No other complications.

If that was really what he was supposed to be doing here. If he was really Durand.

Durand started seeing things again—people and faces at the edge of his vision—but he was convinced they would go away once he'd gotten some sleep.

Thumping music from a dozen venues reached him from across the bay. Saturday night. The party was in full swing.

Durand turned in along the strand. There were almost no waves here in the cove. He decided to avoid marinas altogether and just drive the boat up onto the beach and walk away. There were already some water-jet taxis nosed up onto the sand. He'd fit right in.

Beyond the beach loomed a five-meter seawall of interlocking boulders dotted with palm trees and topped by a pedestrian path with lights. Sea rise in the past few decades had clearly affected the city—but rather than move their prime nightspots, Pattayans apparently had decided to put in a barrier. This meant Durand could see only the second story and above of the buildings fronting the beach—and even these were partially blocked by the silhouettes of people walking the pedestrian path. However, the glittering lights and noise coming from beyond the wall showed there was plenty to distract people from Durand's arrival.

The long-tailed macaque stared out at the lights and music, chattering excitedly.

"Well, pal, if you're real, it's time we parted ways."

Durand turned the boat in toward the beach and eased the throttle down to just a few knots. Moments later the bow of the cigarette boat crunched up onto the sand. He powered down the electric water jets.

Durand cast one more look over the boat and then slipped over the port side, lowering himself onto the beach.

Behind him the monkey screeched and raced about, clearly upset. It launched off the boat, onto the sand, and up toward the illuminated palm trees blowing in the sea breeze.

Durand walked toward the steps, passing by chaise longues and beach umbrellas folded and locked up for the night.

A middle-aged Caucasian couple strolled past in the darkness. The man spoke with a British accent. "That's a lovely boat you have there."

Durand nodded silently and climbed the steps.

Up top he looked out at the busy beachfront street packed with pedestrians, scooters, autonomous electric cars, and songthaews overflowing with drunk tourists. Thumping music warred for people's attention. Fast-food places, restaurants, bars, dance clubs, strip clubs, massage parlors, and VR dens lined the street. On the sidewalk stood lines of young women in short skirts, interacting with LFP links and also talking to real men passing by.

Every light pole, palm tree, and wall along the street seemed to be slathered with video stickers running short clips of bands, sex acts, and pop divas. The cheap electric stickers had been illegal in Singapore for years—viewed as visual pollution. Now Durand knew why. Even if he hadn't been nearly crazed with exhaustion, the stimulation would have been too much.

He descended the steps. Drunks everywhere. It reminded Durand of every shore leave he'd ever been on.

He noted a police pickup truck moving through the crowd with several Thai officers, male and female, standing in back clutching the roll bars. They wore vests marked "Tourist Police" in English.

A sensor array stood above the cab. Durand had no doubt it housed license plate readers and facial detection orbs, but he suspected they were largely tasked with dealing a light touch to drunk expats. Finding repeat troublemakers. They didn't look anywhere near as threatening as the Singapore police. However, Durand also knew that more serious tactical units were just an emergency call away.

He descended the steps to street level and moved through the crowd. He was sweaty and a bit sunburned, but he'd kept reasonably clean during his journey using the boat's onboard water systems.

It felt surreal to be among human beings again. Exhaustion had his mind playing tricks on him—the hallucinations were coming fast. A hypersexualized manga girl in a miniskirt and stockings winked at him and jiggled cartoon breasts. Other computer-generated fetish models motioned for him to enter their clubs.

And then it occurred to Durand that he wasn't hallucinating—there were simply no laws about public LFP projection here. These were rogue AR models being beamed into his retinas. In his current state he almost thought he was going insane.

He passed by a sex club and a young Japanese half cat, half woman whispered to him with an Asian accent, "Sex with me. Soft robotics. Clean-machine VR . . ."

Sex with cartoons. The logical endgame of high-tech fanboy culture.

Dozens of languages passed by Durand. Hindi, Arabic, Mandarin, Japanese, Korean, French, German, all sorts of English. Pattaya was an uneasy mix of family beach fun and red-light district sex market.

But a quick glance was all Durand merited from passersby. People skirted around him and moved on to some new, unusual sight seconds later.

Good.

Durand was suddenly accosted by a gigantic cartoon bear in a Russian hat waving a liquor bottle and motioning for him to enter a walk-in freezer vodka lounge. Moments later, a large meatball with toothpick arms and legs walked past, smiling and carrying a sign that read: "Deathless Meatballs—400 baht."

"Goddamnit . . ." He'd forgotten how annoying unregulated AR could be. The cities in Africa were much the same. Durand shielded his eyes from the adparitions, and moved across the street toward a twenty-four-hour minimart.

The older Thai proprietor smiled at him and offered a slight wai, peaking his hands at his chest. "*Sawasdee krap.*"

Durand wai'd back and was relieved to notice he still had a bitring on his finger. "Mirror glasses, please."

The man grabbed a pair from a rack on the wall.

Durand noticed a bin of burner phablets next to the pay terminal. They were cheap, flexible, disposable devices that tourists used so none of their vacation activities could be easily tied to them.

Durand grabbed one and tossed it onto the counter. His ring had thousands of Singaporean dollars loaded. He hoped to hell the old man was honest.

He fist-bumped the pay terminal and the transaction cleared—and for only a few hundred baht.

"*Khop khun krab.*"

"Thanks." Durand headed out the door, donning his mirror glasses. His visual field calmed a bit, but the video stickers affixed everywhere still assailed him—often ten identical ones looping alongside one another.

There would apparently be no cessation of the visual stimulation in Pattaya City.

Durand moved to the edge of the sidewalk and powered up the phablet. The boot sequence was a parade of advertising—almost all of it sexual in nature.

"C'mon . . ."

Finally he got a main screen and entered the chat client. In his exhausted state he strained to remember Frey's one-time number. But he'd had plenty of time to repeat it in his head. He composed the following message:

> *Our mutual friend screwed up, but I made it here anyway. In*
> *town. Ready to meet. Contact me at this number ASAP.*

He sent the message and hoped it reached Frey. He put the earbud for the phone in, and double-checked that the sound levels were sufficient to hear over the thumping music in the street.

Just then his phablet chirped, and he pulled it out to read a message.

> *Sanctuary of Truth. 1 pm, tomorrow. Dress biz casual.*
> *Respectable. I'll approach you (assuming you haven't changed*
> *again).*

Durand felt his irritation at Frey rising already.

Chapter 24

Despite thumping music, shouting, and laughter all around his room, Kenneth Durand fell into a dreamless sleep almost immediately. He'd rented a sanitized cubicle bed for the night in an automated hostel in the red-light district. For this not-quite hotel room, he wasn't required to provide a passport—no doubt a concession to privacy-seeking tourists.

He maxed out the twelve-hour rental timer and closed his eyes. The next thing he heard was a loud female voice speaking in multiple languages set to a background of techno music. Looking up, he saw it was 0830. He'd slept straight through. The female voice was now pitching a VR sex parlor near his current location—loud enough that he was soon awake. From his sound patterns and the accelerometer in the phablet, the device also now knew he was awake and began leaking his data to local merchants. Breakfast pop-up ads rolled in fast.

He showered and shaved in a common bathroom for another fee— going so far as to shave the stubble of hair on his scalp. He wanted to look clean. Orderly.

Finished, he headed out into the street, ignoring the autonomous songthaews and cabs, opting to walk; there were facial recognition and security cameras everywhere, but he knew from experience how quickly that data piled up. He guessed it was mostly used to up-sell tourists or track down people after crimes were committed in a certain location. He'd find out if he was right soon enough.

He bought an Aussie bush hat from a street vendor to give some measure of cover against street cameras, and walked Pattaya Beach Road along the seawall, grabbing degan khao kai jeow—rice and a cultured egg omelet—at a market stall.

He moved with surprising ease among the Sunday morning expat retirees, embezzlers, vacationing gangsters, and locals. Bleary-eyed tourists were emerging into the daylight from VR parlors. Tourist police rousted junkies and drunks from sois and troks. He felt irrationally calm and confident in this strange body—strong, healthy. The sense of surreality his exhaustion had brought on was gone. He was ready to meet these Luk Krung. To get back to himself.

Eating on the move, Durand pulled out his phablet. He'd already researched the Sanctuary of Truth the night before, and he had plenty of time before the meet. First he needed to get a change of clothes. Frey had requested business casual, and a more prosperous look was probably a good idea to keep the police off his back. It took only a moment to locate a nearby clothing store, and he made his way there on foot.

Durand arrived a half hour early to scope out Pattaya's Sanctuary of Truth. The ornate temple was located on a stony cape near the city's seawall and surrounded by a high, mildew-stained wall of its own. He had to pay admission to enter, and inside it became clear the place was a combination garden/temple/adventure park. There were electric all-terrain cycles and elephant rides, VR parlors and food stalls. Durand felt overdressed in his button-down shirt, jacket, khakis, and mirrored glasses. The security guards he saw looked bored, out of shape, and distracted. If there were police here, then they were doing a good job of concealing themselves.

Ahead, through the trees, Durand could see a massive, Khmer-style wat with multiple curving roofs rich with ornamentation. Only when he got closer did he see that the entire structure was fashioned of wood—its peak easily a hundred meters high. It was segmented into four wings. Various parts of the exterior were fading and weathered. Others were brand-new. But almost every inch of the temple was decorated with carved faces and mythological forms from both Buddhist and Hindu faiths.

He entered through a richly carved winding stair, passing beneath multiple porticos braced by leaning Chinese, Thai, Indian, and Khmer figures. In the shade of the sanctuary, tourists from all over the world sipped drinks and took selfie scans.

A sign near the door read "No camera drones inside" in multiple languages.

Durand wandered the different chambers, on the lookout for police or gangsters. But everyone looked like distracted tourists, watching the wood-carvers or looking up at incredibly detailed woodwork.

After a while, Durand started reading plaques to kill time. He tried to use his phablet to translate the Thai script of one, but his low-cost phablet OS kept inserting ad copy for strip clubs into the middle of the translation.

"Brushing up on Thai history, I see." Bryan Frey stepped up alongside Durand, likewise dressed in a button-down shirt, slacks, and a jacket.

Durand spoke without turning. "When do we meet these people?"

"So much for pleasant chitchat."

"I didn't come here for chitchat. When we do meet the Luk Krung?"

"Shh." Frey looked around. "Outside . . ."

Frey brought them toward the exit and out in the sun. They moved away from the temple and tourists taking photos of elephant rides and walked along the breezy seawall.

Frey glanced around to see that they were relatively alone. "I've rescheduled with the Luk Krung twice already. You certainly took your sweet-ass time getting here."

Durand looked down at Frey, lifted up his mirror glasses, and glared into the dwarf's eyes. "People died so I could get here—do you understand?"

Frey drew back. "Died? What the hell happened?"

"Rad screwed up. He didn't factor in how badly the police wanted Wyckes. They set up roadblocks on the highway. I had to make my own way here."

Frey grimaced. "Goddamnit, Rad. He's not much of a criminal, you know. So how *did* you wind up getting here?"

"I hired traffickers to take me by boat. They collected DNA samples from the passengers and figured out who I was out on the water."

"How on earth did you escape in the middle of the ocean?"

Durand put his mirror glasses back on. "I did what I had to. Let's just leave it at that." He looked back at the ornate temple.

Frey processed this. "I see." He walked along for several moments in silence. "I did have an opportunity to sequence your current DNA and your past DNA."

Durand looked back at him with interest.

"It proves beyond a shadow of a doubt that you are Kenneth Durand. You'll be happy to know your heart and most of your internal organs are unchanged. By my calculations your DNA is still 99.994 percent original."

Durand heard the news with a mix of satisfaction and dismay—glad to hear he was still mostly himself, but knowing also that the most recognizable parts of his identity had been erased.

"I thought the news that you're mostly unchanged would be better received."

"When are we meeting these people? I want out of this skin. I don't like what I'm capable of in this psycho's body."

"Well . . . again, your mind and vitals remain unedited. So whatever you've done or haven't done is—"

"When are we meeting?"

Frey glanced into his designer light field glasses. "The car should be here in a few minutes. I've arranged for a consultation in their showroom."

"Showroom?"

"Yes. Pattaya City is a destination for medical tourists. The Luk Krung run several very fine hospitals."

"This city is an R-rated beach town."

"Yes, if you stay down near Walking Street, but the city diversified in the last few decades—moved upscale. It turns out medical tourism is more profitable than sin. The nicer part of town now caters to medical tourists from all over—and also parents looking for truly novel genetic edits for their children-to-be."

Frey gestured to the city skyline. "Certainly you don't think massage parlors paid for all this. Lots of wealth from around the world has come here. This is a thriving genetic marketplace, Mr. Durand—most of it quite legal, which, I imagine, is why you never found it."

Durand studied the city. "This Luk Krung gang . . . you said they do radical genetic edits."

"What they do will be self-explanatory, but for god's sake, let me do the talking. Don't even speak in the car on the way over. It's their courtesy vehicle. As far as they know, we're a married couple from Canada who've adopted an embryo that we want substantially modified."

Durand narrowed his eyes at Frey. "Wait. I thought we were going to see them because you've worked with them before. That we were going there specifically to discuss my situation."

"You can't expect me to just ring them up and say, 'Hey, guys, I've got a buddy who's been transformed into Marcus Wyckes—can you change him back?' I need to show them proof of what's happened to you—which, thanks to you, we now have—and go from there. This adoption cover story gets us in the door."

Durand stared. "Let me get this straight . . ."

"By all means . . ."

"We're going into this place as a couple of scumbags who would adopt someone else's embryo and then modify it to suit our tastes—like a *kitchen*."

"You surprise me; I thought you were going to be upset that I told them we were married. Fortunately for us both, public affection is frowned upon in Thailand so—"

"You are on thin ice with me, Frey."

Frey pointed. "Right there: it's exactly that sort of pissy attitude that will *sell us* as a married couple."

Durand leaned down, pulling off the mirror glasses completely. "You get us in there and get us to their top person. Because I'm telling you right now: if I discover you're trying to betray me, we will have a serious problem, you and I."

"I assure you—"

"I killed three men to be here."

Frey put up his hands in acquiescence, then looked up to see an autonomous electric Mercedes with black-tinted windows roll up the drive near the entrance.

"Here's our ride. Act like a genetic tourist. Look entitled. And remember, no unnecessary talking."

With a grim expression Durand followed Frey, who approached the silver-and-black sedan as it glided noiselessly to a stop at the curb.

Frey opened the door for Durand. "After you, my dear."

"Fuck off." Getting inside, Durand looked around to realize that the windows were even more opaque when viewed from the inside. Blacked out, in fact.

Frey got in after him and closed the door with a *thwup*. Interior lights came on.

Durand narrowed his eyes. "We can't see out of the car."

Frey put a finger to his lips. "Yes, dear. They'd rather we not know where we're going. Your devices won't work in here, either." He rapped the leather-inlaid door with his knuckles. "Faraday cage, you see. I hear it's standard in this line of business. Can't have the clientele knowing where the lab is. Otherwise, they could get raided."

Dressed in street clothes, Corporal Bank of the Royal Thai Police Central Investigation Bureau stood in the gift shop of the Sanctuary of Truth, pretending to examine caged doves. He wondered if his daughter would like one of them. They were put on sale specifically to be released near a shrine, he knew, but perhaps one would make a nice pet? He glanced up at the inset video on a rear-facing camera of his LFP glasses.

There: the suspect was departing with the second man—getting into a very fine autonomous sedan. He'd affixed pin cams to the walls outside as well. He was getting good video. There must be big things afoot for his commander to be personally involved. Word was that Bangkok was behind this one. Some international manhunt.

Bank calmly watched the Mercedes depart and then spoke into his LFP uplink. "The suspect rendezvoused with a second individual. Photos sent. Both suspects departed Sanctuary of Truth in autonomous vehicle, license number X2-3-82. Add this car to autotracking."

There. Bank had done his part. The devious little *farang* hadn't lost him—though the bastard had certainly tried to shake any tails. If this dwarf was a big fish, perhaps Bank would get a commendation. Maybe it would give him the boost he needed to make sergeant. Better kickbacks as a sergeant.

He decided he was buying this dove, after all. A sergeant could afford a pet dove for his daughter.

Chapter 25

After driving in silence for at least fifteen minutes through the sound of dense traffic, horns, and general city clamor, the Mercedes sedan entered a quieter place of screeches and echoes, heading down.

A parking garage, Durand guessed.

After rounding several ramps, the Mercedes came to a stop. The left door opened to reveal a smiling, attractive young Thai woman in a business suit, along with two smiling women in lab coats. They all bowed with their hands peaked before their hearts. "*Sawasdee ka.*"

The woman in the business suit stepped forward. "Mr. and Mr. Anderson. So good to have you as our honored guests." She motioned for them to follow. "Please. Enter. No need to remove your shoes. We follow the Western custom here."

Durand glared at Frey before exiting the car. Frey joined him on the red carpet as a server in a silk tunic extended a tray holding twin champagne flutes.

"Champagne, sirs?"

Frey smiled. "Don't mind if I do . . ." He grabbed one and passed it toward Durand. "Champagne, dear?"

Durand shook his head. "Let's get on with this."

Frey returned one flute but sipped the other. "Right. Please keep an open mind . . ."

They walked through tinted glass doors flanked by palms and a babbling water feature and fieldstones. Inside they found a stylish lobby done in grown materials, plants, and more natural stone, with soft, perfectly imitated sunlight streaming in from artificial skylights. The beams focused on the lab's logo—a single Thai letter in the form of a small living tree, no doubt genetically engineered to spell out the name of the enterprise.

Durand wondered if it was Desai's handiwork.

Another beautiful young Thai woman in a business suit approached them wearing designer LFP glasses. She performed a wai as well. "Gentlemen. Our sensors indicate you both possess mobile devices. We must hold these for the duration of your visit. They will, of course, be returned to you upon your departure."

She held out a metal lockbox and opened the lid.

Durand and Frey looked at each other.

Frey shrugged. "Of course . . ." He removed his LFP glasses and his belt processing unit, placing them both in the box.

Durand tossed his cheap phablet into the box as well, to Frey's obvious embarrassment.

"He likes his burners. Bit of a privacy nut, my husband."

The young woman smiled sweetly as she locked the box and handed the key to Frey. "Not at all uncommon, Mr. Anderson. Enjoy your visit with us today." She departed.

The original hostess motioned for them to follow her.

Durand had always had the impression that these embryo clinics were backroom affairs done in the dark. As he looked around, this place was nothing like what he had imagined. It looked like a high-end fertility clinic.

They entered a sizable lounge area, where dozens of other would-be parents stood speaking with lab counselors—male and female—at small standing tables. The clients ran the gamut in age and ethnicity. There was the occasional pair where one partner was much older—either the man or the woman. He heard British-, American-, South African–, and Australian-accented English. There were Russian, Chinese, Arab, Indian, Japanese, and Korean couples. All of them fashionably dressed. These were no ordinary customers. People from the Bubble—executives, lawyers, bankers, and doctors.

Another young Thai woman approached them as they were shown

to a standing table. She wai'd. "*Sawasdee ka.* My name is Ms. Meow, and I will be your personal counselor. So good to meet you, Mr. and Mr. Anderson. We are honored that you consider entrusting us with your most precious gift. Since you're our last arrival, we are now ready for the floor presentation."

Durand raised an eyebrow. "Floor presentation?"

Frey tapped Durand's arm. "Didn't I mention that, darling? Ah . . . I should have."

The young woman smiled brightly. She spoke American English with no accent whatsoever. "You will need this . . ." She extended a thin film tablet framed in synbio ivory to Durand. The device had a slick-looking AR-based UI on its surface beneath the lab logo. It must have had an integrated glim because AR objects floated above the tablet in an impossible-looking, hyperrealistic way.

"While you enjoy the show, this portal will permit you to mark your favorite genetic selections for later review during our personal one-on-one consultation. And of course, we can always replay the floor presentation afterward to find the genetic options you found most desirable."

Frey nodded. "Very much appreciated, my dear. This will be one of the most difficult choices of our lives. It's nice to know we're in capable hands."

She smiled engagingly again. "I am here to be of service." She looked up to see that the other counselors were bringing their clients toward a double set of oxidized bronze doors. These opened noiselessly like the entry to some ancient temple. "I see we are ready to begin. If you'll please come with me, gentlemen, I'll bring you to your table."

Durand cast an impatient look at Frey.

"After you, my dear." He gestured for Durand to go first.

Meow brought them into a ballroom dotted with dozens of small cultured-wood cocktail tables and matching chairs. They were clearly grown in their present shapes, since not a seam or joint was visible—a subtle demonstration of genetic mastery.

The center of the room contained a fashion show catwalk and small stage with pinpoint lights illuminating its length. The entire showroom was decorated with the finest synbio hardwoods, glass, and grown fabric decor. Artificial sunlight poured in from skylights above. It was convincing enough to make it seem like this was all happening in the light of day, instead of several stories below ground.

Ms. Meow escorted them to their table. As they sat, she placed a hand on each of their shoulders. "I will see you gentlemen after the show. I cannot wait to plan your special one." She nodded toward a waiter standing by in a silk tunic, then departed.

The Thai waiter wai'd to them. "Gentlemen, would you care for a cocktail or perhaps a light repast?" With a gesture, a menu appeared from thin air above their ivory tablet, turning toward them as they looked at it. "Might I recommend the beluga caviar?"

Durand cast an annoyed look at the waiter. "*Caviar?* You're serving caviar?"

"The highest-grade *degan* caviar, sir—biofactured at our own facility and 100 percent carbon neutral."

Frey laughed dramatically. "Such a stickler about sustainability, but that's one of the things I love about you." He turned to the waiter. "Please bring us some. And also a mineral water for my husband, please. Preferably fresh from a fusion reactor."

Durand rolled his eyes.

"Of course, sir." With that the waiter moved off.

Durand glowered at Frey.

"Being married, I, of course, know you're a degan, but I'm just a bit surprised that you would make it an issue *today*—especially given everything else on your plate, so to speak."

"I'm trying to get back to myself. Abandoning my closely held beliefs isn't going to help that."

Soft music rose, and a spotlight shone down on the stage.

Durand leaned closer to Frey. "When are we—?"

Frey held up a finger for silence and pointed to the tablet, whose AR magic was shrinking away, so as not to obscure the show about to begin.

Durand held his tongue but sighed in irritation.

The music expanded into earwormy K-pop music. Gorgeous Thai women in sequined leotards emerged from both wings of the stage—with huge, plumed headdresses of rare (though undoubtedly cultured) feathers.

The audience applauded as spotlights focused on the center curtain, with a Thai-accented woman's voice intoning, "Ladies, gentlemen, and transgender, give a warm hand for your host, Mr. Vegas!"

A middle-aged Thai man with long, free-flowing black hair emerged from behind the curtain. He wore a perfectly tailored brocade tuxedo and a small headset microphone that in this day and age was wholly unnecessary—except that it identified him immediately as the emcee.

The audience applauded as the emcee clapped right back at them, wai'd, then clapped some more. His black hair shimmered as it flowed down his shoulders. He resembled one of those magicians who don't actually do tricks.

"Very good! So good to see you today! Welcome to our dream factory." He bowed slightly, smiling. "*Sabai dee mai?* You honor us with your presence."

The applause died down as he moved forward with confidence, walking the catwalk.

"This day, we would like to help you conceive the child of your dreams."

The emcee studied his audience. "I see we have a wonderful group. You've come from all around this world to be with us today, and I think I know why. Where most clinics show you mere images of what *could be*—we bring you the real thing. Children who already have undergone the edits you desire. And what better way to begin than by turning over the emcee duties to . . ." He gestured stage left, where a spotlight shined down. "Kimberly!"

At that moment an adorable six-year-old Caucasian girl with blond hair and blue eyes emerged wearing a sequined gown and her own microphone headset.

Vegas welcomed her, clapping too. "Age six, recipient of our proprietary DLG and MPP line of intelligence and memory edits . . ."

Kimberly smiled brightly and waved calmly to the crowd like a pro beauty contestant, speaking in one language after another: "Hello, everyone! *Dobryy den´ vsem! Dàjiā xiàwŭ hăo! Kon´nichiwa, min´na! Buenas tardes a todos! Guten Abend allerseits! Bon après-midi, tout le monde!*" Her pronunciation was flawless, and whenever she spoke another language, the ivory tablet on Durand's table projected subtitles in English into his eyes. The little girl transitioned seamlessly from one language to the next as though it was second nature, finally settling back on English. "Welcome! We know you're here because you want to give your future child the very best start possible. And from firsthand experience, I can tell you . . ." She grinned coyly, accentuating her perfect dimples. "It's pretty darned nice having quality genes!"

The audience laughed and clapped as the little girl soaked up the applause, encouraging them. She strode to the head of the catwalk beneath a spotlight as Vegas disappeared into the shadows and the adult showgirls melted away behind the sequined curtains. She stood alone.

"As Mr. Vegas says, I benefited from proprietary in vitro modifications that greatly improved expression of my DLG3 and MPP6 genes, re-creating a rare natural mutation enjoyed by just a few. I'm told these genes play an essential role in intelligence and memory and are associated with the guanylate kinase protein family. Specifically, they manage clustering of NMDA receptors at excitatory synapses—which are required for learning and memory through their role in synaptic plasticity following NMDA receptor signaling." She smiled disarmingly. "But then again, I'm only six—what do I know?" She held out her hands and shrugged adorably to uproarious laughter.

Durand realized the little girl was his daughter's age—and yet she seemed almost alien in her intelligence. Mia was inquisitive, hardworking, and intelligent. This Kimberly seemed effortlessly brilliant.

The tablet on Durand's table highlighted gene selections ready for "favoriting."

There was something too "uncanny valley" about this little girl. He leaned over to Frey and hissed into his ear, "Are you kidding me? This place needs to be shut down." His finger jabbed into the table.

Frey smiled and laughed lightly with the rest of the audience. "Now, now, my dear. You wanted to see the edge." Frey stopped smiling and turned toward Durand, whispering back, "And this is it."

The show continued as the precocious Kimberly finished telling a dirty joke in Russian, delivering the punch line—which was immediately translated by superscript hovering above her in AR: "Whatever you do, don't have the fish!"

The audience laughed—especially the Russians.

The little girl then spoke in Mandarin, with perfect accent and diction. This, too, was instantly translated to a language appropriate to the viewer and beamed into individual eyes by glims on every table.

Durand guessed that software was monitoring his eye activity and pupil responses for interest—and a possible sale. But also perhaps for subversion and informants.

Durand tried to watch without perceiving Kimberly as an abomination. After all, this was an actual, adorable little girl. None of this was her fault. She hadn't asked to be created as a genetic wunderkind.

Kimberly smiled as she moved to the side of the catwalk, still soaking up laughter from a joke she'd just told in French. Then she paused, getting serious. "But it's not fair for me to take up all your time. You've come a long way to see the true potential for your own children. So without further ado, let me share with you our entire line of CRISPR edits for 2045!"

The K-pop music returned. Laser lights flashed, and a spotlight shined down on the sequined rear curtain.

"Please remember to mark your preference cards. Our trained counselors will advise you on the likely results of your preferred traits in combination with the unique genetics of your source embryo." She gestured. "Now, ladies and gentlemen, *Damen und Herren, Nǚshìmen xiānshēngmen*, meet six-year-old Samson!"

The curtain parted as a little boy with the physique of a bodybuilder strode onto the catwalk to music, lights, and applause.

Kimberly accompanied his posing with sales patter. "Samson's displaying the potential for our MYH3 and MYH11 line of smooth and skeletal muscle edits. Look at those arms! Samson has a glorious athletic career ahead of him. These muscles can also be made less voluminous, with greater power-to-mass performance, for those who prefer a sleeker runner's physique."

The little boy posed, his muscles glistening under the lights as he flexed while the music pulsed in sync.

He quickly made a return on the catwalk, passing twins—a little Asian boy and girl—emerging from the curtains. They appeared to be Han Chinese, but with blond hair and blue eyes. They wore lederhosen and dirndls. Their facial features and perfect, parchment-like skin were projected onto virtual screens that materialized to either side of the stage to provide an unmistakable close-up of the Aryan features of these Asian children.

"For those who prefer lighter hues with Asian features, we present our hybrid 'blond Chinese' line of KRT75 edits. An exceptional combination of fair complexion and traditional Sino phenotypes."

Durand turned again to Frey. He felt the outrage starting to burn and struggled to prevent his tattoos from appearing. He glanced down and saw his hand begin to shade. Through focused concentration, he willed the genetic tattoos back into invisibility.

Frey noticed. He pushed the tablet away from them and leaned toward Durand, meeting his gaze. He whispered, "I needed you to see this."

Durand hissed back, "What on earth does this sick display have to do with changing me back?"

"Who exactly do you think will be helping you do that? The very people who are capable of creating what's on that stage are the same people you need. And it's not just the proprietors. Look around you. Who do you see in the audience?"

Durand glanced around. The room was filled with what the Thai would call *farang*—foreigners. In fact, he didn't see any Thai people here beyond the staff.

Frey continued. "No, they've all come—like you—from inside the Bubble. Out here to where the laws are stretched thin. To get what they want far from the all-seeing IoT eye. The Luk Krung didn't invent CRISPR, and I'd be willing to wager they didn't put up the investment capital for this enterprise, either. They're just serving a ready market. And when your fashionable friends and neighbors go home with their perfect child implanted in their womb, everyone will pretend this never happened."

Durand returned his gaze to Frey. "Why are you telling me this?"

"Because I know you want to shut this place down. I can see the revulsion in your face. I'm guessing you *will* shut it down. But if I'm going to do this with you, I need to know you will fulfill your promise to me. That I will get what I came for."

"And for that you're making me sit through this?"

"I wanted you to see that what we want is the same—you and I. And it's not unlike what these people want."

"I'm nothing like these people."

"You don't get to judge." He nodded toward the others around them. "You came here to be personally edited into the human you see in your mind's eye. I came here for the same reason. Now, I'd agree that editing a helpless embryo to suit a parent's personal tastes is pretty fucked up. I didn't like my mother's taste in *drapes*, so I sure as hell wouldn't want her choosing my cheekbones . . ." He gestured to the stage.

Durand could see a line of half a dozen boys there displaying a range of numbered cheekbone heights.

"But we—you and I—came here to break the law and get what we both want. There is no turning back from this once we begin. You can't go halfway with the Luk Krung. If you have lingering doubts, tell me now, and we will leave. And I will pass to the authorities genetic proof that you are . . . mostly . . . Kenneth Durand and not Marcus Wyckes. But if we do that"—he gestured to Durand—"like *this* you will remain. Now is the time to decide. But your decision must be final."

Durand considered this as he watched the stage. A small child was doing backflips like an Olympic gymnast, traversing the stage to wild applause.

He suddenly wondered what *Kenneth Durand* was doing here. Kenneth Durand ate deathless meat because it was better for the environment, and he didn't want anything to die for his dinner. And yet he had killed people to reach this room. What was happening up on that stage was one of the most disgusting displays of unethical genetics he'd ever seen. And not only had his algorithms *not* detected this place, but now he was here as a client. A customer looking to serve his own needs.

But it was Marcus Wyckes who had done this to him, and if this

Thai cartel could somehow reverse engineer the Huli jing's in vivo edits, rewriting him to his original DNA—what then? Wasn't he giving this gang the ability to do in vivo edits as well? Like Desai said: this was worth hundreds of billions. Trillions. He would be helping this technology to spread. A technology that could destabilize the world by rendering identity itself obsolete. Creating a *post-identity* world. What then?

Durand could feel the ethical quicksand pulling him under. As much as he pictured himself saying, *I refuse; I cannot do this*—he remained sitting at the table as the degan caviar was placed before them. The only image that kept coming into his mind was of his wife and daughter and the idea of who Kenneth Durand was—father, husband—alongside them. His rational mind told him it was merely an evolved preference for his own genes, but then what else *was there* in the natural world but a compelling drive to propagate one's genes? What made them *his* genes? Chance?

Yet he knew deep down in his being that they were his genes. And now they had been stolen from him.

He was tempted to pull out the photograph of his wife and daughter, to look at it, but he didn't dare just now. He could see it in his mind clearly enough.

How would they look upon him if they knew what he'd already done?

There needed to be a brief exception in his life—an ethics time-out. A moment of selfishness. Just one, and he would get back to who he'd been. He felt the quicksand swallowing him as he realized he was going to do this. That, in fact, people had already died so that he could reach the seat he was in right now, in this macabre showroom. He watched Frey calmly spooning caviar onto a cracker.

Why wasn't he punching Frey in the face? Why wasn't he calling the police and having this place raided?

Here Durand sat, and continued to sit. That was the simple fact. And each passing second he wasn't getting up and leaving made it all the more true. Was he really the ethical man he presented to his daughter and wife?

The Kenneth Durand he'd thought he was would never have considered this.

But then, that Durand hadn't seen and felt his face and throat and arms and entire body change around his consciousness. That Durand could hug his daughter with his own arms—not those of a sociopath.

It would be better to be dead.

Then why hadn't he killed himself? He could have leaped from that under-construction high-rise in Singapore. Or out in the Gulf of Thailand—why hadn't he just tied an anchor around his neck and plunged into the sea?

He'd *killed* to get back to himself.

How was that even possible? Kenneth Durand didn't even *fish* because blood upset him. Killing—especially after the thousand hours of gun-camera footage he'd seen in Africa—had been completely unimaginable. And yet he'd viciously stabbed two young men to death. He had no concrete memory of doing so—though he knew he had.

He realized for the first time that his own life was more important to him than the lives of others. It was a truth that he'd never had to face before—one every rational person wanted to avoid. Deathless meat was the ultimate expression of that reluctance.

Frey was right about one thing: Durand was just like the rest of the clientele here. He saw what the Luk Krung was doing, but he was still determined to seek their help for himself.

And he *was* going to do it.

"I'm a hypocrite. Is that what you want to hear from me?"

Frey grimaced. "I want to hear that there is no moral difference between what you and I want. That you will willingly help me to derive the change agent that may still be in your DNA or somatic cells so I can cure my achondroplasia. Do you agree to this?"

Durand nodded. "I agree."

"And will you make certain to help me, just as I will help you?"

He met Frey's gaze. "I will."

"Very well. Now we are neither of us blameless. No matter what happens from here on." Frey reached for the ivory tablet. "It's time I spoke to the management of this establishment about the real purpose of our visit." He tapped an AR button to summon their genetic counselor.

In the interval Durand watched the stage numbly. The little emcee was presenting a child wearing geisha-like makeup and costume who suddenly erupted in a stunning operatic singing voice—to great applause.

Chapter 26

Thick-necked Thai security men in suits and LFP glasses accompanied Kenneth Durand, Bryan Frey, and their genetic counselor, Ms. Meow, down an echoing concrete corridor. It was unlike the plush spaces they'd been in before—clearly the business end of the operation.

Durand glanced back at the Thai security men warily. "This guy really calls himself 'Mr. Vegas'?"

Frey shook his head. "He didn't. His parents did. Birth nicknames are a Thai tradition meant to confuse evil spirits from stealing newborns. But they've gotten rather fun in modern times. I know a Ms. King Kong and a Mr. Laser as well. You can work for years with someone in Thailand and never know their real first and last name."

Ms. Meow was stone-faced as she brought them through a steel door into a well-appointed sitting room lined with leather sofas, surrealist paintings, and a well-stocked bar. "Gentlemen, please take a seat."

Frey looked around with concern that no one was there to meet them. "Does Vegas know it's me who's come to see him?"

A male voice answered. "Mr. Vegas does, Bryan."

Frey and Durand turned to see the male emcee, Mr. Vegas, enter through a different door—the same man who'd opened the fashion show. He still wore his brocade tuxedo and nodded, bowing slightly to them both. He turned back to Frey. "It has been some time since we saw you last."

Frey bowed slightly as well. "*Sawasdee krap*, Mr. Vegas. It is good to see you. I'd heard you expanded your product lines into human edits, and so I've brought a very interesting client along with me."

"Our new partners have indeed enabled us to move beyond what we did in the old days. No more editing pets and plants."

"The modeling load must be enormous."

"It is."

"Your product line is quite impressive. And my compliments on your showmanship. It far exceeds the dog and cat shows you put on years ago."

Vegas stared, unreadable for a moment. He then turned to Durand. "You've brought along a commercial client. No doubt one who wishes to remain anonymous."

Frey spread his hands. "For now, yes."

"In the market for 'radical' edits. Is that correct?"

"We're here for something even more serious than that. We've come to discuss the radical edits my client has received. Edits you might be interested in seeing yourself."

"This is not the preferred means of contacting us. Entering our facility under false pretenses." He returned his gaze to Frey. "Under a false name."

"Of course, but as you'll see, secrecy was required."

Vegas moved to the bar and began to pour himself a scotch. "You know, Bryan, you should see what we've been up to since you left. You and I got started in this business together, after all. I think you will find it interesting."

"Perhaps another time. We should instead focus on why we—"

"Nonsense! I insist." He downed his two fingers of scotch and clapped his hands, motioning. "Come! Let me show you just how far our little enterprise has come from our days of editing poodles and shih tzus!" He let out a screechy laugh and opened the side door.

The security men nodded for Durand and Frey to move forward. Their genetic counselor let herself out the opposite door without looking back.

Durand gave a concerned look to Frey, who motioned for calm.

"If you insist, Vegas. We'd be happy to tour the operation."

"Excellent!" He entered an echoing and brightly lit double-height concrete corridor lined with numbered sliding metal doors on rails. "All of this was financed by our international partners. Whereas I once had to rely on you alone for guidance, I now have two dozen genetic engineers designing product lines."

"Where did you find your partners?"

"They found us."

"They manage your computational load?"

"We have remote access to state-of-the-art systems—cloud-based photonic exascale computing available to us on demand."

"So that's how you were able to scale so quickly?"

"More than that. They supplied us with designs. Our younger selves would be amazed by what we routinely achieve today."

"The changes are indeed coming faster every year."

Vegas pressed a button, and one of the heavy metal doors slid open with a low grinding sound. He led them into what looked like a light manufacturing operation, with wheeled conveyor lines for moving cardboard boxes. Pallets of boxes stood nearby.

Arranged in a circle stood half a dozen six-year-old children of varying ethnicities—both boys and girls. They wore simple blue work smocks with cheap plastic sandals. They didn't even glance up as Vegas and his guests entered. Instead, the children focused on passing cardboard boxes from the conveyor line, on to another child, and then to a third child, who added it to the stack of boxes on a pallet—whereupon a child on the far side removed a box from the pallet and placed it onto the conveyor line, starting the loop all over again.

It was a bizarre imitation of work.

Vegas gestured to the little workers. "Our other DLG3 line of edits. We call it 'Worker Bee.' Creates laborers of low IQ. Low food requirements. Designed for docility. They can be trained to perform tasks too simple for robots to perform cost-effectively. Sterile, of course."

Frey and Durand stopped cold.

Frey's initial look of shock was quickly replaced by a ready smile. "You really have changed your business."

"Look . . ." Vegas leaned in to take a box from one of the children, interrupting their work. The young girl he took the box from barely noticed, and instead waited for the next box to be handed to her. "Put them through the motions, and they imprint quickly. They can be taught to understand spoken language, but do not themselves speak. And so can keep secrets."

Durand noticed several more thick-necked security men enter and fold their hands in front of them patiently.

Frey's eyes darted around the room. "And do these . . . workers mature?"

"Yes, of course, Bryan. They will grow to become full-sized adults—though devoid of sexuality. This product has only been in existence for six years. It shows great promise. They can be produced at a highly competitive cost to typical industrial robots, and are more easily 'programmed' by unskilled staff."

"But . . ." Frey's voice trailed off.

Vegas turned to him. "Yes?"

"I'm given to understand that there are plenty of slaves already in the world. Huge populations of refugees on the move. Wouldn't that make for a . . . challenging market for this product?"

Vegas nodded. "Indeed. But unlike slaves, as you can see, these workers will not rebel. Or demand rights. Docile—susceptible to suggestion and lacking self-interest. This achievement was accomplished through research on Devil's Breath."

Frey stared out at the workers. "Scopolamine."

"Yes. It has a fascinating effect on the human brain. Zombifies the mind, making it receptive to external suggestion. Our partners have perfected embryo edits to create the chemical naturally within the brain. With these children, such susceptibility to external suggestion is permanent. They will hold their hand over a flame if you tell them to."

Durand felt nausea. Right here—this was the reason for the Genetic Crime Division. It's what had motivated his old self. Before he'd gone on this insane quest, his job had been to prevent abominations like this. He'd had a noble purpose. Now he was standing here petitioning monsters for assistance.

This was *devolution*. Humanity was devolving a portion of itself into a slave subspecies. He had to put a stop to this. It could not go on. The evil on display here was too great.

Frey nudged Durand roughly.

Durand looked over at him to see an expression of impatience on Frey's face.

Frey turned to Vegas. "This is a radical shift from editing pets, Tang. I'd heard you'd gone into the baby mill business, but you have to admit, this is pretty goddamned extreme."

Vegas nodded. "Yes. Yes, it is, Bryan." He turned an unfriendly eye toward Frey. "But then, I have changed, too. I was given little choice by my new partners. And I was in an economic predicament. It seems I made a bad bet on someone."

Frey looked momentarily concerned before his easy smile returned.

"A certain freelance genetic engineer I'd employed had badly handled his work. He said he was headed to Singapore. That he didn't need me anymore."

Frey held up his hands. "You cannot still be sore about that, Tang."

"It's *Mr. Vegas* now."

"I was full of myself back then. It was a very big opportunity. Very advanced. They—"

"You were soon dismissed."

"That was a misunderstanding. The investors had unreasonable expectations, and—"

"To expect *anything* from you is unreasonable. Or so I have found." Vegas approached Frey. "The edits you designed for me had serious flaws. You were to deliver the genome for a long-lived shih tzu."

"I did! The computer model indicated those dogs would live thirty years. Reduced likelihood of—"

"Yes, you did indeed fulfill the letter of your contract." Vegas's expression turned angry. "But by six months of age the dogs smelled like Stilton cheese."

Frey raised his eyebrows. "Really? That is . . . surprising . . . to some extent."

"Surprising!" Vegas slapped a cardboard box violently out of one of the docile children's hands. The child didn't even flinch. "By the time it was apparent how shoddy your work was, you were gone. With my money. Most of the edits you sold me were not as advertised. I was nearly bankrupted. Money had to be borrowed. From dangerous people."

Frey put a finger to his chin in thought. "You know, I think I know how that shih tzu error happened."

"It's too late. I was very glad to hear you had come to me."

"I can see that you're angry, Tang."

"*Mr. Vegas!*"

Frey held up his hands in a conciliatory gesture. "I'm perfectly willing to repay any and all costs. Especially when you see—"

"It is too late."

Durand observed Frey's increasing desperation with a strange detachment. He could see how quickly this was unraveling. Looking around him, he realized that there were far too many security people in here for a tour. Things were about to go very wrong.

And yet he felt an eerie calm—even as his anger rose.

"It was a simple mistake. Genetic modeling before photonics was extremely expensive. And your computer modeling budget was alarmingly inadequate."

"Was it? Well, fortunately my new partners have expanded those capabilities. Let me show you one of our biggest sellers . . ." Vegas gestured to his guards, and they opened a side door.

Six small boys entered wearing military fatigues and tiny caps in digital jungle camouflage, marching obediently. They carried MP6 submachine guns strapped to their chests, tiny hands clutching them as they stared straight ahead.

Vegas shouted as they drew alongside. "Halt!"

The boys snapped to, and slapped their boots on the ground as they stood at rigid attention.

Vegas paced around them, resting his hands on the shoulders of the diminutive soldiers. "You like them, Bryan? They're knockout mice of a sort—only the genes we've knocked out this time are those that support compassion and empathy. HTR2A. SLC6A4. BDNF. DRD2. And don't forget CRHR1—shrinking the fear center of the human brain. These children are designed to grow into reliable soldiers. They will not fall prey to conscience, or be tormented by memories of horror. Nor do they fear death. They obey and tell no tales of what they've done. Likewise sterile. Don't want these nasty fuckers breeding."

Durand felt a boiling rage within him. He visualized burning this place to the ground—but then realized he had to notify the authorities. That's what Kenneth Durand would have done. And he *was* Kenneth Durand. This place could not be suffered to exist.

Still he watched, almost as if he were having an out-of-body experience. Frey spoke, but the sound seemed muted somehow. He watched the dwarf's lips moving as he tried to evade his doom—a pointless endeavor, Durand now knew.

Durand's anger grew more intense. Anger at this evil. Anger at his own presence here.

Frey held up his hands again. "If you'll just listen, we are here for something very important—"

With a wave of Vegas's hand the child soldiers obediently chambered rounds in their weapons and aimed them at Frey and Durand both.

Durand felt steady as he stepped forward.

Men all around them produced guns.

But Durand could already feel the marks appearing—he willed them into existence with his anger. He glared at Vegas as he slowly approached. Unhurried.

Vegas's eyes widened as he saw the tattoos.

Durand tore his shirtfront open to reveal the dark Huli jing fox, trefoil knot, butterflies, and more surfacing across his chest and stomach. He was certain he felt the tingling of Asian script appearing on his bald scalp.

The men around the room slowly lowered their weapons even though Durand walked right up to Vegas—looming over the small man.

Vegas looked suddenly terrified.

Durand's dark eyes bored holes into the man. "I am your 'partner,' am I?"

Vegas studied the tattoos still appearing before him. They were clearly marks he knew. He dropped to his knees, bowing his head, hands peaked before him. "Master Wyckes. Please forgive. You change shape like the clouds in the sky. I did not recognize you." Vegas motioned frantically to the others.

The men around the room holstered their weapons and bowed deeply, offering wais. At a hissed command, even the child soldiers lowered their weapons and bowed.

Durand stared at the bowed heads but spoke to Vegas: "You're going to do something for me . . ."

Chapter 27

Silently hovering behind an air-duct louver, a tiny drone transmitted grainy video and scratchy audio of child soldiers and "Vegas" Tang Chalpat bowing before Marcus Wyckes—the burly, tattooed leader of the Huli jing.

A kilometer away Detective Inspector Aiyana Marcotte recognized the diminutive Bryan Frey standing at Wyckes's side. She sat in a surveillance truck with Royal Thai Police General Prem Syriyanond, commander of Region Two, Chonburi, Pattaya City—a special self-governing municipal area focused on expats and tourists. An AR conference line was also open to the Royal Thai Metropolitan Police Special Investigations Unit in Bangkok, and in attendance were the head of Thailand's Arintharat 26 anti-terror unit, as well as the subinspector of Thailand's Interpol National Central Bureau Foreign Affairs Division One. It had taken half a career of bridge building to get this much political clout in this van, and Marcotte suspected there were as many unseen motives and agendas here as people in attendance. But here they were, and the Thai political machine was finally focused on her target: Marcus Wyckes and his Huli jing. For her reasons or theirs, she did not care. She only cared that their support for Interpol's case would last. Certainly the Huli jing had spread enough money around Thailand to muddy the already silted political waters.

Marcotte exchanged weary looks with Sergeant Michael Yi Ji-chang; they'd both been working phones for the past twenty-four hours to arrange this raid. Yi sat among several surveillance technical officers who controlled the equipment in the van.

The Thai police command studied the surveillance video beamed from the drone.

Marcotte recognized the drone type from its feed and movements—a tiny CICADA model. The overly cute acronym stood for Close-In Covert Autonomous Disposable Aircraft, and the little devices had pro-liferated around the world in recent years, used in everything from police work to tabloid journalism. You could find them washing up on beaches in areas where espionage and adultery took place, or wherever celebrities were found. There were probably more CICADAs than tuna floating in the South China Sea these days.

Marcotte studied the grainy imagery closely and decided to push for action. "Any questions, General Prem?"

He spoke English with a British accent. "No. I have seen more than enough."

Thus far the video evidence from the CICADAS was shocking—even before it revealed the presence of Marcus Wyckes. Dozens of the tiny devices had been set loose to map the air ducts of the subterranean embryo lab. The police version of the firmware was designed for this sort of thing, and they left some of their number behind as relay stations to ensure their transmitters/receivers could daisy-chain their way to the surface. The video they provided was furrowing the general's brow deeper every moment.

Live genedited children as floor models, complete with a high-production-value fashion show. That was a new one. Usually the cartels just had CGI mockups. Vegas had apparently spent years *growing* sample children—for which the Luk Krung would pay dearly under international law. But more importantly, the Luk Krung appeared to be controlled by the Huli jing.

Marcotte closely observed the revulsion on the face of the police general in charge of Thailand Police Region Two as he watched through LFP glasses; the grainy image of Marcus Wyckes loomed over the kneeling Mr. Vegas—the underboss pleading for forgiveness. Software was analyzing the tattoos on Wyckes's bald head.

Yi looked up. "Positive ID on Wyckes, all right."

Marcotte would have Wyckes. But the more surveillance video she

saw, the more she wanted this place shut down as well—and those children rescued and rehabilitated to the greatest extent possible. The computer models for their genetic edits destroyed. If Wyckes managed to get
himself killed in the meantime, that was no great loss to humanity. But
this raid needed to go down. And it needed to go down *now*.

She turned to General Prem. "Will you command Arintharat 26 to
go in, General?" Marcotte wasn't a fool. She knew there'd been payoffs
made to the police at many levels—but she'd arranged enough national
political power to be present on this operation that she thought there was
a chance no one would weasel out of taking action, lest the optics hurt
their careers—and their international reputations. Marcotte also knew
General Prem had grandchildren—Yi had provided her with that tidbit,
which he'd gleaned from one of the general's assistants in casual conversation. Marcotte was ready to bring up those grandchildren if necessary
to push the man to action.

But it turned out to be unnecessary.

The thin, balding, and gray-haired commander shook his head in
disgust. "*Farang*. They come to our country to commit their sins. They
think their money buys everything."

"Will you order the special tactics team to go in, General?"

General Prem turned to her with an intense gaze—but spoke to his
second in command, a burly Thai police lieutenant with a dour
demeanor. "Launch the raid. I want *everyone* arrested. Do not let the
Provincial Police within a kilometer of the target. We will make exam-
ples of these people. I want only vetted men on this raid."

"Yes, sir."

"And, Lieutenant . . ."

The officer turned.

"Cordon off a two-block radius. No vehicle traffic comes in or goes
out of the area. Pedestrians are to be stopped, identified, and searched.
Suspicious individuals detained. I want this entire rat's nest eliminated,
and none to escape justice. Do you understand me? *None*."

"I understand perfectly, sir." The lieutenant started issuing orders via
radio.

The other commanders and political liaisons began relaying this decision across the police and Interpol hierarchy.

Marcotte unclenched just slightly. Justice would be done today. Too many eyes. Too many lines crossed. For once, things were going her way.

She stared grimly as the grainy drone video continued. Marcus Wyckes's image wavered from the tiny camera's receptor. It might be the last time she saw him alive. But as long as his body could be retrieved, her mission here would be a success. And the world would be a safer place. It might even mean the beginning of the end for the Huli jing.

She turned to Yi. His eyes bored into the surveillance image of Wyckes. "Sergeant, I'll be going in after the site is secured to put eyes on Wyckes. Notify Singapore police; they'll want to prepare extradition papers in case he survives. And when the raid goes down, I want you in here as my eyes and ears."

"Will do, Inspector."

Marcotte exited the command truck.

Chapter 28

Kenneth Durand stared down at Mr. Vegas. "Get up."

Vegas meekly rose from his kneeling position. He waved the security men away. "Get out of here!" He looked up at the catwalks above. "You! Get to your posts."

Most of the men started filing out. As did the child soldiers, marching smartly.

Suddenly a familiar child's voice echoed from a steel catwalk above them. "Vegas!"

Everyone looked up to see Kimberly, the precocious six-year-old girl who emceed the fashion show. She still wore her small sequined gown with a tiara, but she looked annoyed as she pushed past exiting security men on the catwalk above. She frowned. "What have you done now?"

Vegas threw up his hands. "I had business."

She marched down a metal staircase to join them. "I told you I had something important to discuss. The next thing I know, you've disappeared to do something stupid."

"Daughter, we have guests."

"I know that." Kimberly somberly approached Durand and bowed. "*Sawasdee ka*, Khun Marcus."

Bryan Frey stared back and forth between Durand, Vegas, and the little girl—clearly knocked off balance by the sudden turn of events.

Vegas looked aghast. "Kimberly, you *knew* this was Khun Marcus?"

"I recognized him from the stage. What sort of fools are running reception? His face is all over the news. Your people are not doing their jobs." Kimberly again turned to face Durand. "Our apologies, Khun Marcus. How may the Luk Krung serve the fox with nine tails?'

Durand narrowed his eyes at the little girl—whose opinion seemed to be held in high regard here.

Frey looked to Durand quizzically.

Durand felt his tattoos almost pulsating. His anger was not ebbing. "The authorities are pursuing me. I must change form before proceeding."

Kimberly's eyes grew wide. "You will be changing form here?"

"Your people will assist me."

Vegas wai'd deeply once more. "Khun Marcus, you honor us. I was told the change agent would not be permitted outside of Naypyidaw. To use it here—"

Naypyidaw. Durand committed the name to memory. He pressed. "We have a police informant among the Huli jing. They betrayed me, and I will find them."

Vegas and Kimberly looked concerned.

"I assure you, there is no police informant here, Master."

"That may be." Durand leaned toward Vegas. "But my right hand is close by and waiting. If I'm betrayed here, there will be no mercy."

Vegas blanched. "Otto is here? In Pattaya City?"

Kimberly's face scrunched up, and she actually began to resemble a little girl. To Durand's horror, tears began to flow down her face. He felt his tattoos start to waver.

Kimberly looked up at Vegas with actual fear. "The Mirror Man isn't coming, Papa, is he?"

Vegas moved over and hugged her close, patting her tiara. "There, there, daughter. Otto has no reason to come here. As Master Wyckes said, Otto is only looking for a police informant." Vegas looked up at Durand. "And there is no police informant here. On my life. We are not fools."

Durand also took note of the name of Wyckes's right-hand man: *Otto.* It was obvious the man was greatly feared. There was value in that.

Frey had started showing signs of intellectual life again—coming out of his paralysis at the complete reversal of his fortunes. He observed the crying girl with interest. "You call Otto the Mirror Man?"

She sniffled and buried her face in Vegas's brocade jacket.

"You have not yet met Otto?"

Frey spoke carefully. "No. I just met . . . 'Master' Wyckes . . . a few days ago."

Durand noticed his tattoos were beginning to fade now at the little girl's tears. He moved Frey bodily aside and spoke to Vegas. "We don't have time for this. I need your technicians to reverse engineer the change agent. There should still be traces of it in my blood."

Vegas and Kimberly exchanged startled looks. She looked up and wiped away her tears.

Vegas asked, "Reverse engineer? Khun Marcus, do you not have the change agent with you?"

"Not here. And because there's a traitor among the Huli jing, communications are suspect." He pointed. "You will keep silent about my arrival."

"Of course. You have our word."

"I brought a genomic sequence I want to transform into. Dr. Frey here will work with you using my blood sample to search for traces of the change agent. And we'll take it from there."

Frey nodded weakly at first—and then more assertively to the others. "Just show me to your labs."

Kimberly and Vegas looked doubtfully at each other.

"We will happily do as you ask, Khun Marcus, but—"

A klaxon and strobing lights suddenly went off.

Frey glanced around. "What the hell is that?"

Someone shouted, *"Tamruat!"*

Vegas blanched. "A police raid? But they have been paid . . . They have all been paid!" He manipulated unseen virtual objects in his LFP glasses, apparently checking surveillance camera feeds. "Arintharat antiterror teams . . . Why are—?" He gasped, then turned in fear toward Durand.

Durand was momentarily shocked, but recovered quickly enough to glare at Vegas. "If you've betrayed me—"

"No, no, Master! It was not me. I swear it. We only just now learned of your presence. And we will get you out safely! This will prove our loyalty. I swear to you! I have a private escape route. Follow me!" With that, Vegas grabbed Kimberly's hand and ran toward the sliding industrial door.

Durand and Frey exchanged confused and worried looks.

Frey pointed. "We need to go. Apparently someone somewhere recognized you."

Durand and Frey followed Vegas out the door and down a side corridor.

Vegas waved frantically as the alarms continued. "Hurry! This way!" He brought them through a storeroom abutting a commercial kitchen. They could hear panicked screams of clients fleeing the ballroom.

Pops of gunfire or perhaps doors being breached.

Durand shouted at Vegas, "Tell your men not to shoot at the police. Tell them to surrender."

"Surrender? But, Khun Marcus, the police must be delayed. We need time to escape! Evidence must be cleared from memory. Genetic material destroyed."

"The quicker the police take control of this lab, the sooner they'll be focused on gathering evidence and not chasing me. The only priority is for *me* to escape. This facility means nothing."

"But, Khun—"

Durand silenced him with a glare.

Vegas nodded uncertainly. "I cannot guarantee my men will surrender. The jail time alone—"

"Tell them the Huli jing will look after those who obey. But only those who obey."

Vegas struggled but finally started shouting commands in Thai into his LFP comm link.

Frey whispered, "What on earth are you doing? We need to escape."

Durand hissed, "This place needs to be shut down, and I don't want police officers or civilians to die in the process."

Up ahead, Kimberly had stopped at a blank wall in a corner. She made several somatic gestures to a surveillance camera, and a hidden door opened.

Vegas shouted, "This way!"

Durand and Frey followed.

Otto walked through double glass doors into the refined lobby of the Luk Krung clinic. His tactical police escort stood nervously to either side— local officers in balaclavas, helmets, and black body armor bearing yellow "Police" labels in English. Their weapons at the ready.

Corrupted men all—too tempted over the years by the unlimited money the Huli jing could offer. Now regretting, Otto knew, their years of payoffs; they could not now, even on a day like today, refuse their true masters. Too much evidence could be used against them.

The corporal on Otto's left swore under his breath as he looked ahead to see a dozen heavily armed Arintharat anti-terror teams moving in formation down the corridors of the lab, long guns out, tactical lights on, clearing rooms and shouting at unseen people to get on the ground.

The corporal turned toward Otto, but soon looked away—clearly spooked by the young man's disturbing aura. "We should not be here, sir. Our orders are to stay clear of this lab."

Otto shook his head slowly as he straightened his pale green silk tie in a nearby mirror.

"Sir, they will ask me who you are. They'll analyze surveillance video. We will be found out. All of us arrested." He paused. "Sir, please. Listen to me. I am on your side."

Otto noticed a bronze plaque indicating a restroom. The door was wedged open; chalk marks on the wall showed it had been cleared by earlier teams. "Before we go, I need to use the restroom."

"Are you kidding?" The corporal sighed in frustration and motioned for his two even more skittish companions to follow.

"Is he really using the bathroom?"

The other whispered, "We need to leave . . ."

Otto strolled calmly toward the restroom. "Come with me."

They reluctantly followed. The sounds of doors being broken in and screams echoed in the corridors farther on.

The restroom was nicely appointed—tasteful, muted stone and wood tones. A small water feature with water lilies occupied one corner. Otto stepped in front of a large mirror while his tactical escort stood nervously nearby, their radios squawking.

Otto took a comb from a tray on the counter and began to carefully comb his slicked-back hair.

"Sir, this is not the time . . ."

"I'm the only one who needs to be concerned about the time, Corporal."

Otto removed a silver flask from his jacket pocket and placed it reverently on the stone countertop. He took a deep breath and then opened the unusually complex cap—unlocking its several different seals. He then poured out a clear liquid onto his hands and slicked the liquid into his hair, combing it in fastidiously.

There were gunshots in the distance.

"Sir, please!"

"Unlike apaxi variants, lioxol is not a contact biotoxin—but an aerosol. Extremely powerful, and even more so as it evaporates." Otto then rubbed some of the liquid on his neck and then again onto his hands.

Confused, the corporal stepped forward, clearly having had enough. "Sir! We must—"

He never finished the sentence. Instead he collapsed face forward, hitting the counter hard and rolling off onto the floor. The other two officers rushed to help him, but they themselves staggered—and then collapsed. One of them had a momentary seizure, then went largely still, his booted foot spasming as his last breath left him.

Otto gazed at his own reflection in the mirror as he placed wireless earphones in each ear. He turned up the volume on Bach's glorious Cantata BWV 19 and conducted the soaring arias with his hands. He'd only recently learned of it, and it filled him with joy. What humans were sometimes capable of always amazed him.

Otto left the restroom and moved deeper into the Luk Krung clinic. He strode down the corridor with his hands held open and outward in surrender.

A balaclava-wearing tactical officer guarding a line of zip-tied prisoners glanced up to see Otto approaching. The prisoners sat, weeping—

middle-aged Brits, Germans, Chinese, French—well-heeled and well-dressed clients from around the globe.

The officer raised his weapon at Otto and shouted, "You! Down on the ground! Now! Down on the ground!"

At least that's what Otto guessed the man said. He couldn't hear him over the music. But Otto knew the drill. He complied immediately—hands still raised.

"Hands on the back of your head!"

Otto did so.

Another tactical officer joined the first, and they rushed toward him, a thicket of zip ties ready on their utility belts. One grabbed Otto's wrist with his gloved hand.

But a moment later the officer staggered, then collapsed.

Otto's hand was suddenly released. Almost simultaneously the officer in front of Otto crumpled, twitching.

Otto rose to his feet again—then stared at the shocked and zip-tied tourists. They started babbling at him in their native languages. Otto could see their mouths moving—some angry, others terrified. But Otto could not hear them. All he could hear were the blissful strains of the cantata.

Otto walked alongside the dozens of zip-tied lab clients, running his fingers through their hair and meeting their confused expressions. An antisavior. He could feel their lives evaporating beneath his fingertips. He was convinced he could feel it.

He walked onward, the line of dead growing behind him, leaning on one another, extending down the corridor.

Otto walked on, conducting a soaring chorus.

He turned a corner and almost immediately came upon a large breaching team with heavily armed tactical police with bulletproof shields, body armor, ballistic helmets—blinding light stabbing out from their guns. They led a dozen suited and zip-tied, tattooed Luk Krung gang members back toward the lobby.

The moment the police spotted Otto, lights and guns focused on him. He raised his hands high. He couldn't hear their voices over the music, but behind their black balaclavas, he could see their jaws moving. Shouting at him.

Otto complied with commands he knew well. He knelt in the hall. Placed his hands on the back of his head as the team moved over and around him—grabbing his hands roughly. They soon surrounded him.

And then he felt them slipping away. First one fell. Then five, then ten more, staggering as the long guns dropped from their hands. The last one hit the wall and slid down into a crumpled heap.

Only a few molecules of lioxol in the olfactory channel. That was all it took. Death followed moments later as the central nervous system shut down.

Otto calmly stood and approached a dozen handcuffed and kneeling Luk Krung members. Their faces were portraits of terror as he approached. They knew who Otto was. Some among the doomed men wept, praying to the spirits of their ancestors in Thai.

As Otto moved through them, continuing down the hall, he rubbed their bald, tattooed scalps.

He did not wait to see the bodies drop.

There would be no witnesses. No living evidence. No outward sign of the outrages here. Only the dead.

And Marcus Wyckes would be among them, putting to rest, once and for all, the search for the leader of the Huli jing.

Otto continued down the corridor—toward the concealed rooms that he knew Vegas kept.

Durand and Frey followed Kimberly and Vegas down a narrow utility corridor lined with power and HVAC conduits.

Vegas glanced back, urging speed with a flurry of his hands. "You and I will depart, Khun Marcus, while Dr. Frey and Kimberly remain behind."

Frey shouted, "The hell I will!"

"There is only so much room. You will see!"

Kimberly shouted, "You promised me!"

"Kimberly, you are a six-year-old child. They will not punish you. You can pretend to be a simpleton."

She punched him in the ribs ineffectually. "I think that might prove easier for you."

Vegas glanced back at Durand. "The girl will be sent to a foster home. We'll have her back immediately."

Durand stared darkly. "Dr. Frey is going with me. You stay behind."

Vegas looked horrified. "But I can be of great help to you, Khun Marcus! I can do so much to assist you if I am not captured by the police."

They reached the base of a metal staircase. Durand vaulted up the steps, passing Vegas and emerging in a small warehouse with a painted concrete floor.

A small helicopter sat in the middle of the room on a marked helipad—though there was no obvious exit. The chopper was made of a white chitinous material—probably a grown shell—with a bulbous tinted windshield. Outboard on each corner of the craft were dual counterfacing propellers, about a meter in diameter—eight in all.

Frey moved alongside Durand with Kimberly and Vegas. Frey nodded to himself. "I'll be damned. An Ehang."

Vegas nervously motioned to it. "Very complex. You'll need an experienced hand to get it working."

Kimberly pouted and folded her arms. "He's lying. It's autonomous. Programmed for a preplanned escape route."

"Damn you, child!"

Durand had seen vehicles like these flitting over Singapore in small numbers—a commutation option for the well-off. As he approached, the interior lit up, followed by the passenger doors opening.

A synthetic voice spoke: *"Please enter and fasten your safety belts."*

Frey looked inside. "I think we can manage that, Tang."

Sirens could be heard through the nearby corrugated metal walls.

Vegas shouted hopefully, "We need to leave, Khun Marcus!"

Frey nodded. "Yes. And *we* will."

Durand walked around to the far side of the Ehang. "Where will it take us?"

Vegas's eyes lit up. "A place only I know. I can—"

"Can I use it to get back to my headquarters?"

"In Myanmar! Oh, no, Khun Marcus. Naypyidaw is much too far—and the waypoints and exchange sites are already programmed."

"Exchange sites?"

"The escape all preplanned. You really should take me with you. Dr. Frey is—"

"Dr. Frey has the knowledge I need." Durand glanced up at the ceiling. It wasn't much over ten meters. He entered the chopper anyway.

Frey climbed in on the other side and began strapping himself in.

"Can this thing really maneuver in here?"

Frey shrugged. "It got in here somehow." He noticed a leather satchel secured between the seats and unzipped it. Inside were thick wads of Thai baht. "Vegas's go-bag, apparently. He really did think of everything."

Just then the synthetic voice returned, saying pleasantly, "*Stay clear of the doors. Stay clear of the doors. Launch sequence commencing . . .*"

Vegas shouted over a whining sound that kept increasing, "Please, Master! Take me with you!"

Kimberly stood nearby and rolled her eyes dramatically.

Durand shouted, "Don't worry, you'll be taken care of!"

A moment later the doors eased shut, and conditioned air filled the cabin.

Frey looked around at the cultured leather seats. "This is rather nice."

The electric motors whirred to life, and an integral glim displayed AR gauges and maps into their retinas—none with any apparent inputs. They were merely passengers.

Then the twin quad-mounted rotors spooled up, a roar and a wind building in the hangar.

The AI voice said calmly, "*Prepare for combat takeoff.*"

"What's a combat—?"

Frey didn't get a chance to finish his sentence. The Ehang lifted off the floor and nosed downward all in one fluid motion—and started hurtling toward the corrugated metal wall.

"Shit!"

The wall slid aside in two sections as if on explosive bolts, and the autonomous chopper roared into the sunlight—and then *down*.

Frey screamed, and Durand felt his stomach drop as they hurtled toward a street choked with emergency vehicles and flashing police lights. Then it pulled up, rotated violently, and roared down the narrow city street at an angle—just centimeters away from a tangle of utility lines.

Frey pressed his arms against the cabin wall. "Jesus H. Fucking Christ!"

The chopper lurched upward, soared through an open atrium between hotel towers as tourists ran screaming for cover. The chopper then streaked out over a decorative pond, then down over a rail line, emerging beneath power lines, and then up and out across a vast container yard, dodging between construction cranes.

"No, no, no, no, no . . ."

Durand shoved back against Frey's clawing hands. "Would you stop grabbing at me?"

G-forces again slammed Durand and Frey into their seat backs as the machine kept accelerating, dodging around buildings, under power pylons, and around cranes.

"I'm going to be sick . . ."

"Don't you dare, Bryan." Durand gritted his teeth against the g-forces.

A glance to his left, and he noticed a lawn-mower-sized police drone on their tail as the Ehang arced in a steep turn. The police drone's camera array gleamed in the sunlight. "Police drone!"

Frey sucked in a breath, still pressing with all his might against the cabin wall. "What the hell do you expect me to do about it? I'm busy trying not to shit myself!"

They began curving out across the harbor front at what seemed like a meter above the water—literally dodging between pleasure boats and floating restaurants. Tourists dove into the water as the chopper roared toward them.

"Oh god!"

They turned sideways, zipping between the faux funnels of an imitation steamboat-themed restaurant.

They then rocketed between autonomous container ships, under rope lines, and finally in a curving trajectory that crushed Durand back into his seat, air expelled unwillingly from his lungs.

Frey shouted, "I should have let Vegas go with you!"

Vegas stood in the hangar, watching the open doors and the police drones hovering beyond. Humid heat began to invade the room. He could hear sirens and shouting voices on the street below.

Kimberly poked him in the ribs. "Were you really going to leave me behind?"

Vegas sighed. "I would never leave you behind, daughter. At least not for long. You are my treasure."

But then Vegas felt a disturbing sensation—as though a bad spirit had come near. He turned toward Kimberly.

Tears were running down her cheeks, and her mouth stuttered. She visibly trembled.

Despite his fear, Vegas moved to hold her. "What is it, child? What's wrong?"

She sucked for air amid terrified sobs. "The Mirror Man is here."

Vegas turned to see a face he did not recognize rise slowly up the staircase behind them. Each step on the metal staircase echoed. Vegas's heart began to thunder in his chest. Even though Vegas knew what Otto was, he still felt a primal dread that went beyond reason. Some things humans have evolved to fear.

Vegas held Kimberly close, her sobs now uncontrollable. "We helped the Master escape, Otto. He is safely on his way back to Myanmar. I gave him my own chopper."

Otto stood still five meters away—the humid breeze blew in past Vegas from the open hangar doors. The man's slick hair did not move. Neither did his grim expression change. "Then he is gone."

Vegas nodded. "Khun Marcus is gone. Yes. He is gone home."

Otto did not respond immediately.

"He said we would be taken care of. I cannot go to jail. My daughter needs to be cared for."

"You will not go to jail. None of you will."

Otto started walking toward them. Vegas noticed what looked like beads of sweat over Otto's face—though he had only been in the tropical air for a few moments.

"Wait! Otto, you know that we would never betray the Huli jing. We are loyal servants. We will tell the police nothing!"

"You won't have the chance."

"No, please!" Vegas found himself hoping for the police—for the Arintharat 26 to come rushing up the staircase and gun down the otherworldly Otto.

But that did not happen.

Kimberly trembled, gripping Vegas's arm, sobbing, "I'm afraid! I don't want to die!"

Otto stood next to them. "Then you are one of the lucky ones." He ran his fingers through her hair. "Most who I visit beg for death."

Vegas and Kimberly collapsed onto each other in the middle of the concrete floor. Their dead eyes stared at the ceiling.

Lingering just a moment, Otto looked out the open hangar doors, nodded to himself, and descended the stairs again.

Frey gripped his armrests and stared in terror as the Ehang chopper roared between three-story strip malls, under flyways. Each time the chopper seemed a split second away from crashing headlong into a wall or colliding with light poles or wireless towers, it turned away with stomach-churning suddenness.

To their relief, the Ehang finally raced out across the countryside, past temples, chedis, stupas, and long rectangular rice paddies. Only here did the chopper finally relax its crazy zigzagging flight path and instead soar in a beeline across the fields, barely a meter above the tips of the rice stalks waving in the wind.

Durand looked around them through the bulbous, tinted canopy. An AR display also provided a virtual rearview mirror. "Looks like we lost the police drones."

Frey still gripped the armrests. "I don't think even they could keep up with this thing." He nodded toward the windshield. "Any lower and we'll be harvesting this goddamned rice."

They whizzed past farmers, who shook their fists and shouted.

Frey's face dropped as he turned forward again. "Oh god, no . . ."

A raised berm between rice fields approached. Numerous scooters traversed its length—but the Ehang roared toward it at three hundred kilometers per hour.

"No, no, no!"

The chopper streaked through the gap between scooters, and they raced out over the fields beyond.

Frey closed his eyes. "Why the hell do I even look? It's only going to upset me."

Durand gazed at the rice paddies unfolding before them. It was going to be difficult for anything except fixed-wing aircraft to catch up to them now. And those would take a while to scramble.

The Ehang gained a bit of altitude and began to curve rightward.

Frey groaned. "What now?"

The chopper flared back, bleeding off speed with its rotor wash as it descended—then pitched forward to fly straight through the opening doors of a nondescript, corrugated metal warehouse.

The chopper rotated before setting itself down in a marked space alongside a second Ehang chopper—this one red with yellow stripes instead of clean white.

"Thank god . . ." Frey unbuckled his safety harness.

The doors to the second chopper opened—beckoning—and its electric motors began to spool up.

Their own chopper rotors whined down only slightly as the doors opened. A synthetic female voice said, *"Second vehicle waiting. Second vehicle waiting."*

Durand jumped out, shouting, "It's an exchange. Grab the go-bag and get moving!"

"Goddamnit . . ." Frey took the bag and practically fell out of the first chopper. He ran on unsteady feet toward the second.

"Looks like Vegas programmed vehicle changes into this journey." Durand got into the waiting aircraft.

Frey crawled in on the far side. "We don't even know where we're going!"

The doors closed.

"Anywhere's better than back there. And Vegas clearly seems to have planned for the worst."

The rotors whined up, and the new chopper lifted off the moment Frey fastened his safety harness. It nosed through the doors that opened on the far side of the warehouse.

Looking back, Durand could see their original chopper racing back the way they'd come, gaining altitude in an apparent effort to attract attention and lead away any pursuers.

The new chopper raced low across the rice paddies, heading north, and away from Pattaya City.

Chapter 29

Word came down, and Aiyana Marcotte followed a second wave of Thai police into the now secured Luk Krung clinic facility. She wore a tactical vest with the word "Interpol" stamped across the front and back in large white letters. Her group included evidence technicians, uniformed Royal Thai Police officers, a couple of media camera teams, and a high-ranking Thai police official in formal attire. They entered through the parking garage, where the glass doors of the clinic led into a tastefully decorated lobby.

Marcotte spoke to Sergeant Michael Yi Ji-chang through her LFP phone link. "They're finally letting us in with the evidence teams. Any word on Wyckes?"

"*Hang on . . . Something's up, Inspector. The commanders are shouting at each other in Thai now . . .*" The sound of men shouting at one another was audible in the background. "*There's been some sort of problem. A big one from the sound of it.*"

A shout went up near Marcotte. She walked forward to see a police official shouting at camera crews, who were filming dozens of human bodies splayed across the corridor—some of them handcuffed European and Chinese civilians and others black-clad Thai tactical police. Their dead eyes stared. More shouting as the officials pushed the camera crews back.

"Holy hell . . ."

There were at least three dozen bodies in the main corridor, but none of them had visible injuries. There was no blood.

"What the . . . ?"

"*What are you seeing?*"

"Sergeant, there are dead people everywhere in the corridors—civilians and police. What the hell's going on?"

"*I don't know, but I think the command center just discovered it.*"

"Just discovered it? How the hell did they not notice? This place isn't secured."

Police teams moved forward with handguns raised, and as soon as they came around the corner, they moved back, alarmed. "More dead! Dead everywhere!"

"I need information, Sergeant."

There was more shouting in the background of Yi's phone.

Close to Marcotte a police official lifted his head from a radio and shouted, "Poison gas! It's poison gas!"

The politicians, media, and police panicked equally, stampeding back toward the exit.

Marcotte followed. "Someone's saying there's poison gas in the lab. Is that true?"

"*I just got the word. This is bad.*"

Marcotte moved out through the parking garage. "Information, Sergeant. Now."

"*They're reviewing CICADA footage. They've got people down all over, Inspector. It's looking like someone released poison gas inside the lab. There are civilians dead. Maybe a lot of them.*"

She walked up the concrete ramp with dozens of other police—most of whom were pushing away media cameras in a very threatening way. Others clutched handkerchiefs to their faces in the vain hope this would somehow stop nerve gas.

"From what I saw in there, it would have to be a nerve toxin."

"*I'm looking over their shoulders at surveillance video right now. There's a guy walking around with no gas mask or anything. People are just dropping dead as he passes by them. He's dressed like the game show host from hell.*"

"He's not spraying anything on them?"

"No. He just walks within a few meters, and they drop."

"That sort of toxicity level—just a breath or two—how could he be immune? That's impossible."

"Well, I'm looking right at it."

"Where is this guy now?"

"They're reviewing footage." A pause. "Oh my god. Inspector, it looks like we've got mass casualties on our hands."

Marcotte felt like punching a wall. *Wyckes.*

Someone else was shouting in the background of Yi's phone now. "The political shit has really hit the fan here. I'm being shoved out of the command truck." Yi shouted to someone, "We weren't the ones who planned this!"

"Goddamnit. Yi. Yi!"

"Yeah."

"What's the status of the breaching teams? What about the civilians?"

"They're bringing hazmat teams in. Robots. But they're pulling everyone out for now. Distributing MOPP gear."

"There are scores of civilians in that lab. Children. The Luk Krung could be using this opportunity to incinerate evidence. And what about Wyckes? Has anyone seen Wyckes? He's the one behind all this."

"An autonomous chopper took off from one of the nearby buildings a couple minutes ago. Looks like it's been modded. It's flying below radar— literally at treetop level all over the city."

She pinched the bridge of her nose in frustration. "How the hell did the recon teams miss a *helicopter* on the roof? That's the first thing they should have secured."

"Apparently it came out of some hidden hangar. They have no idea who was in it. Police drones are in pursuit."

"Goddamnit! Find out if anyone has Wyckes. And get me the status of that chopper pursuit."

"Will do."

Marcotte moved out of the parking garage and into the open air. Reporters were swarming the police now, with additional police coming in to push the reporters back. Police sedans whooping their sirens came up to collect the officials. More police formed a blockade at the mouth of the parking garage, shouting for reporters to stay back.

A police officer walked past distributing black S10 gas masks. He pushed one into Marcotte's hands, shouting, "Must wear. Orders."

Marcotte grabbed the mask and looked at the gathering media circus. As soon as they saw the gas masks, they all dove for them, trying to be the first to do a live remote masked up.

The media. Dozens of dead civilians and police was an unmitigated disaster to the task force. Not even she would have guessed that Wyckes would be evil enough to release poison gas just to cover his escape.

Marcotte felt a sinking feeling. Had she caused this? Were people dead because of her?

She glanced up as she heard a shout behind her. Three Thai motorcycle police officers manning the roadblock at the end of the street aimed their pistols at a well-dressed man who had just emerged from a stairwell door to the parking garage. Marcotte perked up since the man had to have come from the Luk Krung clinic. There had been tactical units guarding the stairwell—but no longer, apparently.

She moved toward the scene as the motorcycle cops shouted in Thai.

The man looked to be an Asian businessman—Mongolian perhaps. He wore a tailored pin-striped suit, his jacket splayed open as he raised his hands. He calmly obeyed orders to kneel, then put his hands on his head as the officers moved in for the arrest.

Suddenly the lead officer collapsed facedown onto the pavement, alongside the suspect. The other two staggered. One dropped his gun. And then they both collapsed as well.

The man looked over to Marcotte as he calmly got to his feet.

A wave of adrenaline spread through Marcotte. She barked into her LFP link, "Sergeant! He's here!"

"Who is? Wyckes?"

She turned to the cluster of reporters and shouted, "Gas masks on!" Reporters already puzzling over their masks ran screaming. Cops who hadn't gotten them yet fled as well.

Marcotte watched the suited man climb onto a parked electric motorcycle. He calmly pulled a civilian helmet on.

She ran toward him, reaching by reflex for the small of her back and the gun that wasn't there. *Damnit.*

Instead, she removed her LFP glasses in order to slip on the S10 gas mask and immediately lost her link to Yi. She stuffed the LFP glasses into a pocket in her tactical vest and cinched the gas mask straps. By the time she reached the scene of the dead officers, the suspect was racing away down the street.

Marcotte could clearly see one officer's dead eyes staring skyward. She ran for one of the three nearby police motorcycles. It, too, was an electric bike—which was good. They'd retired gasoline bikes before she did her two years in the LAPD. This one looked somewhat similar to her old patrol unit. It had an old HK416 assault rifle locked into a rack on the rear strut.

She raised her LFP glasses to her mask and shouted muffled words to Yi. "Call General Prem! Get him to follow me! Tell him I'm in pursuit of the poison gas suspect!"

"What? I didn't copy that, Inspector. Please—"

She stowed the LFP glasses again and thumbed the bike's safety and power. With that Marcotte screeched forward, rapidly accelerating after the suited man.

She weaved through traffic and turned on her lights and siren. Marcotte looked for the police radio link, but then realized it was in the officers' helmets—back where they had fallen. Their pistols were back there, too.

Stop screwing up, baby.

Her foster mother's voice came to her at times like these. The woman was a tough cop, and she didn't care for excuses.

Keep your shit together.

Marcotte tried to take deep breaths to calm herself and focus her vision inside the suffocating mask. She was a skilled rider, but she'd never performed a high-speed pursuit in MOPP gear. Her lenses were partly clouding up in the stifling humidity.

Marcotte hugged the electric bike close and accelerated past confused scooter drivers and tourists stuck in dense traffic caused by the police blockade. They craned their necks to look after the black-skinned woman in an Interpol flak jacket and gas mask racing between cars on a Thai police motorcycle, its sirens whooping and warbling.

Focusing through the cloudy lenses of the mask, Marcotte could see the man's bike a couple hundred meters ahead. He glanced back and clearly saw her. He slipped between cars, but she was gaining. Nobody was dropping dead around him as he passed by. Maybe his poison had been used up. Or perhaps it was because he was traveling fast.

You can't stop him here, baby.

Marcotte nodded. And her foster mother would have been right. She had to get the suspect away from these crowded streets. If she collared him in the middle of all these people, he could unleash a toxin. A crowd would gather. She had to hang back.

Did she risk taking off the mask? Asking for backup? If so, now was the time to risk exposure.

Marcotte pulled the mask up and grabbed for her LFP glasses and slipped them on momentarily. Their lenses immediately started translating Thai road signs for her, but she shouted into her open link to Yi. "Sergeant!"

"*Inspector, what the hell's going on? Why are you moving away from the lab?*"

"I'm pursuing the suspect in the gas attack."

"*How do you know what he looks like?*"

"Because I just saw him kill three motorcycle cops in the street. He must have some sort of airborne nerve agent. He's racing through the city on a motorcycle. I'm following."

"*For god's sake, don't catch him.*"

"I've got a gas mask. I have to put it back on. And soon."

"*Inspector, just hang back. Hold on . . .*" She heard Yi shouting to someone.

Marcotte was gaining on the man. He glanced back at her again, then ducked along gutters and sidewalks as necessary to maintain speed.

But she was still gaining.

"*Inspector, police command says only to follow him. Right now all their drones are pursuing the escaped chopper. But if this guy's got a nerve agent on him, they need him out of populated areas above all else."*

"Right."

"Just hang back and follow. Stay away from him."

"Call you when I can." Marcotte hung up. She pulled down the gas mask and cinched the straps as best she could with one hand.

The suspect glanced back at her again, then suddenly turned right down a soi, one of the narrow side streets common throughout the city.

She approached the turn and leaned into it, heading down a lane lined with parked cars, hanging laundry, and garbage bins. The suspect was rocketing down the soi far ahead—quickly disappearing around a bend. Marcotte accelerated as people poked their heads out of windows and over balconies to see her race past, sirens blaring. Her powerful electric bike whined down the lane.

She curved right, crossing a short bridge over a brown-water canal, and suddenly saw the suspect coming straight at her.

Marcotte slammed on her brakes, skidding to a stop. The man skidded to a stop a few meters away and stepped off the bike, letting it drop.

Marcotte did likewise, slipping off it as it slowed.

They stood in the lane, now just a few meters apart.

Her foster mother's voice in her mind. *You call that hanging back?*

Pigeons clustered on a power line nearby began to drop off the wire en masse, dead before they hit the pavement, or rolled off the railing into the canal below.

The nerve agent was clearly still potent.

The man removed his motorcycle helmet and tossed it aside as he walked slowly toward her. His suit was impressively tailored. He had a silk handkerchief tastefully folded in the breast pocket. His confidence unnerved her. He seemed unhurried.

Marcotte's rapid breathing was deafening inside the gas mask. She pointed and shouted in a muffled voice, "Down on the ground! Now!"

He did not comply.

His face was broad, skin pale, eyes narrow. His hair slicked back. He looked like a young Central Asian bureaucrat. This was the first high-level member of the Huli jing she'd ever seen alive.

But there was more to it than that.

The *wrongness* hit her like a riptide, rolling around her and nearly knocking her off her feet. Was it the nerve agent acting on her? She pulled at the gas mask straps, yanking them tighter.

The feeling didn't go away. There was something unnatural about the man standing before her. She'd never believed anything more strongly in her life.

"What the hell are you?"

He stared with unliving eyes. "I am the future."

He moved toward her.

She backed up. "Get down on the ground! You're under arrest!"

"Inspector Marcotte. I recognized you. You stand out here in Thailand."

She halted. He knew her name. This unnatural creature knew who she was.

Civilians peered from windows and doorways. Locals approached on the sidewalk.

Marcotte shouted through her gas mask. "Get back! Danger! Get back!" She waved like a lunatic.

The people ducked back into their flats or edged away, but stayed watching.

The man laughed. "You're on my list. You've saved me a trip." He extended his hand. "I'll have that gas mask."

Karate had long been Marcotte's passion—something her foster mother had introduced to her. A means of personal self-defense in a world where, at times, no help was coming. One thing she learned in childhood was to never be helpless again.

He moved in. She stepped aside and grabbed his wrist—delivering a series of rapid kicks to vulnerability points in his abdomen, side, and groin, grunting defiance with each hit.

But his touch sent a jolt of revulsion through her body. She felt her bladder release. The wetness spreading.

She ducked below another grab for her mask, then leaped up and gave a roundhouse kick to the side of his head that sent him reeling.

He slammed into the side railing of the bridge. Then quickly righted himself. Shaking his head and wiping away blood from his rapidly swelling lip.

"Get on the ground!" She felt urine running down her legs. Her heart hammering in her ears in terror. Her hands shaking.

You can take him. I know you can, baby.

He moved toward her. "You can hit me. But all I need is to lift your mask just once . . ."

She weaved around him.

"Look at you . . ." He pointed at her hands.

She could clearly see that her own hands were now glistening with poison.

"It only requires a few molecules in your olfactory channel."

Fear flowed through and around her.

"You are dead, Inspector Marcotte."

You can beat this son of a bitch, baby.

"And you are death to all those who come near you."

Her eyes narrowed. "You got that right, motherfucker . . ."

She lunged toward him, then ducked under his grasp, clearing his legs out from under him, and hammered the side of his head with her elbow as he tried to get up.

He rolled clear while she pursued him, kicking his ribs.

"I don't care if you are *Satan* himself—I will kick your goddamned ass!"

He rolled back to his feet, blood flowing down his nose. His right eye reddening.

He took a moment to assess her. Then he glanced aside. "Do you hear that?" He moved away from her.

She followed. She could hear children laughing. Lots of them.

"Do you hear them?"

A bolt of fear ran through Marcotte. She lowered her hands.

He ran now, down the lane, and she ran after him, struggling for breath in the gas mask after all the exertion. Running was suffocating her. She came around a house to see a schoolyard thirty or forty meters away. Dozens of Thai elementary school children in neat uniforms played in a fenced yard there.

The suited man wiped away blood from his nose and pointed. "Follow me, and I will run toward them. And through crowded places. I will slay hundreds."

She sucked for air. Taking off the mask meant instant death. She could see the toxin glistening on her hands. She looked up into the unnatural man's dead eyes and took a measure of pride that one of them was swelling. "Crawl back into hell—but I will find you one day."

The man laughed, then backed away from her, while she moved between him and the distant children. The thing righted his motorcycle, gathered his helmet, and with one last look at her accelerated away.

A friendly dog approached Marcotte, wagging his tail and barking beyond a chain-link fence.

"No!" Marcotte fled back toward the bridge, running along the lane, waving off curious onlookers. She felt her lungs burning as she sucked for more from the mask, but nonetheless sprinted the last few meters to jump off the bridge into the brown water of the canal.

Chapter 30

A jet-black Ehang autonomous chopper soared above the evening skyline of Bangkok. Other than its gold stripes, it looked identical to the previous four they'd ridden in a circuitous route all afternoon.

Seated next to Durand, Frey sighed and looked upon the city. "That's a sight I didn't think I'd see again. I've made a few enemies here."

"Is there anywhere you haven't made enemies?"

Durand gazed out the window. He'd never been to Bangkok, and the city looked beautiful as the sun set. From five hundred meters up the Chao Phraya River coiled through the midst of it like a metallic snake. The navigation lights of long-tail boats, barges, and the occasional fishing boat speckled its length.

Their chopper navigated between glittering hundred-story office and residential towers, passing by other autonomous time-share choppers, ferrying well-heeled passengers across town. Bangkok, too, had benefited from the Gene Revolution, and lots of business was being transacted here, as a gateway between China and the rest of South and Central Asia. Corruption was an issue. It was a place to do business if you couldn't do your business inside the Bubble.

And it was breathtakingly beautiful to fly over at night.

Before long, the Ehang descended toward a spire of mirrored glass— a residential tower overlooking the illuminated Bhumibol suspension bridge. A private helicopter pad came into view on a broad terrace near a swimming pool. The multistory residence appeared to take up the entire top of the building and was more opulent than anything Durand had ever seen up close.

The Ehang masterfully maneuvered past potted palms and alighted in the center of the helipad. The rotors immediately began to wind down, and as they did, the doors remained locked.

The synthetic voice said, *"Please wait."*

Normal safety rules were apparently being enforced again.

When the rotors had finally stopped, the chopper doors whirred open, and the voice said, *"Thank you for escaping with us. Please exit the aircraft."*

Durand grabbed the leather go-bag; then he and Frey stepped out, relieved to see no other chopper waiting for them. Frey spread out his arms at both the expansive nighttime view of the city and the river a hundred stories below. He then turned to encompass the three-story ter-raced penthouse behind them.

"Would you look at this place?"

Each floor was smaller than the one below, creating a series of large terraces. They currently stood on the middle one, overlooking an illumi-nated swimming pool and bar, while on their level were gardens and patio furniture—along with another bar. Above them looked to be bed-rooms. All of it was softly lit and designed with a modern art aesthetic: clean curves of polished cement and glass, along with a profusion of living things and trickling water. The plants had clearly been modified to grow into Thai cultural motifs—chedis and temples.

As they followed steps down from the helipad, the Ehang's doors closed and its rotors wound up again. They watched as the chopper took off into the evening sky, soon lost among dozens of other choppers flit-ting about the skyline.

Then it was relatively quiet again.

Durand dropped the go-bag onto a nearby patio table, while Frey approached a second impressive bar, done in the style of an ornate Bud-dhist stupa, in direct contrast to the modernity of the surrounding pent-house. Somehow the juxtaposition worked.

Frey's short frame disappeared around the bar, but his hands could be seen grabbing for several bottles. There was a rattle, and in a moment his upper body appeared behind the bar. He was obviously standing on something.

"I must say, the pay scale for evil is impressive."

Durand collapsed onto one of the cultured-wood patio chairs. "Don't even joke about that."

"Care for a drink?"

"I think I need one."

"I'll make you my specialty."

"Whatever. After today, I don't really care."

"Quite the day."

Durand looked above and around him. "We can't stay here. The police could arrive any minute."

"I'm not sure I agree with that assessment." There was a tinkle of glasses.

"How do you figure?"

"Well, this was Vegas's *safe* house—the operative word being *safe*. The place he would flee to if things went to shit. Which would likely mean it's owned through a series of shell corporations that have no ties to him. No doubt lots of bribes were paid to keep it off the books . . . This is Thailand, after all."

"What about the data trail for the choppers?"

"What trail? That bootlegger OS they were running seemed less than legal. And don't overrate Interpol's influence in Thailand. We'll be long gone before your colleagues dig up this place. No, I think we're safe here for the time being. Safer by far than parading around the streets of Bangkok."

Durand considered this and finally leaned back into the patio chair. "Fine. But we need to get to the capital of Myanmar somehow."

"Naypyidaw."

"Right. That's where Vegas said the change agent was. That must be the elite black market those rumors mentioned."

"Interesting city, Naypyidaw."

Durand looked at Frey in surprise. "You've been there?"

"No. No one's 'been there.' I meant the city's history is interesting. I saw a documentary about it once. Half a century ago the military junta decided its citizens were annoying, so they built a new capital city out in the middle of nowhere. Huge buildings. Wide streets. But not many actual people. You can't just fly in there. It's locked down tight."

"Nonetheless, we need to go there."

Frey poured two drinks into frosted martini glasses. "Well, let's not eat boiled rice from the middle of the bowl, as the Thai people say."

"Which means what exactly?"

Frey walked from behind the bar. "It means, let's not act without preparation. Why it means that, I have no idea, but it does." He passed a glass to Durand, raising his own in toast. "To well-programmed escapes."

Durand clinked glasses, but then examined the bright red drink. "What is this?"

"I call this a blastocyst injection. Mekhong whiskey and Krating Daeng. I suspect it's been responsible for more than a few pregnancies."

Durand drank and winced at the strength of it.

Frey got into one of the incredibly comfortable patio chairs. "Just look at that view."

Durand sat for several moments lost in thought, staring out at the city. After a minute or so he turned to see a wary expression on Frey's face. "What?"

"You had me going there for a bit back with the Luk Krung."

"You didn't seriously think I was Wyckes?"

"You were alarmingly convincing."

"If I hadn't convinced Vegas, we'd both be dead right now. Or arrested—which in my case is the same thing."

Frey was silent for a few moments. "You're really serious about going to Myanmar?"

"Yes, I'm serious. It's where the change agent is. And it's also where the real Marcus Wyckes is."

"And what will you do even if you reach Naypyidaw? It's not like the Huli jing will have a Yelp listing."

"What's a Yelp listing?"

"Never mind. It was a thing. My point is that the Huli jing are probably protected by the junta there."

"Myanmar became a democracy decades ago."

"There are a lot of democracies that aren't. The Myanmar military can countermand anything the civilian government does. That's why there's a multidecade insurgency still going on there."

"Then don't go. But I'm going—because I refuse to stay like this."

"Things really could be worse for you, you know."

"Oh, really, how? Has anyone stolen your body, Bryan?"

"No, but neither has anyone spent weeks breaking me with torture. Make no mistake: a military junta is the real power in Burma, and the Huli jing has probably paid them off. If they find you, they're liable to do terrible things. There's a reason there are two million Shan, Karen, and Hmong people in refugee camps along the border with Thailand. And what's more, you don't speak the language. You aren't exactly going to blend in. Do you even have a plan?"

Durand pondered the question. "If I could get direct evidence of what the Huli jing is doing and bring it out to the rest of the world, then perhaps international pressure could force action."

"The world has been ignoring the situation in Myanmar for fifty years. What makes you think they're going to start noticing it now?"

Durand gestured to his body. "Because this change agent will affect everyone on earth. Like you said: this can't have been developed just to be used on me. And the Huli jing is hiding it there, in Myanmar, where no one can see it."

Frey paused and then raised his eyebrows. "Scaring the bejesus out of the world. I suppose that might actually work. But if what you're looking for is evidence, why not just use yourself as evidence? We have DNA proof that you're mostly Kenneth Durand."

"I need to get changed back before I provide evidence."

Frey grunted. "I keep forgetting." He took another sip of his drink. "Okay. So what constitutes 'evidence' of this change agent?"

"A sample, I suppose."

"Of the intact change agent? Ready-to-use?"

Durand nodded.

"There's a major insurgency going on in Myanmar. Did I mention that?"

"You did."

"Not thrilled about going."

"I told you, you don't have to go."

"Oh, but I think I do." Frey grimaced. "The Thai police apparently followed you and me to the Luk Krung clinic. Which means I am now a known associate of possibly the most wanted man in the world."

"Marcus Wyckes."

Frey nodded. "So I can't go back to where or who I was. Or anywhere really."

Durand sighed. "Shit. I'm sorry I pulled you into all this, Bryan."

"You didn't do it. I did. Or more accurately Rad Desai did. Bastard hasn't even returned my messages. Probably in hiding waiting for this to all blow over."

Durand brooded.

Frey took another sip of his drink. "Besides, you and I had an agreement."

"Even after all this, you still want to get edited?"

"Especially after all this. It's starting to sound like reinventing myself is the only viable option." He looked approvingly at his drink. "And I can help get us over the border."

"I thought you were clueless when it came to smuggling people over borders."

"Normally, yes, but in this case I have connections."

"Your last 'connection' wanted to kill us."

"Tang did take my departure harder than I thought. But no, the Shan people and I get along famously."

"The Shan people."

"Indigenous hill tribes. Theravada Buddhists. Four or five million of them spread across Laos, Thailand, and Burma. They're at war with the Burmese central government, as are the Hmong and the Karen people and half a dozen smaller indigenous tribes. Seems they're all in the way of resource-development projects."

"And how do you know these Shan people?"

"I did freelance work for their resistance a few years back."

Durand couldn't mask his surprise.

"Now, now. I wouldn't want to ruin your negative impression of me.

I was paid. And paid well. Black markets love wars. I edited LOC_OSO7 and p-SINE1 rice strains for the Shan to counteract Burmese government gene drives—some of which were developed by major biotech firms on the down-low, in violation of UN treaties."

"I'm familiar with gene drive weapons. I spent eight years hunting bioterrorists."

"Well then, you know how ugly shoving undesirable traits onto victim populations can be—in this case, sabotaging rice to create famines. Destroy the food supply in a clandestine way—make it look like a blight. Wrath of god, what have you. Nothing the media hasn't seen before. Better optics than land mines and air strikes. It also drives tribes out of a whole region. But the Shan hired black market genetic engineers of their own to create competing gene drives to keep their crops viable."

"Genetic warfare."

"All genetics is warfare."

"And you still have contacts among these Shan."

Frey nodded. "If they're still alive. I read that the government bought hunter-killer drones and set them loose in the jungles last year."

"Lovely."

"I'll reach out to the Shan later tonight. I've got a rather ponderous encrypted address book out there on the Interwebs. I'll need to crack that open. I'm sure Vegas has some prepaid telecom equipment around here. He was always privacy-obsessed."

"So you got your start with Vegas."

Frey looked wistful. "I lived here in Thailand for years. When I first left the States."

"Then you speak Thai."

He laughed. "No. When I say 'live,' I mean like an American."

"Why'd you leave the States?"

"Why did you leave?"

"I asked first."

Frey shrugged. "I could see which way the wind was blowing. I got the sense they were going to start burning witches again, and big things were happening in my profession elsewhere."

"Big things—like children who've had compassion edited out of their genome?"

Frey just gave him a look. "See, that's not a helpful attitude. You *world policemen* want to declare everything illegal, but in the final analysis people will use every tool at their disposal to obtain advantage. You can't legislate morality."

"You're not seriously arguing that Vegas had the right to create sterile, remorseless child soldiers?"

"Of course not. I'm arguing that what can happen *will* happen, but that it's better that the research take place in the light of day rather than in the dark corners of the world."

"They're creating a whole new subspecies of human. They're minting sociopaths, is what they're doing, and they'll mingle into the general population."

"And I'm certain the purchasers of these 'remorseless children' will have buyer's remorse. Leading an army of sociopaths is incredibly dangerous. I might be a genetic engineer, but I think the demise of natural selection has been greatly exaggerated. Nature did not select for empathy and social bonds because Nature was kind—but because those were survival advantages. Completely selfish, unfeeling people don't care for the greater good. They don't appreciate goals beyond themselves. And that limits them."

Durand stared. "Then explain Wyckes. He sure as hell seems to be succeeding."

"Mark my words: Mother Nature has a hell of a backhand."

Soft jazz music suddenly started playing all around them.

Durand and Frey both froze in alarm.

Swirling mood lights illuminated the patio, creating a party-lounge atmosphere.

A beautiful young Thai woman in an ornate silk robe and sandals emerged from inside, walking confidently across the patio. She was stunning. Her smiling face fell when she noticed Durand and Frey—who were quite clearly not whom she had been expecting.

"You're not Gino."

Frey sat up straight. "Sadly, we are not."

She checked her comm bracelet, tugged with long polished nails at a virtual screen. "I got an alert that said Gino's chopper had arrived." She looked up, businesslike. "He's not with you?"

Durand shook his head.

Frey shrugged casually. "Gino sent us ahead. Told us to wait for him here. I'm sure he'll be along in a day or two."

She sighed in irritation. "He's not answering his phone."

"He was quite busy when we left him. And you are?"

She looked irked but said, "Gardenia."

"Gardenia. What a lovely name."

"I'm with Gino."

"Of course. I'm an old associate of Gino's from back in the '20s."

"I didn't think anyone knew Gino from that long ago. You must have some interesting stories."

"None I can tell, unfortunately."

She nodded. "I was going to take a swim."

"Don't let us stop you."

She shrugged and slipped off her robe, revealing her perfectly toned body in a bikini. She walked toward the water, kicked off her sandals, and dove in.

Frey sighed. "Such a lovely view out here."

Durand finished his drink. "I need to get some rest. You should do the same—after you reach out to your hill tribe." He got up, examining the glass walls on the floor above. "I'm going to find a bedroom."

"Looks like there're plenty." Frey raised his glass again.

Durand followed a wide teakwood staircase upstairs into a long hallway. He wandered from door to door until he found what seemed to be a guest bedroom with a glass wall looking down on the pool area below and the broad sweep of the city lights. It appeared that all the rooms had glass walls. He wondered how people got privacy. Or how they slept in. But he was too tired to think for long. Almost as soon as his head hit the pillow—and a very fine pillow it was—he fell asleep.

Durand awoke suddenly in the middle of the night to commotion. It took him a moment to orient himself, but he finally recalled where he was, and as he looked around in the semidarkness, a screen glowing on the wall pulsated in sync with rock music—a pounding beat.

The text at the base of the pulsating colors read "Iggy Pop—Gardenia." He glanced down at the pool area through the plate glass and could see Vegas's Thai mistress and Frey dancing with reckless abandon, poolside, a champagne bottle in his hand.

Durand put a pillow over his head and rolled back to sleep.

Chapter 31

The dream was always the same. She is six again. Aiyana's mother calls to her in their two-room, windowless mud brick house. Aiyana kneels at the hearth, baking kissra—the thin, fermented bread of her childhood. She bakes on a sheet of tin pulled over the mouth of a cut oil drum glowing with coals. The aroma of the bread tantalizes her. But she responds to the second call of her name, entering the front room to see a man in a crisp white thawb and kaffiyeh made of fine cotton standing in their doorway, not entering, for this would be *haram*—forbidden. Instead, he stands in the rubble-strewn street. Aiyana's mother wears a dark toub wound about her body and her hair and speaks to him quietly. This, too, is a sin, but Aiyana's father never came back from the war—the all-consuming, ever-expanding war that Aiyana cannot understand. She imagines the war as a monster that eats people. People fear it. Men go to fight it and never return. Or they come back mangled.

The man holds a satellite phone. He also wears a glittering gold timepiece on his wrist that is the single most beautiful thing Aiyana has ever seen. A blue SUV, coated in mud, is parked some ways behind him in the lane.

The man says nothing to Aiyana, merely looks her over while Aiyana's mother and brothers stand nearby. Eventually the man nods, and Aiyana's mother leans down to her. Her mother's face is always blurry in the dream. Aiyana can no longer recall her mother's face.

"Go with this man now. Do as he says, and be a good girl."

The man takes Aiyana's hand, and Aiyana looks back again,

bewildered, as she is pulled away, out the door, and her mother's eyes watch her go from the darkness of their hovel. Sadness? Relief? What is the expression on her mother's face? Aiyana would give anything to know now. Maybe that is the reason for the dream.

Her brothers look on, for once not teasing.

But the beautiful timepiece is there, right next to her face, wrapped around the man's thick, hairy wrist. She reaches to touch the watch face, and the man smacks her hand away. She begins to cry.

Inspector Aiyana Marcotte woke from the dream as she always did—crying. She fumbled for the light on the hotel nightstand, and then grabbed the medallion on a silver chain she knew was there. She looked upon the dull bronze medallion beneath the light.

A Saint Anne medal. The patron saint of the childless. She had found it in the envelope of her foster mother's personal things—after her adoptive mother passed away in the hospital.

Marcotte had never known that her foster mother wore it. Not until that day.

How long had her foster mother prayed for a child? How long had Marcotte prayed for a mother? What did it mean that Saint Anne was also revered in Islam? In the Qur'an she was known as Hannah. Different religions but the same prayer.

Marcotte sat up and wiped her face. Collected herself. She looked down at the second medallion she had since added to her foster mother's silver chain.

Saint Peter Claver. The patron saint to slaves. It steadied her. She looked up at the window and the sunlight rising above Bangkok. Then she grabbed her LFP glasses from the charger and put them on.

The newsfeeds were on fire. The story was everywhere. Two hundred and thirty-six dead. Thirty-one of the victims Thai police—among them members of the country's most elite anti-terror unit. Prominent civilians from around the world dead. Children dead. Every member of the Luk Krung dead.

And everywhere in the feeds, not the face of Marcus Wyckes but instead the face of the young suited man the media had dubbed the "Angel of Death." Somehow clinic surveillance camera imagery of the

Huli jing assassin had leaked. The same *thing* Marcotte had fought in the street had its face at the top of every media feed. *His touch meant death . . .*

It wasn't a he. It was an *it*. She remembered its unliving eyes. Headlines screamed that his skin oozed poison.

There was a sharp knock on her door.

She walked wearily to the peephole. Her skin was still raw from the decontamination chemicals and harsh brushes they'd used to scrub off the first layer of her skin. The biohazard team had incinerated her tactical vest. Her clothing. Her head was bald after they'd shaved off every lock of hair. She was clean. Alive.

She peered through the opening and saw Sergeant Michael Yi Ji-chang with several grim-faced Thai men in suits. Detectives, no doubt.

Marcotte closed her robe and opened the door.

Yi nodded. "Morning, Inspector. No doubt you've seen the news."

She nodded back.

"General Prem's been sacked. They want us out of the country by nightfall."

She nodded again.

"I'll come and collect you when you're ready." He waited for a response, but finally shrugged and moved away.

"Sergeant."

Yi turned.

"Wyckes committed this atrocity to stop us. We do not stop. Do you understand? We pursue him. He will go to ground somewhere, and when he does, I want him to hear our hounds on his trail."

Yi nodded, looking relieved, and then headed for the elevators with the Thai detectives close behind.

Chapter 32

Well after dawn Kenneth Durand lay staring at the view of downtown Bangkok through his feet. The glass wall made it seem as though he was lying on a ledge overlooking Bhumibol Bridge with its golden, pointed spires.

What troubled him most was that he hadn't thought of his wife and daughter the moment he awoke. Instead, he'd stared out at the city, just grateful to be alive. What he should have been grateful for was his chance to continue—to keep striving to get back to himself. His growing comfort in this form angered him.

A knock on the bedroom door interrupted his troubled thoughts. The knock was followed immediately by Bryan Frey walking in and jumping up to sit on the edge of the large bed. "Sorry to pester you, but the world has apparently not stopped turning. And there's news you need to see."

Frey made inscrutable gestures above a new bracelet he wore, causing LFP projectors to descend from pods in the ceiling. These began shining content into Durand's retinas. A virtual two-hundred-inch video screen appeared, superimposed before the view of Bangkok. Acoustic beams brought sound.

The screen displayed newsfeeds and audio, all in Thai. But with a gesture Frey converted it to English. Harrowing scrolling headlines rolled past beneath grim-faced news reporters: "Pattaya City Massacre. Over Two Hundred Dead. General Prem Resigns in Disgrace."

Durand sat up. "What the hell . . . ?"

Frey watched the images. "After we escaped. It seems Wyckes wasn't content to let his people fall into the hands of the police. Either that or he'd hoped to eliminate you."

Durand felt a wave of horror sweep over him. "Those children . . ."

Frey muted the video. "Police. Children. The clients. And Mr. Vegas—along with his Luk Krung."

"Jesus . . ." Durand's breathing increased, and he could feel his tattoos surfacing all over him. He sat shirtless before a screen filled with sickening headlines. Headlines he had caused. "We killed them all."

"No. Don't say that." Frey pointed at the screen—at a crystal clear surveillance image that was in heavy rotation on all the feeds: the Angel of Death. "*He* killed them. A man 'dripping in nerve toxins.' That's who we need to talk about." Frey froze the image with a gesture.

Durand frowned at the screen. "Nerve toxins . . . ?"

"You remember Vegas was afraid of Wyckes's right hand—the man he called Otto?"

Durand nodded.

"That little Einstein girl, she cried at the mention of Otto. She called him the Mirror Man. Do you remember her saying that?"

"Yes."

"I thought it was strange for her to use such a mystical name. Especially because she was so brilliant."

"She was still just a child." Durand studied the face of the killer. "I think I've met this man before. In Singapore."

"You *met* the Angel of Death?"

"I'll remember those eyes for the rest of my life. Dead eyes. I recognize some of the face. He's changed, but not entirely." Durand turned to Frey. "This was the man who injected me. I'm certain of it."

Frey pondered something. "It's making more and more sense. He's immune to biotoxins." Frey popped a pill from a half-empty blister pak.

"What are you taking?"

"I printed up a batch of nootropics. Improves brain function. It's making things clearer. Follow me on this . . ." Frey pointed. "This is indeed Wyckes's 'right hand.' Do you get it: *right hand*?"

Durand just stared.

"He's an *enantiomorph*."

Durand kept staring.

"*Mirror life*. That's why he isn't affected by biotoxins. He wouldn't be affected by human viruses or parasites or diseases, either. Because he is the opposite of life."

"I don't understand."

Frey snapped his fingers, searching for words. "Chirality. Handedness. Molecules, like amino and nucleic acids, have a 'handedness'—not literally hands, but orientations of a molecule's atoms. They can be reversed—from left to right, to right to left. They could have the same chemical formula, but be mirror images of each other. And thus have different interactions, even though they are technically the same compounds."

"So you think this man—"

"Is an opposite. *All* complex organisms on earth are comprised of left—or levo—amino acids. Nobody is entirely sure why that is, but that's the way life evolved." Frey pointed at the screen. "I think the Huli jing created an opposite form of life."

"Why?"

"That's the question, isn't it?"

Durand looked again at the killer's face. "I can't describe it, but there was something about him that was terrifying. It's like he was alive but shouldn't have been."

Frey nodded to himself, riding the nootropics. "Fascinating. I would have guessed it would be no different from a racemic mixture." He looked up. "Which is a mixture of both left- and right-handed enantiomers." He held up a finger. "But . . . perhaps some aspect of mirror life evokes an evolved revulsion in us—some survival instinct that is repelled by its presence. This 'Otto' . . . antiperson—he would have no connection to any other living thing on earth. He wouldn't even be able to digest normal food."

"It can't have been a coincidence that he was there. He must have followed me."

Frey looked grim once more. "It wasn't a coincidence. Radheya Desai is also dead."

Durand snapped a look at Frey. "Dead?"

"Yes. Gruesomely, too. The news said it was a gang killing. But I think it was Otto looking for you."

Durand lowered his head into his hands. "I've gotten all these people killed."

"No." Frey pointed at the screen. "It is this person—or this antiperson— who's done this. It's Marcus Wyckes who's done this. Not you."

"I caused it to happen."

"You degans are always so willing to accept guilt. You were just trying to survive, Ken."

Durand gestured to the image of Otto on the screen. "He was there because of me. All those people died because he had come there to kill me."

"And what about the police? What were the police doing there?"

"I don't know." Durand lowered his head into his hands again. "I don't know." Durand looked up. "And what does it matter if this man is 'mirror life' or just a killer? All it shows is how twisted the Huli jing are— to create this abomination."

Frey crawled toward Durand across the bed. "Ah, that's where you're wrong, my friend. I think there might be a link between your transformation and this Otto. Look . . ." He poked the trefoil knot tattoo still visible on Durand's arm. "Why is the Huli jing lab symbol a trefoil?"

Durand examined the tattoo. The single looping line.

Frey tapped it. "These are Wyckes's tattoos. Tattoos are personal things. We've been wasting an incredible source of intelligence about Wyckes that's woven right into your skin. Unless he was on a bender when he got these, he didn't choose them by chance."

Durand looked down at his arm again.

Frey jabbed a tattoo. "A trefoil is significant. I don't know why it didn't occur to me before. A trefoil knot is the simplest chiral knot in existence—meaning it is not identical to its mirror image. And DNA trefoils have major implications in intramolecular synapsis of—"

"English. English, please, Bryan."

"Right. That's the nootropics talking." He stood on the bed examining Durand's tattoo array, studying them like a psychic reading a palm. "What

I'm saying is that I think the trefoil holds the key to the change agent's morphology." On Durand's blank look, he explained: "Its structure."

Durand nodded. "Okay."

"But there's more." Frey pointed at the screen. "What do you see on Otto there? On his neck. Do you see it?" He zoomed the image in.

Durand saw a tattoo of a gray-white-and-gold butterfly on the man's neck. There were other tattoos, but the butterfly was most prominent.

"Just like yours, probably not visible unless the blood's up—like yours is now. But . . ." Frey stretched the skin over Durand's butterfly, comparing it to the tattoo on the screen. "He and Wyckes got matching tattoos. Check it out. Same species and everything."

"But that doesn't tell us what it means."

Frey poked him. "Maybe it does. Huli jing—if we had bothered to read up on our mythology—is a shape-shifting mythological being. A mischievous spirit that can—"

"Take any form. Yes, I know. I sat through a briefing on the Huli jing the day I got injected. Interpol thought the name meant Wyckes's organization wanted to remain hidden."

"Clearly the name—and the tattoo—was chosen for its literal meaning." He tapped his finger on Durand's butterfly tattoo again. "And I think this butterfly was as well. What do butterflies undergo?"

"Metamorphosis."

"Right. *Metamorphosis*—changing from a caterpillar into its final form. Do you know something interesting about caterpillars and butterflies that not a lot of people realize?"

"What?"

"A caterpillar and its butterfly have the same genetic sequence." Frey pounded his fist into his hand. "Same exact DNA and completely different forms. How is that possible?"

Durand realized he'd never known that. And it did seem puzzling.

"Epigenetics. Gene expression. Turning genes on and off. That's what happens during the butterfly's metamorphosis. It builds a chrysalis and secretes chemicals that cause it to fall into a comatose state as its body changes."

"Like my coma. After they injected me."

Frey nodded. "I think that's what the Huli jing discovered—not only how to edit DNA, but how to turn genes on and off on demand, not simply write them into the chain. After all, computer code doesn't do anything unless you execute it." He stabbed at Durand's butterfly tattoo. "I think *this* was the butterfly species that helped them figure it out, and why Wyckes and Otto wear it as a tattoo: *Archon apollinus*. The False Apollo."

"What did you just say?"

Frey turned to him. "*Archon apol—*"

"No, the other name."

"False Apollo."

Durand got to his feet and paced. "Christ . . ." He rubbed his hands over his bald, tattooed scalp. "Get rid of his damn face, please."

"Oh. Sorry." With a gesture, the television screen blinked out of existence. Frey watched Durand. "What's up?"

"False Apollo. Is that really this butterfly's name?"

"I checked it this morning. I've been busy. Talk to me."

"I worked on an anti-bioterror team back in the '30s. Naval Intelligence. We were searching for nihilistic terrorist groups. Or brilliant idiots. People who might accidentally or purposely create genetic weapons that could wipe out humanity. Either directly or by crippling our ecosystems."

"So, what about this False Apollo?"

"They briefed all the teams on it. False Apollo. It was the name of a multibillion-dollar illicit biodefense project. It was a big deal. They shut it down."

"It was a *military project?*"

"It was unclear who was running it. Government. Industry. No one knew. It spanned borders."

"What was False Apollo's purpose?"

"To create a universal defense against an extinction-level pathogen."

"In other words: mirror life."

Durand shrugged. "I don't know. Like I said, they shut False Apollo down. I never saw it. Maybe parts of it got out into the world. We were warned to keep a lookout."

"Well, fuck me . . ." Frey pondered the implications. "The name fits. Apollo was the Greek god of music, healing, and light. But he was also the god of plagues." Frey looked up. "So the Huli jing might be remnants of a rogue biodefense project?"

Durand paced. "No wonder they had so many connections. We've got to get moving."

Frey nodded. "Gardenia and I were able to transact some business last night."

Durand gave him an exasperated look. "I'm not interested in your—"

"Not that sort of business. I mean *business*. She was more than a little concerned when she learned of Vegas's demise, and she was eager to exchange the baht we had for biocoin. She might be heading to her home village to lie low for a while."

"Can we trust her?"

"We're going to have to trust her. Vegas trusted her, and she was more than helpful. Look . . ." Frey held up a gleaming piece of obsidian etched with a gold stylized aircraft logo. "She showed me where he kept his credit fobs."

"What is that?" Durand took it.

"A hideously expensive, zero-memory, on-demand autonomous electric jet service—Jet Black. This will bring us a lot closer to Myanmar."

"We won't be able to get near an airport."

"We won't have to. Vertical takeoff and landing. We can use the helipad outside. Costs a goddamned fortune, but it's not our money." He took the credit fob back. "More importantly, I got in touch with my Shan contact last night. They're still alive, and they said they would agree to smuggle us over the border and through the Burmese highlands—although it's going to cost us."

Durand started to get dressed. "How much?"

"Half a million US dollars. Pretty much everything we had."

"How do you know these Shan people of yours aren't going to just kill us?"

"Their payment is contingent on our safe arrival in Naypyidaw. With Gardenia's help, I converted all our cash into a single encrypted wallet, and gave the Shan a down payment of a hundred thousand. They get the balance when we arrive safely."

"They could torture the code out of you."

"They'd have no reason to. They're making the trip anyway, and I've helped them a great deal in the past—which is the only reason Shan938 agreed to take us."

"Shan938—that's the name of your contact?"

"It's the only name I was ever given. I've never met any of them in person."

Durand narrowed his eyes. "How do you know these aren't just criminals? Or scammers?"

"Because they've paid me considerably more than this over the years for genetic editing of their crops. And this account holder had the encryption keys and digital signature to prove they are who they say. You must understand, these Shan are a spiritual people—Buddhists. The central government keeps trying to kill them, and they just want to be left alone. They're not criminals."

"What do they know about us?"

"I told them you and I need to get to the capital of Myanmar, and if the central government knew what we planned on doing there, they'd probably try to kill us."

"And they didn't ask what we'll be doing?"

Frey shook his head.

"You conducted this exchange over an encrypted line, I hope."

"Now I'm insulted. I break the law for a living."

"What route will we be taking?"

"They didn't say what route we'd be taking. Operational security. They'll want to be certain we're not working with the Tatmadaw first, of course. All they gave me was GPS coordinates and a date and time to meet: three o'clock this afternoon."

Durand shot a concerned look Frey's way. "*This* afternoon? That's cutting it close, isn't it? What is that, four hundred miles away?"

"Yes, but we'll have a jet. Shan938 said if we arrive in anything else or with anyone else, we'll be shot out of the sky."

Durand just stared at Frey. "What time did you get up this morning?"

"I didn't sleep . . ." Frey brought up a three-dimensional satellite map of the Thai-Burmese border region, projecting it where the video screen was. The entire glass wall was replaced by an aerial view of hundreds of square miles of jungle-choked mountains and brown, snaking rivers. A yellow dot highlighted a mountain clearing fifteen kilometers from the Burmese border. "That's where they wanted to meet."

Durand pointed at the bracelet Frey was using to control the video screen. "Where'd you get the comm bracelet?"

Frey went into the hallway and came back with a box brimming with dozens of phablets, bracelets, circlets, and LFP glasses. He dumped them on the bed. "Like I said: Tang liked his privacy. These are all prepaid. Bought by surrogates from all over Thailand. He even kept receipts." Frey smirked. "You know what they say: when privacy is criminalized, only criminals will have privacy."

Durand poked through the pile. "I'm not who you think I am, Bryan. I'm no more a fan of total surveillance than you are." He grabbed a pair of LFP glasses and looked back up at the map projected over the glass wall. "These Shan people of yours, you're confident they can smuggle us to the capital?"

"They smuggle everything. The Burmese military has declared foreign biofacturing tools and software illegal. The resistance brings in high-tech equipment, weapons, money."

Durand turned the mountainous map model this way and that. It looked like seriously rugged terrain. "You said the central government deployed deep-maneuver weapons in this region?"

Frey gave him a blank stare.

"Autonomous drones. Robotic weapons."

"Oh, right. Last year. It's a regular arms bazaar out there."

Durand grunted. "Those might be a problem. The worst ones generate their own energy—grow their own algae biofuels from decomposing plant matter. They can remain in the field for months. Sometimes years. Waiting."

"Why am I not surprised you know about this sort of thing?"

"I didn't say I approved of them. I just know about them." He looked back at the map. "Let's summon this Jet Black of yours."

• • •

They waited on the patio for nearly an hour, but finally they heard the hissing sound of an approaching jet. The Lilium electric jet was sleeker than the Ehang chopper—predictably black, with wings that extended from the rear of a lozenge-shaped cabin and smaller ducted electric fans up front. A line of dozens more small-ducted fan jets ran the entire length of both wings. Apparently it utilized an array of massively redundant smaller jet engines instead of a few big ones.

The aircraft rose above the railing from below, rotated, and settled with uncanny accuracy in the center of the helipad. Its jets wound down while a voice called out loudly, *"Stand clear. Stand clear. Stand clear."* Red lights flashed.

Once the engines fell silent, the tinted gull-wing doors opened, as did a luggage compartment. *"Call me Jet Black. Welcome."*

Durand watched with some consternation as Frey dragged two large duffel bags across the pavement. He struggled to heave them into the jet's cargo bay. "What's all that?"

"If you're concerned about theft, let me remind you that the former owner was a criminal. So it's already stolen—I'm just moving it."

Durand shook his head and climbed into the passenger compartment. Again a two-seater, it was even more finely appointed than Vegas's fleet of Ehangs. The seats looked to have been handmade with real, organic leather.

Frey followed a moment later. As he sat down, the synthetic voice spoke: *"Aircraft overloaded by twenty-seven kilograms. Please remove at least twenty-seven kilograms of weight."*

"Damnit." Durand got out before Frey could beat him to it. He opened the cargo hatch and pulled out the first duffel bag. It was unwieldy. He unzipped it. "What the hell is in here?"

Durand pulled out what looked like a portable pharmaceutical printer.

Frey came up alongside him. "The Shan could make good use of that. Korean-made. It's high-quality gear, and it'll only be confiscated by the police if it remains here."

Durand pulled out a dozen bottles of expensive-looking liquor, packages of vaping supplies. He tossed them onto the patio, then shoved the half-empty duffel bag back into the cargo compartment.

They both climbed back in and buckled up in frosty silence.

Frey finally said, "That wasn't all for me, you know. There are gift protocols in Asian society that one should try to follow."

"Half a million dollars makes a damn nice gift."

"Say 'Jet Black' and tell me your desired destination."

AR maps and gauges appeared in front of them both. Frey began to manipulate the map to enter destination coordinates.

Durand stopped him. "Don't enter the coordinates now. Plug in a popular destination nearby. A tourist spot would be perfect."

"I've got the GPS coordinates right here."

"If anyone's tracking us, we don't need to give them hours to prepare a reception committee. Give it a destination that isn't going to set off any red flags, and we'll change it at the last minute when we get close."

"I suppose I should listen to a man who spies on people for a living . . ." Frey spoke to the AI. "Jet Black: Fly us to . . . Chiang Mai Airport, please."

"Why do you say 'please' to these things?"

"Because it's polite, that's why."

"They sell that information to advertisers."

"They sell the fact that I'm polite to machines?"

"They sell the fact that you're susceptible to technical animism."

"So what if I am?"

"Tell me that after your machines start to sound wounded if you don't buy something."

The electric duct fans hissed to life, and a synthetic voice spoke: *"Your journey to Chiang Mai International Airport is estimated at two hours and thirteen minutes. Please prepare for liftoff, and feel free to call my name if you need anything while we are en route."*

Chapter 33

The Lilium electric jet was smooth and quiet. They cruised along at three thousand meters altitude going several hundred kilometers per hour. Durand reclined, consumed with his own thoughts, while Frey snored, sound asleep just minutes after takeoff.

Durand watched the mirrored office towers of Bangkok's CBD recede quickly behind them. Before long they soared past the last residential block and golf course and set out over a patchwork of long, rectangular rice fields. Durand could see orange robotic farm machinery in the shallow rice paddies. The wide central plain of Thailand spread out before him, traced by glittering rivers and dotted with golden temples.

Despite his deep concerns over what lay ahead, Durand found himself thinking about how much his daughter, Mia, would have loved this flight. He suddenly felt very homesick—but also relieved to feel that again. He tried to keep his focus on who he was: he was Kenneth Durand. Examining his arms, he was comforted to see that his tattoos had hidden themselves again. They seemed to be appearing more and more lately.

As the Lilium jet traveled north, the rivers multiplied and hillocks appeared in the plains, until green jungle foothills drew in from either side. Mountainous regions were barely visible beyond the humid haze. The occasional gleaming golden pagoda caught the sun's light. Whitewashed stupas and the stepped roofs of temples mixed in with office buildings and shopping malls. The little jet raced northward for hours until around midday a large city came into view ahead. The AR mapping system labeled it Chiang Mai, with cultural markers popping up like mushrooms.

Soft chimes sounded. *"I hope you're enjoying your flight. We've begun our descent to Chiang Mai International Airport autonomous transport terminal, and should be on the ground within ten minutes."*

Durand nudged the snoring Frey as the jet began to descend.

Frey snapped alert. "Yes. What is it?"

"Time to enter your coordinates."

"Chiang Mai already?"

"Yes."

"Damn. I want to bring this seat with us. Let me sleep for just a few more minutes."

Durand elbowed Frey sharply in the ribs. "Up! Key in the coordinates."

Frey sighed and sat up. He manipulated a few invisible objects in his glasses. "Jet Black."

"How can I help you?"

"Substitute new destination."

A larger map appeared before them. *"Surcharges may apply. Where would you like to go?"*

"Travel to these GPS coordinates: 19° 35' 26.18" north latitude and 98° 0' 54.96" east longitude. Desired arrival time: three p.m. local."

"Please wait . . ." After a few moments the onboard systems calculated their path and displayed a map into their retinas. The synthetic voice said, *"Your selected destination lies inside a safety advisory zone. Additional insurance charges will be . . . 400 percent of the standard rate. Do you accept? Please indicate."*

Frey raised an eyebrow. "Just an extra forty-two thousand US dollars in insurance? Why not? I don't think Vegas will mind." He clicked the "Yes" button hovering in midair.

"A rerouting surcharge of 25 percent also applies. Do you accept?"

Frey gritted his teeth and clicked "Yes."

"Thank you. Estimated arrival time at new destination, three p.m. local time. Enjoy your flight."

They curved left, away from Chiang Mai, heading up toward the mountains to the northwest.

The weather was clear as the jet sailed over jungle-filled ravines, waterfalls, and rapids. Treetops raced past the viewports at their feet. And suddenly a golden stupa dome appeared, glittering in the sunlight, but then gone as they raced still upward past more jungle. When they crested the first mountain, a vast terrain of rugged jungle wilderness stretched out before them. Rainstorms were visible in the far distance, with flashes of lightning and dark clouds and shadows, but here it was still clear. Steam rose from various pockets in the dense forests below.

Durand scanned the horizon. It was becoming clear how vast this jungle was.

Frey grimaced. "Why do I get the feeling we're not dressed properly for this?"

Durand looked down at their business casual clothes and loafers. "We'll deal with it."

"At least we'll be the best-dressed people in the resistance."

They soared within fifty meters of the highest ridge. A golden Buddha statue passed below inside a tiled, peaked roof at the summit.

Beyond it the land fell out beneath them. Ahead tall peaks still loomed. Their destination appeared in AR as a glowing green dot, beamed into their eyes. They were going in. The jet's engines decreased.

"Jet Black here. I hope you're enjoying your flight. We're beginning our descent to coordinates 19° 35' 26.18" north latitude and 98° 0' 54.96" east longitude. Please prepare for landing."

The jet glided downward, rocking in minor turbulence.

Frey glanced at the clock. "Look at that: 2:59 p.m. See? That's what I like about machines—precision."

"Tell me that when we're facing killer drones."

The jet rocked a bit more before it entered a sloping valley surrounded on all sides by much higher jungle peaks. They turned, spiraling down toward the only clearing in sight. It was ringed by tangled brush and short, broad-leafed trees. There were no structures or people in sight.

The jet's forward thrusters kicked in, and they went into a hover just above the landing zone. The grass billowed away from the jet wash.

The synthetic voice said, *"There is no standardized landing pad here.*

In order to land do you agree to accept any and all liability?" A "Yes/No" pop-up appeared.

Frey sighed. "Yes." He stabbed at the button.

Another pop-up instantly appeared.

"Do you agree to an additional 800 percent insurance surcharge? Please indicate."

Another "Yes/No" pop-up appeared.

"Jesus, I'm stealing the money, and I still feel like I'm getting robbed."

"Just hit the button."

Frey tapped the "Yes" button.

"Thank you. Please prepare for a potentially rough landing. And in any event, thank you for flying Jet Black."

The jet rotated, hovered a moment more, then gently descended, touching down perfectly on a gently sloped clearing. The jet motors began to wind down immediately.

It was precisely three p.m.

Frey smacked the dashboard. "After all that it was completely safe. What a waste of a hundred thousand dollars."

"Would you prefer we crashed?"

"At least we'd be getting our money's worth."

Durand opened his door, and a wave of heat and humidity hit him. It made Singapore seem pleasant.

They both exited and crunched across flattened cane grass to the front of the Lilium, examining the jungle hilltops all around them.

Frey scowled. "I'm gonna miss that air-conditioning."

They both removed their suit jackets.

There was a deep thrum of insects, the calls of birds and screeching macaques. The din of living things here was relentless. The clearing they stood in obviously had been hacked out of the jungle, because all around them was deep, tangled brush and trees.

"Where are these friends of yours?"

"Observing us, no doubt."

Just then a sound like a large insect approached, expanding into a deep hum. They turned upward to see a purple consumer quadcopter drone hovering ten meters above them. It carried a camera on a gimbal that turned to survey them and then their jet. The drone then descended and hovered a few meters in front of them.

A synthesized male voice emanated from a speaker somewhere on it. *"Dismiss your aircraft."*

Frey looked to Durand.

Durand spoke without emotion. "We're either dead, or we're going to Myanmar. Either way, we don't need the jet."

Frey nodded but spoke to the hovering drone. "I need to get equipment out of the cargo bay first."

A moment of silence.

Then, *"We did not agree to bring your equipment. Just you two."*

"Some of our gear will be useful. You can come and examine it, but let me just pull the bags out first."

The drone said nothing, but instead edged away from the jet. Durand took the initiative and opened the Lilium's cargo bay, pulling out the two duffel bags. "Disregarding their instructions is a bad way to start."

Frey manipulated an AR interface just outside the jet's doorway. "You've been whining about those bags since we left this morning, but you'll end up thanking me."

The Lilium's synthetic voice said, *"Jet Black here. You have opted to cancel your return journey. I want to be sure you understand that this will end your rental, stranding you here. No refund will be granted for your . . . full-day . . . rental. Additional services and emergency pickup will be charged at triple prime-time rates. Do you still wish to cancel your return trip?"*

"Yes." Frey stabbed at an invisible interface with his index finger.

"Let me reconfirm: Do you wish to cancel your return trip, stranding you here and incurring maximum return-flight charges?"

"Yes, goddamnit!" He turned to Durand. "The very last thing I thought I'd be doing in the Burmese jungle is arguing with an AI about surcharges."

"Okay, I've processed your request. You have now canceled your return trip for a total nonrefundable charge of . . . five million, two hundred and forty-three thousand baht. Please stand clear of the aircraft, and thank you for flying Jet Black."

"Yes, and if I ever need to get royally screwed, I'll be sure to call on you."

Durand and Frey stepped back as the duct fans wound up, splaying the grass in every direction and kicking up debris. Moments later, the aircraft lifted into the sky and peeled away to the southeast, quickly climbing toward the ridge.

"I'm surprised it can lift off with so much of our money."

Once it disappeared over the summit, the jungle returned to relative quiet—except for the ever-present thrum of insects and animals.

The small drone returned. The synthesized voice said, *Follow me.*

Durand grabbed the heavier duffel bag and passed the half-full one to Frey. They followed the drone as it slowly drifted beneath the canopy of jungle, moving along a barely discernible path through the tangled undergrowth.

Almost immediately mosquitoes began eating them alive.

Frey slapped his neck. "Goddamnit! I can't believe I didn't bring bug spray."

Up ahead, the drone had turned around and was waiting in a widened section of the path. Artocarpus trees leaned in from either side, concealing the path from the sky.

As they reached the drone, they both dropped their duffels.

Moments later Durand noticed a squad of a dozen well-camouflaged men slowly move in on them from two directions, emerging from the bush with long guns aimed and ready.

Durand elbowed Frey and raised his hands.

Frey did likewise. "Hello . . ."

The Shan soldiers wore camo bandanas over their faces, though it was possible to see from their eyes that they were brown-skinned—clearly Southeast Asian. They all wore traditional cinched baggy gray-and-pale-blue pants and tunics of homespun cloth, as well as the traditional conical woven bamboo hats known as kups. But along with these they each wore modern camouflaged web harnesses loaded with spare clips, grenades, radios, and other equipment.

Their weapons Durand recognized as aging M4s (or at least M4 knockoffs) with holosights and tactical infrared flashlights—so they probably had night-vision gear somewhere. All of them wore low-slung military packs.

Durand could see no light machine guns with them, so they were probably a fast-moving recon team. Either that or they had overwatch on the ridges above—which on second thought seemed likely.

Only four of the Shan soldiers came directly up to Durand and Frey; the two on either side kept their weapons aimed, while a man in his twenties lowered his bandana and grabbed the drone from midair, stowing it in his pack as soon as its motors cut off. He smiled and spoke English with a slight accent: "Which one of you is Dr. Bryan Frey?"

Frey nodded. "I am."

The man smiled warmly. "So good to finally meet you in person, Doctor." He bowed slightly, putting his hands before his chest in a pyramid, offering a wai greeting.

Frey lowered his arms in relief and wai'd back. "Shan938, I presume?"

"Only partly."

Durand studied the other soldier standing in front—and noticed the eyes above the bandana were clearly female. Her dark eyes met Durand's gaze—and stared back at him with undaunted intensity.

He lowered his gaze and his hands, putting them together before his chest as he bowed lightly to her.

She tugged down her bandana, revealing an attractive woman in her late twenties or early thirties. She did not smile. Instead she gave a cursory bow and barked at the man who'd greeted Frey—who was still smiling.

"My elder sister, Aye Su Win. She commands. I am Thet Ko Lin. Interpreter. The two of us are Shan938. You have been speaking to her through me. I translate her words. She speaks no English."

Frey looked happily surprised. He bowed to her. "Then all these years I've been conversing with you, Nan Win."

"Bo Win," Thet corrected. "'Bo' means 'commander.'"

"Bo Win. My apologies."

She eyed him and spoke rapidly to her brother in the Shan dialect.

"My sister says you did not mention you were a dwarf."

Frey smiled diplomatically. "Tell her I did not think it relevant."

Thet conveyed this to her, and she looked irritated. A moment later she barked back a string of words.

Thet listened and translated as she spoke. "We have a cousin with your condition, and walking long distances can be an issue for him. It was relevant information."

"Well, surely we're not walking all the way to Naypyidaw."

Thet paused before conveying this to his sister. As he did so, all the men erupted in laughter. She did not laugh.

Durand muttered, "Charming the locals as usual."

Frey whispered back, "I would think five hundred thousand US dollars would at least put us on the back of a truck."

She spoke to her brother but looked squarely at Frey—pointing at him menacingly.

Thet smiled and laughed nervously. "So sorry, Dr. Frey, but my sister says if you withhold any more relevant information from her, she will leave you and your friend behind." Thet laughed nervously and bowed again. "So sorry, but my sister does not . . . how do you say . . . fuck around. Do you see?"

Frey nodded grimly. "Yes, Thet. I see."

Win stepped forward and between Durand and Frey, moving them aside to look at the duffel bags on the ground. She muttered something in irritation as she tried to lift one.

Thet translated. "She says you have brought seventy kilos of what, exactly?"

She unzipped the first duffel to find wads of bank-wrapped Thai baht notes.

Frey looked to Durand. "I was going to tell you about those."

"Were you . . ."

She found two automatic pistols—both Sig Sauers, with oak handles. She slid the action back to find that they were loaded and cast a dark eye at Frey.

"Tell your sister that those are intended for much later—after we've parted company and are inside the capital. And even then, only for personal protection."

She confiscated the guns, unloading them with practiced ease and tossing them to one of her men, who caught them and quickly stashed them in his pack.

"Of course, you'll hold on to them for us."

She also tossed the wads of baht notes to another soldier, who caught them and secured them.

Frey kept nodding. "For safekeeping. Good idea."

Durand spoke under his breath. "Please tell me you don't have narcotics in those bags."

"Would you stop with the narcotics? You sound like my mother. I'm not on narcotics. They're nootropics."

Thet motioned for silence. "Is there anything else in these bags my sister should know about?"

Frey sighed, clearly feeling set upon. "Tell her there's a portable multiplex DNA sequencer with reagents and supplies. A pharmaceutical printer with an array of precursors. A lovely hypersonic music system, and various recreational materials intended as gifts for all of you."

Thet listened intently and conveyed this to his sister, who was already going through the final duffel bag—finding the DNA sequencer. She nodded at it appreciatively and spoke to her brother.

"We will purchase this from you. The price can be taken off your travel cost."

Frey stepped forward. "I only need to use it twice, ideally. After that, you may have it. Consider it a gift to the Shan people."

Thet smiled as he conveyed this.

Win studied Frey, and then called out to another soldier sharply.

The man rushed forward, opening his pack to withdraw electronic equipment.

Thet knelt next to Frey. "Do not be alarmed, Dr. Frey. This will only take a few minutes. It is quite painless."

"*What* is quite painless?" Frey tried to move away but soldiers grabbed him by the arms.

Durand raised his hands but stepped forward.

Two guns were immediately aimed at him from a meter away.

Bo Win shouted, and everyone froze.

Durand looked to Thet. "I won't allow you to harm my friend, Thet. Please tell me that's not what's about to happen."

"No." He turned to face Durand. "We have not been introduced. So sorry."

Durand bowed slightly to Thet, peaking his hands. "I am Kenneth Durand."

Thet bowed as well. "Pleased to make your acquaintance, Mr. Durand."

Behind him a soldier placed what looked like an encephalograph cap onto Frey's head. It rather comically resembled a tanker's helmet.

Durand nodded. "Near-infrared."

Thet smiled. "Yes. You've seen this?"

Durand turned to Frey. "Relax, Bryan. They're just going to interrogate you."

"Why would I relax if they're going to *interrogate* me?"

"It's a portable unit—like we used in the Horn of Africa back in the '20s. With suspected insurgents. It uses near-infrared light to penetrate a few inches into the brain and examine blood flow. It's like an fMRI unit, but lower-powered and portable. The software on the handheld unit has algorithms that detect brain activity associated with dissembling."

"You mean lying."

"Yes."

"Then why the hell didn't you just say 'lying'? You world policemen are always using five-dollar words. No wonder there's a deficit."

"I said, relax. It's not going to hurt you. Just don't lie to them. You have nothing to hide, right?"

Frey was getting his breathing under control as they sat him down.

Thet listened as his sister spoke quickly, then turned to Frey. "My sister wants to know if you are a spy for the Tatmadaw or the central Burmese government, Dr. Frey."

Frey sighed again. "No. I am not a spy for the Burmese army or government, or any government. I'm not keen on central government, frankly."

Win looked at the display on a unit being held by the system operator. Satisfied, she asked another question.

"Do you intend to harm the SSA or the Shan people?"

"No, I do not."

Win watched the display, then spoke again.

Thet turned to Frey. "Is your companion a spy for any government?"

Frey turned to Durand and shrugged. "I don't know, ask him. If you think *I'm* suspicious, wait until you hear his story."

"Thanks, asshole."

Thet relayed this information to Win as she watched the display. She turned to Durand.

The soldiers took the sensor cap off Frey's head and pushed him toward Durand.

As Frey walked clear, brushing himself off, he glared at Durand. "All yours. I'm kind of curious, myself, to see if you're full of shit."

Durand ignored him and walked up, bowing to make it easier for the smaller Shan men to place the cap on his head. The soldiers were clearly keyed up around him; he looked decidedly dangerous in close quarters. Several M4s were aimed at him.

Once the equipment operator was ready, Win spoke quickly to her brother.

Thet turned. "Mr. Durand, are you a spy for any government?"

Durand spoke calmly. "I am a spy, but not for a government. I work for Interpol as the lead geospatial data analyst of their Genetic Crime Division. I search for illegal genetic editing labs."

Thet blanched and turned to his sister—who looked unperturbed by the readings on the machine. Thet spoke to her.

The soldiers murmured among themselves. Bo Win looked darkly at Durand and barked a stream of words at her brother.

"My sister wants to know why you are here. Are you here to disrupt the Shan cause or the Shan people?"

Durand looked directly into her eyes, not Thet's. "I'm not here in an official capacity. I came here on my own—because of what a cartel named the Huli jing did to me. I came here to destroy the Huli jing. As a personal matter."

As Thet related this, the other soldiers again murmured. Win studied the machine's screen.

Win answered and Thet translated. "This Huli jing is well known to us. They have done unspeakable evil to our people. And yet you and your dwarf friend plan to—all by yourselves—destroy them?" She sighed in irritation. "There are enough crazy foreigners in my country already. I will not import more."

Thet smiled and bowed slightly. "So sorry, Mr. Durand. So sorry. I merely translate."

"I understand, Thet. I don't blame your sister for being skeptical."

Thet relayed this to his sister.

Durand kept his gaze locked on her. "It sounds crazy, I know. But of all the people on this earth, I am uniquely equipped to infiltrate the Huli jing, to gather evidence of their crimes and bring the condemnation of the whole world down on them."

Thet relayed Durand's words.

Win studied Durand and spoke.

Thet said, "The outside world has abandoned us for decades. What makes you think you will make them care about what's happening to our people?"

"Because the Huli jing created something that will disrupt the foundation of all civilization. I just need to get into their genetic labs and obtain evidence of it."

Thet translated.

Win answered. "Huli jing labs are secured by hundreds of soldiers. You would not get within kilometers of them."

Durand focused on her eyes. "I disagree. I think I will get into their labs. Because genetically I'm identical to the leader of the Huli jing—Marcus Wyckes."

Frey winced. "Oh, dear . . ."

Thet was momentarily speechless, but then translated at the urging of Durand. Meanwhile, Durand pulled off his shirt.

As Win's translated words reached their ears, Durand concentrated—willing his tattoos to surface on his skin. And seemingly without effort, the chromatophores began to appear, spreading across his chest and shoulders and neck. He looked up to face the group—now the warlord of the Huli jing. The Fox with Nine Tails.

Cries of alarm went through the men. The entire squad of Shan raised their weapons, and hurled threatening commands at Durand in the Shan dialect.

Bo Win silenced them all again with a terse command of her own. She looked at the intricate and extensive tattoos that seemed to have magically appeared across Durand's muscular frame. Then she spoke.

Still in shock, Thet translated as she did so. "She would think you a demon if she believed in such things. My sister asks, what are you?"

"I am a victim of the Huli jing's genetic experiments."

The men and Bo Win listened to Thet's translation.

"If you have an Internet connection at all—via satellite or otherwise—you'll discover there is a massive manhunt for the leader of the Huli jing. You will find this face on those news reports." Durand pointed at himself. "I'm wanted in a hundred and ninety countries as Marcus Wyckes. But I am *not* Marcus Wyckes." Durand stared intently into her dark eyes. "The Huli jing have discovered a way to edit a fully grown human being. They edited my DNA to transform me into Marcus Wyckes—hoping I would die in the process. And they gave me these marks . . ." He extended his arms. "Genetic tattoos that they use to recognize each other. But I didn't die, and now I'm coming for them."

Durand had to nudge Thet to take the shocked look off his face and have him convey the message to his sister. Again murmurs of confusion went through the soldiers, which Win silenced with another command.

She barked orders at a soldier who had antennas running from his backpack. The man was already working a large-screened, flexible phablet. Moments later he passed it to her with a grave look on his face.

Win held up the phablet screen to see an image of Wyckes in the news compared to the man in front of her.

Whispered comments were already moving through the squad.

Win growled for silence and got it. She glanced again at the interrogation-system screen. The operator shrugged at her. His expression said, *He's telling the truth.*

She approached Durand with the phablet still in her hand, holding the screen right up next to his face. Her face only a foot away from his. Her men held their weapons ready.

The resemblance was undeniable. She flipped from major newsfeed to major newsfeed—BBC to Xinhua to Reuters. Finally she lowered the phablet and spoke to Durand while Thet translated. "If this is true—that the Huli jing have acquired the ability to edit the living—why would they edit your DNA to match their leader?"

"I was doing work for Interpol that was responsible for shutting down hundreds of Huli jing labs. That's why the Huli jing transformed me. Now my own people are hunting me, and if I die, the manhunt for Wyckes will end."

She absorbed Thet's translated words and paced. Her men were hanging on her every movement. Win stopped. "Why should I trust you, shape-changer?"

Durand slowly reached into his pocket as a dozen weapons snapped alert. He held up his other hand and produced the photo of his old self, posing next to Mia and Miyuki. Durand held it up for Win to see.

"This is the real me. And this is my wife and child."

Win stopped cold. Her hand reached out. Durand only reluctantly let the photo go. She studied Durand's real face in the photo and clearly tried to connect it to the one in front of her.

"I need to get back to myself. I cannot exist like this, and I need to make sure this never happens to anyone else. The Huli jing made the mistake of transforming me into the image of their leader—to take the blame for his crimes. I intend to use that to destroy them."

Win still studied the photo.

Durand perceived a softening of her hard eyes.

Thet spoke to Durand. "My sister . . . she had a boy . . . and a husband. Tatmadaw drones killed them."

Durand lowered his head. "I cannot imagine her pain."

Win steeled herself and passed the photo back to Durand, who eagerly took it. She then spoke to her brother.

Thet turned to Durand. "My sister says you have a lovely family. You should be very proud."

Durand felt himself on the verge of tears, momentarily undermining his menacing appearance. "Thank you. I exist for them."

She studied him and removed the interrogation cap from his

head—noticing the tattoos underneath that also traced across his scalp. Win then spoke.

Thet relayed her words. "She says . . . the decision to help you is far above her authority, but she will consult our leaders once we are inside Shan territory. She can promise nothing, but if what you say is true, all things are possible."

Durand nodded. "Thank your sister for me, Thet."

In answer Win wai'd again, which Durand returned with sincerity, touching his nose to his peaked fingers.

With that Win circled her hand and whistled.

The squad of men rushed to get moving.

Chapter 34

hey moved single file along jungle trails that crisscrossed the hills. Monsoon rain started toward late afternoon, with large drops cascading down broad tropical leaves in sizable rivulets.

Kenneth Durand walked in wet, baggy, pale blue pants and a tunic of homespun cloth, as well as the traditional kup hat and sandals. The clothing had been supplied by the Shan, and was thankfully loose-fitting enough to fit even Durand's muscular frame. The sandals did surprisingly well on the muddy track, draining out water instantly.

Durand glanced back at Bryan Frey, who trudged along with surprising aplomb. The Shan had adjusted tunic and pants to fit him in short order as well—though the kup hat looked outsized on him. He'd found a short walking stick of fallen hardwood, and kept up with the Shan resistance fighters, laden as they were with heavy packs.

Minutes after they left the jet landing site, Durand watched as Bo Win coordinated with her outlying teams by burst radio. He was surprised how far sophisticated military equipment had spread. Back when he was in the service, these encrypted handsets were expensive and difficult to maintain. But now they were available all over the Internet—could, in fact, be 3D-printed from Deep Web designs, along with their firmware.

An hour after they began, they linked up with a dozen more Shan resistance fighters, who led donkeys laden with what appeared to be boxes of ammunition or weapons. Durand had a general knowledge of the conflicts in the region, and he knew that Thailand was sympathetic to the cause of the indigenous people in Myanmar—not least because of their friction with the Burmese military, going back centuries.

Another side effect of the ongoing conflict in Myanmar was the hundreds of thousands of refugees fleeing over the border. As the group crested a ridge, through the rain Durand made out the lights and camp-fires of a shockingly massive refugee camp in a valley to their east. Kilometers away, it was still readily visible.

Thet nodded toward it as he noticed Durand's gaze. "UN refugee camp. Seven hundred thousand people. Shan, Hmong, Karen. Many more."

"The Thai authorities host it?"

Thet gestured dismissively. "Once you enter there, very difficult to leave. Camp is twenty years old. Keeps growing."

Durand gave it one more look and compared it to what he knew about the monster refugee camps in Kenya, Malaysia, Turkey, and on and on. There were a hundred million people in official camps—with no good plan for what to do with them. He'd always been daunted by the magnitude of the problem, but he'd never actually laid eyes on one of the camps. It cast a dark cloud over his mood to add to the monsoon rain.

The group camped behind a hill before nightfall. The men used dehydrated food with enclosed heating units for rations. One of these was passed to Durand, along with a water filtration straw. He sat on a log next to Frey and across from Thet, who'd taken a keen interest in them. Frey and Thet had been talking for much of the afternoon.

Durand asked, "How far to the border, Thet?"

Thet smiled. "Just a couple kilometers."

"Will we cross in the night?"

"Oh, no. Darkness has no advantage. Machines see better than we at night. We like day. Rain like this during the day, perfect weather against fighting machines. Worse for them. You should rest." He mimed sleep. "We leave just before dawn."

Soldiers strung up thick, black netting between the trees around the camp.

Frey noticed them working and turned to Thet. "If those are mosquito nets, I'd hate to see the mosquitoes."

Thet laughed good-naturedly. "Anti-drone netting. Snares surveillance units. Sets off alarm."

Men behind him laid out bamboo mats, and soon the group huddled in several different spots under camouflaged tarpaulins in the rain, while others kept watch. Durand recognized the tarp material as a thermal insulator. It would conceal their heat signature from the air. Likewise, he'd seen motion and acoustic sensors set up on their perimeter, scanning the jungle around them for threats, interpreting movement and myriad sounds.

Even here, out on the Thai-Burmese border, algorithms ran the show. He considered this as he watched a stream of rainwater rush a foot past his head in the semidarkness. Durand drifted off to sleep.

They crossed the border near dawn in a mild drizzle and scattered fog. Durand thought the border would be marked in some way or cleared of trees—maybe even fenced, mined, and drone patrolled. Instead, he only heard about their crossing after it was over. He passed by Thet standing next to a tree.

The amiable translator smiled. "Welcome to Myanmar, Mr. Durand."

Durand looked up at the sky. The fog was thick, but he knew they weren't far inside the border. "Aren't you concerned about military drones guarding the border?"

"Tatmadaw seeks to avoid incident with Thai military. Their machines are not so precise in determining enemies. They stay clear of the border. We will face them further in-country—once we reach the Daen Lao Range tomorrow. Rough country there."

Durand looked back at a line of men and donkeys moving up a steep, muddy trail flowing with rainwater.

Frey approached, clinging to the back of a small gray donkey. "You hear that, Ken? We'll be getting to the rough country *tomorrow*, he says."

Durand said nothing, instead looking down at the tattoos half visible on his wet skin. With some effort, he willed them to go away.

•   •   •

Around midday the rain let up, and a humid heat enveloped them. Monkeys and birds began calling again, and a deafening chorus of insect life returned.

As Durand passed Thet and Frey on the trail, Thet pointed at a phablet map that showed roughly where they were—about eight kilometers into Myanmar after nine hours of heavy slogging. Durand was easily able to keep up with the toughest of the soldiers—but also felt guilt for admiring his new body's strength and endurance.

Late in the afternoon, the column stopped, and men readied their weapons. Looking down into a ravine, Durand could see a reddish dirt road, muddy from the rain. They were apparently crossing it in bounding groups, while the others kept watch. Durand could see Thet sitting with his back against a tree, manipulating the remote controller for his quadcopter drone—which was nowhere in sight. Thet wore LFP glasses, which Durand knew would provide a full-immersion VR effect. Apparently he was scouting the road.

Before long, Durand's group was waved onward, along with a line of pack donkeys. As they crossed, recent large truck tracks were visible in the mud. The treads looked deep, suggesting either military or logging vehicles.

From the road Durand could see a line of steep jungle mountains ahead. The beginning of the eastern Burmese highlands—the Daen Lao Range. Durand knew the highest peak there rose roughly 2,500 meters, and they were only in the foothills.

They moved upslope into the steaming jungle, Shan soldiers cutting a path with machetes fifty meters in from the road.

In the late afternoon and a thousand meters uphill, Frey collapsed next to Durand as soldiers prepared camp around them. Durand felt almost unaffected by the march.

Frey groaned. "I finally understand what *saddle sore* means. These are muscles I don't use much. I'm constantly having to counteract whatever Tuk is doing just to stay on his back."

"Tuk is the donkey?"

"Yes, the donkey, and I've come to realize Tuk can make my life miserable for me if he wants."

Durand noticed Bo Win moving through the camp, issuing terse orders to soldiers. As she came up on Durand and Frey, she coldly appraised Frey's obvious exhaustion.

Frey perked up. "Thank you for the donkey, Bo Win. Most appreciated."

She moved past without responding, issuing more orders to men stringing up anti-drone nets.

Durand accepted a self-heating food packet from a soldier passing them out. "I think she's starting to like you."

The next day dawned with monsoon rain. Durand and Frey sat huddled under giant taro leaves among the Shan soldiers, sipping chemically heated tea and scooping sticky rice into their mouths.

Thet sat next to them. "Your tattoos intrigue the men, Mr. Durand."

Durand glanced at his own arms and was relieved to see the tattoos weren't visible.

"You say they are part of your genetic code?"

"Part of Marcus Wyckes's genetic code. Not mine."

Thet nodded.

Frey interjected, "Mr. Durand's skin is biologically like that of a chameleon, Thet."

"Ah. Then you can make your tattoos appear and disappear at will? May I see them again?"

Durand cast a wary look Thet's way.

Frey waved Thet off. "They usually appear only when Mr. Durand is agitated."

"I see. Curious." Thet chewed for several moments, deep in thought. "Tattoos are very important in Shan culture." He pulled up the sleeve of his own tunic to show dragons and other inscrutable symbols lining his arm.

Other Shan fighters around them did the same—displaying their ink. Every one of them was tattooed in several places—one even stuck out his tongue to show a dark swirling pattern on it.

"Tattoos are a rite of passage into adulthood for us—for men and women. A sayah uses a brass-tipped stick to inject 'magical' ingredients beneath our skin. To give us power over illness, or evildoers, or weapons."

Frey cast a skeptical eye in Thet's direction. "And do you believe your tattoos are magical, Thet?"

Thet laughed. "No, Dr. Frey. But some do believe this." He paused. "In fact, some of the men think Mr. Durand's tattoos carry powerful magic."

Durand and Frey exchanged concerned looks.

A whistle went up, and the men started breaking camp.

Monkeys screeched in the distance. By midday the rain had stopped, replaced by shimmering heat and humidity. Nothing about or on Durand was dry. Bugs were everywhere.

A soldier gave a slight whistle to Durand, snapping him alert. The man pointed at his eyes, then directed his fingers ahead. Durand followed them, and as they came around the towering roots of a dipterocarp tree, Durand saw the tangled wreckage of a large military drone, its wings sheared off and scattered in the brush. The gray laminated fuselage was split open like a wasp's thorax—the nose driven into the ground. Vines were already growing around its Russian language markings. A faded Burmese military insignia was visible on its tail fin.

As he walked past, Durand and the others stared at the robotic carcass with foreboding. He had expected the Shan fighters to walk jubilantly past the wreckage, but it looked as though they realized there would always be more drones.

He kept moving downslope and didn't look back.

By midmorning the sound of rushing water was unmistakable. Soon they reached the bottom of a narrow valley, down which a small, fast-moving river flowed. Its brown water was cluttered with logs and leafy debris. The Shan column followed it west.

Durand looked ahead to see Bo Win standing on a rock, looking skyward with some sort of optics. She keyed a radio and then listened.

They had eyes on the sky, then. Good.

Durand fell in next to Frey's donkey as they moved along the river's edge on a freshly hacked trail.

They traveled for several hours in a somnolent state, Durand listening to Tuk's hooves scramble over rocks and squish into the red mud. They trudged one step at a time, torpid in the heat, bathed in sweat.

Then suddenly a shout went up from ahead. Durand saw men rushing for cover. Fifty meters downriver, Shan fighters fell back from the forest toward the riverbank, unslinging their rifles.

More shouting. Then the crackling of automatic gunfire.

Durand moved behind a tree. He peered out to see a metallic, spiderlike object the size of a dog scrambling with remarkable swiftness over rocks and among a group of Shan fighters.

Then it exploded, sending an echoing boom across the valley. The detonation hit Durand like a physical object, and he dropped to the mud as a piece of shrapnel whined past in the trees.

Frey's donkey brayed and bolted, tossing him into the mud.

Screams came from downriver. Someone was in great pain. Smoke billowed from a crater. More shouting in the Shan dialect.

Durand looked up from the mud to see soldiers scanning the trees upslope as medics moved toward the injured. He turned to see Frey concealing himself behind a river rock.

"What the hell was that?"

The screaming continued.

Durand moved alongside him. "Spider mine."

"That's a thing now?"

"Used in anti-insurgency operations. They usually program them to listen for enemy dialects. It lays out a web of microphones, and it'll hone in, aiming to detonate itself in the middle of the enemy."

"Fuck me. I thought I never wanted to go to a war, and now I'm certain I don't."

Durand noticed that his own tattoos were on full display on his forearms and no doubt elsewhere. Not surprising, given how fast his heart was beating.

The screaming had ceased—either due to painkillers or worse.

Frey rolled onto his back. "I hate this evil shit."

Thet came running toward them, his M4 out and ready. "Mr. Durand. Dr. Frey." Thet seemed to ignore the reappearance of Durand's tattoos. "We cannot remain here. The mine will have sent a coded signal prior to exploding. Drones will be coming. We must go. Quickly."

Durand got to his feet and grabbed Frey, picking him up entirely.

"Let go of me!"

"Not the time, Bryan." Durand leaped over rocks as he carried Frey past a scene of blood-smeared rocks and human intestines, while medics worked furiously on a wounded soldier who appeared unconscious. The coppery smell of blood, sulfur, and butyric acid filled his nostrils for a moment as he rushed past with a column of other Shan fighters.

He saw Bo Win studying the skies again and shouting at them. He didn't need to understand her language to know she was telling them to *move*. They crashed through the underbrush, heading upslope.

His body felt strong, despite the heat and Frey's considerable weight in his arms. Due to Frey's foreshortened legs and arms, he couldn't put the dwarf on his back, but instead held him to his chest like a child.

"I'm not comfortable with this, Ken."

"Shut up." Durand surged uphill, using what trail was made by those ahead of him. They soon turned westward, higher up the valley wall and moved double-time along the slope. A few kilometers later, exhausted, the men took refuge beneath a thick stand of bamboo.

Durand still felt strong. He put Frey down and stood with a group of panting fighters. They stared at his sharply defined array of tattoos—whispering among themselves.

Frey straightened his tunic.

Fifteen minutes later Durand's tattoos had faded, but they hadn't disappeared entirely. By then the rest of the group had arrived, first the donkey train, followed by Thet and two stretchers, one containing a wounded man, the other with a green biofilm, vacuum body bag strapped to it.

Bo Win brought up the rear with her radio team. She listened to earphones and hissed orders. Men rushed to deploy thermal tarps.

But after a half hour of tense sky watching and listening to radio reports, she eventually ordered the column to move out again.

The rest of the day was spent moving along the valley wall, parallel to the river. They could still hear the water below them. At some point Durand passed Win watching her men walk by, clearly inspecting each one of them, voicing encouragement.

As he passed her, she nodded to him, and he to her.

A dozen kilometers later the exhausted soldiers made camp in a thickly forested valley bottom. The Daen Lao Range rose all around them now—a rugged jungle wilderness.

As Durand sat in the gathering darkness, watching Frey bandage his many blisters, Thet approached and sat down with them. He wasn't his usual smiling self.

"How's the wounded man, Thet?"

"He died as well, unfortunately." Thet gestured across his own abdomen. "The shrapnel pattern is designed to cause internal bleeding."

Durand said nothing.

"Tomorrow we cross the Salween River. It runs north to south in our path—two hundred and fifty meters wide."

Frey sighed. "Do I even want to ask what's waiting for us there?"

"The Salween is always our biggest barrier. It is watched, but our people watch it as well. No one is better at getting supply chains across the Salween than my sister. But I wanted you to know what's coming tomorrow."

Durand nodded. "Thank you."

"Pray for rain and fog." With that Thet moved away to speak with the other men.

Durand could also see Bo Win moving from group to group, listening to them. Durand could see she had the men's respect. She had undoubtedly earned it.

In the night Durand and the entire camp were suddenly awakened by a spine-chilling shriek that ripped past overhead. It sounded like a chainsaw cutting corrugated tin, and almost as quickly as it had arrived, it faded away down along the valley.

Looking across the camp, Durand could hear the clatter of weapons as men huddled beneath their thermal tarps. Whatever it was, it wasn't going to be held back by anti-drone nets. He figured it had been going a few hundred kilometers per hour.

He turned to see Frey's eyes in the darkness.

"What in the living Christ was that?"

"Probably something looking for us."

Durand peeked out beneath the tarp to see lights in the sky and more horrific sounds like tearing metal. He tried not to think about the large stretch of water they were going to cross come daylight.

Before dawn Bo Win walked among the men. They got up, hastily ate rations, then broke camp without a word necessary from her. They headed upslope, trudging all morning toward a ridgeline they couldn't see through the thick canopy of trees.

But finally they crested the ridge, and for a moment, Durand could see through the treetops, down into the valley and the massive brown river flowing between jungle mountains below them. It was like something from another age. No development lined its banks. No ships appeared on the several-kilometer stretch he could see.

And then he was moving downhill, back beneath the trees.

Unfortunately the day dawned clear. By early afternoon Shan fighters lay concealed behind trees and boulders as sunlight shined through the trees ahead—marking the river's edge.

Several of the men stole glances at Durand. He looked at his forearms and could see that his tattoos had never truly faded from the night before. He felt them keenly now—as though they were becoming more a part of him.

Thet moved at a crouch to Durand and Frey, who were lying with their backs against a vine-strewn boulder. "Our transport has arrived."

Frey looked relieved. "So we're not crossing the river on our own?"

"No. Local people have fished and worked the Salween for

centuries. Their boats move up and down the river. They help us. We will stagger the crossing so as not to draw attention. We load the weapons and ammunition in a nearby stream. On the far bank of the Salween we will be met by more of our people."

Frey took a deep breath. "How many times have you and your sister done this?"

"Many times." Thet smiled. "Follow me."

Durand and Frey fell in behind him as they moved along a line of other fighters, readying their weapons. They emerged onto the bank of a calm stream that flowed into the wide body of the Salween. Waiting for them there was a colorful long-tail boat piled with crates that were covered by a purple tarpaulin, lashed in place by nylon cord. A small cabin stood just ahead of the engine, which resembled nothing so much as a car engine bolted, open-air, into the bottom of the boat. From it a differential linked it to a long pole, at the end of which was a propeller that the operator steered like a rudder.

The entire length of the boat was painted green and red, with highlights of gold leaf and ornamental Burmese script.

They climbed the gangplank and took places inside the small cabin, joining three other Shan soldiers.

Thet smiled. "The first boat is already across. My sister is waiting on the far shore. The second boat is nearly there as well."

Frey looked reassured.

The powerful engine rumbled to life, drowning out their conversation for the moment. Several men pushed the boat into the stream, where the pilot quickly lowered his propeller and hit the throttle.

Durand watched the trees race past with surprising speed. He'd ridden in navy go-fast boats. This vessel wasn't far off their pace.

They roared out of the tributary and turned in against the Salween's current, still driving upriver with impressive speed. Thet motioned for them to remain low as they plied along, looking to casual inspection like a local bringing goods to market upstream.

Glancing ahead, Durand could see the wake of similar boats here and there along the Salween's silty brown water. So the river wasn't deserted. Likewise, he could see a small village with bamboo docks and thatched roofs upriver on the far shore. It was like something from a previous age.

The air felt cooler here on the water, and the breeze flowing around them felt even better. He glanced over at Frey, who was leaning back, enjoying it.

Frey laughed. "I didn't think it was going to be this nice."

Durand turned back upriver and studied the looming mountains to the north. The Salween wound its way through them from up near the Himalayas. Here, they were far from just about everywhere. Africa had never felt this remote. This inaccessible. And it occurred to Durand that he would likely never return from this journey.

This thought darkened his mood considerably despite the sun and fair breeze.

A shout came from up on deck. Durand looked up to see a man on the bow pointing. He followed the man's gaze toward a distant object hoving into view around a bend in the river. It soon resolved into some type of hydrofoil craft—a vessel whose propulsion and stabilization lay beneath the water. These lifted the body of the vessel out of the water at speed—eliminating most of the resistance and enabling fast movement.

Thet stiffened and drew compact binoculars. "This is a problem."

Frey looked up with a start. "What is it?"

Thet passed the binoculars to Durand. "Patrol drone. They sometimes move submerged for stretches. It must have gotten past our lookouts."

Frey sat up straight. "A drone boat?"

Durand aimed the binoculars upriver and saw what was unmistakably an unmanned patrol boat with what looked like a twenty-millimeter cannon up front.

Thet shouted something at the driver.

Durand looked back to see the man was unsettled.

"We duck down and rely upon our cover. It is an autonomous vehicle—unlikely to open fire on locals who don't match its target pattern."

Durand ducked low but looked ahead to see the hydrofoil veering to their port, heading in toward the lead boat that was half a kilometer ahead of them. "What's it doing?"

Thet watched with obvious anxiety.

The lead long-tail boat took evasive maneuvers and made a beeline for the far bank. Durand immediately knew it was a mistake. Algorithmically, flight was likely to elicit a pursuit response from an autonomous weapon. The boat pilot had panicked.

Thet muttered. "No. No . . ."

An orange tracer round suddenly raced out from the stable platform of the drone gunboat—with a rapid series of cracks reaching them a moment later.

The lead long-tail boat ripped apart—its cargo exploding and casting flaming debris high into the air.

Frey dove for the deck.

Thet shouted at their pilot, motioning to head straight upriver.

Durand watched as orange tracer rounds suddenly streamed out of the jungle from various places on shore, skipping off the water and past the hydrofoil as it arced back toward its prey.

A rocket suddenly streaked out from the far shore as well. It impacted the hydrofoil aft, causing its rear foils to buckle. The vessel rolled at speed into the water, breaking apart in a geyser of white foam.

Thet shouted up to their boat pilot, motioning toward the far shore.

But already Durand noticed movement in the sky. Apparently something had been waiting for them after the incident with the crawling mine. "We've got incoming, Thet!" Durand pointed. He focused the binoculars, though it was hard to keep them steady.

Autonomous choppers—torpedo-shaped gray slugs heading over the ridgeline and across the water.

The long-tail boat leaned into a turn, and soon they evened their keel, making a run for the far bank, just a hundred meters away now.

Suddenly the supersonic snap of bullets ripped the air around them, shattering the nearby window, piercing the wood with spots of sunlight and sending splinters everywhere. One of the three soldiers slumped over as Durand and Thet dove for cover next to Frey. The other two soldiers climbed out on deck.

The long-tail boat pitched right, then left again as the soldiers moved to the gunwales and opened fire on an incoming drone chopper.

Tracers still streamed out of the jungle toward the evasive, fast-moving aircraft.

Thet looked to the stern of the boat, shouted, then got up and raced aft.

Durand turned to see that the boat's pilot was missing—the entire rear of their boat had been speckled with bullet holes. The engine was still running, but unattended, the long-tail propeller slalomed from side to side. They were making little progress toward shore.

Thet crawled across the deck to grab the throttle.

Durand moved to check the pulse of the soldier who'd slumped over in the cabin. He laid the man down next to Frey and could see there was a sucking chest wound. The unconscious man struggled for breath with his other lung, blood spilling out of him.

Durand pulled a can of wound sealant from the man's web harness, bit the cap off, and inserted the sterile tip into the worst of the bleeding—pressing the actuator. The medical coagulant oozed out, covering the wound. He shouted at Frey, "You're a doctor, aren't you?"

"Not that sort of doctor!" He covered his head as more bullets snapped in.

The soldiers fired their M4s into the air just outside.

Between shots and the roar of the engine, Frey shouted, "We need to get off this goddamned river!"

Durand looked back at Thet directing the long-tail's rudder.

A chopper flew past, ripping the deck with bullets and detonating the fuel tank. Flames roared into the cabin as Durand hit the deck again. The flames receded, but the boat's engine died.

Durand looked up to see that Thet was gone. The aft deck was on fire.

Durand raced toward the stern, past the smoking engine, and looked out behind them, through the flames.

Thet's body lay facedown in the current some ways back. Glancing over his shoulder, Durand could see the boat was nearly to shore—and clearly had the momentum to reach it.

Durand tossed his kup and pulled off his tunic, then dove into the silted river. He surfaced, feeling the current draw him onward—away from the flaming boat as it impacted the riverbank.

Durand swam as fast as he could toward Thet's body, rolling with the slow current. As he did so, he saw yellow and green tracers rip across the sky. One of the choppers pinwheeled in flames a thousand meters downrange. But he also saw more choppers cresting the distant ridge.

Durand swam harder, and heard the same buzz saw sound they'd heard in the middle of the night, and only now realized it was what you heard right before one of these damn things flew over you.

Durand dove deep into the water and heard high-velocity rounds whip into the water all around him, slowing almost instantly. Moments later he burst back to the surface to see the fiery turbofan at the tail end of a receding chopper—racing across the water, chased by tracers streaming from both shores.

Durand reached Thet and grabbed him by the tunic collar, rolling him faceup. He then wrapped an arm around the man's chest and pulled him backward, as he'd been trained in innumerable navy rescue drills. His arms felt powerful, capable, and he pulled for shore, simultaneously checking Thet for visible wounds. He didn't see any bullet punctures on the front of the man's tunic, but he did see a nasty, bleeding gash on Thet's head. He focused on pulling him to shore as chopper engines, gunfire, and bullets tore up the air overhead.

Minutes later Durand came into the shallows under the shade of thorny acacia trees, roughly five hundred meters downriver from where the long-tail boat burned on shore.

He strained to pull Thet up onto the bank, and then did a fireman's carry to bring him into the jungle. There, Durand laid Thet down, and checked for breathing and a pulse. He found neither and started doing CPR, pressing the heel of his palm at a measured pace as river water bubbled out of Thet's throat and his head wound bled.

Durand heard thrashing in the brush nearby and looked up to see two Shan resistance fighters emerge. They put down their weapons and came to assist. Durand pointed at the bleeding scalp wound before returning his focus to CPR.

The men broke out field dressings and applied pressure while the gunfire still raged out on the river.

Moments later Thet coughed out the last of the water and gasped for air. Several moments after that, he opened his eyes.

Durand stopped the compression. He looked into Thet's eyes. "You see me? Do you see me?"

Thet nodded.

"Follow my finger. What's your name?"

"Thet Ko Lin."

"Good." Durand looked up to meet the gaze of the soldiers. "Go see if Dr. Frey is okay."

Thet coughed again, and to Durand's surprise, he translated Durand's instructions to the two men.

The two soldiers put Thet's arms over them and followed as Durand blazed a trail back upriver. The gunfire and chopper noise had begun to die down. After several minutes of thrashing through the undergrowth, they could hear orders being shouted. It was a voice Durand recognized.

Bo Win.

They emerged from the brush to see a dozen soldiers pulling boxes out of the still-burning long-tail boat.

One of the soldiers shouted and pointed at Thet being carried. Several of the men moved to help. Win raced to the front of them, talking fast.

Thet waved her away as she tried to examine his head wound. Durand watched them go, while others remained to unload the weapons and ammunition from the boat.

"I'm alive, in case you're curious."

Durand turned to see Frey holding a bandage against his own bleeding scalp.

"I could use some sealant, I think."

"We need to get inland."

A shout went up at the sound of approaching jets. The Shan grabbed the last of the crates, motioning for Durand and Frey to move.

• • •

That night unseen aircraft crisscrossed the skies for miles around their camp—thundering jets and autonomous choppers—but the Shan fighters lay concealed beneath a rock outcropping, hemmed in close by artocarpus trees and a heavy jungle canopy.

Most of the weapons and other supplies had made it across the river, but several of their fighters had been killed, wounded, or were still missing. Likewise, a couple boats were still hiding in tributaries on the eastern bank. But they would follow in coming days. Still, Durand counted at least twice as many people now and saw new faces. Apparently they'd linked up with some other group.

Durand could see Bo Win speaking gravely with another Shan commander as they examined maps on LFP glasses over near the base of the rock face. Word had come down that the supply column would be moving onward at dawn.

Thet was in a makeshift infirmary tent, among other wounded. Frey and Durand had lost their interpreter for the time being. Instead, Durand heard the Shan fighters whispering as he passed by. They smiled and bowed wais to him.

He knew his tattoos were still visible. A glance at his arms showed they had not faded at all, even hours after the river crossing.

Later, while Durand sat in the darkness, trying to remember the contours of Miyuki's face, he became aware that the men around him were making room for someone walking through.

He looked up and barely discerned Bo Win's features from the reflected light of a three-quarter moon. Durand stood and bowed, peaking his hands.

She stood silently before him for several moments, then put her hands together and bowed, looking back up at him. She said in halting English, "My thanks . . . for brother . . . Mr. Durin."

He bowed to her again.

Her expression softened for just a moment; then Win moved on, slipping between her soldiers—who all looked back at Durand in the darkness. He could feel their eyes on him.

Durand longed to be home. To be himself. And yet the trajectory of his life could be very different. He sensed how thin the cord was that tied him to himself.

Frey sat up from the shadows nearby. "You saved Thet's life?"

Durand nodded.

Frey's eyes followed Win. "Good." He got comfortable on his bamboo mat. "I rather like Thet."

Chapter 35

Morning brought rain again and low cloud cover, but the men broke
camp in good spirits because it wasn't drone weather. The column
marched in silence along freshly hacked trails and into a broad jungle
valley, parsed by streams and swamps. The ground churned almost
immediately to mud with the passage of hooves and feet.

Midmorning Durand came alongside Thet's litter. Two soldiers carried the man on a folding carbon fiber frame.

Thet smiled broadly. "Mr. Durand. They say you saved me."

"Then we're even, Thet; you and your sister are saving me right now."

Thet pointed. "Your tattoos—they are visible today."

Durand looked down at his arms and nodded—unsure whether
they'd ever go away again.

"The men believe your tattoos protected you from the drones—back
at the river."

Durand said nothing. Instead, he bowed a wai to Thet and moved
ahead.

Soon Frey, riding Tuk, fell in behind Durand. "What's going on
with you exactly?"

Durand walked in silence.

"It's rather easy to notice when you're upset. You wear it on your
sleeve."

Durand cast an annoyed glance at Frey. "I can feel myself slipping
away. That's what's going on."

"Are you losing your connection to the chromatophores?"

"I'm having trouble remembering what *I* was like. How it felt to be Kenneth Durand." He examined his arms. "There are things I don't even think about anymore . . ."

Frey contemplated this. "So, tell me something about Kenneth Durand."

"I told you I—"

"Surely you remember Kenneth Durand's life. *Experience* makes us who we are. So where did Kenneth Durand come from anyway? And what possessed him to go to the Naval Academy, of all things? It seems a rather jingoistic choice. Enlighten me."

Durand walked in brooding silence for a bit. "It wasn't a choice. It was a goal. We were poor. I told myself that my mother and my brother and sister were counting on me to succeed."

"Well, you did succeed. You should be proud."

"But I never really came back." Durand picked up his pace and moved ahead in the column.

That evening they camped in a narrow defile with a waterfall and idyllic pool of water nearby. Durand moved through the camp to smiles and nods. He noticed that Thet was sitting up and drinking tea now, laughing as he spoke to the other men.

While helping to string up the anti-drone nets, Durand put his comprehensive knot skills to use and demonstrated a quick-release highwayman's knot several times to the Shan fighters, who observed his hands closely. The language barrier made it easier to focus on his actual hand movements. The men were fast learners, and they soon put that clever knot to use, smiling at him.

While crossing camp, Durand passed Bo Win. They nodded and continued—though he felt their shared gaze linger a moment longer than necessary. He spent the remainder of the night with an unsettled feeling. In the darkness he pulled out the photo of his family, but he could not see it. Instead, he thumbed its surface.

• • •

After a fitful sleep, Durand awoke in the predawn. The chorus of insects drowned out the thin waterfall nearby. He eased out from between the other sleeping fighters and walked toward the pool of water. He splashed the cool water over his face and ran his hand through it. In the evening he hadn't noticed that the water was so clear—the first clear water he'd seen in this mountainous, mud-filled jungle.

Predawn and it was already in the high seventies, and he could see tunics drying on branches. He pulled off his own tunic and eased into the water. It was only a couple meters deep. He swam along the bank, feeling the coolness seep into him. He rolled over to gaze at the canopy above. He listened to the calls of tropical birds. Water cascaded down from a cliff face fifty meters high.

He suddenly wondered if there were poisonous snakes in the pool. It startled him upright in the water. Durand turned toward the bank and noticed Bo Win standing there.

At first he thought she might be angry with him for taking a swim, but her expression remained neutral.

He reached for the bank and pulled himself up through the brush. He wai'd to her silently. She still stared at him.

Durand looked around to see if the camp was stirring, but the sun had not yet touched the eastern horizon. Only the sentries on the perimeter were awake.

He felt her hand brush his arm, and he looked down to see she was there next to him, a head shorter than he. Close.

Win spoke softly in the Shan dialect. Just then Durand wanted more than anything to understand her as he watched her beautiful eyes catch reflected light. The desire he felt began to consume him. With effort he recalled his family. His wife and daughter.

He *knew* it shouldn't require effort, but at that moment Kenneth Durand seemed more like a man he once knew than his true self. This was becoming his real life.

And it fit him. He felt at home in chaos.

But that wasn't true. He knew it wasn't. He'd loved everything about his old life—even if he couldn't see it now.

But a realization nearly crushed him.

Was he going through the motions? Striving toward a goal because Kenneth Durand wanted it? There was a *void* where his rage had once been. He felt the driving force of it fading.

This had to be some evolved trait. Some plasticity of the human mind to adapt to new circumstances. He felt his grip on Durand weakening.

Win was looking with concern into his eyes, and she seemed to sense that he was struggling with intense emotions. She clasped his hand.

He took a deep breath and closed his eyes. He tried to imagine his wife's face.

He could not.

He opened his eyes to see Win. If she moved to him, he could not resist her. He knew that now. And he knew she sensed it, too.

Win gazed at him for several moments and then leaned her head against his shoulder. He stroked her hair as they stood this way for a moment.

And then she pushed slowly away from him, looking up with eyes that seemed to say, *In some other life.*

Win then turned and moved silently toward the camp.

Durand felt as if he teetered on the edge of a precipice he had only just now noticed. He knelt on the ground—the faces of his wife and daughter coming to him clearly now.

The realization that he'd been ready—willing—to leave them behind brought tears to his eyes. He wept silently.

He needed—*needed*—to get his identity back. The anger had returned. But he could not help wonder how much longer it would remain. How long would he be able to perceive his current self as the "other"—before his old self started to fade?

But then he noticed his arms in the dim light.

The Huli jing tattoos had faded. Suddenly gone.

He stood and focused his mind. He was Kenneth Durand. Kenneth Durand.

• • •

Durand **marched with** the lead fighters that day, staying near the front, keeping his thoughts to himself as they came down out of the Burmese highlands. Through occasional gaps between the trees he could see low foothills and a broad valley ahead—miles across with the far side lost in haze.

The men seemed more at ease here, and sure enough, Durand could see a patchwork of rice paddies on the valley floor ahead.

By evening they walked along a berm with rice paddies to either side. Water buffalo wallowed in brown creeks nearby, and they could see farmers knee-deep in water waving welcome.

The fighters waved back.

Eventually, the column entered a small village like something from a bygone age. The thatched roof huts were raised on bamboo stilts, and yet there were solar panels and satellite dishes, too. Durand could see 3D printers in tool sheds and a gray-haired man wearing LFP glasses, motioning with his hands as he manipulated virtual objects.

Bo Win moved past Durand, heading to the front to meet the village elder, who came out to greet them, along with barking dogs and lots of barefoot children in T-shirts and tunics. There was smiling and hugging.

Frey's donkey came up along with the rest of the pack train, and he laboriously dismounted to the great amusement of the children, who gathered around him, laughing.

"Ah, yes, the funny little dwarf. The honesty of children. How refreshing." He smiled at them.

Durand watched Bo Win. She saluted a trim, dignified-looking man in military uniform who had emerged from a corrugated metal building with several other soldiers, automatic rifles slung over their shoulders. After listening for a few moments, they invited her inside.

"What do you figure that's all about?"

Frey walked up alongside. "Reporting in. She'll pass along information about us, no doubt."

Durand watched the door close behind her.

• • •

That night the resistance fighters sat around a long wooden table, sharing platters of rice, stir-fried vegetables, wooden bowls of soup, and bottled beer. The men laughed and spoke over one another. They seemed elated to have survived another supply run. Glad to be near home.

Durand watched them, envious.

Frey sat next to Thet—who was up and walking now, though with a line of pale blue wound sealant running across his scalp.

"Tell me, Thet, where do we go from here?"

"Most of these men will head north tomorrow. My sister awaits instructions from superiors."

"Regarding us?"

Thet nodded.

Frey gestured to the pork rice Durand was eating. "I thought you were a degan."

"Fuck off."

Thet raised his eyebrows. "You prefer deathless meat, Mr. Durand?"

Durand looked up. "I didn't become a degan for spiritual reasons. It was for my daughter. It's better for the environment."

Frey snorted. "*Our* environment, he means—not the pig's, clearly. Because that's what we mean when we say 'the environment,' right?"

Durand cast an annoyed look Frey's way.

"Though I suppose transhumanists might use this 'change agent' technology to edit their lungs to metabolize a different gas mixture— then there will indeed be a big struggle over saving the environment. *Whose environment?* I'd say we're heading toward an increasingly disordered world, Thet. Though the local picture in places like Singapore and London might be very pleasant indeed, I don't imagine we are going to remain a single species for much longer. Pity."

Thet pointed.

Durand and Frey turned to see Win emerge from the communications shed. She motioned to her brother in coded hand signals.

He nodded back at her. "I will need to make preparations. Apparently you are going north."

Chapter 36

The next morning they boarded a long-tail boat on a nearby canal under a sky that threatened rain, thunder rumbling ominously in the foothills. Most of the other fighters had moved on before dawn. Accompanying Durand and Frey were Bo Win, Thet, three resistance fighters, and a farmer piloting the boat. All of them were dressed in indigo-dyed tunics made of homespun fabric, with baggy pants cinched beneath their shirts. More importantly, they all wore the conical bamboo hats as they clambered aboard, with Durand and Frey shielding their faces from the sky.

Given the resolution of drone surveillance platforms—and the amount of both Western and Eastern equipment sold to the regime—Durand knew that security was a real concern.

Moments after boarding, the powerful engine of the long-tail roared to life, and they soon raced down the canal at a considerable speed. Water buffalo fled onto the banks as they approached.

Keeping the kup on his head took considerable effort with the wind, but Durand poked his head up high enough to gaze out onto mist-filled rice paddies to either side.

He noticed Bo Win doing the same. She met his gaze without intent. Whatever had passed between them two days before, she had moved on.

Bo Win must have made the case to bring Durand and Frey to her leadership. She had put her reputation on the line for him.

The boat soon joined a narrow river that snaked through the low foothills of the Burmese highlands. Reeds and bamboo forests closed in on either side. Ruins of ancient brick temples rose from the bush— overgrown and shattered from either time or earlier conflicts. Durand guessed they must have been centuries old.

The temple ruins increased in number, and as they came around a bend in the river, they soon emerged into a large lake. They left the coast behind and raced out over the dark blue water.

Durand could make out rounded hills kilometers away on the far shore. Traditional fishermen were already out on the lake, standing on one leg in their narrow wooden boats and rowing a stern oar with the other leg as they cast homemade nets.

It was a scene that must have been occurring here every morning for a thousand years. The sense of permanence calmed Durand.

In the water behind these fishermen stood whitewashed domed stupas and chedis. They rose from the water's surface, creating a maze. Some lay in ruins; others were still bright white. Some even had gold pinnacles, catching the sun's light as it crested the horizon.

They passed between the holy sites, their wake lapping against the aging brick at the waterline.

By midday, the boat approached a large Buddhist monastery with curving tiled roofs. Saffron-robed monks walked the grounds, and a massive, vine-choked stone temple rose behind it.

The boat slowed, and the farmer eased the bow onto a gravel beach. Young, bald-headed monks came to assist them in disembarking, reaching to hold hands as the passengers hopped down. Yet they did not touch Bo Win, instead keeping a respectful distance—whether by social custom or due to her position, Durand did not know.

The monks had no outward response to Frey's dwarfism, and assisted him out of the boat and onto shore with great care.

Frey joined Durand on the beach, looking back at the young monks. "They seem nice."

Durand nodded toward Thet, who was motioning for them to follow.

Win was already well ahead. Her men remained back in the boat, weapons concealed. Durand and Frey caught up with Thet.

Durand took in the enormity and age of the ornate structure as they walked beneath its stone arches. He could see dozens of robed monks of all ages watching them and smiling, some of them bowing in greeting. "Where are we, Thet?"

Thet put his hands together. "So sorry. I cannot say, Mr. Durand."

He brought Durand and Frey deeper into the ancient building. Soon the sights and smells changed from incense to something more like a hospital. As they followed Win, Durand was shocked as they passed wards containing deformed children playing on the wooden floors, or sleeping in cribs, while robed monks cared for them.

The children ranged in age from infancy to six or seven years old—Bamar, Shan, or Karen, Durand couldn't tell. But their genetic deformities made him wince despite his best efforts. Double-faced or with multiple extra arms and legs, misshapen bodies that curled upon themselves. This wasn't some random situation. He knew it was the result of reckless genetic editing. His heart sank at the sight of them. Children crying in discomfort and intractable confusion tore at his parental instincts.

"Thet . . . My god, what is this?"

"The Huli jing. They experiment on embryos to . . . how do you say? Map gene expression. They allow all their experiments to gestate to birth, and carefully record the results. Most are destroyed. Some, like these, are discarded."

Frey moved into one of the doorways, and looked as though he was on the edge of a breakdown. He gazed out upon the children, his mouth moving wordlessly.

There were dozens of children in view, and possibly many more in the rooms and wards beyond.

Frey finally said, "The monks care for them."

Thet nodded. "They say they are trapped in these bodies for this life."

Frey appeared on the verge of tears. "This wasn't karma. They didn't deserve this. No child deserves this." He turned to Thet. "I have some medical training. Some may be suffering from disorders that can be ameliorated. My skills might be of some use."

"I am certain the monks would be very glad of your assistance, Dr. Frey."

Frey looked out at the ward again. "To be an active intellect impris-
oned in a nonfunctioning body. I sometimes forget how fortunate I am."

Thet tugged at Frey's sleeve. "We must follow Bo Win, please."

Frey nodded, and they all three continued down the corridor, past
genetically monstrous children playing with smiling monks.

They walked through towering, carved wooden doors into a room
lined with representations of the Buddha in many manifestations, some
fashioned in gold, jade, and opal, others in wood or stone.

Bo Win had removed her kup, and both Durand and Frey did likewise. She turned and spoke rapidly in the Shan dialect as they approached.

Thet translated. "My sister asks that you release your final payment,
Dr. Frey."

Frey's face fell and then morphed into irritation. "Standing as we are
in a place of spiritual enlightenment—and so recently passing through a
place of severe human suffering—I'm not particularly of a mind to discuss money right now, Bo Win."

Thet relayed Frey's words, and Win's face hardened. She replied
immediately.

"My sister says that—"

"You can tell your sister that the deal was that I would arrange for
payment when Mr. Durand and I were both safely arrived in Naypyidaw.
This does not look like Naypyidaw."

Thet spoke for several moments, exchanging terse words with Win.

"My sister says that the arrangement changed when Mr. Durand
revealed that he has been genetically transformed into the leader of the
Huli jing."

Durand interjected, "How has it changed, Thet?"

Win turned to Durand. She spoke in Shan but looked into Durand's
eyes.

Thet's English words overlaid her own. "I have beseeched my leaders on your behalf. I await word from them. My people may do a great
deal more than merely deliver you to the capital. We may try to help you
succeed."

She added in English of her own, "Mr. Durin."

Durand felt shame. The intensity in her eyes had many dimensions.

Was it faith in him? Conviction of her cause? He looked down and then placed his hands together before him, bowing deeply to her.

Durand then spoke to Frey without looking. "Give her the money."

"What do you mean, give her the money? We're not—"

"We're alive because of her. I trust her and Thet with my life." He looked up. "You should, too."

"Oh, and you're a great judge of character all of a sudden?"

"I trusted you, didn't I?"

Frey was about to argue but stopped.

"Give her the code for the wallet."

"The entire four hundred thousand?"

"Yes. Let's be done with this. They'll need the money. Look around you."

Frey was already nodding. "Okay. I'm just not used to changing a deal." He looked up to Thet. "Can you please give me a pen, Thet?"

"Yes, of course." Thet searched in his shoulder bag and came up with a pen and a worn leather-bound notepad.

"Oh, I like this. Can I keep this?"

"Bryan."

Frey cast an irritated glance at Durand, then jotted several codes onto the paper. He stabbed the last dot with a flourish before handing over the pad and pen. "There you go."

Thet nodded and placed his hands together. "Thank you, Dr. Frey. The money is very much needed by our cause. Particularly in light of upcoming expenses." He spoke to Bo Win as he handed her the notepad.

She examined it and then nodded to Frey and finally turned to Durand. She then departed.

Durand watched her go. "What now, Thet?"

Thet grimaced. "It will take some days until our leaders make a decision. Until then, we have concealed rooms in the monastery. Please follow me."

Chapter 37

Over the next several days Durand walked the grounds among ancient wats, stupas, and crumbling statues. Thet insisted Durand remain out of sight—though the same prohibition wasn't extended to Frey, who had taken to working with the genetically altered orphans in the ward.

At times Durand could see Frey interacting with patients through grillwork that provided a veiled view into the main hall. It was as though a stranger had possessed Frey. Durand barely recognized the gene hacker he'd hired back in Johor. Frey was kind and patient with the deformed children in his care. Making kid jokes that another monk translated. Durand supposed Frey could identify with these children— trapped as they were in bodies they did not choose.

It was an increasingly common malady.

Durand remained hidden, pacing around a courtyard, circling the base of a towering Buddha damaged in some ancient war. Burmese cats were his main companions. No one else seemed to come to this place. The cats climbed onto his lap to sleep, and purr. They distracted him from his anxieties for a time. But then he'd remember his daughter's toyger and start to worry about the Shan leadership's decision. And what was taking so long.

Two days had already passed since their payment.

On the third day, late in the afternoon, an elderly monk wearing printed plastic eyeglasses and a saffron robe entered through an ironbound wooden gate. He looked to be in his late eighties and clicked along with a cane. His exposed shoulders still looked fit.

The monk's expression changed from serenity to apparent surprise at the sight of Durand. It occurred to Durand that very few knew he was here.

The elderly monk bowed a shallow wai in greeting, smiling.

Durand stood up from a stone bench, a cat leaping from his lap. He bowed a deep wai in return.

The monk then commenced slowly walking around the base of the Buddha shrine, deep in contemplation. He worked beads in his free hand as he did so. Every so often he would pass in front of Durand as he walked ancient stone slabs.

On one of his laps, he looked to Durand and softly said, "*Dukkha.*"

Durand looked up. "Sorry, I don't speak—"

"The word refers to suffering," he said in English. He gestured with his free hand. "A longing for what isn't. I see it on your face. Worry."

"You speak English."

The monk spoke with a British accent. "Some still learn English." He refocused on Durand. "You are consumed with worry."

Durand nodded. "I have good reason to worry."

"Do you?" The old monk moved over to him and eased down onto the bench. "And what do you worry about?"

Durand looked toward the mountains. "I need to get home."

"Craving leads to disappointment and sorrow. This we call *dukkha.* Suffering. It is one of the two characteristics of *sankhara*—'conditioned phenomena' through which we perceive the physical world."

Durand sighed in irritation. He appreciated the old man's concern, but at the same time, platitudes weren't going to solve anything. "I'll bear that in mind."

"What you do is up to you. But be conscious of what you do. Why do you worry?"

Durand recalled the compassion these monks displayed to the disfigured orphans in their care, and he took a more conciliatory tone. "I worry that I will never see my home or my wife and daughter again."

"But at some point this will be true. No matter what you do."

Durand paused. "Very powerful people want to make sure it happens now."

"And so you suffer."

Durand nodded.

"I was a biochemist until my fifties."

Durand looked up in surprise.

"Oh, yes. In Hyderabad. That was fine for many years."

"Why did you leave it?"

"Because everyone I loved perished. In a flood."

"My god . . . I'm so sorry."

"No one was to blame."

Durand remained silent.

"Theravada Buddhism follows the Pāli Canon—a collection of the oldest Buddhist texts. They teach us that life has but three characteristics, the first of which is *anicca*—impermanence. All conditioned phenomena are subject to change: physical characteristics, assumptions, theories, knowledge. Nothing is permanent because all things are bound together, recursively, and as one changes, so, too, do the others. It is the longing to stop this change that causes the second characteristic— *dukkha*. Suffering."

"Why wouldn't we want to stop some change? If you could go back, wouldn't you? To be with those you love?"

"But I cannot go back. And if I did, I am already a different person than the one they knew."

Durand stopped himself. An image of stabbing a man repeatedly in the back came into his mind again. His voice hoarse with rage. Of standing in the darkness next to Bo Win.

He looked back up at the monk.

"I'm losing myself. I can feel the person I knew slipping away. I need to get back."

"And if you did get back, Mr. Durand . . ."

Durand cast a wary look at the old man.

". . . would you *be* back?"

Durand strained to answer honestly. He finally straightened and looked into the elder monk's eyes. "That doesn't matter. I don't matter. I want to be there for them. Even if I'm not completely the same."

"They tell me you have been genetically edited."

Durand suddenly realized he was not speaking with merely an elderly monk. "Yes. This"—he gestured to his body, his face—"isn't who I am."

"And you believe your genomic sequence is intrinsically your identity?"

"Part of me. Yes."

"It is not something you chose but something the universe thrust upon you. Yet you call it you."

"It's the form my daughter calls Dad. And it's half her DNA. What I brought to the union my wife and I made."

"*Anatta*—the third characteristic of life. The not-self. There is no permanent *atta*—or self. From the moment we begin, all entities—including living beings—are subject to a process of continuous change."

"I understand that wise men might tell me it's foolish to cling to the physical. That all things turn to dust." He gestured to the ruined stone statue. "But I want my body for as long as I can have it. I will let it go. But not yet." He searched the monk's eyes. "Being a husband and father, that was taken from me not by fate, but by *men*. Selfish, cruel men who enslave millions—who have created and cast away the deformed children you care for. I want to take back from them my physical form and make certain they never do this to anyone else." He shook his head. "You may be wiser than me, and I may have a lot to learn about suffering and impermanence, but I would crawl through fire to get back to my wife and child. To see them look at me with love in their eyes just one more time. I would give anything for that. *Anything.* Am I a perfect man? No. I'm not even a particularly good man. I have in the past done . . . horrible things. I lie awake at night thinking of the harm I've done to people I'll never know. But just this one thing that is wholly good that I helped create—my little girl. I promised my wife that I would try to make the world a better place for her. And if I'm going to die here, then let me at least do that. Help me destroy the Huli jing. Help me stop them, even if it kills me."

The monk sat in silence regarding Durand for several moments. Then he got to his sandaled feet. "Bring an end to your suffering, Mr. Durand."

With that, the elderly monk clicked his cane on the slabs of ancient stone as he walked away, through the gate and into the monastery beyond.

Chapter 38

That evening Durand, Frey, and Thet sat in Durand's tiny cell eating wooden bowls of a chicken-and-coconut curry. Thet refused to discuss the elder monk Durand had met, but he was willing to discuss the Huli jing.

"You've seen the results of some of their experiments. They do this to those they've enslaved, in prison camps outside the city. But there is much going on inside the city. Private jets come and go at all hours. Foreigners from around the globe. Our people check the tail numbers. Many are untraceable."

Durand looked to Thet. "Do these planes have windows or no windows?"

Frey looked up. "You think they might be renditions?"

Thet shook his head. "These planes have many windows. Very luxurious service staff. Many domestics. Some are big planes—Boeing, Comac, Airbus. Privately owned. Many bodyguards. Arab. Russian. Chinese. American. Many nationalities."

Durand pondered this information. "Some services people are willing to pay big money for."

Just then a monk in saffron robes appeared in the doorway and bowed, smiling. Incongruously he held a device shaped like a laser pistol. He spoke rapidly to Thet, who got up from his perch in the window frame. Thet nodded and accepted the device from the young monk, who then departed, closing the door.

Thet turned to Durand and Frey as he powered on the device. "Gentlemen. If you would please disrobe."

Frey raised his eyebrows. "Excuse me?"

"What's going on, Thet?"

"I need to scan your bodies. For an accurate reading"—he tested the scanner against the wall, red laser light splayed across it—"you should ideally be nude."

The next day Durand and Frey were confined to their shortened wing of the monastery. The confinement was to all evidence voluntary, but Thet asked them not to leave their rooms, and they honored his request.

Instead Frey spent his time pacing back and forth in Durand's monk cell while Durand lay on the cot. It was mercifully not as hot near the lake, but their shutters had been closed, sealed from the outside, making it stifling just the same. It was beginning to feel as though they were prisoners.

Frey stopped. "What the hell did you say to that old monk, anyway?"

"We talked about impermanence . . . and dukkha—suffering."

"From what I've experienced, suffering is reliably permanent."

"I think he just wanted to meet me."

"Do you think you've worn out our welcome?"

A knock.

They both looked up to see the door open. The elder monk stood in the doorway with several other monks in robes standing behind him. The elder monk nodded to Durand and then Frey, then entered, clicking his cane on the stone floor. The younger monks followed and began setting up what looked like mirrors and folding dressing tables.

"Good evening, gentlemen."

Durand stood and bowed a wai, as did Frey.

Frey asked, "Pardon my asking, but are we your prisoners now?"

The monk laughed and shook his head. "You have been exceptionally kind to our lost children, Dr. Frey. You help make the burden of life easier for some."

"I'm glad I could make some use of the machines I brought. And children usually find me hilarious."

"What's all this?" Durand gestured toward the monks, who were laying out what looked to be expensive dinner jackets, black bow ties, and shoes.

The elder monk turned. "Your new identities. An American businessman and his colleague are missing tonight in Rangoon. They had an appointment with the Huli jing. You might wish to take their place."

Durand stood and examined the black-tie outfits. "You're helping us?"

The monk motioned to another monk, who produced a corrugated carbon fiber briefcase with a chain leading to an open handcuff. He also held the key. The young monk placed the briefcase on the bed and clicked it open, stepping back.

The elder monk looked to Durand. "A great deal of corrupt money has entered our country. It poisons men's hearts."

Durand and Frey walked up and looked into the case. Inside were individual jewel sleeves snugged into slots in a black velvet interior. Durand drew out one and pressed its sides to open its mouth. He drew a breath, then poured a dozen large rubies onto the bed.

Frey examined the dozens of other packets, peeking into several, weighing them with his hands. "My god, these must be worth millions."

"Forty-three million US dollars at current prices, Dr. Frey."

Momentarily speechless, Frey turned to look at the elder monk.

Durand slipped the jewels back into the sleeve, and the sleeve back into the case. He snapped it shut. "Why?"

"It is the cost of entry to the Huli jing facility. Thirty million, up front, nonrefundable to create an account. Up until now I did not have anyone who would be able to pass for clients of the Huli jing—whom I could also trust. But you, Mr. Durand, and your genetic consultant"—he nodded to Frey, then turned back to Durand—"will seem like just another couple of devilish foreigners here to take the change agent. To become someone else. In fact, the businessman's invitation fob is in this jacket."

Durand pondered this. "They'll have biometrics on the client. Iris, fingerprint—"

"You forget what the Huli jing is doing, Mr. Durand. Anonymity is what they're selling. *True anonymity.* A post-identity world. A cleansing of earthly sins. There are no fingerprints or iris scans or even DNA scans that can identify their clients. There is only money and desire."

Frey nodded. "It does rule out the lookie-loos."

Durand gestured to the case. "And once we're in, what then?"

The monk moved to the dinner jackets. He opened one coat and motioned to the sleeve. "Concealed pockets—made specifically to hold ampoules of their change agent. We know the precise size and shape of the glass ampoules because we've ambushed their supply trucks before. The reagent itself does not seem to leave the facility. But we hope you and Dr. Frey will change that."

Frey's brow furrowed. "How on earth are we going to get away with samples of their active change agent? I don't expect they'll be letting us into their labs."

"That's where you're wrong." The elderly monk moved Durand in front of the mirror. "Realize that among the Nine Tails of the Huli jing, faces and ethnicity are always changing. Instead, they have other means of proving their identity. Their marks of rank."

"Tattoos."

The monk nodded. "We are told Huli jing chromatophores reflect light at varying frequencies—notably ultraviolet. The patterns represent a unique three-dimensional key that, combined with its spectrographic signature, identify the bearer who activates them."

Durand pulled off his tunic and stood looking at his bare chest in the mirror. As he focused his will, he saw the tattoos begin to fade in. The more he concentrated on the Huli jing and what they had taken from him—on the stranger's face in the mirror—the darker his tattoos became.

Soon he stood before the mirror as Marcus Wyckes, leader of the Huli jing.

The elder monk gripped Durand's muscular shoulder. "You will become your enemy, Mr. Durand, and you will go where you will within his domain."

Frey cleared his throat. "Surely clients are watched at all times."

"In fact, they are tracked at all times, Dr. Frey. Every Huli jing client wears a tracking bracelet. Which is why we've included these in your coat . . ." The old monk removed a long Vantablack glove from one of the coat pockets. It looked like a two-dimensional hole in reality. "Slip this over your bracelet arm. It will act as a Faraday cage—blocking the client-tracking signal."

"But security guards—"

"There will be a diversion to make it easier for you. The Huli jing facility will come under attack by rebel forces tonight at 2100 hours. If you have not found your opportunity by then, perhaps that will create one."

Durand turned to the monk with concern. "Resistance fighters are going to attack the Huli jing—in the capital?"

"They will create enough of a diversion to keep the focus off you. When you've obtained your samples, you will resume your identity as a Huli jing client."

Durand pondered the plan. "Your people might get killed."

The elder monk just stared. "Some undoubtedly will. Knowing this, all have volunteered. They are willing to face the risk, Mr. Durand."

"Bo Win volunteered, didn't she?"

The elder monk stared. "That is not important."

"It's important to me."

"Mr. Durand, there is little time if you are to make your client appointment."

Frey stepped between them. "And what about me? What about the edit I came here for?" He gestured to Durand. "And that he came for? You know it will require weeks or months for a transformation. How's that going to work? We steal an ampoule and then what? Hang around for months in a coma?"

Durand was about to speak, but Frey cut him off. "Don't act as though you're pure of heart. You came here to get edited. To be restored to your original self." He turned back to the monk. "Where does what we both came for fit into your plan?"

The elder monk remained unmoved. "Your initial appointment this evening is a consultation. The actual edits are usually scheduled later. Bring us the change agent on your return, and the rest is up to you both."

He turned. "Whether to change yourselves will be your decision to make."

Durand and Frey looked at each other.

Durand and Frey walked through the corridors of the monastery in bespoke black tie and dinner jackets—the attaché case of rubies hand-cuffed to Durand's left wrist. Both men were immaculately groomed, with Durand's head shaved close and Frey's unruly mane for once tamed. The laser scanner made for a perfect fit with their clothing in every dimension. Durand had to admit it was a good look. It made him feel confident, as daunting as their task seemed.

Frey brushed something off his sleeve. "Black tie. Unusually old school."

"It's what the invitation requires."

They passed a young monk in saffron robes who ushered them toward a rear entrance. They moved through kitchen areas until they emerged behind the monastery, where an electric Maybach limousine awaited them. Standing next to it was Thet, dressed in a chauffeur's uniform with a cap.

He smiled. "Good evening, gentlemen. You look quite prosperous." Thet opened the rear door for them.

Frey climbed into the backseat.

Durand stopped and gripped Thet's shoulder. "You don't have to do this."

Thet shook his head. "Not for you, Mr. Durand. For me. For my people. You need to succeed. I will get you there."

Durand nodded. Another squeeze of Thet's shoulder, and he got inside.

Thet slid into the driver's seat.

Frey reclined in back. "I could get used to this. Thet, where on earth did you get hold of this car?"

He looked into the rearview mirror. "Many foreigners come. Some make bad decisions."

With that ominous-sounding comment, Thet brought the car

silently forward, down the monastery's drive, falling in behind a black SUV. Another just like it came up behind them—completing the appearance of a VIP security detail. Durand couldn't see through the SUV's blacked-out windows and had no idea who was coming along with them.

Frey grabbed a scotch from the minibar. He raised his glass. "Here's to good fortune."

Chapter 39

They drove for nearly forty minutes, passing through rural military checkpoints without difficulty. Durand didn't know whether that was because they were well-dressed in a chauffeured, million-dollar car with security escorts, or whether the soldiers were disloyal. In between the checkpoints they passed burned-out military vehicles and bullet-riddled police stations. In the distance he could hear occasional gunfire and explosions.

To maintain appearances Thet had closed the glass partition between them. Durand pressed the intercom. "Thet, are those Shan forces?"

Thet's voice came over the speaker. "No. Some fighting every night. Army. Rebels."

Durand gazed out the window as they entered the capital itself. Here, the depth and complexity of the military cordon increased. Their leading and trailing security SUVs parted ways with them, returning back the way they'd come.

Thet brought the Maybach toward the city, slaloming between speed bumps and concrete blast walls. Their car was scanned by automated devices. Mirrors were passed beneath its undercarriage by soldiers as well.

But soldiers did not request Durand and Frey's papers. Instead, they would briefly shine lights into the passenger compartment, only to see the case handcuffed to Durand's wrist as he held up the Huli jing fob. Another flash onto his face and black-tie attire, and their car was invariably waved through.

Apparently the Huli jing did not like their clients hassled and had the connections to make that so.

Beyond the concentric rings of military checkpoints, the Maybach finally reached modern, wide, but nearly deserted city streets. Well-lit signs proclaimed in Burmese and English that they had arrived in the capital city: Naypyidaw.

Suddenly the battered LFP glasses Durand had picked up at Vegas's penthouse chirped from his pocket to indicate an Internet connection was available. It was the first time in days.

He and Frey exchanged surprised looks.

"Civilization." Frey pulled a pair of LFP glasses out of his own coat pocket. "Might be interesting to see what's transpired while we've been in the Middle Ages . . ." He started flipping through screens only visible to him.

"Don't connect to any accounts linked to you."

"I was evading the law well before I met you, Agent Durand. Besides, I'm just checking newsfeeds."

A thought occurred to Durand. He put on his own pair of LFP glasses and opened the device's messaging client.

He decided now was probably his last opportunity to send a message. He was, after all, still an Interpol agent. Durand couldn't recall Inspector Aiyana Marcotte's old-time email address, but he remembered her saying she used it because she wanted to be reachable by impoverished, trafficked people—which meant it had to be discoverable. Using a proxy, he did a brief search for Marcotte's name and title and soon found her public email address and PGP key. He then began typing a message with the virtual keyboard.

Detective Inspector Aiyana Marcotte:

The trail to Marcus Wyckes has led me to Naypyidaw, Myanmar. The Huli jing is headquartered here, taking advantage of ties to the military to hide in plain sight. Tonight I will attempt to infiltrate the Huli jing labs to obtain a sample of a change agent capable of genetically altering live human beings.

You once briefed me on the Huli jing and mentioned that the Nine

Tails—the Huli jing's inner circle—regularly die off. I now know that the Nine Tails are not dying; they are constantly changing. I suspect they genetically edit themselves and slay others—from among the many slaves they traffic—to take their places. Thus, you will not ever be able to bring a case against the Huli jing leadership. Focus on the chromatophores in their skin. This is their identification. This will provide the key.

I have reason to believe the Huli jing are the remnants of an illicit biodefense project named False Apollo—shut down in 2032 (Sergeant Yi should be able to access records for it). It was created with the cooperation of powerful organizations and/or governments with the goal of creating a universal defense against human extinction. I'm concerned that the Huli jing might have perverted this goal for some much darker purpose.

I am going to destroy this device after I send this message, but I will contact you again from a different address if I survive. I trust you to pursue this matter with discretion and dedication no matter what my fate. I wish us all luck.

Sincerely

He left the signature blank, encrypted the message, and tapped "Send." After it was confirmed, he removed his LFP glasses and bent them in two. He turned to Frey. "Yours, too. Destroy them. They won't allow devices in there, and we don't need the scrutiny."

Frey sighed. He pulled off the LFP glasses, and Durand twisted them into wreckage for him.

They looked out at the downtown. It was weirdly posh, with towering, architecturally exotic office buildings but streets far too wide and empty. They saw only army vehicles and high-end luxury cars like their own on the road—and not many of these, either. Nor a pedestrian in sight.

Thet's voice came in over the intercom. "We are arriving. Good luck, Mr. Durand, Dr. Frey. I will look for you when you are ready to depart. It has been my pleasure knowing you gentlemen."

They both nodded to Thet through the etched partition glass.

The Maybach turned down a cobblestone drive leading to an office tower, outlined in organometallic light. A trefoil knot logo glowed from nearby shrubbery. Soldiers in body armor with long guns and guard dogs roamed everywhere.

The Maybach stopped under a marble portico. The armored doors unlocked.

A suited valet opened the door and tipped his doorman's hat to Durand as he got out. "Good evening, sir. Your invitation, please."

Durand bumped his invitation fob against a pad the valet held out to him. The man glanced at an unseen screen, then smiled. "Very good, sir."

Frey got out next to Durand.

"Through those doors, gentlemen. The reception staff will assist you."

"Our car?"

"We know which car you arrived in, sir. We will summon your driver when you are ready to depart."

Durand looked down at Frey. They both straightened their ties, then walked up marble steps along a red carpet runner, moving past lines of soldiers in randomized digital camouflage and carbyne helmets, standing to attention on either side. The soldiers appeared ethnically diverse but had a definite Soviet-era vibe. Staring ahead, unseeing. Automatic rifles slung across their chests. At the ready. There were scores of them.

The glass lobby doors opened, and Durand and Frey crossed a surprisingly gaudy lobby, again lined with two dozen heavily armed soldiers standing at attention. A red carpet led down its length.

At the end of the carpet stood an imposing reception desk of black marble. The trefoil knot symbol was set in brushed gold on the wall behind it. There was room to pass on either side.

Standing before the desk in a full-length black gown and gloves was a gorgeous young blond. She wore a diamond necklace whose jewel-encrusted pendant was also fashioned into a trefoil knot.

She smiled as they approached. "Good evening, gentlemen. Welcome."

Frey nodded happily. "Good evening, young lady."

"Are you seeking personal or third-party revisions this evening?"

Durand and Frey looked at each other. Then the woman. They spoke in unison.

"Personal."

"Very good. I see that neither of you are wearing electronics. Please be aware that no phones, cameras, or other recording devices are allowed anywhere within this facility. It is important that this rule be observed closely, and there will be no exceptions. Do you understand?"

They both nodded.

"Excellent. Allow me to assist you with your marker." She gestured to Durand's handcuffed case and patted the black marble countertop. "Please place and open the case here, sir. And unlock the cuff."

Durand placed the attaché case on the counter. He then produced a key to unlock the cuff, and clicked in a code to unlock the case itself. He then turned it toward her.

As he did so, she deftly slipped a carbon fiber bracelet around his wrist, fastening it on him like a concert pass.

"This device will identify you to staff members as well as track your movements throughout the facility." She flipped open a cover to reveal a button. "If you have need of a staff member for any reason, simply tap this button. If you attempt to remove or tamper with the device, it will send out an alarm." She smiled. "You don't want that."

She viewed the contents of the ruby-filled case with the indifferent eye of someone accustomed to seeing vast wealth. She then wrapped a companion bracelet around the attaché case handle. "We will scan your gems for clarity, cut, and size to determine their value. It will only take a few moments."

She handed the case to another young woman in a gown who emerged from a side door. She then turned to Frey. "Your right wrist please, sir."

"Yes, of course." Frey reached up, clearly enjoying her attention. "Miss, has anyone ever told you that you are the spitting image of a young Margot Robbie?"

She smiled. "I should think so. I have 99.993 percent of her DNA."

Frey laughed good-naturedly. "You naughty girl."

She turned to Durand and motioned for him to look into a nearby, wall-mounted glim. "Here is your balance, sir."

He followed her gaze and saw the number "$40,293,083 USD" floating in midair next to the words "On Account."

Durand cast a steely look her way. "That's about three million short by my calculation."

She smiled brightly. "You may, of course, depart with your jewels, sir. But this is the sum our systems are prepared to credit for what you've brought us today. Rubies are, after all, not as portable or fungible as cryptocurrencies."

Durand waved her off. "Fine. I'll accept it."

She smiled again. "You are all set for consultations on personal revisions." She gestured. "Please proceed to the elevator. And enjoy your time with us."

Frey grinned broadly. "I'm sure we will."

Durand and Frey walked around the massive stone reception desk and found a single elevator car done in mirrors and brass waiting for them. They entered and the doors closed. As expected there were no buttons. It began to ascend.

Frey sighed. "Well, we've just been relieved of forty million dollars. Macao isn't half as efficient."

Durand turned to see the view through the glass wall behind them.

Frey fished in his pocket for a moment, and then produced a small chip case. He extended it to Durand.

"What's this?"

"Some data you're going to need. Your original genomic sequence, digitized."

Durand took the chip and held it in the palm of his alien hand. On the device was the key to getting back to himself.

Frey pointed. Durand looked out at the city falling away beneath them as the elevator rose quickly and silently.

Frey no longer seemed festive. "Ken, no matter what happens tonight, I want to thank you for bringing me here. For bringing me this far."

Durand nodded.

The elevator slowed, and then the doors opened on the fiftieth floor.

Chapter 40

They emerged into a marble hall with crystal chandeliers and wood-paneled walls. A six-foot-high vase overflowing with fresh tropical flowers occupied the center of the room. Standing nearby was a tall, thin Caucasian man in his thirties in a dark blue suit, with flowing red hair. He had the orderly look, sharp features, and suave manner of a professional cocktail party guest.

"Gentlemen. Welcome. You may call me Thomas." He had a slight French accent. "I will be escorting you to your consultations and answering any questions you may have along the way."

Frey nodded. "Good evening, Thomas."

"I hear you're considering personal revisions."

"Indeed we are."

"Excellent. I, too, have undergone considerable revision, and I could not be happier."

"Have you . . . ?"

Durand and Frey exchanged looks. The man had a striking though not classically handsome appearance.

He nodded. "I realize I look rather unique. However, Thomas Jefferson has been a lifelong passion of mine."

"Thomas Jefferson?"

"Yes. The DNA was not easy to obtain, I assure you."

Before Durand could answer, a young Scarlett Johansson pushed past him, arm in arm with a young Charlize Theron. Both ladies wore sequin gowns, jeweled necklaces, and white gloves.

Frey pivoted to watch them go. "Good Lord . . ." In backing up, he nearly collided with half a dozen more Scarlett Johanssons laughing and smiling as they moved past and around him, entering a crowded lounge.

One of the Johanssons turned around and leaned over to pinch Frey's cheek. She said with a thick Asian accent, "You 'dorable!" And moved off.

Frey pointed. "That was a flock of Johanssons."

Thomas watched them go. "Yes, some of our most popular third-party revisions. For best results we recommend using a source individual who is a native speaker of your desired language."

Frey kept pointing. "Young Scarlett Johanssons."

"Of course, the age is dependent on the age of the recipient." Thomas gestured, ushering them to the entrance of the lounge area.

The room was furnished with a series of sofas and armchairs and a grand piano, where a pianist played jazzy, festive music. Standing or sitting on divans were multiple Hollywood and Bollywood celebrities, K-pop stars, and more—with multiple copies of each. Laughing and sitting among them were a few older men—Arabs, dour-looking Yakuza or Triads in business suits, and an Eastern European man in a ridiculously ornate military uniform.

Frey stared in amazement. "Who on earth is this for?"

Thomas stood next to them at the edge of the room. "We do not judge here. Slavery is perfectly legal in certain jurisdictions. Likewise, some willingly surrender their identity to further career goals. Our third-party revision team is able to accommodate almost all interests. Of course, they can offer secure confinement for involuntary revisions, where necessary. Such is the world."

Durand stood in shock at the doorway.

Frey recovered his senses first. "Where do you get the source DNA?"

"We have an extensive collection network and keep up with popular tastes by monitoring social media. If there is a public figure you desire, we most likely have their DNA in our database."

Durand did a double take at a young Brad Pitt wearing a leather jacket and leaning on the edge of a baby grand piano. The real Brad Pitt was in his eighties. Next to the young Pitt stood a line of Pitt variations—

a Latino version, an African, an Indian, and then an Asian Brad Pitt. There were a few flavors of Denzel Washington nearby, too, all chatting amiably.

"We can accommodate different tastes for different markets. Anyone you control can be customized to suit your tastes."

Robed sheiks and the military dictator seemed to be eating up the "own your own celebrity" pitch.

Durand felt numb. Did people want to look like movie stars? Perhaps some people did. Did the celebrities have any idea their DNA had been stolen? He guessed not.

Looking around the room at the faux celebrities, he wondered who these people were born to be. Would their own mothers ever recognize them again? How did parents react to having their genetic legacy discarded like a coat?

Durand felt a tug on his sleeve. He looked to see Frey motioning him onward. Durand followed, down the main hallway and away from the third-party lounge.

Frey walked alongside Thomas. "How long do those types of revisions take?"

"It varies greatly. The celebrity transformations you see here were quite significant—two years or more to safely effect the required DNA edits. Some will be going to clients soon. But as with any genetic procedure, there is a minor risk. Toxic shock. Hemorrhaging. Mutation. Mutations can be corrected in most cases. We have strict quality control."

The broker brought them into a room where 3D computer models of the nude bodies of young men and women spun in place, while much older clients pointed at various features. A technician made adjustments, and the image changed—either pleasing or displeasing them.

"It is a common complaint of our clients that their servants do not match their preferences. These servants can now be customized like any other prized possession."

Durand looked on as a technician modified the computer model of a young Southeast Asian woman like clay.

"As you can see, gentlemen, we model the edits using our proprietary bioinformatics systems, and then prepare the reagent to your precise specifications. You'll learn more about the process during your own consultation."

Frey nodded vigorously. "Yes. As you can imagine, I am eager to make some revisions."

"Very good. Our genetic engineers have worked such wonders before. Please follow me." He brought them through double doors and into a richly adorned corridor. The doors closed behind them as they walked.

"You gentlemen may not be aware that certain legal aspects of the international genetic market are changing."

Durand cast a suspicious look at the man's back. "Changing? How so?"

"Our partners—large biotech consortiums—have for years been gathering genetic data from billions of human beings. This has been the Trefoil Labs mission: Other partners have been gathering and storing genetic data on untold numbers of flora and fauna." He looked back at them. "You should invest now. I would invest more if I could. You are fortunate to be men of means."

"Invest. In biotech?"

"No. In genomic sequences."

Durand and Frey looked at each other.

"I would immediately purchase my own genomic sequence at the very least." He glanced back again. "Before someone else does. Personally, I'd rather own a slightly inferior genetic sequence than lease a more desirable one."

Durand narrowed his eyes. "What in hell's name are you talking about? The Treaty on Genetic Modification is—"

"Is a relic. Live editing will render germ line editing moot. Genetic edits can be reversed—even in mature organisms. The TGM is a dead letter—and quite soon."

Frey interceded as he apparently noticed Durand was getting agitated. "Humor me, here. What exactly are you saying?"

"The international legal groundwork is being laid, copyrighting and patenting genomic sequences for proprietary algae, bacteria, and yeast organisms—the factories of the fourth industrial revolution."

"What does that have to do with human beings?"

"DNA is DNA. Merely information. Which means that human beings are merely information. And there is a long-established legal precedent that information can be owned."

It took everything in him to keep his tattoos from appearing. Durand felt them rising along with his rage. He stepped to the side, turning against the wall.

"Are you okay, sir?"

"Yes. Yes, I'm fine."

Frey was right at his elbow, casting a dark expression his way.

"Just the travel. It upsets my stomach." Durand calmed himself and stood straight.

"That weakness can be fixed." Thomas pushed open a heavy wooden door. "Smart people will make certain to own and copyright their blood-line: 51 percent ownership in a certain sequence of DNA would be a controlling interest. There are all sorts of fractional ownership scenarios."

Durand said, "Slavery 2.0."

The broker turned to him. "Ah, except that it requires no reference to species—merely sequences. One merely owns information. If that happens to define a human being, then that human being was not very smart not to own himself."

Durand realized that the theft of his own identity was almost minor compared to what was occurring here.

Chapter 41

They arrived in a beautiful lab with tropical hardwood cabinets and marble floors and countertops. A middle-age Eastern European woman in a white lab coat smiled as they entered.

"Here we are. Our personal revision department." Thomas put a hand on Frey's shoulder. "May I introduce you to your genetic counselor, Ms. Rita. She will bring you through the transformation process."

Rita smiled again. "Good evening, sir."

Frey looked a bit overwhelmed and smiled wanly.

Thomas turned to Durand. "Unfortunately your counselor is still with a client; however, he will be available quite soon. In the meantime, may I—"

Frey grabbed Durand's sleeve. "Good! I mean, don't leave just yet. I'd like you here with me."

Durand spoke to Thomas. "I'll wait here."

Thomas spread his hands. "As you wish, gentlemen. I will return shortly."

Durand and Frey ignored his departure.

The genetic counselor extended her hand to both of them in turn. "Gentlemen, it is a pleasure." She examined Frey. "We are preparing edits for you today?"

"Yes. I'm going to let you guess what type."

She moved her hand. Glims in the ceiling and countertops beamed AR images of human forms and double helices of DNA into their retinas. "This is where we develop an editing plan to effect your desired revisions."

Frey looked around at the floating virtual objects. "How long does it take you to calculate the edits and their sequence?"

"It depends, of course, on the complexity of the revisions, but our photonic clusters can usually return complete edit solutions within an hour."

Frey looked shocked. *"An hour?* My god. I used to have to wait days for edits to proteins."

She laughed. "Now you're dating yourself. So you were in the trade?"

Frey shrugged. "I dabbled. But I never had a setup like this."

She smiled, looking around. "It is quite something." She took hold of his hand gently. "I'd like you to see something." She extended his index finger and guided it over to a device resembling a fingerprint reader.

Frey winced at a slight sting and withdrew his finger.

"Just a little blood, and . . ."

Suddenly a rough 3D computer model of Frey's body appeared. It had no surface color, but was a gray graphical primitive—anatomically correct as it was.

"Well, that's rather personal."

"Nothing I haven't seen before." She adjusted controls on invisible displays, moving her hands in midair. "Let's give you some lifelike colorization." Moments later Frey appeared, nude and in living color, on-screen.

"Now it's even more personal."

"Will we be addressing your achondroplasia first?"

"You were able to distinguish my condition from—"

"Our systems recognized the precise genetic error immediately." She turned. "Would you like to see what you'd look like with it corrected? To see the man you were meant to be?"

Frey's face flushed. "You can model that—right now? Here and now?"

She smiled and tapped a virtual button.

The floating AR model of Frey fluttered for several moments, and then a photographically detailed model of a handsome, well-proportioned man floated in space before them.

Frey's hands began to tremble. And then tears flowed from his eyes. "That's me."

She checked invisible readings. "Six feet, two inches." She looked up. "My, you're a handsome fellow. With just a few genetic edits, too. Most of our clients aren't so lucky."

Durand could not help but be affected as Frey reached out toward his ideal self.

Frey wiped his tears away. He tried to regain a professional air. "How many edits?"

She studied an unseen screen. "Achondroplasia is a more interconnected malady than geneticists suspected. It took a lot of experimentation to follow the—"

"How many?"

"Eighty-six unique edits."

Frey nodded eagerly. "And that would cost how much?"

"Five million six hundred and thirty-three thousand US dollars."

Frey stared at the image.

Durand remained silent.

The genetic counselor said, "You have more than enough in your account. We could explore additional improvements."

Frey simply stared, mesmerized.

Thomas suddenly returned. He tapped Durand on the shoulder. "Hanif is ready for you now, sir."

Frey could barely take his eyes off the model.

"I need to take care of this, Bryan. I'll be back."

Frey still stared as Rita made small revisions.

"Bryan."

Frey looked up. "Yes. Yes, I will be here."

Reluctantly Durand followed Thomas.

Chapter 42

I am most pleased to meet you. My name is Hanif." The slim, middle-age Indonesian man in a white lab coat studied Kenneth Durand's muscular frame. "My goodness, you look as though you have already had some refinements. Is this not so?"

Durand didn't know what to do with this question, so he shook his head. "I have very specific requirements. I want this . . ." He passed Hanif the data chip Frey had given him.

"What is this?"

"It's a complete genomic sequence."

The man examined the chip. "You've brought a genomic sequence, sir?"

"Yes. That contains the letters of the person I need to be revised to."

Hanif looked skeptical. "Is it a complete genomic sequence or merely sequences you wish to edit?"

"It should be a complete genomic sequence."

"This could be dangerous. We need to be certain there are no neurological—"

"Just load it."

The genetic counselor sighed, and after manipulating some unseen screens, he slid the chip into a slot on the edge of the countertop. He waited for several moments. "Let's see what we have here." He glanced up, and a gray graphical primitive of a human form appeared before Durand.

Even though it was similar to modeling clay, Durand could

immediately recognize it as his old self. His heart raced as he watched it slowly revolve. "Make it lifelike."

Hanif was studying his screens. "What's that, sir?"

"I said, give it a lifelike skin tone. Make it photorealistic."

"Very well." He clicked around, and finally a virtual Kenneth Durand stood before him. Durand lowered his head. He was so close. He had come so far. He looked up and saw himself staring back for the first time in what seemed like an eternity.

Hanif looked up from his virtual screens and jumped as if he suddenly had a Siberian tiger sitting before him. "My god. I deeply apologize, sir. I . . ."

Durand gazed down at his hands and immediately realized his error. He looked at his reflection in the glass-fronted cabinets. His Huli jing tattoos were all on display.

Hanif was flustered. "Please forgive me, sir. If this is a test, I assure you, I am most loyal. I would never—"

Durand held up his hand. "Calm down."

"But I do most humbly apologize, sir. If there is any doubt as to my loyalty."

Durand pointed at the image of himself rotating before them both. "Do you see this?"

"Yes. I do see, sir."

"Synthesize this into a change agent, and do it immediately. Do you understand?"

"Yes, I do. I do very much, sir." The man got busy. "Of course, I will need you to place your finger in the receptacle, sir."

Durand looked over to see an indentation in the counter with a green light flashing from it. He inserted his index finger and felt the barest pinch. Moments later he saw an image of his current self—Marcus Wyckes—floating right alongside Kenneth Durand. It was his internal struggle made visible.

"There is some interesting overlap here . . ."

"Never mind the overlap. Just make me into that first one."

"Yes, sir. I will prepare a change agent."

"How long will it take?"

"To compute the edit plan or to synthesize the reagent?"

"Both. Tell me the time for both."

Hanif interacted with unseen UIs. "It looks as though we have previous computations on file for this sequence . . ." He glanced up at Durand. "Of course. You must have transferred the other way. I see. This will save us a tremendous amount of time. We can merely reverse the previous edit plan. I should be able to synthesize the reagent in a couple hours. But then we would need to schedule the procedure, discuss a recuperation—"

"I want the change agent put into an autoinjector."

".Into an ampoule, sir?" Hanif gazed at the records. "Ah. Like before?"

Durand turned away from the image of his old self to stare at Hanif. He nodded. "Yes. Like before."

As Durand walked around staring at the virtual images of Kenneth Durand and Marcus Wyckes, he heard a beep and a security door behind him slid open.

Durand turned to face it and noticed a corridor leading through a laboratory space. He glanced back and noticed that Hanif was focused on a virtual interface—clearly aiming to impress. Walking forward to the edge of the open door, Durand could see a green light on the door security pad. He glanced down at the tattoos on the back of his hand and remembered what the elder monk had said about his tattoos being a three-dimensional key—in ultraviolet frequencies. Visible through his clothing, then.

Hanif spoke behind him. "I would not recommend such an aggressive pace of revision, sir." He read a virtual display. "Oh, my. How on earth did you survive this?" He looked back at the tattooed Huli jing before him. "I do not mean to offend. And please forgive me—but I would suggest reducing the pace by at least two-thirds."

Durand nodded. "Fine. Just prepare the autoinjector."

Hanif moved his hands over unseen screens. "I humbly beg your forbearance . . . but an admin code. Without it, the system will charge—"

Durand held up his wrist and pointed to the carbon fiber band. "Apply it to this account."

"This is most—"

Durand pounded the counter. "Do it!"

The man's hands moved swiftly. "This is eleven million—"

"Do it!"

"Yes. Yes, sir."

"I'll return."

"Yes, of course, sir."

As he moved toward the security door, Durand removed the Vanta-black glove from his jacket pocket and pulled it on over his tracking bracelet. He then moved through the security door, tattoos still prominent, and walked down the service corridor beyond.

It apparently joined all the client consultation rooms to a central processing lab.

Technicians and robots here worked in glass-walled labs to either side. Robotic arms moved ampoules in and out of refrigerated units filled with rows of thousands more. As Durand passed each lab door, the red light on its security pad would turn green.

He had complete access.

Durand pushed into a glass-walled storage room occupied by only a robotic arm busy retrieving ampoules from storage. The door chirped as he did so, and the robotic arm immediately ceased activity, pulling away into a corner.

As he walked along the glass refrigerator doors, a glim in the ceiling found his retinas and began beaming AR information to him. Durand gazed at thousands of sealed glass ampoules in racks, each filled with perhaps half an ounce of honey-colored liquid.

Who were they meant for?

The lights on the refrigerator doors also flipped from green to red as Durand passed. He finally stopped before one marked with the AR label "Involuntary Third-Party Revisions." The racks here contained ampoules with autoinjectors.

Durand opened the door and clinked around for a bit, and removed one marked with an inscrutable client code. As he stared at the AR label, it soon expanded into the image of an African man with accompanying physical stats.

Durand held the ampoule up to the light. He could see a short needle encased in glass on the nib end. Like the old morphine injectors used in the military.

Durand slipped the ampoule into the side pocket of his suit jacket.

Suddenly there was the sound of a distant explosion. The ampoules in the rack in front of him shivered.

Durand looked up. The chatter of machine gun fire followed.

He closed the refrigerator and exited the glass-walled lab, walking calmly and turning back toward the client consultation lab.

The staccato crackling of multiple machine guns and booms of explosions echoed over the city. A larger explosion made the floor vibrate.

Suddenly Durand noticed several heavy-set, suited security men move into his path in the corridor ahead. He walked forward confidently—imperiously. Relying on his markings to complete his disguise. He gestured for them to get out of his way.

Instead, they drew nonlethal weapons and aimed them at his chest. Shock devices from the look of them.

Durand slowed to a halt. "Out of my way."

He heard the door to a lab behind him open, and a familiar sensation of dread came over Durand. He heard more heavy footsteps and turned to see half a dozen security men there as well, nonlethal weapons also raised.

These men parted as the familiar uncanny sensation increased. Otto emerged from between them, wearing a charcoal suit with a red tie. His double Windsor as perfect as ever. However, he sported a slight bruise under his right eye.

"Mr. Durand."

Even Durand's newfound calm during a crisis crumbled in the enantiomorph's presence. "False Apollo."

Otto's confident expression momentarily cracked. "I have never liked that name. There is nothing false about me."

Distant machine gun fire rattled.

Otto stared at Durand—and then Otto's own tattoos faded into sight across his neck and the back of his hands.

"Those marks don't belong to you."

Durand gazed down at his own hands. The tattoos burned on his skin. He felt hatred coursing through him. "I didn't ask for them."

"Nonetheless." He stared at Durand but spoke to the guards. "Mr. Wyckes wants to see him."

Another distant explosion.

The guards moved in on Durand from both directions—hitting him with shock devices before he could rush them. His muscles frozen by spasms, Durand let out a howl of rage, but a dozen sets of hands grabbed him and held him down. He was soon zip-tied.

"Otto, I know what you are!" Durand's face was pressed against the floor. "I know why they made you."

Otto said nothing.

The security men dragged Durand away. As they emerged from the lab, he saw another group of men escorting a stone-faced Bryan Frey down the corridor. Frey's own hands were also zip-tied behind him.

"Bryan."

Frey did not respond. He stared ahead as if catatonic.

The doors to a freight elevator opened. There was room for them all.

Chapter 43

The elevator doors opened onto a lavish rooftop patio area. Planted palms lined a walkway, waterfalls flowed into pools of indigo-lit water. Swarthy men in navy blazers stood nearby, weapons ready.

Behind them, the night sky was stitched by orange and green tracers. The echo of distant gunfire. The occasional flash and delayed BOOM of an explosion.

The security escort pulled Durand and Frey past an empty rooftop cocktail lounge, up a series of short stone steps toward a viewing platform equipped with a covered telescope. Along the steps stood eight men, four to either side. They wore tailored business suits and ran the gamut of human diversity—from Asian to African to Caucasian to Latino. They all stared as Durand and Frey were dragged past.

Each had Huli jing tattoos running along his hands, neck, and scalp.

When Otto walked to the top of the steps and took his place there, Durand realized these were the Nine Tails of the Huli jing.

Standing at the railing was a man in a red sweater and slacks. Smoke curled around him as he observed the city below.

The security guards halted and pushed Durand and Frey down to their knees.

Frey looked miserable, with his head drooping toward the ground.

The man at the railing turned. He was in his thirties, his face giving hints of many different ethnicities. Durand had never seen someone so resolutely . . . everything. The man's eyes were almond shaped, but his complexion was fair. His hair was curled, but his nose aquiline. And he had a complement of Huli jing tattoos identical to Durand's.

The man tossed his cigar over the railing and blew out the last of the smoke.

In the distance gunfire continued.

The man approached Durand, unperturbed. "Now, that's a face I haven't seen in some time." He looked up. "Well done, Otto. Well done as always."

Durand hissed, "Wyckes."

Wyckes leaned down some distance away, hands on his knees. "You can't prove that." He laughed.

So did the Nine Tails around him.

"But *you*—well. Sucks to be me." His hands swept across the city view. "You're just in time to see the fireworks. Seems the locals had a bit of a plan. Completely pointless, of course. As you might imagine, we have people inside their organization. We can be anyone."

Otto handed Wyckes a sheet of paper.

Wyckes laughed and held it up. It was the Interpol Red Notice with Durand's current likeness on it. "Interpol's biometric scan made it very easy to identify you. And of course, Otto knew you were coming. So all your long journey did was cost me billions of dollars in lost equipment and business. Do you realize how many people are looking for Marcus Wyckes right now?"

He tossed the paper aside. "Perhaps your own colleagues will identify your body."

"They'll arrest you eventually, Wyckes."

Wyckes stared down on Durand. "Arrest whom? And why? There isn't even a legal basis to arrest me anymore. In fact, I'm going to use your laws against you."

He moved around Durand. "Laws are so inflexible. Personally, I find constant, incremental change to be a tremendous advantage—both in Nature and in business. I'm surprised you've made such a fuss about it. I gifted you my *own* original DNA—I'm like a father to you."

Rage caused Durand to struggle to his feet and against his bonds.

Unseen hands pushed him back down. Durand seethed. "I came all this way just to get your DNA out of me."

"Ah. You make me sad."

"Change me back, Wyckes!"

"Personal transformation is very much our business, but in your particular case I'm afraid that's not possible. It's vital that you remain exactly the way you are. Mr. Wyckes has committed heinous crimes, and it's important that he face justice."

Wyckes took notice of Bryan Frey. Frey stared far off at a remote dais on the roof. Wyckes followed Frey's gaze toward two clawed, half-horse, half-eagle, pony-sized monstrosities growling on chains there.

"Dr. Frey, I see you're admiring our latest product."

Frey stared in utter shock. "Hippogriffs."

"You know your mythology." Wyckes walked down the steps and halfway toward the beasts. "A hybrid of two distinct species. Big seller with Arab sheiks. They love these things." Wyckes leaned over to a nearby barrel and grabbed a raw piece of meat—which he tossed toward the hippogriffs.

The monsters shrieked and clawed at each other, fighting for the meat. Tearing it to pieces in seconds. "Unsurprisingly, they can't fly. Ancient people had no sense of aerodynamics. Sterile. Unpredictable as hell, batshit crazy. It's their braincase—too small. Probably in constant pain. But then, after a certain age, aren't we all?"

Durand shouted at the ground, "The world will put a stop to what you're doing!"

Wyckes laughed. "No, the world won't, Mr. Durand. Everyone wants to reinvent themselves. In this world of mass surveillance and constant tracking, who wouldn't want the chance to become a new person? After all, anyone of consequence has done one or two things they'd rather put behind them."

Wyckes walked around behind Durand, gripping his shoulder. "That's true of you, too, I think. Isn't it?" He leaned next to his ear. "How many people had to perish so you could be you?"

Durand tried to pull away from Wyckes's grip, and from the memory of the people he'd killed or caused to be killed.

"None of this would be necessary if it wasn't for the ubiquitous surveillance of the modern world. People used to be able to reinvent themselves the old-fashioned way—but now? Now I'm the only game in town."

"You're changing people who have no choice."

"The slaves, you mean? Very profitable. They tell me it's legal in some places—and soon enough elsewhere, too. And even if it isn't, who's to say I did it?" He thought for a moment. "In fact, I think *you* did it. The law will back me up on that."

Frey replied before Durand did. "Life without personal accountability."

Wyckes turned to Frey.

Frey met his gaze. "A bit like turning the entire world into an Internet chat room, isn't it?"

Wyckes laughed. "Yes. Certainly the powerful will no longer have to keep apologizing for their behavior."

Durand gritted his teeth again. "They're going to stop you."

Just then a large explosion lit up the downtown area. Gunfire crackled, followed by several more explosions.

Wyckes walked toward the edge of the rooftop and surveyed the city. "Isn't this a charming country? It's uncanny how many of my close associates are blood relatives to powerful men in the unstable precincts of the world. Blood has an almost mystical power over warlord cultures."

Helicopter lights approached in the distance.

Frey looked up at the approaching chopper. "I'm surprised you're not sticking around, Wyckes. Don't you have a squad of genetic supersoldiers to protect you?"

"I'm not going anywhere, Dr. Frey. These attacks happen all the time. Didn't the insurgents tell you that? And by the way: the world doesn't care about what goes on here. That's why this place suits us." He surveyed the tracers arcing across the skyline. Then he turned back toward Frey. "And supersoldiers? That whole supersoldier thing is overrated. Biology is all about trade-offs. Great strength comes with great caloric and hydration requirements. And let's face it: bullets *kill elephants*—so what's the point of a supersoldier? Give me twenty thousand skinny guys with AKs. We're making so much money, we can always buy more.

"Speaking of money . . ." Wyckes walked up to Frey. "I should point out that, although I cannot help Mr. Durand here, you, Dr. Frey, we can certainly help. And you've got plenty of money on account."

Frey furrowed his brow. "I'd appreciate it if you did not toy with me."

Wyckes motioned to a nearby guard and accepted a glim from the man. Wyckes tossed it on the ground in front of Durand and Frey. Moments later a glowing thermal image of Frey expanded in front of them. It was video of the moment Frey first saw his potential genetically corrected self in the lab.

Red colors flowed through every corner of Frey's face in thermal view.

"You see that, Dr. Frey? Right there. That is what joy looks like from a physiological perspective. Pure, unadulterated joy. There's no concealing it."

Frey gazed longingly at the image of himself viewing himself cured.

"You're a genetic engineer. You can be of use to us. And what else do you have to look forward to? You are wanted everywhere in this world. We could change that."

Frey stared at the image for several moments more.

"Why not make a change, Dr. Frey?"

Frey nodded, tears running down his face. "Yes."

Durand felt his heart sink.

Wyckes nodded to a guard, who lifted Frey to his feet. The sound of steel, and Frey's zip-ties were cut free.

"Bryan! What are you doing?" Durand glared at him.

Frey rubbed his red wrists. "You have no right to judge me—I told you from the beginning what I wanted. Between the two of us, at least I haven't killed anyone to get here. And thanks to you, I'm wanted by the police everywhere." He grabbed the Interpol Notice fluttering near his feet. "Even *here*, apparently!"

Durand hissed, "You know what they plan to do."

Frey raged at Durand. "And what exactly do you expect me to do about it? It's not just them. It's the tide of the world. This is what's *happening*, and I can either stand in front of it and get crushed—with you— or I can get on board. Those are my only choices. And I've made my choice."

Durand slumped down.

Frey reacted to Durand's expression. "Look, I'm sorry about what happened to you. But that isn't my fault. I tried. You *know* I tried. I risked my life for you. But what makes your life more important than mine? Or the lives of anyone else?"

"They're going to enslave you."

"The other genetic engineers didn't look particularly miserable. And being six foot fucking two will go a long way toward relieving my depression."

With that, Frey nodded toward a guard who came up to him. "Goodbye, Ken. I'm truly sorry. But it's too much for you to ask me to die with you."

Frey headed back toward the elevator with several guards.

Chapter 44

After **Frey had** gone, Durand knelt in despair.

Wyckes turned to Otto. "Best not to have his body found in Myanmar. Too close to our operations."

Otto nodded. "I will bring him to—"

"*You* won't be leaving this facility. The 'Angel of Death' is still on every newsfeed. Until your face changes more, it will be difficult for you to move about." A grin escaped. "Boy, she really gave you a shiner, didn't she?"

Otto didn't laugh. "Marcotte will pay for it."

"I'm sure she will. But not quite yet." Wyckes turned back to Durand but addressed the guards restraining him. "Interpol must log Marcus Wyckes as finally and truly dead.

"His DNA must be intact. Take him anywhere rule of law holds and kill him. Toss him out of a helicopter over Hong Kong, for all I care, just make sure the police find his body. And put your eyes on his corpse. Make sure he's dead."

The guards all nodded solemnly.

A helicopter touched down on a helipad on the far end of the roof.

Durand looked up. "Wyckes. How did False Apollo go from preventing human extinction—to this?"

Wyckes reacted in surprise. But then he laughed. "False Apollo! My god . . ." He snapped his fingers and pointed at Durand. "That's right. You were a bug hunter. Navy intelligence. I'm impressed you made the connection."

"It was intended to stop genetic terrorism."

"Who's to say what its purpose was?" Wyckes shrugged. "Besides, I was just a contractor. And what would have happened to poor Otto's people if I hadn't been around? Who would have preserved all those embryos?"

Durand narrowed his eyes. "What embryos?"

"Ten thousand mirror people." He turned to Otto.

Otto nodded grimly.

Durand was momentarily speechless. He finally said, "Why?"

"Because Armageddon is getting cheaper every year, that's why. There is a die-off coming. Billions of angry people—one of them is bound to do something stupid with pathogens. Otto's people will continue the human race. You and I will go the way of the dinosaurs."

Wyckes nodded to the guards and rough hands pulled Durand to his feet.

"Is that what you tell Otto, Wyckes? Or does he already know he's obsolete?"

"Get him out of here."

Durand shouted, "Otto! The change agent means that *nothing* can wipe out humanity anymore. Don't you realize that? Humanity can change at will. No pathogen or virus can wipe us out!" Durand shouted even louder as they pulled him toward the helicopter, "Armageddon isn't coming!"

Otto stared hard after Durand.

Wyckes moved as if to clap Otto on the shoulder—but apparently could not bring himself to do so. Instead he simply said, "He's desperate, Otto. He'll say anything."

Otto continued staring.

Several guards dragged Durand toward the chopper. They pushed Durand aboard and climbed in after him. The chopper lifted off, heading away on the far side of the building from the fighting—racing across the eerily empty, well-lit city.

Durand sat, hands zip-tied, watching the city blocks roll past below. In a few minutes, they circled over a large modern airport with conspicuously little activity. The chopper descended toward the tarmac and a waiting private jet.

Before Durand could fully realize what was happening, he was on the ground and being half dragged, half carried toward the jet, up its steps, and shoved into a comfortable leather seat. The security detail closed the door and spoke briefly with the pilots. The engines started to spool up.

Durand stared into a mirror, set—by some cruel irony—right in his line of sight. Wyckes's original face stared back at him, as if mocking. Durand wanted to smash his own teeth in.

He gazed around as the security men strapped themselves into their seats in preparation for takeoff.

It occurred to Durand that he could do more than simply wait for death.

Durand stared back toward the mirror. He shook his head slowly as he shifted to the side to grab at the autoinjector ampoule in his jacket pocket. He started smiling—laughing, in fact, as he gazed at the reflection of Wyckes's face.

He shook his head to his own reflection.

Durand saw the tattoos appear on his skin again. Perhaps for the last time. He laughed harder.

The security detail cast strange looks at him.

"Be quiet!"

But Durand felt steady. As the private jet taxied onto the runway, he gripped the autoinjector between his fingers under the fine suit fabric.

The jet engines throttled up, and Durand pressed the ampoule against the side of his leg. He felt the glass tip snap.

And then he thrust the exposed needle into his leg.

The pain was shockingly severe. He screamed as what felt like acid spread through him.

The jet rolled along the taxiway.

A voice behind him. "I said be quiet!"

Durand felt his face already beginning to swell. He started to cough, and sweat coated his skin. But he also started laughing uncontrollably.

One of the guards nearby shouted, "Shit! Stop the plane!"

He heard seat belts being undone as the guards raced over to him, running their hands over him.

"He dosed himself!"

In a moment one of the guards located the spent ampoule under a wet spot on his jacket. He held it up for the others. The exposed needle and empty vial said it all.

Durand began to have trouble breathing, but he still laughed just the same. His wrists swelled against the zip ties. He panted, sucking for air. "I don't think Mr. Wyckes . . . is going to be very happy . . . about losing his patsy."

The guards looked at one another gravely.

Durand started a wheezing laugh again and blacked out.

Chapter 45

Kenneth Durand awoke strapped to a table. He was racked with pain, and his face and body felt tight with swelling. When he looked around, it was obvious he was back in the Huli jing labs. In a familiar room.

He heard voices and closed his swollen eyes again. Male voices. Angry.

"We could all get killed if you screw this up."

A more familiar voice. "It will take time to figure out how far the change agent got before neutralization. Then I'll need to compute a new edit plan to undo the changes."

"He was your patient. You should have most of his bio-data already."

"The editing process was only under way for a half hour or so."

The familiar voice countered, "The agent triggers many changes early in the process to prepare for metamorphosis. How did he get ahold of an ampoule?"

"That doesn't matter."

A different voice. "This needs to be done now! Do you hear?"

Yet another voice. "If you do not fix this, you will be the first to die. And it won't be quick. I promise you."

"Forgive! Please forgive! I can fix it! It will take time to synthesize a correction. But I promise you—"

"Mr. Wyckes wanted this subject dumped tonight. He should already be on a plane."

"Tonight? That is too soon."

"Just get it done."

Durand heard retreating footsteps.

Then someone approached his table.

Durand opened his eyes. He saw a very nervous lab technician staring at the ground. It was Hanif—the genetic counselor he had seen earlier in the evening. Durand tried to speak—but it was surprisingly difficult. "Hanif . . ."

Hanif's eyes darted away. "Do not speak to me."

"Hanif."

"Do not speak to me. Please." He got busy moving his arms to virtual interfaces.

"Don't."

"I have no choice. They will kill me." He leaned into Durand's field of vision. "And you lied to me."

Durand's somehow even more alien voice croaked, "I'm trying to destroy the Huli jing."

Hanif paused. Then he got busy again. "It's impossible. Just let me be. Have you not done enough already?"

But then Durand noticed Hanif stiffen. He stood up straight and raised his shaking hands.

Bryan Frey's voice came from close by. "Untie him."

Durand looked to the side. "Bryan?"

Hanif cursed in a foreign language and began unbuckling Durand's restraints. "They will kill me. You realize that, don't you?"

Frey walked into view wearing a medical gown and holding a wicked surgical knife. "You're the one who signed up for this, Hanif."

"I did not sign up for anything. They took my passport. I have been a virtual prisoner for four years."

Durand craned his neck toward Frey and spoke through swollen lips. "You son of a bitch, I thought you sold me out."

Hanif took the last strap off Durand's ankle. Durand tried to sit up.

Frey narrowed his eyes. "How is my not wanting to die selling *you* out?"

Durand successfully sat up, but with difficulty. "You said—"

"No, I stand by what I said back there. You must admit it was the rational decision. I thought I might have a chance to save myself. I wasn't going to work for the Huli jing. But getting revised would certainly have helped to start a new life."

Hanif shook his head. "You would never have escaped."

Machine gun fire and explosions rattled the glassware.

"The Shan attack is still under way."

Hanif whispered, "Gentlemen! You are going to get us *all* killed."

Durand examined his hands, which were hideously swollen. So was his body.

Frey gestured toward him. "I barely recognized you when they wheeled you past."

Durand looked at his own reflection in the cabinet glass. The tightness he was feeling in his face wasn't just swelling. The left side of his face looked partly deformed. Asymmetrical. Other parts of his body felt strange or painful as well. Bruises ran down both his arms. "Shit."

Hanif moved about, gathering items from cupboards. "It is nothing that cannot be fixed." He grabbed Durand's swollen hand. "If you help me, I will help you. Please help me get away from here. I, too, have a family. Back in Indonesia. But where can I go? The resistance is throughout the countryside. They would kill me. I cannot leave through the airport or roads, either. I am a prisoner here. Help me."

Frey lowered the surgical knife. "We know people in the resistance. We can get you out."

"I have your change agent, Mr. Durand. It finished while you were away. I can bring it with us." Hanif moved toward refrigerated cabinets and started rifling through them.

Frey shouted, "Get mine as well!"

"I want immunity! For what I've done. I did not do it willingly. Many people here are wishing to bring an end to this madness."

Durand held his deformed arms out. "What did I do to myself?"

"You injected a sheik's bodyguard's DNA, Mr. Durand. It is fixable."

Frey pointed. "Ah. I can see a hint of it. On the left side." He dropped the knife onto a tray and called out after the lab technician, "You'll find my own change agent is being synthesized in the lab next door. The name is Bryan Frey."

Durand jerked his swollen head. "Go with him, Bryan. We can't trust him just yet."

"Oh, right." Frey nodded and grabbed the surgical knife again as he followed the man.

Durand got up from the table and nearly fell. His legs were swollen, and his rib cage felt strange. He could see his blurry reflection in several polished surfaces throughout the lab, and none of them looked good. To make matters stranger, he was still wearing his dinner jacket and torn shirtfront, only parts of which still fit.

The lab side door hissed opened.

Durand felt another presence in the lab now. That same feeling of dread. He closed his swollen eyes in resignation and turned to see Otto standing in the doorway. The full complement of Huli jing tattoos was still displayed darkly against Otto's neck and hands.

Durand glanced down to see no tattoos at all on his own warped skin. It was strangely a relief. He looked up at Otto. "Wyckes lied to you."

Otto approached.

Durand felt the fear building, but he faced those undead eyes. "I know you're alone. I know you've always been alone."

Otto stopped just a foot away.

Durand's swollen, discolored hands trembled. He held them up. "But I know that inside you're a person. Like me."

"Your kind is an abomination."

Durand nodded. "We are. Sometimes we most definitely are." He caught his ragged breath. "But our minds are the same as yours. If nothing else, we can share knowledge."

Otto stared.

"Humanity isn't going extinct, Otto. I'm sorry. Wyckes will never raise your people."

Otto pounded on the bench and got in Durand's swollen face. "A lie!"

"How do you know those embryos even exist?"

"I saw them! He showed them to me."

Durand trembled, but he faced the uncanny visage. Felt Otto's unliving breath upon him.

"Embryos in cryo. Whole mirror life ecosystems. Preserved. Waiting. I am the first of my kind. The first of many."

Durand, still trembling, said, "How long ago did you see them?"

Otto's dead eyes glared.

"I'm guessing years."

Otto said nothing.

"Go and ask Wyckes, Otto. Ask to see them again."

Just then Frey and Hanif returned. Hanif dropped a metal tray and fell to his knees at the sight of Otto.

"Please forgive! Please forgive!"

Frey stood warily. Obviously taken aback. "What's going on?"

Otto's gaze did not waver from Durand.

"Ask Wyckes to show you the mirror life in cryo. He won't be able to. Because after they had the change agent, they didn't need the False Apollo Project anymore. They incinerated everything when they shut it down. They showed us video of the labs. I didn't know what they were destroying until I met you."

Otto's stare faltered and he looked down.

"I'm sorry."

An explosion outside rattled the glassware again.

Otto spoke to the floor. "What color were the walls in those labs?"

Durand contorted his swollen face. "The walls?"

Otto's terrifying eyes got right up to Durand's as he screamed, "The walls, damn you! What color were the walls of the False Apollo labs? If you really saw them, you'd—"

"Blue!" Durand shook in fear to have Otto so close. "They were light blue! The floors, the walls."

Otto's fierce expression faded, and he staggered back.

"I don't know why everything was blue. But it was."

Otto stared at nothing. His voice was calm. "It had to do with filtering reflected light on test samples."

The room was silent for several moments except for gunfire crackling in the distance.

"Leave this place, Mr. Durand." Otto moved toward the door.

Hanif and Frey leaped aside, pressing against the wall as if a grizzly bear were marching past.

Otto stopped in front of them. He pointed at an emergency biohazard station on the wall. "You will want to use biohazard suits. The atmosphere in here is going to become unsuitable for old life."

Chapter 46

Hanif sealed and locked the lab doors behind Otto after he left. "We must depart if Mr. Otto is going to use what I think he's going to use." Hanif broke open the biohazard station and started pulling out the protective gear. He tested the oxygen mask.

Durand struggled to walk as Frey gathered ampoules and vials of reagent.

"We have more than enough here to provide evidence of what they've been doing."

Hanif ran about frantically. "We must leave! I suspect very bad things are about to happen."

It took them nearly ten minutes to gather all their materials and suit up in biohazard gear. Frey's protective suit looked particularly alarming since the arms and legs were mostly empty. At some point a klaxon went off—whooping as biohazard strobes flashed.

Hanif looked at Durand and spoke through his mask: "We must hurry!"

Hanif entered the corridor pushing the wheeled lab table. Both Durand and Frey were piled onto it as if they were corpses. Durand looked out through his visor at the passing hallway.

Hanif shouted through the radio in his gas mask, "Biohazard! Stand back! Biohazard!"

As they moved through the corridors, Durand saw security guards and clients lying motionless here and there. They showed no obvious signs of injury, but they didn't appear to be breathing.

The biohazard strobes still flashed and the alarms wailed. Distant machine gun fire and explosions filled the gaps. Hanif rolled the gurney partly into the elevator, and then pulled a dead body out of the elevator car before trying again.

Durand could hear his own ragged breathing through the mask as the elevator doors closed and they descended to the lobby.

When they got to the ground floor Durand could see through his gas mask that some of the lobby windows had been shot out. There was glass all over the floor. Several soldiers lay dead—blood everywhere. Other soldiers tended to the wounded.

The sounds were all muted through the biohazard gear.

Hanif shouted again, "Biohazard! Stand clear! Stand clear!"

The soldiers kept their distance.

As Hanif reached the portico, there was no longer any valet. Bullet-riddled cars were scattered about, some burning. Frey pulled off his hazmat headgear and waved like mad for Thet somewhere out there in the darkness.

Durand sat up to help, but Frey stopped him. "No offense, Ken, but I don't think Thet will recognize you."

Soon the lights of the Maybach appeared, and Thet nodded toward them as he brought the car to the edge of the drive.

Wyckes stood near the window in his office, watching the attack still under way. The military was driving the insurgents off, but there was something wrong. He could feel it.

When the biohazard alarms went off, he *knew*. And when there was less and less activity on their comm network. Clicking through the surveillance confirmed his fears.

He waited. And prepared.

Soon enough, the double doors to his office opened, and Otto entered, his tattoos visible. "Marcus."

Wyckes stood up from his desk chair. He wore a full biohazard suit with the hood flipped back to reveal his face. His own markings on display.

Otto stopped ten meters away across the wide floor. In the conservatory nearby the butterflies flocked away from him as best they could. But then they dropped, fluttering, to the floor dead.

Wyckes shook his head. "What have you done, Otto?"

Unlike the eyes of everyone else he'd ever known, Otto's eyes were unreadable to Wyckes. They always looked dead. Unfeeling.

"I need to see them, Marcus."

"Who do you need to see, Otto?"

"My kind."

Wyckes hesitated. "There are things you need to understand . . ."

"Do you realize how much I want to not feel this anymore? This world is a *hell* to me. Do you understand?"

"You're upset."

"You told me my time was coming. That old life on earth would end. You told me I would cleanse the world."

"Otto—"

"I'm tired of waiting. It's time to begin."

"Otto—"

"Show them to me!"

Wyckes sighed. "I didn't want you to find out this way."

Otto laughed ruefully and withdrew a flask from his pocket. He unstoppered it and began to pour the liquid over his arms.

"You were meant to be a savior of mankind."

Otto just laughed.

"You were meant to be humanity's last hope."

Otto tossed away the silver flask. "That's what you've been telling me since I was a child." He extended his arms and smiled his uncanny smile. "You were like a father to me—embrace me. For once let me feel your touch . . ." Otto walked toward Wyckes.

Wyckes flipped the hood of his biohazard suit closed—then lifted an automatic pistol from his desk. "Stop."

Otto halted his advance.

"There is what you were meant to be and there is what you are."

"Give me my people."

"I incinerated your 'people' the first chance I got. Once they were no longer necessary, those embryos went into a furnace."

Otto's icy grin faded, and he lowered his arms—for once looking truly wounded. He then curled into a kneeling position in the middle of the floor and hugged himself while rocking gently. A soft groaning sound came from him.

Wyckes lowered his pistol. "You're no longer a child, Otto. Even then I found your terror at this world pathetic."

Otto continued rocking.

"But it's almost over. I want you to know something before the end."

Otto kept rocking back and forth, groaning.

"*You* are the abomination. As a boy, they gave you to me to be destroyed."

Otto kept rocking.

"But I thought I could get some use out of you first."

Otto rocked harder, groaning louder.

"I'll have to burn your body. Do you know why?"

Otto paused.

"Because not even maggots are willing to eat your flesh."

Otto curled up tighter and groaned again.

"You're no longer a child, Otto. Stand up and face your death like a man."

Otto replied softly, "No, I'm not a child." Then, more confidently, "But neither am I a man."

Wyckes noticed the gun muzzle beneath Otto's arm too late. He tried to react, but just then realized how inferior the reflexes of this body were to his original self. It was like moving through water.

He'd barely raised his pistol when a powerful BOOM threw him back into his leather office chair. His gun clattered to the floor.

Wheezing, Wyckes sucked helplessly for air. It felt like a boulder was resting on top of him. He looked down to see a small hole in the chest of the biohazard suit.

Otto approached with an automatic pistol in his hand.

Wyckes had never seen Otto use a gun in his life. He frowned in confusion through his biohazard face mask.

Otto leaned close. "I have always hated all life on earth. Except for you, Marcus." He leaned closer. "But I was wrong about you."

Otto's hand gripped the biohazard face mask as Wyckes still gasped for air. "My kind of life was created once. It can be re-created. I'm sure the information is in the Huli jing cloud somewhere."

Wyckes felt his breath failing. This body he occupied didn't seem to have half the endurance he remembered as a young man. If he could just sit up.

Otto unclipped the biohazard hood. "Now, before you go, I'd like you to feel my touch just once—for old times' sake."

Wyckes sucked vainly for air as he felt a familiar, all-encompassing revulsion consume him.

The last thing he felt was the horrifying touch of Otto's bare hand against his skin as he let out one last, strangled scream.

FOUR MONTHS LATER

Chapter 47

Durand gazed at the sky through the open monastery window. He saw the same line of palms as always. He lay in bed, a ceiling fan circling lazily above him. It was hot, but he'd grown more accustomed to it. Somehow it felt more and more like Singapore each day.

A moment later Hanif entered with a tray and smiled good-naturedly. "It is time, Mr. Durand."

Durand sat up. "What time?"

"By my calculations, all the rewrites should have concluded. I can find no trace of XNA in your bloodstream. I believe you are—as they say—done."

Durand almost didn't know what to feel.

"The acolytes tell me you've been walking in the room. Recovering your balance fast."

Fear gripped Durand—as it had for several weeks now. He saw the flash of a handheld mirror on Hanif's tray. He started shaking his head. "Get that goddamned thing away from me, Hanif."

"Mr. Durand, you must look upon yourself."

"And is that what it's going to be? Myself? You don't even *know* what I look like! How do you know? I can't look in a mirror, Hanif. I can't do it!"

"You want to go home to your family. I know you do."

Durand pressed his palms into his eyes. "God. I just want—"

"Mr. Durand. Have I not cared for you?"

"That's not the point."

"Are you a man of reason?"

Durand breathed deeply, examining his increasingly familiar arms. And seeing no genetic tattoos despite his deep emotion.

"Does one's identity come from within our hearts or our DNA?"

Durand murmured, "Within our hearts."

"And what is DNA?"

"Data."

"Yes. And your current data now matches your original data."

Durand said nothing for several moments.

"I did not have to know what you looked like. I had your original genomic sequence. You are a man of science. Of reason. Are you not?"

"I was. Once."

He felt the handle of the mirror pushed into his hand.

"No." He pushed it away.

"You must take it. Please. Look."

"No."

"Mr. Durand . . ." Hanif grabbed Durand's chin and held the mirror up to his face.

Before Durand realized it, he was gazing upon his reflection.

And it was his own reflection.

He recalled his nose. His eyes.

He sat up, adrenaline surging. He stroked his chin. "My god . . ."

Hanif held up Durand's well-worn family photo from its place on the nightstand. He pointed to the man in the photo. "Do you see yourself?"

Durand felt tears run down his face and he lowered his head. He then took one more look in the mirror. "My god." He threw off the covers and looked again at his body. His familiar runner's body.

He was still bruised, and smaller in stature than he'd recently been used to, but he recalled this form. It felt comfortable to him.

He put the hand mirror back on the tray. "How is Bryan recovering?"

Hanif winced slightly and made a motion with his hand. "I believe he will start to come around soon."

Durand wasn't liking what he'd been hearing about Frey. Hanif was being far too evasive. "Is he at least able to walk?"

Hanif looked away. "He is in the great room on the first floor."

Durand remembered this was where the monks took care of disfigured children—results of Huli jing genetic experimentation.

"I need to go see him." Durand got up unsteadily. "I need to see if I can help him."

With Hanif's assistance, Durand left the room and limped down a long staircase. They could hear children laughing outside.

Durand moved down the tiled hallways of the monastery, and as they passed several of the children's wards, he was surprised by the number of empty beds. "What's happened, Hanif?"

A young Burmese girl raced past Durand, almost toppling him. She was followed by another two girls, one limping but moving fast on a crutch to keep up.

Hanif nodded. "Ask Dr. Frey."

Durand looked up to see Bryan Frey sitting at the bedside of a slightly deformed boy of about four. Frey looked exactly as he had when Durand last saw him—still in the grip of achondroplasia. Still with shortened arms and legs.

Frey's short fingers nonetheless performed a sleight-of-hand magic trick with a marble for the boy—whose own arms were mildly warped. The little boy laughed as Frey again produced the marble from thin air. "There you go. You might actually be able to make use of that soon enough, little man."

"Bryan."

Frey looked up, peering over old-fashioned reading glasses and finally casting a quizzical look Durand's way. "Who are you?"

He should have expected it, of course, but the realization still stunned Durand. Frey did not recognize him. At least not on sight.

Hanif supported Durand. "Bryan, this is Kenneth Durand."

Durand put a hand to his chest. "It's *me*."

Frey removed his reading glasses and sighed. "I'd gotten used to the old you."

Hanif tsk-tsked him and helped Durand to sit down on an empty bed nearby. "This is indeed Mr. Durand. I transformed him myself."

Frey glanced over at the burn scar still on Durand's arm from the drone cowling from all those months ago. It was the one thing that endured. "I'll be damned. So you are you." He looked up at Durand's face. "I'd say you look good, Ken, but . . ." He chuckled. "You look like a cop, man."

Durand examined Frey. "Why are you . . . ?"

Frey glanced down at himself. "Oh. Why am I still me? How nice of you to ask."

"You know what I mean."

"Yes. I suppose I did go through some inconvenience to get myself transformed."

"Just a bit."

Frey pulled a necklace out from his shirtfront. On the end of it was an ampoule filled with a golden liquid. "I might still one day." He looked around at the half-populated children's ward. "But for the moment, I've too much work to do."

Durand looked around the ward as well. The children in sight seemed markedly improved. The rest were gone. "My god . . ."

Frey jumped down off the chair. "Follow me."

Durand realized he'd been hearing the laughter of children more and more over the months. It had happened so slowly that he hadn't noticed, but he didn't recall hearing any laughter here during his first visit.

Hanif helped Durand move along, but Durand finally shrugged him off. "I can walk. I can walk. Thanks, Hanif." He walked shakily alongside Frey.

They moved out onto a wide patio. Below in the yard children were running around, some limping, others moving gracefully. Young monks in saffron robes tried to keep order, laughing as children tossed balls to one another.

Durand felt a moment of clarity. "My god. Look at them. You fixed them."

Frey nodded. "Still a lot of work to do. And more arrive each day."

Hanif stood alongside. "The survivors of the Huli jing are coming here. Dr. Frey helps them."

Durand gazed out at the children. "But not yourself."

"I couldn't very well help them if I was bedridden. There was a great deal to learn. Hanif has been an extraordinary help. And there's no telling how long the Huli jing photonic cloud servers will still be up. They could go down any day."

Durand marveled at the scene. "How did they recover so fast . . . ?"

"Because I didn't need to do massive edits to them. For many it was just a single edit. It took a whole menu of edits to get you back to yourself." He nodded at the children. "But these kids, they already were themselves. They just needed a little tweak to activate key genes." Frey looked back to Durand. "As I said, Hanif has been most helpful."

They moved back inside, walking past monks performing physical therapy with healing children.

Durand looked around in amazement. "And here I thought this change agent was going to make the world a nightmare."

Frey waved him off. "Only for us early adopters. In fact, your kind might soon be out of a job."

"How do you figure?"

"The Treaty on Genetic Modification—soon everything that gets changed will be able to be changed back. Germ line edits won't mean anything. No more threat of superviruses or gene drive weapons wiping us all out. In fact, I think I have a new line of work for you, Ken."

"How kind of you to think of me."

"What do you think of this? Genetic security service. Like a credit monitor—but for DNA. People deposit their original DNA for reference, and you test their DNA periodically to see if it's changed. You'd still get to wear a suit and stick your nose in other people's business."

Durand nodded. "Sounds right up my alley."

They stopped near the gateway to a temple, where a golden Buddha stood.

Frey pointed. "You'll find Thet through there. He's usually here in the afternoons."

"Thet's here?"

"Go pay your respects. I think he would appreciate it."

Durand's face grew serious.

Frey looked away. "I expect we will not meet again, Agent Durand." He turned. "But if we do, hopefully you'll go easy on me." Hanif moved to join him.

Durand called out to Frey, "Bryan, if we meet again, I'd say the world is in big trouble."

Frey laughed, and then he turned a corner, Hanif on his heels.

Durand moved slowly down into the temple, past burning candles and incense. He soon found Thet kneeling, his hands clasped before him. Smoke curling from an incense burner.

Durand waited nearby.

Thet soon looked up and stood.

It occurred again to Durand that he was no longer the same man Thet knew. Not physically. He placed a hand on his chest. "Thet. I am Kenneth Durand. You know me. I'm sorry to disturb you. Dr. Frey said . . ."

Thet nodded. He smiled weakly and approached. "It is very strange to see you . . . Mr. Durand . . . like this. But Buddhist teachings prepare us for such things. Of course you are Mr. Kenneth Durand. It is good for our eyes to meet again."

Durand looked to the incense burner.

Thet gestured. "Praying. For the spirit of my sister, Bo Win."

Durand caught his breath. "I see." He took another, deeper breath. An indescribable sadness came over him. "Thet, I'm sorry. I—"

"No, no, Mr. Durand. She would be happy." He moved to point toward the wall—then cupped his ear.

Durand heard the children playing.

"We all live many lives, Mr. Durand."

Durand nodded again. He bowed a deep wai to Thet.

Chapter 48

Durand stepped down from the jet and into Singapore's familiar humidity. Several vehicles waited nearby on the tarmac of Changi International. He felt a smile come to his face as he saw his wife, Miyuki, release Mia. His daughter ran to him.

She screamed in joy as he picked her up. "Daddy! Daddy!"

He kissed her and hugged her close. Her fragrance brought him back to himself more than anything yet.

Miyuki was half a step behind. She wrapped her arms around him, and he felt the wetness of her tears. They shared a deep kiss and hugged again.

"I was worried I'd never see either of you again."

Miyuki held his gaze. "We thought we'd lost you."

"No. I'm here." He held them tight, then tucked Mia under his arm. She giggled, and he moved at a stagger toward the others waiting for him.

Michael Yi Ji-chang and Claire Belanger closed the distance—Yi with an almost disbelieving grin on his face.

Claire hugged him and gave him a kiss on both cheeks. "We were elated to hear you were safe, Ken. Welcome back. It is a miracle."

Yi pushed aside Durand's handshake and just grabbed him, slapping him on the back. "Holy crap, buddy. You have no idea. You're not going to believe everything that's happened while you've been gone."

"No, probably not. But I gotta tell you, Mike, I just want to go home right now." He kept a tight hold on his daughter, who was still laughing.

Yi nodded. "Of course. You ring me when you're ready."

"I will." Looking up, Durand could see Inspector Aiyana Marcotte standing next to a chauffeured car, waiting for them. An SPF security detail stood close at hand. Durand put his daughter down, and as his family approached, Marcotte opened the passenger door for them.

"Welcome back, Agent Durand." She extended her hand.

He shook it firmly. "Thank you, Inspector."

"When you're back on duty, Sergeant Yi will catch you up on everything we've been doing. You have a good partner there."

"Yeah, I know. Did he tell you about the whole Korean Han thing?"

She laughed. "He did."

She leaned over the door as Miyuki and Mia got into the car.

"The Myanmar raids appear to have broken the back of the Huli jing. What we discovered in Naypyidaw was truly shocking. And it all came from an anonymous tip."

Durand looked at her. "Did it remain anonymous?"

Marcotte studied him. "Yes, it did. But someone deserves my thanks."

"Someone would say forget about it."

She nodded.

Durand got into the car.

"It's all over the news, you know—a means for editing the living. They say it will change everything. The Post-Identity World, they're calling it. Police work is about to get harder. I seem to remember Marcus Wyckes was down here warning us about that a few months ago. But somehow he got away."

"I wouldn't know anything about that, Inspector." Durand nodded toward his wife and daughter. "Now, if you'll excuse me."

"One more thing . . ." She leaned down. "We found Marcus Wyckes's body in Naypyidaw."

"Don't be so sure."

She studied Durand's expression. "I'm not. We also still need to find this 'Mirror Man' you mentioned in your report."

Durand gave her an exasperated look.

She nodded. "We'll talk more." Marcotte nodded also to Miyuki and

Mia, then shut the door behind them. She watched the car pull away, police escort lights flashing.

Belanger and Yi came up alongside Marcotte.

Belanger spoke to her without turning. "How do we know that's really Ken Durand?"

Marcotte considered the question. "He passed the debrief. Lie detectors. The family seems to think it's him."

"But how do we *really* know?"

Yi watched the car exit the tarmac. "Give me a day or two. If there's one thing I know how to do, it's push Ken Durand's buttons."

Marcotte let a slight smile escape. "Sounds like a plan."

Chapter 49

The banker tried to contain an odd sense of revulsion at her handsome young client. She spoke with a slight Russian accent. "Will you be staying in London long, Mr. Taylor?"

"I just moved here actually." The young man looked up from signing virtual bank documents with a jade stylus carved with dragons. His lifeless gray eyes fixed on her. He was blond with square-jawed good looks, but somehow his presence was unnerving. "My family's originally from the UK, but I was raised overseas."

"Really?" She wanted this to be over.

"After my ordeal I'd like to be closer to family. It's the most important thing to me—a sense of belonging."

"Yes, of course." A pause. "If you don't mind my asking, what ordeal?"

He stowed the jade stylus in his jacket pocket. "I was kidnapped. Held for months by rebels in Indonesia."

True shock registered on her face. "No. You are joking."

"My parents feared me dead."

They probably wished for it, she thought. "How did it happen?"

"Being the heir to my family's considerable business interests does have its downside."

"And your family paid ransom?"

"I was fortunate enough to escape. It took me months to find a way out."

She wondered how anyone could want him back. "Your parents must be overjoyed."

"It's been a bit rocky actually. The drug the rebels used during the abduction impacted my memory—I've lost parts of my own childhood."

Now she felt bad. Was that what was wrong with him? "How terrible."

"But we will be a family again. I'm certain of it."

"Well, you are safe now, at least. And fortunately, as a man of means, you will be able to enjoy all the finer things that life in the London Trade Zone has to offer." She slid his virtual paperwork into an AR inbox he'd made available. "Is there anything else I can help you with?" She smiled, though it took effort.

"Thank you, no." He stood, and one of his two suited bodyguards winced while helping him with his greatcoat.

She rose as well. "Mr. Taylor, it has been a pleasure. I hope to see you and your family soon. And welcome home." She could not bring herself to extend her hand. She hadn't been able to do it when he came in, either. She was appalled at her rude and illogical behavior. She could not overcome it.

Fortunately he turned away without offering his hand. "Yes." He then departed, her gaze following as his bodyguards took up positions behind him. Dressed in a bespoke suit and greatcoat, he was the very picture of establishment wealth—or an old-world vampire. She couldn't tell which.

As he and his bodyguards exited into the winter chill through security doors onto Lombard Street, he noticed not far ahead a crowd of hundreds of people knotting up around some invisible AR content. The growing mob created a choke point on the already crowded London sidewalk.

He moved away from the autonomous Mercedes waiting for him at the curb and donned designer LFP glasses. He walked toward the crowd, gazing up as an enormous AR public news screen appeared on the side of a bank tower. Audio came in through his earphones as the crowd parted uneasily around him. He looked up to watch breaking news unfold.

A matronly anchorwoman spoke beside the latest video from Myanmar—an inset showed dozens of identical movie stars being led away toward buses. *"Recent revelations from Myanmar continue to draw international outrage—and also call into question the security model of the West."*

The screen showed Myanmar officials raiding the vast laboratories of the Huli jing. An Interpol official in a biohazard suit held up an ampoule filled with honey-colored liquid.

"The so-called 'change agent'—capable of transforming the genetic sequence of living people—could radically alter the world as we know it."

As he watched, he felt his anger rise and narrowed his eyes at the screen. But then he glanced down at the back of his own hand to see familiar tattoos fading into place there.

Focusing on the markings, he willed them away again and watched them slowly fade.

The anchorwoman continued. *"This technology could well undermine the concept of identity itself. Who is who, personal accountability—these were until now the foundation of all law. And yet new live genetic editing technology may render such presumptions obsolete."*

He smiled to himself and nodded. With one more glance up at the screen, he walked through the crowd—which parted around him like nervous prey.

Further Reading

You can learn more about the technologies and themes explored in *Change Agent* by visiting www.daniel-suarez.com or through the following books:

Regenesis: How Synthetic Biology Will Reinvent Nature and Ourselves by George Church and Ed Regis (Basic Books)

Evolving Ourselves: How Unnatural Selection and Nonrandom Mutation Are Changing Life on Earth by Juan Enriquez and Steve Gullans (Penguin)

The Gene: An Intimate History by Siddhartha Mukherjee (Scribner)

Tomorrow's Battlefield: U.S. Proxy Wars and Secret Ops in Africa by Nick Turse (Haymarket Books)

Is the American Century Over? by Joseph S. Nye Jr. (Polity Press)

Synthetic Biology: A Lab Manual by Josefine Liljeruhm, Erik Gullberg, and Anthony C. Forster (World Scientific)

BioBuilder: Synthetic Biology in the Lab by Natalie Kuldell, Rachel Bernstein, Karen Ingram, and Kathryn M. Hart (O'Reilly)

Acknowledgments

Building the world of 2045 for this book required research into many subjects—genetic editing, synthetic biology, Interpol, human trafficking, geopolitics, economics, blockchain tech, light fields, renewable energy, climate change, and more. While ultimately a work of fiction, it began from a realistic foundation.

I'd like to personally thank the following individuals for their gracious assistance in making my research easier: Russell Baldwin, for guiding me through DNA processing in law enforcement, and Marc Goodman, for his firsthand knowledge of Interpol and his rather disquieting expertise on the future of crime. To the extent I stretched the boundaries of their respective disciplines for the sake of this narrative, the fault is entirely my own.

Thanks as well to George Church, Ed Regis, Steve Gullans, Siddhartha Mukherjee, Nick Turse, Joseph S. Nye Jr., Josefine Liljeruhm, Erik Gullberg, Anthony C. Forster, Natalie Kuldell, Rachel Bernstein, Karen Ingram, Kathryn M. Hart, Joseph L. Flatley, Christopher Lingle, Carl E. Walter, Fraser J. T. Howie, Antonio Regalado, Jeffrey Bartholet, Rory Buckeridge, Emily Singer, Ian Urbina, Oliver Wainwright, Robinson Meyer, Eric Holthaus, Sarah Zhang, Coco Alcuaz, Szu Ping Chan, Jane Langdale, and Elsa Vulliamy, whose published works informed critical parts of this story.

My gratitude also to the following individuals for providing translation assistance in various scenes: Rodney Van Meter and Amelie Geeraert for Japanese; Palash Sanyal for both Bengali and Hindi; Björn Persson and Thierry Renard for Thai; and Achmad Thamrin for Malay.

Sincere thanks to my longtime literary agent, Rafe Sagalyn, and the entire team at ICM—and also to my sagacious editors at Dutton, Ben Sevier and Jessica Renheim.

However, these acknowledgments could never be complete without a heartfelt thanks to my wife, Michelle—for reasons that would fill a book all their own.

ABOUT THE AUTHOR

DANIEL SUAREZ is the author of the *New York Times* bestseller *Daemon, Freedom™, Kill Decision,* and *Influx.* A former systems consultant to Fortune 1000 companies, Mr. Suarez has designed and developed software for the defense, finance, and entertainment industries. His fiction focuses on technology-driven change, and he is a past speaker at TED Global, NASA Ames, the Long Now Foundation, and the headquarters of Google, Microsoft, and Amazon. An avid gamer and technologist, he lives in Los Angeles.